THE PSYCHIC
OF SACHSENHAUSEN

DAVID TURTON

CURIOUS CORVID PUBLISHING, OHIO

Curious Corvid
PUBLISHING

For Olivia

First they came for the socialists, and I did not speak out,

Because I was not a socialist.

Then they came for the trade unionists, and I did not speak out,

Because I was not a trade unionist.

Then they came for the Jews, and I did not speak out,

Because I was not a Jew.

Then they came for me – and there was no one left to speak for me.

Martin Niemöller

Imprisoned in Sachsenhausen 1938 – 1941.

PROLOGUE

RICHARD - JULY 2021

The feeling flowed over Richard, as it always did, accompanied by brightly coloured lights and the sharp smell of burnt rubber. Head spinning, he sank to his knees, grasped his face and sucked in a slow, ragged breath. Sandy knelt by his side.

"It's happening again, isn't it?"

Richard nodded. He stood slowly and tried to make sense of his surroundings. Disorientation always came before his visions, and now the world looked a different place.

Only hours before, he had enjoyed breakfast at the top of Berlin's famous TV Tower, the views across the city giving him the God-like feeling that he was suspended hundreds of metres above the hustle and bustle, a superior being watching the lowly living their small lives beneath him. Now on ground level, he felt like he was suddenly floating. The atmosphere around him had become soft and tangible, as if covered in translucent film, gossamer thin and reflective. Lights shone out from everyone, bright beams shooting through the tops of their heads. Vivid colours wheeled above passers-by who glanced at Richard with concern as he staggered across Hackescher Market.

"What do you see?" Sandy asked as he grabbed his arm to steady him.

Richard looked at his husband, trying to focus. Dazzling coloured lights rolled like white-hot lava from the head of a nearby tour guide, engulfing him. They swirled and lit up the sky above. The lights called to Richard in a voice that he couldn't recognise, the unspoken words a melody moving through the eye-burning glare. He listened. He sensed. He tried to understand. Then, with a twitch and a loud click that existed only in Richard's head, the lights faded in a slow-motion retreat to nothingness. Richard watched the normal return on a wave of nausea. He bent over and vomited onto the pavement.

The tour guide rushed over. A spectrum of vivid colour spun from his name badge and stung Richard's eyes.

"Sir, are you all right?" An Irish accent rang delicately from the guide. Richard could see the word flow from his mouth in a stream of glimmering colour.

"What tour are you running?" Richard asked him. He focused in on the man's name badge and made out the name Ronan in thick block capitals.

"It's a concentration camp tour, sir. But it involves extensive walking. In your state I don't think. . ."

"Two tickets," Richard said.

"Are you sure?"

"We'll take two tickets," Sandy repeated his husband's words.

The camp was half an hour away from central Berlin by train. They disembarked at the end of the line, a small, charming town called Oranienburg. As they followed the guide, along with a group of American, Canadian and British tourists, Sandy turned to him.

"That's the first episode for two years," he said quietly. "What did you see? Why this tour?"

"Just some lights," Richard told him. "Something about this feels important."

Sandy nodded. Richard knew he understood that he just wasn't ready to share his feelings, that there was more.

Richard's episodes, as Sandy called them, had first hit him at eighteen years old. Doctors thought the visions and lights had been some form of epilepsy, but tests and scans revealed nothing.

Richard simply lived with the random attacks until the day he met up with friends in London. They were about to go into a restaurant when he felt faint and saw a boiling, black cloud with flashing red lights pouring out of the building. Shaken and unsteady, Richard had refused to go in, telling the others he had been struggling with a bug, that he would wait for them in a nearby park, that they should enjoy their lunch without him.

When he closed his eyes, he could still hear the monstrous boom as a terrorist wearing a suicide vest blew the building apart. He took thirty-six souls with him, everyone of Richard's party amongst them. The loss and the gnawing guilt – could he have saved them if he had only listened? – were things Richard had slowly learnt to live with but never forgotten. Now, in his forties, the moments were sporadic, coming every few years.

They reached the camp, and Richard immediately felt his senses filling with dread. Sandy clasped his hand tighter. Ronan, the tour guide, led the group around. He explained the rise of the Nazis in the 1930s, Adolf Hitler taking power and capturing the imagination of the disillusioned German people. He explained how the camp had been built by inmates from another prison. They were shown around buildings, a reconstructed jail block that had once been built in a T-shape to enable three guards to monitor each huge hallway full of political dissidents. The guide relayed a regime of cold brutality, of torture and murder, of the casual cruelty of the SS who broke down their prisoners psychologically and physically until they were shells of human beings.

Towards the end of the tour they came to a structure covered by a protective shell. The guide took them inside to see a large Pieta-style statue and a network of low foundation walls that gave the impression of rooms in a house.

"This is Station Z," the guide said.

The feeling of disorientation hit Richard in a huge wave. He grabbed his head with his sweating hands, fighting the drowning sensation, the feeling his whole body had been plunged underwater. The smell of burning rubber was so strong whole tyres could have been aflame under his nose. Billowing black clouds hung over him, omnipotent and ominous. The foundations of Station Z were suddenly alive, firing inky shafts of darkness in all directions. Soul-wrenching screams ricocheted through Richard's head, and all around the air turned thick and suffocating. The acrid odour of smoking rubber changed to an overpowering stench of hot, rancid meat that made Richard choke and vomit in a violent spasm. He fell onto his back, knowing the smell was human flesh burning, the bubble and blister of skin on fire, of exposed bone scorching in a hellish inferno. His vision wavered, pink lights shone across his eyes.

"Richard! Richard!" Sandy's panicked shouts were a whisper in the background, as if he was calling from the top of a distant cliff. Richard felt like he was sinking, sucked down into a maelstrom of unthinkable pain, of unimaginable evil.

The vague, far off sensation of his husband slapping his face floated through Richard's consciousness, and he sensed more than saw a blur of other faces peering down at him, but he was falling further into that abyss.

Richard would later wonder if he had passed out before the screams and the smoke and the jet-black beams finally faded. He felt his vision become soft, out of focus, until slowly the scene in front of him became sharper. Hazy shapes became people facing him. He was on his feet before a crowd who were clapping and cheering. Richard looked down. He was on a stage in front of an audience, soaking up their ovation. He realised he was smiling, the drowning feeling of disorientation replaced with an immense wave of euphoric pleasure. Richard looked around through eyes whose gaze was firm and steady. He was somewhere else. He was *someone* else.

Chapter One

GARLAND - 1935

Garland crouched in the pin-drop silence of the theatre, his arms outstretched, then stood and looked out at the audience as still as stone in their seats. Sweat dripped from his forehead and his breath came in snatches. He counted the seconds. One, two, three. . . Slowly he bowed, and like patients snapped from a trance, the crowd rose as one and applauded, all 250 of them on their feet, the crescendo of their cheers filling Garland's senses.

He walked from the stage and the theatre manager, Mr Andersen, slapped him on the back.

"What a performance!" he said. "You'll be a fine dancer, boy. The best in Oslo. No, the best in Norway. I've no doubt."

He put his arm around Garland and looked upwards at an imaginary billboard.

"I can see it now." Mr Andersen had squeezed shut his eyes. "Garland Lund – Paris, London, New York. Your name will be in lights, young man."

Garland beamed. His teachers, instructors, friends had all told him he was a wonderful performer. But the faith of old Mr Andersen, someone so well-respected in the theatre world, and now the crowd's reaction had confirmed his talents to himself. Garland let the grin linger. It all felt so special.

He walked backstage and saw Johan waiting. They hugged tightly.

"My best friend," said Johan. "Don't forget me when you're living the high life around the world."

They hugged again.

"Watch it you two, people will think you're a couple of homosexuals," Mr Andersen said as he walked past.

Johan laughed. "Maybe they would if they didn't always think we were brothers."

Garland considered Johan closely. It was true. Even with the difference in their height – Johan was much taller at six feet and had been the strong protector in their childhood – they looked and acted with the closeness of siblings, two young men cast from the same familial mould. Growing up in the same archaic Oslo orphanage would partly explain it, but the rest was pure coincidence. They had identical blond hair and sharp blue eyes that no one could miss.

Their interests, though, were wildly different. Whilst Garland loved to dance and perform, Johan was a born soldier. He had always been hungry for adventure, a fearless chance-taker who lived to push the boundaries of what he could achieve. Sometimes others would fear him. There were boys in the orphanage who were terrified of Johan, cowering when he was near. Garland had never felt his friend was aggressive or a bully. He just had a presence. It was both physical and psychological. And Johan had dished out a few beatings of fellow orphans in the past, actions that led to reciprocal beatings from the master of the orphanage. But it never bothered him; Johan wasn't frightened of anyone. Garland was different though, and he supposed that's what gave them such a solid friendship. He knew he was more sensitive, quieter, with a slight fear of the world around him. The "homosexual" jibes didn't bother him. He'd had people call him queer since he was a young boy, with his love of dancing, his slender figure and handsome face. Name-calling and judgements didn't matter when you had a friend like Johan on your side.

"Garland, I have an idea," Johan said, breaking Garland out of his daydream as they stood in the dusty backstage area.

Garland looked at his friend through narrowed eyes. "Why do I get the feeling that this is going to be another of your big adventures, Johan?"

"Because it is! It's the biggest. I'm moving to Berlin. I've been selected to be one of their guards. It might not sound much, but it's a huge honour."

Garland pursed his lips and nodded. He knew Johan had applied but hadn't believed it would happen this fast.

"Wow, well done. Berlin? That's a big move."

"I want you to come. There's a lot going on there," Johan said, eyes flashing with confidence and an almost childlike excitement. "It's moved on since the war. Everything is cheap, and there are lots of opportunities for people like us. They love Norwegians in Germany. We're like gods over there."

"Jo, things are really starting to happen for me here. For the first time in my life things are looking good. You want me to move to some strange city?"

Johan gave a "come on" shrug, palms up.

"Garland, it's Berlin! The arts are massive over there. You'll have a much better chance of making it. They'll love you, I promise. The recruiting officer said he'd get me in a special branch of their guards. He said if I go now, the rewards will be huge in the future."

Garland looked at his friend, two pairs of bright blue eyes locked together in two seconds of silence.

"What do you say?"

Garland broke out into a smile and hugged his friend for a third time.

Chapter Two

JOHAN - 1935

Johan pulled himself up on the bar, his biceps straining with the effort. Visits to the gym had become more frequent since he'd been accepted by the Germans. The recruitment process had been simple and straightforward. The National Socialists had been in power for two years in Germany and they had plans to make their country great again. Rudi Froch, the head of the Oslo branch of National Socialists, had spotted Johan playing football one Saturday afternoon. Froch, a hard-faced man with slate-grey hair, stopped him after the match and looked him up and down, commenting on his physique, height and stunning blond hair and blue eyes.

Froch had requested a meeting with Johan, in which he continually described Johan as Aryan, the *master* race which would one day dominate the world. As Froch spoke in his slow, deliberate tones, Johan felt a warm rush. An orphan who had never known his parents, Johan had suffered as a child. The beatings and abuse at the Oslo orphanage, where he lived until he was fifteen years old, were routine.

They had left Johan used to defending himself and making himself as physically imposing as possible – and thrown by words of care or kindness. The veteran's praise caught him off guard. Froch was around sixty years old, a big man with prominent red veins tracking across his nose and cheeks like a map of bloody rivers. He smelt of stale tobacco and sweat. When he spoke, he moved his thick-rimmed glasses higher up his nose.

"I want you to go to Germany and help it become the best country in the world," Froch had told him. "Norway is nice. A pleasant, beautiful country. But a man of your talents is wasted in a peaceful country. You should be at the forefront of a new civilisation. These Jews, Blacks, Romani, they are bringing down our way of life. There is a man, Adolf Hitler, who is working hard to turn all of this around. You may have heard of him."

Johan shook his head. Although the name rung a distant bell, he had no idea about politics and current affairs. They held no interest. He followed sport, particularly Oslo athletes and the local football sides.

"Hitler is assembling a brilliant team of people who will lead Germany into the future," Froch told him. "They have learnt the lessons of the Great War. They have identified the backstabbers, the traitors, the enemies of the state. But they have also identified the heroes. The people that will drive the Fatherland forwards. Now, I have a contact who is high up in Hitler's cabinet in Berlin. A fit, young, strong Aryan like you will do well. They don't usually let non-Germans in, but a man with my contacts, I can pull some strings. How does that sound to you, son?"

Johan raised his eyebrows and grinned, flashing his white teeth to the old man. It was faith in him, faith he hadn't ever experienced before, and it immediately appealed. That feeling of belonging, of making a difference. Of being a hero.

"It sounds pretty good, I have to admit," he replied, a cool answer that was betrayed by his blushing cheeks.

"Excellent! This is no ordinary guard duty. The branch are closely aligned with Hitler himself. In fact, their head is a close ally of the Fuehrer. They are the protectors of the people. They are tough, feared, respected. A political force of their own. This is a big opportunity, son. So, what do you say?"

Johan nodded. The words were foreign to his ears. . . Hitler, Fuehrer, Fatherland, political forces. But the adrenaline kick of excitement and heady self-worth made his chest fill with pride. He wanted to be a part of this new world.

"I'll have to move to Berlin? Can I bring anyone with me?"

"Of course," Froch replied, a smile twisted upwards, causing a deep wrinkle on his cheek. "Another Aryan orphan?"

Johan nodded. "Yes, he's like my brother. Mr Froch, these special guards. What are they called?"

Froch smiled widely. It ignited something darker in his eyes. "The Schutzstaffel."

"The Protection Squadron," Johan translated.

Both he and Garland were fluent in German, by fluke not design. The master of their orphanage had been from Munich and forced them to learn his language.

"Yes," Froch said now. "SS for short."

They had arranged another meeting where Johan completed all the necessary forms and paperwork and took a demanding physical assessment. A week later he received a knock on the door with more paperwork: a contract to join the SS in Germany. He didn't hesitate in signing. Oslo held nothing for him anymore. He had grown up without feeling a part of the city's society, and there was little adventure for him here. Garland, on the other hand, took some convincing, but Johan was sure his best friend would thrive in Berlin as much as he had in Oslo. He had heard of Berlin's nightlife when he was younger, the arts shows, the drinking, the theatre and cabaret. Some said it was so lively it was wrong, decadent even. Johan thought his friend would fit in just fine.

Muscles burning, Johan pulled himself up once more, shaking off his daydreams. His arms ached. He had pushed himself too far. Jumping down, he dragged off his T-shirt, covered in oily sweat, and looked in the full-length gymnasium mirror. His chest pumped outwards from his body above a set of rippling adnominal muscles that could have been chiselled from granite. His eyes traced up to his own face. His square jaw and small nose sat below his sparkling blue eyes and neat blond hair, a delicate image that contrasted heavily with his robust frame. The worthless idiots from the orphanage, the master, those who'd written him off, all lesser mortals who would soon be kissing his feet. He smiled at himself in the mirror as Froch's words echoed in his mind.

Tough, feared, respected.

Chapter Three

GARLAND - 1935

The day had finally arrived. Oslo was bathed in unseasonable warmth, the sun large and resplendent in its cloudless sky. A group of gulls soared noisily overhead.

Mr Andersen had come to wave Garland off. A few friends from ballet joined them on the platform at Oslo Station. Neither Johan nor Garland had much baggage. One knapsack each was enough for all their belongings. Material trappings didn't figure highly in the priorities of orphans, even after they'd left their childhood behind.

Garland felt his eyes grow wet as he shook hands with Mr Andersen. The hot steam rising from the train blended with a cooling breeze from the Oslofjord, the tangy smell of oil heavy in the morning air. Andersen handed Garland a written reference for potential employers in the theatres of Berlin.

"Good luck, Garland, and don't forget us little people when you make in big in Germany." Garland smiled and a solitary tear escaped to roll down his cheek. Andersen pulled the handshake into a full-blown hug. He whispered in Garland's ear, his mouth so close that Garland felt his breath.

"Be careful over there, son. I've heard things have changed over the last couple of years. Just keep your wits about you. Make sure your SS friend helps you out if you need it. Maybe it's not so safe for people like us."

Garland pulled away, his brow furrowed. *People like us.* He wasn't sure what Mr Andersen meant but didn't want to probe too much. He'd heard mixed reports about the Nazi Party, but most of the talk was political, something that left him cold.

True, the war was long over and Germany was finally rising from the ashes, but he had picked up different opinions about Berlin life. On one hand, the Nazis kept absolute control over entertainment and ruled with an iron fist. On the other, he heard the city was vibrant and alive, bursting with culture, art and a nightlife wild enough to have some calling it hedonistic.

There were other good signs too. The SS had paid for their train fares and agreed to put Garland up until he found a permanent home in Berlin. Also, as Mr Andersen said, if Johan was heading high up as a guard, he would surely be the solid protector should trouble come knocking at Garland's door.

He said his goodbyes until the tears left his cheeks wet and gleaming in the sun's midday glare. Johan, always more of a loner, simply gave the send-off party a smile and a strong handshake before boarding. Garland stepped onto the train and took one last look at Oslo, its tiled rooftops glimmering in the rays of yellow sunlight. He drew in a slow, deep breath, tasting soot and hot steam on the clear Norwegian air, and let his gaze follow the distant hills that stared back without judgement or favour. Garland shut the train door and waved out of the half-opened window as the engine's wheels squealed into motion.

He was on his way. The long journey ahead would take them down to Sweden through endless stations, onto a boat from Trelleborg to Rostock in Germany and finally another train to Berlin.

Garland followed Johan into a booth, stowed his pack and sat opposite two men reading newspapers. Berlin was hosting the Summer Olympics, and the back page of one carried an interview with Norway's national boxers, hoping to bring home medals and glory from the tournament. Cigarette smoke billowed in the carriage, the two men puffing together with machine precision as Garland and Johan read the article.

"The Olympics," Johan said, turning to Garland with wide eyes and a wider grin. "We should try and go. They've built a massive stadium for it."

"Why not?" Garland replied. But his attention was elsewhere. The man on the left of the pair opposite was in a German army uniform. When he lowered his paper to turn a page, Garland saw the emblem of an eagle, its huge wings outstretched, on his right breast. The eagle was perched atop a circular shape containing a swastika. As Garland stared at the emblem, the world around him suddenly began to change. The atmosphere became thick and cloying, the bite of cigarette smoke now replaced by a smell of burning, a choking stench that engulfed the small booth. Garland reeled like a drunk in his seat and stared wide-eyed as the eagle began to move, its giant wings flapping slowly as it launched itself from the emblem. Twisting its neck to train tomb-cold eyes around the carriage, it lifted from the soldier's uniform in a slow, graceful motion, the swastika glowing a dark, fiery red in its talons, and glided past Garland's ear. He felt the displaced air brush lightly across his face, then saw the eagle drop the pulsing swastika onto Johan. As Garland watched he saw his friend's face change. It shone deep crimson, a mask of dripping blood before the colour sank to black, the skin charring and spitting in hideous slow motion until all he could see were Johan's white eyes and teeth.

"Gar, what's wrong? Why are you looking at me like that?"

Garland heard the words but couldn't respond. He saw Johan's face bloom and stretch, bulging as if something was trying to escape underneath the flesh. Now from the bloated blackness other faces began to come and go in a ghastly flicker-show. Faces young and old whose tortured expressions were scarred with desperation, their black rimmed eyes hollow and haunted, the men with thick unkempt beards, every face gaunt and skeletal and barely human. Garland watched the shadow of another face, eyes blazing, jet-black hair combed over, a thin moustache sitting neatly above lips as taut as razor wire, before Johan changed one final time. The sallow, grinning skull stared back at Garland, its empty sockets death-dark and soulless. Garland heard a high-pitched scream, a blood-curdling sound that seemed to pierce his brain, and in that moment felt the visions melting away. The thick atmosphere lifted and the burning smell vanished, replaced again with the drifting cloud of cigarette smoke. Garland, panting, wretched a single sliver of bile on the floor.

"Get him out of here!" the soldier shouted to Johan. "If he vomits you'll both be cleaning it with your bare hands."

"Sorry, sir," Johan was laying Garland back in his seat. "He's not well. A bug he's been carrying."

He gathered their packs, helped Garland to his feet and held him as they made their way along the swaying corridor until they reached an empty booth.

Johan dragged Garland inside and pushed him onto a seat by the window. He studied Garland with narrowed eyes, anger flashing behind a look of cautious concern. "What's the matter with you? What was all that about?"

"I don't know." Garland's voice was weak. "I haven't ever felt like that before. I think I'm okay now but—"

"But what?"

Garland looked down, avoiding his friend's eyes, not sure he could explain. "Something doesn't feel right about this. Do you know what you're getting yourself into?"

Johan softened his tone.

"Of course," he sounded relieved. "Is that what this is all about? You're homesick already? Where's your sense of adventure? This is an amazing opportunity for both of us. Grasp it. Life is what you make it, Gar. Think positively. No more funny turns. Okay?"

Garland knew then his friend would never understand. How could he when Garland himself didn't understand what had happened? He would let Johan have his "homesick" explanation, let him look forward to a golden future.

But as he clenched his sweating hands and gazed nervously out of the train window, fear was beating a steady rhythm around Garland's heart and a disembodied voice, distant and foreign, whispered in his ear. *Control it. Embrace it,* it said in quiet English. He knew only he could hear it and fought back tears.

Chapter Four

JOHAN - 1935

After hours of travelling over rail and a choppy journey across the Baltic Sea that made both Garland and Johan throw up into the churning water, their train finally pulled into Stettiner Bahnhof Station.

It was busier than any place Johan had ever seen and he fed on its energy. Neither Johan nor Garland had ever left Norway, or even Oslo. Johan beamed with excitement. He was going to make a difference, show everyone that a poor orphan from a small foreign country could make it big in a world superpower. The possibilities in the SS were endless. His star would rise. He might even become a guard to the great Hitler himself! Garland's funny turn had only soured Johan's excitement for a short time, and, although he had been concerned, he felt sure the moment was a physical manifestation of his friend's real feelings about their new life.

Garland had never been fully on board with the idea, and no matter how many times Johan tried to fire a spark of excitement, he sensed in Garland only lukewarm anticipation of the adventure ahead. Garland was weak; it would be something he'd need to shake off if he was to grow into a man. Otherwise he'd be just like those inferior dregs of society, the Jews and the queers.

Granted, Johan was going to a secure and responsible job whilst Garland was taking more of a gamble with his future. But Garland had never shared the intrepid, risk-taking streak that ran through Johan like an unstoppable force. Berlin meant a fresh start where they could reinvent themselves. They wouldn't be judged as orphans anymore, no longer shackled by a past they had been born to endure. Now they would be truly accepted in society and, with time, recognised and even revered. Johan remembered Froch's words and smiled. *Tough. Respected. Feared.* They glowed brightly in Johan's mind.

What a world we live in where an orphan with no qualifications or education can rise to a pedestal above others, he thought.

They stepped onto the platform and saw a severe, dark-haired man holding a neatly-written white sign with JOHAN OLSEN displayed in thick capital letters. The man was unmissable in a black uniform with a matching hat. Various insignias were attached to his pristine jacket, but it was the bright red armband that stood out, the light against dark contrast striking. Inside the red was another eye-catching contrast, a white circle containing a black swastika. Nothing had captured Johan's imagination more than the simple emblem. In his excitement at joining the SS, he would sit in his bunk and dream. He pictured himself in the prestigious force, he and his comrades in their dashing uniforms, all displaying this symbol of the new world. Johan would sketch the thick black swastika over and over, perfecting his technique. He couldn't wait to wear the uniform himself, to be accepted as one of them.

The officer smiled as Johan and Garland stood to attention in front of him, but it failed to soften his features, the wrinkles on his face giving him a tough, stark look.

"Well, well, well. What fine specimens of young men we have here. At ease," he told them, his Berlin accent quite different to the Munich tones they were used to. He eyed them up and down and placed his large, rough hands on Johan's shoulders. "Blond hair, blue eyes, well-built. Two Aryan men of unerring quality. Welcome to Germany, gentlemen. I am Squad Leader Fischer."

Johan smiled and surreptitiously nudged Garland. "Thank you, sir. Looking forward to getting started, sir."

Fischer held his gaze on Garland. "I understand you are not joining the SS. Is that right?"

"No, sir," Garland replied. "I mean, yes. That is correct. I wish to further the Nazi cause by my theatrical talents." There was a pause and Johan noticed a sheen of sweat appear at Garland's temples despite the cold January air. Again, Johan silently cursed his friend's trepidation. After a few seconds, Fischer spoke.

"Excellent," he said, the smile back in place. "The SS is not for everyone. Dr Goebbels looks after all the theatre in Germany. He will be delighted that a young, talented Aryan is willing to lend his talents to our cause."

Johan smiled. "He is modest, sir. He's the best performer in the whole of Oslo."

"And so he shall be in Berlin," Fischer replied. "Now, come, your lodgings await. Mr Lund, I understand that we have agreed to put you up in temporary accommodation in Berlin until you find a permanent residence?"

Garland nodded.

"Excellent." It was a word Fischer overused, his accent giving it a snappish sound, like a knife being sharpened against granite. "I hope you'll enjoy your new life. I'll provide you with the contact details of the best theatres in the whole city. I trust you have references?"

"Yes, sir," Garland replied, reaching into his knapsack.

"Not now, Mr. Lund. But you will need them when you begin. Berlin theatre is a most competitive arena. I myself go regularly and you will find no better performers in the world. You've certainly come to the right place to make your mark. And, when the time comes, maybe we can make a soldier of you too. No reason why you can't do both."

Johan held his breath and threw a nervous glance at Garland. He knew his friend could think of nothing worse than going into battle, killing others, firing weapons. He hoped he would play along and not show him up in front of this high-ranking officer. Garland had to work on his weakness.

"Yes, sir," Garland replied. "I will certainly look to do that, especially when I've secured a place in a theatre."

Johan quietly exhaled and afforded himself a tiny smile.

"Good. Now, let's move."

Fischer led them to a car parked outside the station. The vehicle was black and had a perfect shine, as if had been polished for days on end. The streets thrummed with cars, bicycles, and pedestrians, crowding roads and footpaths beneath buildings that seemed to stretch to the sky. Some had the imposing Nazi flag draped over the stonework, the bright red and thick black swastika proud and glorious. Johan felt overwhelmed, almost giddy with excitement. This was his city now and just being here, soaking up the atmosphere, looking at the people, made him feel invincible. The emotion surged through his veins, making him feel stronger, taller. The new smells, the colours, the different faces all swirled together in a euphoria in his mind; it was almost too much to take in at once. A liveried chauffeur opened the passenger door and bowed. Who would bow to him in Oslo? Johan struggled to stifle a laugh of disbelief.

Johan and Garland took their places at the rear of the vehicle. Johan ran his hands across the smooth leather seats as the chauffeur eased the car out of the parking bay.

"Mr Lund, we'll drop you off at a hostel not far from here in the Mitte district, where you'll find easy access to the city's theatres by foot or bicycle. You have two weeks to find somewhere else. This is a generous offer which we do not accommodate to most."

"And I thank you for it, sir," Garland replied.

"Mr Olsen, you will come with me to the SS offices where we will go through your documents. And from there you'll board a bus to a town a few hours from here, to Dachau, just outside Munich, where you will take residence for six months and complete our SS training programme. You will then be allocated a station depending on whether you pass and we identify any competencies that fit certain roles."

Johan grimaced and looked over to Garland. All the colour had drained from his friend's face.

I hope to God he doesn't have another episode.

Johan had wondered where his training might be. Although he had assumed in would be in Berlin, being Germany's capital, he thought there was a chance it would be elsewhere. He had kept the possibility from Garland, and whilst he felt a pang of regret, he didn't feel guilty. This was Garland's chance to make something of himself in a new, prosperous city, one that would be the epicentre of the world in times to come. Someone needed to drag him from his comfort zone, and if Johan was to be the man, then so be it.

Garland glared back at Johan, his forehead gleaming with perspiration.

"Y - You said that—"

Johan interrupted him by putting a finger to his mouth.

"Something wrong, boys?" Fischer asked from the front seat. He turned to face them.

"Not at all, sir," Johan replied.

'No," added Garland, shaking his head unconvincingly.

"You know," Fischer began, "I envy you two boys. Young, good-looking. In the peak of your youth, I'd say. Coming to a city like this when it is on the threshold of glory. The Olympics will come this summer, did you know that?"

They nodded, Johan grinning and bobbing his head so rapidly he looked exaggerated and cartoonish.

"The best of the best doing battle. The strongest, fittest men on the planet fighting to see who comes out on top. And do you know something? This will prove once and for all that we are superior to all other races. Let the Jews, the Blacks, even the Romani come and compete. Let them fail and fall at our feet." He spat his words so viciously small globules of saliva flew from his mouth as he spoke. "Let the world see us in all our glory. Then they'll know that we have risen like the phoenix. Then they'll know we unshackled ourselves from the burden of a thousand years of impure, inferior races dragging us down. Then they'll know all right. Heil Hitler!" The last two words were said with such ferocity it made the chauffeur jump, the car jolting as his hands flinched on the wheel.

"Heil Hitler!" the chauffeur echoed.

"Heil Hitler!" Johan repeated loudly. He looked over at Garland, eyebrows raised in silent instruction.

"Heil Hitler," Garland said, with as much enthusiasm as he could muster.

Johan looked out of the window and saw another draped Nazi flag, the rippling of the thick material in the morning wind only adding to its splendour.

Johan smiled and closed his eyes. *Heil Hitler,* he thought...

Chapter Five

GARLAND - 1935

Although his senses had slowly returned, Garland couldn't shake off his episode on the train. He had spent the rest of the journey in unsettling silence, much to the annoyance of Johan, whose excitement was uncontained. The feeling of sickness had faded, but every now and again, colours still swam around the edge of his vision, and he was sure the murmur of a quiet voice chimed somewhere deep in his consciousness.

The conversation with Fischer had done nothing to lift the anxiety gnawing away like a bad memory in his stomach. Meeting him had also made Garland wish he had done more to improve his German. It was ironic that Johan, who had struggled to master reading and writing even in his native tongue, was more confident speaking the language than Garland, infinitely more educated thanks to home-schooling by one of the more nurturing masters at the orphanage.

Something about the SS squad leader had made Garland uncomfortable, but he couldn't quite put his finger on it. Perhaps, Garland considered, he was embarrassed to admit to the officer he wasn't SS material, but Fischer seemed to accept his explanation without judgement. Garland's unease hadn't been helped by the swirling colours that stirred on the fringes, blurred black, white and red smudges ebbing and flowing like a tide trying to pull him under. The skull-and-crossbones symbol above the brim of Fischer's hat seemed to Garland like a gateway to despair, and the vague smell of burning grew stronger the more time he spent with the man. When the car had been rolling through the busy Berlin streets, the sight of the blood-red flags and harsh black swastikas had made Garland's head spin so much he feared what happened on the train was about to happen again. The revelation that Johan would be stationed on the other side of Germany had sickened him even more. He had assumed they would at least be in the same city, even if it was at opposite ends. The thought of tackling everything alone made him feel scared and homesick.

In Oslo he was making waves. Yes, the opportunities in Germany were much greater but he would have enjoyed being a big fish in a small pond. Here he was anonymous, a stranger. He had to start again in a place where no one knew him, with only a sheet of paper to show Mr Andersen's approval, no doubt written in patchy German, and the advantage of his Aryan appearance, which seemed to be a fast-track ticket to success in this country.

Now he looked around the hostel that would be home for the next two weeks. It was basic, his bed one of thirty in a large, shabby room.

Strong odours of dirt and sour sweat wafted around him, unpleasant but to Garland a welcome change to the burning smell that had been so strong when the visions had struck.

"Hello, my friend." A voice came from behind him.

Garland turned to face a small man with dark brown hair. He was wearing gloves and a thick coat. "I still can't get used to the cold winters here," the stranger said, sensing Garland take in the warm clothing. "My name is Gianni. I'm from Rome."

Garland looked at him and smiled. Gianni hardly fitted in with the Aryan look that was supposed to be the ideal in this country.

"Garland Lund. Oslo," he said and shook the Italian's hand.

"Garland. An odd name for a Norwegian?"

"Yes. Long story. How long are you here?"

"I've been in Berlin for four years. This hostel for two weeks. It's not too bad as hostels go. Could be a lot worse. What brings you here, Garland Lund?"

"The theatre. I'm a performer. Ballet."

"Wonderful," replied Gianni. "You're in the right place. Lots of theatres in Berlin, although not as many as before. Before 1933 you couldn't move for them. Some of the stuff going on there was a bit odd though. Men dressed as women, homosexuals running most shows. Then Hitler came and put Goebbels in charge and, well, let's just say it's a bit more controlled now. But still, some good opportunities for the right people."

"So I'm told," Garland said and smiled. He liked Gianni immediately. He had never met an Italian but had heard much about people from the country, particularly Rome. Gianni had a natural charm, his dark hair was impressively neat, with a strand falling delicately and deliberately over his forehead. His brown eyes were large and sparkling, and his smile revealed a set of gleaming white teeth. He looked older than Garland, but still no more than twenty-five.

"Come on," Gianni said, flashing his bright smile. "I'll give you the grand tour of Berlin."

They walked and talked for hours. Gianni was a cook at an Italian restaurant, the Taverne, which was run by a head chef known as Seadog Willy, a swarthy, aggressive German whose ignorance of true Italian cooking was a constant source of irritation to Gianni. The nickname had been born whilst he was a ship's cook on various vessels, his reputation for hard drinking and fist fights, which he invariably won, a badge of honour.

"It's a job," Gianni told Garland. "It pays okay. Not enough to get a decent place to live, but enough to clothe me. And to get free food. I might be able to sneak you some."

Garland liked the sound of that. As a Norwegian he was used to a diet heavy in fish, so the idea of Italian breads and meats, even if poorly prepared, whet his appetite. Gianni's company had lifted his mood. He soaked up the sights of Berlin, the imposing buildings, the impressive Brandenburg Gate and the wonderful cathedral. The swastika flags still made Garland feel queasy, but walking swiftly at Gianni's side, the sensations passed as soon as they came.

They went for a drink at a local *bier keller,* a popular spot bursting with revellers laughing, singing and chatting in voices raised to match the low roar of noise that reached the rafters. They ordered two steins, which they made last for two hours, and sat on wooden seats outside. Although the beer tasted crisp and refreshing at first, Garland struggled to finish the final third when it became warm even in the cool air. He noticed Gianni shivering as a gust of wind blew against his face.

"You don't have this weather in Italy?" Garland asked.

"No," Gianni replied. "Well, not this cold in the winter in Rome, anyway. I imagine you're used to it further north?"

Garland smiled. "This is nothing, my friend." He slapped Gianni's back and felt the thick, rough material of his coat.

"So, now we are getting to know each other, I am intrigued," Gianni said, his dark eyebrows dancing with mischievous excitement. "Your name. Where does it come from?"

Garland sighed. He was never good at lying or keeping secrets. He was too soft, Johan always used to tell him. Maybe it was his theatrical side. To perform at the highest levels, you had to feel emotion, passion, empathy. And with the smooth came the rough; sometimes Garland felt too much emotion. Sometimes he took things too hard.

There were moments he wished he could be more like Johan, protected by a hardened edge, able to take whatever life flung at him with a smile, fearless and brave as a bear ready to fight. Instead Garland worried, he cried, and he couldn't tell a convincing lie. The guilt of passing a simple fib overwhelmed him, and even if he tried, he was found out. On Garland, deception blazed like a warning flare. He could fool no one, even in the name of self-preservation. Telling Gianni the truth was the easy option.

"I'm an orphan. My mother was a young woman in Oslo when she had a two-week affair with a British soldier on leave. He swept her off her feet, treated her like a princess and then left."

"Ah, took off into the night. Shirked his responsibility and left your mother high and dry. A familiar story, I'm afraid," Gianni replied.

"No," Garland heard the edge in his voice. "He never knew I existed. My mother carried on loving him until she died. I was six years old, but she thought so much of him she didn't want me to ever forget him. So, she gave me his surname, Garland, as my first name. He was called Daniel Garland and he was an officer. My mother told me he had won medals for bravery, he had fought gallantly in the Great War and he was a hero in England. Even though growing up without him hurt me deeply and still does, I'm proud of where I came from and proud to carry his name. I suppose it's also why I feel so close to the English."

The words had flowed free like a dam breaking, and Garland felt his face heat when he realised he had made a speech.

"It's a nice story," Gianni said quietly, "but the English have got that cold blood running through their veins, much like the Germans. Not like my prime, hot Italian blood!" He slapped the underside of his wrist, emphasising the large blue vein that ran against his skin.

Garland smiled. "Well, we can't all be perfect, can we?"

"Now, let's finish these beers and make our way back. My generosity doesn't stretch to another stein I'm afraid."

Garland was pleased to move on. The beer had bloated him and begun to churn his stomach, which was running on empty. They walked along the streets. The long red flags hanging from the silent buildings looked sinister in the winter moonlight, and Garland quickened his step, forcing his gaze away from the black swastikas that adorned them.

Chapter Six

JOHAN - 1935

Standing on a gravelled hill path at the eastern edge of Dachau's

perimeter, Johan surveyed his surroundings.

Dachau was a different experience. Although it did little to dampen his enthusiasm for his new beginning in Germany, the environment came as a shock. The large training base was attached to a prison camp, where inmates were forced to carry out hard labour.

The work was hard but the treatment from the guards was harder. Johan could smell fear mixing with the grimy fug of sweat and exhaustion. He noticed that birds never flew around the camp, that nature seemed to have abandoned the place completely. Often in Oslo, Johan and Garland would challenge each other to identify birds, even playing a game where the first to correctly name one could swing a free punch at the loser's arm. Of course, if the guess was wrong, the punch would come the other way. But Dachau was no place for games. It was cold and hard and unforgiving.

Training was an ordeal on mind and body but almost a gift compared to the inmates' agonising existence. When Johan saw their suffering, his own hardship felt like a blessing.

He had been surprised at the amount of time the recruits spent on words as well as work outs, the sessions on the Nazi regime and what it meant to be a follower. He learnt about the Jews, the Romani, the superiority of the Aryan race and the future of the Reich. Johan was even tested on his beliefs in an exam. He was determined to prove himself in this world, to take on these ideals and punish those people who didn't deserve to breathe the same air as their superiors. He trained himself day by day to hate the Reich's enemies. They were his enemies now.

He looked down on the prison camp and saw one inmate flogging another under the watchful eye of a guard urging him to strike harder and harder. When the prisoner was too gentle, the guard pushed him to the ground, snatched the whip from his hands and lashed both men twenty-five times. Johan counted the strokes and grimaced at each one. Even from his vantage point twenty metres away, he could see the raw marks tearing into their flesh as the men's screams pierced the solemn morning air.

Johan heard a crunch in the gravelly dirt and looked across to see Weber, his training officer, walking towards him. He stood to attention.

"At ease, Olsen," he said, softly. He strolled over to Johan's side and together they watched the prisoners stand on unsteady legs whilst the guard bellowed insults in their faces.

"They're not human, you know," Weber said evenly. "Never forget that. When it comes to killing - and trust me, Olsen, you will kill many of them, maybe even thousands - do not take it to heart." He tapped his chest as he said the words. "Some of the hardest men struggle to handle it. Some refuse and are dealt with accordingly. But back home in Oslo, if you had a problem with vermin, what would you do? Would you welcome a rat into your house, feed him, clean up his shit? Or would you poison him? Better still, would you throw his body into your garden so that his body will nourish your plants? Think not of these people as men but as rats, Olsen. Rats add nothing to our society. They spread disease, they litter our streets and multiply, causing us only problems. We should dispose of them, but more importantly, we must see that their demise is part of the cycle of success."

Johan realised Weber was preaching more than speaking, no trace of doubt in his words, no sympathy in the sermon.

"These Jews," Weber continued, pointing to the two prisoners, "will die. And very soon by the looks of them. But how would simply killing them, or worse, imprisoning them, benefit us? No, we must use them for all they are worth. We must squeeze them until Germany has had the full benefit of their existence. And then, only then, will they be released by their own demise. And it's not just the Jews. Do you know who is worse than a Jew, in my humble opinion?"

Johan shook his head. He was listening intently, rhythmically switching his focus from Weber's hard face to the two prisoners now back on the ground being kicked and punched by the guard with cold disdain.

"A homosexual." Weber's eyes were on fire. "Homosexuals have no place on this earth. They actively choose a life that does not progress our nation. They'll never father a child. They go against God in every single way. They turn their backs on humanity. I was a guard down there until last autumn," he nodded down to the yard, Johan following his gaze. "One of the last things I did was to take care of a homosexual. He was a big, strong boy. A good worker, too, so I used to lay off him a bit with the beatings. Other guards, they felt he could be rehabilitated. Maybe even make a good soldier. But I hated him, Olsen. I hated him more than I have hated any man I ever met. On my last day, I celebrated by ordering another prisoner to hang him, naked, by his arms, for all others to see. Then I ran my knife down his belly."

Weber traced a line down Johan's stomach. The light touch, even through his thick training uniform, felt like ancient ice that made his shoulders shiver.

"His guts fell to his feet. You could smell them, Olsen. The man bled out but only after three hours. *Three hours!* His face was hanging down, so all he could see in the last miserable moments of his sinful life were his own hot guts splashing onto his feet. That was the best day of my SS career."

Weber paused, eyes closed as he savoured the memory.

"Now, son, how does that make you feel?"

Johan took a heartbeat to glance again at the prisoners below, then pushed out his chest.

"Good, sir." His voice sounded steel strong. "Like you say, the homosexual deserved it. I can't wait to do the same."

Johan gulped once, hearing the words and wondering if they were true.

Weber looked across at him, taking a couple of seconds to consider the response.

"*Wunderbar!*" he finally said, slapping Johan's back so hard Johan stumbled forward, kicking up grit with his boots. "Not long to go and you'll be stationed somewhere like that. Maybe even Dachau itself. Just remember. They're nothing but rats that need to be used and disposed of in the most painful, humiliating way possible. There is no room for tolerance in this world. We begin tolerating the Jews, the homosexuals, the rest of the vermin and where will that get us? They will destroy our nation, boy. Now, I will see you at five hundred hours tomorrow morning for weapons training. Heil Hitler!"

"Heil Hitler!" Johan replied, saluting as Weber turned away. Down in the camp, a third inmate was pulling a creaking barrow slowly across the silent courtyard, the lifeless bodies of the two beaten prisoners a tangle on top of the stained wooden planks, arms and legs locked together in their final freedom.

Chapter Seven

GARLAND - 1936

By the time Garland came face-to-face with Joseph Goebbels, he had already been to the brink of ending his Berlin adventure.

In the early weeks, full of hope, he had trekked from theatre to theatre with Mr Andersen's reference, but expectation slowly died under the weight of endless rejections.

The theatre managers all raised their eyebrows with interest when they met a muscular young Aryan asking if there were any vacancies, but their enthusiasm quickly wilted once they realised his speciality.

"A man performing ballet? A few years ago, maybe, but not now," said one flamboyant impresario at a small, quaint theatre in the Mitte district.

The message became a refrain, and Garland began to curse the dance that had made his name in Oslo.

Whilst disappointment dragged through his days, the nights were spent pot-washing in the Taverne, a favour from Gianni. Here he experienced the hideous Seadog Willy for himself, a hulk of a man who would scream at his staff and even spit in the food of customers he took against. Willy wore his anger and bigotry like a tattoo across his heart. He called everyone *queers* and *Jews* whether he thought they were or not. More than once, Garland had seen him punch a luckless barman for a simple error. Whilst Willy raged, Garland and Gianni kept their heads down. Always.

As the weeks dragged on, Garland kept up his search, but he was running out of hope and options. Only a handful of theatres were left on his dwindling list.

That was the moment everything changed. The moment fate suddenly slid from the shadows to nudge Garland down a different path.

It happened during his weekly stein with Gianni and in the middle of conversation coming rapidly to the boil.

"What do you mean you might give up?" Gianni had said, the words a breakneck blur behind extravagant hand gestures. "This is Berlin. Anything can happen. Please, you must keep trying. You must!"

Garland had looked back at him silently, unconvinced.

"Come on," Gianni demanded. "Give it two more weeks, please. Just two weeks. Promise?"

"You don't understand." Garland shook his head. "In Oslo I was really something. I was the best ballet dancer in the biggest city in

Norway. Here, they don't want to see a grown man dance. They just want actors and singers."

"Then act! Sing! Can you not?"

"Not to the same standard." Garland could feel the heat in his voice rising. "Consider the best chef in Rome, Gianni. Can you picture him?"

Gianni's face wrinkled with pleasure, his mind filling with the sights and smells such a chef could conjure. "Yes," he replied, opening his eyes.

"This chef is a speciality pasta chef. He cooks the finest pasta in Rome and probably the best pasta in all Italy."

"No," Gianni said sternly.

"No?"

"No. The best pasta chef from Rome? Ridiculous. Any Italian would tell you, the best chef of any pasta would be from Bologna. Always Bologna."

Garland paused for a second and sighed.

"Okay, okay," he carried on. "The best pasta chef in Bologna and probably the whole of Italy. Can he also make risotto? Yes. But take him away from pasta and let him only cook risotto, and what happens to his status? What happens to his reputation as the finest in his field? It disappears! You take the speciality away and he becomes the same as everyone else. Make me an actor or a singer and could I pay my rent? Could I impress? Maybe. Would I excel? Would I bring real joy to my audience? I doubt it."

Gianni took a large swig of his stein with an audible gulp and wiped the foam from his mouth. He belched, then clapped his hands together slowly.

"Bravo, Garland Lund! Bravo!" He reached forward and slapped Garland on the back. "Poetic and spoken like a true Italian. Now I understand. You dance ballet because that is your calling. That is. . ."

"I might be able to help you."

The voice came from somewhere behind Garland.

"Hey, *compagno*, have you ever heard of a private conversation?" Gianni said dryly.

Garland turned and saw a man dressed in a suit that didn't appear particularly smart. His clothes seemed tired and hung off him. His face looked weary, tinges of sweat glistening on his temples. Garland saw a white, pasty substance smudged at the edge of his jaw-line.

"Forgive my Roman friend," Garland said. "In what way could you help me? Did you hear my predicament?"

"You are a ballet dancer, the best in all of Norway," the man said it with a hint of derision. Garland turned back to Gianni and forced an embarrassed smile. "You are quite correct, of course. Since Goebbels took over responsibility for entertainment, opportunities for male ballet dancers are somewhat limited. Tell me, young man, how do you feel about comedy?"

"Comedy? Like, acting?" Garland replied, caught off guard.

"Like acting, like dancing. A mixture of the two. Farcical situations, gymnastics, slapstick. Making people laugh."

Garland looked down at his stein and tried to picture himself in front of a laughing crowd. The idea, to his surprise, appealed to him. It wasn't ballet, but it was still an attractive proposition.

"There is a vacancy in my company. One of our performers had to leave, unfortunately. Are you interested? If you're half the dancer you say you are, the rest should come easily."

Garland had wondered at the man's logic but heard himself agreeing to audition at nine o'clock the next morning.

It had taken him a while to get used to his new role, but he learnt quickly. The four other men in the company were experienced performers. He was the youngest by almost a decade. They refused to speak of the man he had replaced, although Garland gleaned he was a similar age to himself. He guessed he had left after some kind of disagreement.

The show was fun and Garland enjoyed expressing himself, tumbling theatrically from an oversized bicycle, tripping over another performer's foot and acting out comic scenes that took advantage of his supple physique and rhythmic movements. The production gathered pace through word of mouth, and soon Garland was appearing at bigger venues in front of ever-growing crowds. Barely six months after arriving in Berlin, and with thoughts of a retreat to Oslo long forgotten, Garland found himself performing a week-long run in the Scala Theatre, one of the most famous in the city.

Now a full house filled the Scala with rapturous applause as he stepped from the stage.

Garland wiped sweat from his brow and smiled.

He was still smiling when he walked into the cluttered dressing room and flopped into a chair.

"What are you doing?" Tomas, the man who had recruited him, was uncharacteristically smart for the end of a show. "Don't you know who is here?"

Garland shook his head.

"Dr Goebbels is in the audience! He wants to meet us backstage. He'll be here any minute!"

Garland jumped to his feet in excited panic, darted to the mirror which hung above a porcelain sink, and tried to smooth his hair. He was still splashing water on his white-painted face when he heard the door creak open and the sound of several pairs of boots drumming against the tiled floor.

The performers all stood to attention, Garland immediately self-conscious at his half made-up face.

Four burly men in smart plain clothes strode in and stood opposite each other, forming a human corridor down which Dr Joseph Goebbels, Hitler's minister of propaganda and the man who controlled all arts and media in Germany, now walked. He had an uneven gait, a limp that made him appear as if he was about to topple over with each step. Garland looked at him and was taken by the glittering intensity in his eyes. They were dark and piercing beneath neat black hair slicked back in a way that was both smart and menacing. The familiar queasy feeling begin to stir deep within Garland – he had ridden its waves more than once since that first turn on the train to Berlin – and saw daggers of blackness in the corners of his vision. His unease increased the nearer Goebbels came.

"Good show, gentlemen. Hilarious! One of the best comedy acts I have seen." Goebbels spoke in a harsh but positive tone.

He walked up to each performer, shaking them by the hand, until he came to Garland. He stood the same height as the German, who leant closer. Garland was fearful of inflicting even his breath on a man of such high importance.

Dark colours swirled in Garland's eyes and his stomach turned, but he reached somewhere deep inside himself to keep control. He couldn't have an episode before this important man. Garland wasn't sure whether it was his paranoia or the silent war he was waging for composure, but Goebbels seemed to linger opposite him longer than with any of the other performers.

"You are not German?" he asked. The dark, intense eyes looked almost accusing.

"No, Dr Goebbels. I'm from Oslo in Norway."

Goebbels looked above Garland's eye line to his blond hair, which was matted with a paste of make-up and sweat. Garland swallowed loudly.

"Of course you are. Welcome to Germany. I'm pleased you have chosen this great country, and our great city of Berlin, to make your home. I hope we have helped you settle in."

"Yes, sir. Very much so."

"Excellent." Goebbels's smile lit nothing in the blackness of his eyes. "Well, keep up the good work, boys."

He slapped Garland on the back and walked out of the door, followed by his four black-suited guards.

Garland looked at Tomas and his fellow performers in silence for a few seconds after the door had shut behind the last soldier. Then the spell was broken and they burst out laughing, hugging each other as they danced and jumped around the cramped room.

When Garland slumped back down he was exhausted, not only by the evening's performance but the mental toll of meeting one of the most powerful men in Germany. He sighed heavily and looked up at the ceiling, thanking the saints he had controlled his disorientation. He shook his head in disbelief at the scene that had just passed, meeting the famous Joseph Goebbels.

And to think I nearly threw this life away and went back to Oslo.

He thought of Johan and wondered how many famous German officers he had met.

He decided to write to his friend.

Chapter Eight

JOHAN - 1936

Johan held the letter in his hands and laughed out loud. He had felt pangs of guilt, of course, after misleading Garland, but he had always believed things would work out. And now Garland had met the great Goebbels!

Johan shook his head as he tried to picture the encounter.

Trust Garland to meet a top Nazi.

Here was Johan, training until he dropped and working guard duty at Dachau, and it was *Garland* getting an audience with the big cheese.

Johan had been stationed at the camp for four months now. In training, he had sailed through every physical challenge, always in the top five in his class for strength, stamina and speed. The officers loved his power, his physique. *The perfect man*, Weber called him. The words made Johan stand two feet taller, his chest puffed with pride. His only failings were the intelligence tests. Weber wanted to get Johan into the top ranks of the SS and worked harder and harder with him each day on the political force of the Reich and the enemies that stood before it.

Hitler would love you, he had told him.

But that demanded more than physical excellence, and although Johan performed well on the philosophy of the Nazi Party, he struggled with some of the basic academic sessions that other, less physically capable trainees breezed through.

Guard duty at Dachau, though, was easy work. Johan enjoyed the sense of power. The way the prisoners looked at him, full of fear, filled Johan with a dark energy. He fed on the panic that flared in their eyes, cornered animals with nowhere to run.

The beatings he dished out quickly became routine. If he couldn't crack the intelligence, he could impress his superiors by attacking their enemies. It was the Jews he targeted most. As time went on, he began to enjoy delivering pain to them. The art was hurting and humiliating them just enough without affecting their ability to work. The feeling of bones cracking under his fists was a wonderful, almost spiritual, release. It took his mind back to his early days at the orphanage. Those who tried to taunt him. Those who didn't realise he was destined for great things, a man of power. And he loved correcting them.

The more Johan punished, the more he embraced the feeling of absolute superiority.

Jews cowered when he walked near them. Johan even perfected his own *death stare* a pitiless expression he reserved for the most abhorrent prisoners in Dachau. Some guards targeted the homosexuals, others went for the communists. But Johan loved beating the Jews and he felt no guilt. These so-called men were lucky they weren't executed on the spot. A beating was a favour, a blessing that was Johan's gift to bestow.

Johan was shaken out of his daydream and almost dropped Garland's letter as Officer Weber clapped him on the back.

"You're moving out, Olsen."

Johan jolted to attention and moved his eyes towards his commander.

"Sir?"

"You're going to Berlin."

Johan turned to face Weber, his jaw dropping open with surprise. He remembered himself and faced forward. "Berlin, sir?"

"A new camp has been built there. A good move for you, son. It will be the administrative centre of the whole SS. Himmler himself visits it regularly, so I'm told. An excellent opportunity for a young Aryan officer."

"Thank you, sir."

"You will be stationed at Sachsenhausen, Oranienburg from 1st August. You will have the whole of August off, a gift for our best men from the Fuehrer himself. But you'll want to be in Berlin for the first of the month."

"Sir?"

"It's the Olympics, Olsen," Weber told him. "The best athletes on the planet will be in our great country. We've secured some free tickets for our SS recruits in Berlin."

Weber winked at Johan.

"I've got a couple for you and a friend. Go there. The Fuehrer himself will attend. Enjoy. There'll be much hard work to come in Sachsenhausen."

"Thank you very much, sir."

"Heil Hitler!" Weber yelled, spittle flying from his lips.

"Heil Hitler!" Johan replied.

Weber left and Johan realised he still had Garland's letter in his hand. He was going to Berlin, to the Olympics, and he knew exactly who he was taking with him.

You think meeting Goebbels is impressive, Garland? How about Hitler and the greatest athletes in the world?

He grinned and his eyes sparkled. Johan was going to see his friend once more. And, even better, he was starting to make real progress in the mighty SS.

He rushed to his living quarters, grabbed a pen and a wad of paper and began to write.

Chapter Nine

SACHSENHAUSEN - 1936

The sun set across the western horizon of Germany and a hazy darkness engulfed Oranienburg.

A colony of bats fluttered and flitted across the bright beam of a spotlight that scanned the large triangular shape of Sachsenhausen.

An SS guard walked nonchalantly across the dirt and inhaled deeply. The sharp smell of the newly constructed wooden buildings hung pleasantly in the air. The guard stroked his rifle longingly. He stopped to tie his shoelaces and squinted as the spotlight swept past his eyes. He took it in, the silence. Soon the camp would be bustling with prisoners, guards, yells, gunfire. The calm was eerier for the sombre fact that it wouldn't last.

A strong breeze blew from the north, causing the tall trees that lined the camp to lean and bend in unison and the bats to scatter erratically in the night's cool air. It was as if the camp was inhaling in anticipation.

Waiting.

Chapter Ten

GARLAND - 1936

Garland sat at a table, tapping his feet nervously against the stone floor. He lit a cigarette and washed down the harsh smoke with a cup of strong, bitter coffee. He had chosen a table facing the door so he could see all who entered the small café, which was on an alleyway off bustling Friedrichstrasse.

Grimacing each time someone who wasn't Johan walked through the door, Garland fixed his gaze on the entrance, beyond the smoke that was curling up from the burning cigarette. A lively stream of people hurried their way through the main street. The Olympics had arrived in Berlin, and with it came an excitement so strong you could feel it in the air, electric and sharp.

He looked away. The more he wished for Johan to appear the less likely it seemed he would. Of course, he had told Johan about the theatre company and every detail of his meeting Dr Goebbels, but to tell him to his face, to *see* his reactions, that would be precious. At the same time, he wanted to hear about his friend's adventures; from Johan's letters it sounded like he was doing well. Very well indeed.

Most of all, Garland was excited the two of them would finally be living in the same city. It had taken eight long months but it would be worth the wait.

The company had a brand new performance that was even better than the last, one with more acrobatics and dance than before, and Garland loved it. Who knows, maybe even more Nazi dignitaries would come and see him perform. He could get free tickets to the theatre for Johan too.

Stubbing out his cigarette, Garland looked over to the clock on the wall and saw that Johan was now almost ten minutes late. He rapped his fingertips rhythmically on the oak table. *What if he'd been called up on urgent duty?* It was the Olympics after all. There was a large police presence around the stadium, and Hitler himself was attending many of the events. Johan may have been ordered to work an extra shift. He had the address of Garland's hostel. Maybe he would call to see him later.

Just as Garland was working out how much longer he should wait, Johan Olsen strode through the door, ducking his head slightly to avoid cracking it on the low frame. Garland felt a surge of emotion, part happiness and part anxiety, as he suddenly wondered if they would still share the same brotherly connection, the natural spark that had brought them together as boys. He stood to greet Johan and was immediately reminded of his friend's impressive stature. He seemed to have grown since January. Hunks of muscle bulged like rock formations from his chest and arms, stretching his tight shirt. Something about his face looked different. There was a glint in his eyes that seemed to belong to a man much older, somehow.

"Gar, great to see you brother. Or should I say *wunderbar?*"

Garland held out his hand and was shocked by Johan's crushing grip, sharp ripples of pain shooting up his arm. Johan eyed Garland apologetically, realising the deliberate show of SS strength wasn't necessary with his old friend. Instead he pulled him into a tight embrace.

"Sorry you've been waiting," Johan said as they sat down. "Had a bit of a late one last night with some of the boys. They've put us up in a brilliant hotel. The barmaid locks the doors and lets us drink steins until we can't talk anymore. And she's pretty easy on the eye if you know what I mean."

Johan talked about the prisoner camp. It seemed exciting, like something from a film. But Garland realised he would never be cut out for the SS when Johan eagerly described the beatings.

"The Jews and the queers, we give them the worst," Johan said, blowing on his coffee to cool it. "We keep them in check. Rehabilitate them so they're ready for German society. It's a tough world, but ultimately, we help them, at least the ones who want the help. Some are too far gone. Those animals we make sure can work and still contribute to society in a safe, confined place."

It was another world to Garland's own experience of Germany, and he was glad he'd never chosen a soldier's life. It sounded hard and unforgiving. Garland had seen the posters, caricature images of Jews who were only out for themselves, selfish backstabbers who would bring down the community of Germany. He'd never really considered it as anything other than politics, but hearing Johan speak of them in such a way made him feel a little sick.

He was swallowing down the negative emotions whilst Johan spoke of his experience of the Olympics so far, the opening ceremony, standing only thirty metres from the Fuehrer himself as he shook the hands of the German athletes.

As Johan talked, Garland's mind drifted again, and his eyes rested on a Nazi flag draped from a building opposite the café. It rippled and shimmered in the breeze, the movements a dance without music. Suddenly, as Garland watched, rivers of red exploded from the flag, the colour shooting in a starburst that swirled over the rooftops of Friedrichstrasse, menacing and ominous. A smell of burning rubber rose, like a mist, thickening and twisting before him as the blocks of the swastika began expanding outwards. Garland watched the cross stretch and widen, a black force blossoming to block out the light. Garland felt its soulless, deathly power as icy fear rose in his heart.

The visions had been visiting him more and more over the past few weeks, followed by nightmares and apocalyptic visions that left Garland dripping in sweat and racked with an unbearable sadness.

Swastikas made the visions more severe, and they had worsened again after he met Dr Goebbels.

The sound of Johan's voice dragged him back from the maelstrom unfolding outside the café window.

"You listening, brother?" – and as if he was reading Garland's thoughts – "You still get those funny turns?"

Garland looked back at Johan, remembering the train to Berlin. He nodded slowly.

"You should really get that checked out." Johan sounded only concerned. "Maybe it's something to do with your eyes."

Garland agreed, knowing something else, something beyond his grasp and understanding, was to blame. He lit a cigarette and downed the rest of his coffee.

"You smoke now?" Johan asked, an eyebrow raised in surprise.

"Yes, picked it up here. Everyone smokes in Berlin."

Johan laughed. "Who'd have thought? I have to bust a gut persuading you to come here and you're the one that turns into the real Berliner! I'd probably join you, but the boys who smoke don't do so well in the running sessions. They say it cleans out the system but the way some of those boys cough, Gar. Just leave me to the beer, that's the only vice I need. Well, the beers and the women, eh? And on that note, let's hear how many have fallen for the Garland Lund charm!"

"None at all really," Garland replied after a few seconds of silence.

"Just one then? Someone special?"

Garland shook his head bashfully.

"Too busy, I suppose." Johan shrugged, the moment awkward.

Garland thought about his life. It was true he had dedicated himself to his performances, spending long hours perfecting routines, the timing and dynamics that turned good to great, the single-minded drive for excellence. The rest of his time he spent with Gianni. The thought of taking women out didn't really appeal. Of course, some chatted to him after performances, but all he saw in their interest was hassle. Even though he loved his work, the pay still only stretched to his bed at the hostel and a few meals out. Throw a woman into the mix, and it would surely cost him Reichsmarks he could ill afford. And he just didn't find them attractive. Something about this was bubbling up from a part of his brain he was ignoring, and Garland dismissed it again. He wasn't interested in women whatsoever, but he was reluctant to tell Johan. His friend simply wouldn't understand.

"Well, maybe we'll change that now your big brother is here." Johan grinned. "Come on, we'll have to set off soon if we're going to make the start."

They left the café and joined the throng of people on the main street, heading for the S-Bahn to the Olympic Stadium. They bustled through the crowds onto the train and it rumbled its way to the Olympiapark. They disembarked and shuffled their way along amongst the hordes. The Nazi flag was hard to miss, the colours pinned to clothes and hats and even held aloft by several in the moving crowd. Each glimpse made Garland feel queasy, red flashes bursting out to blend with the dim morning light.

Garland had seen the stadium as it was being built, a gargantuan creation that gave him new admiration for the construction workers who scuttled like ants amongst the towering superstructure. They must have risked their lives at such heights.

Now the size and scale of the arena gave him a rush of pride for his adopted city and its friendly, hard-working people. Berlin was at the centre of the world, all eyes on the place he called home. Garland believed Berliners deserved it for their sense of adventure. At the same time, the moment seemed a recognition of the risk he himself had taken, leaving Norway behind just when his career was thriving.

He was more determined than ever to make the move a success. He might not have a soldier's fighting heart and edge of steel like Johan, but Garland Lund was no quitter. Maybe, Garland reasoned, it was the genes from his English father that had planted a "never say die" spirit inside him.

As they entered the stadium, shoulder to shoulder with other spectators, Johan turned to Garland and patted him on the back, the strength of the friendly contact again firing a bolt of pain across his shoulder blades.

"You're going to love this, Gar," Johan told him. "Breathe it in. Prepare to be blown away, brother!"

They walked up a wide flight of stone stairs and Garland immediately understood. The sight that opened up before them was spectacular. Garland had never seen so many people in one place, the numbers alone overwhelming. The spectators at the other side of the stadium were so far away they looked like tiny pink dots in the distance. The atmosphere was super-charged, the buzz now a tornado of vibrant emotion, the dizzying cauldron of sight, sound and smell taking Garland's breath away. A huge Nazi banner had been hung from one side of the stadium, several smaller flags running above and below. Garland felt his heart sink as the colours began to leak like tentacles whipping and writhing through the crowd, but he shook the vision to the back of his mind.

"It's really something, isn't it?" Johan said, putting Garland's shudder down to disbelief.

"It really is." Garland meant it. "Thank you so much for the tickets."

They made their way to their seats and scanned the programme they had each been given at the entrance, agreeing with a grin that Norway and Germany would share their allegiance.

"It's the one hundred metres sprint I'm really excited about," Johan said, eyes back on the programme. "The winner of that race really can call himself the fastest man in the world. Just imagine that, Gar. The fastest human on the planet!"

Garland smiled and looked across the field stretching in front of them, thinking of his ballet career. Could he have been the best in the world? Ballet wasn't the same as sport, the blood and thunder battle for medals, the winning and the losing. But he could have been the best in his field. Maybe there was still a chance. After all, he had found an admirer in a man as powerful as Goebbels.

The events were fascinating. Garland watched most of them wide-eyed and slack-jawed, the athletes all toned specimens of physical perfection. Most of the men – and even some of the women – made Johan himself look like a skinny schoolboy. The Germans were well-supported, but Garland found his admiration drawn to the Americans and the Soviets. There seemed nothing they could not do well.

When the time came for the men's one hundred metres final, Johan jumped to his feet and roared.

Excitement rippled like electricity across the packed crowd, the atmosphere raising the hairs on the back of Garland's neck. The wild cheers for Erich Borchmeyer, the German sprinter, seemed to crackle.

Garland bounced on his heels, his skin breaking out in goose bumps as the runners limbered up on the orange track below. Even at the distance, he could see their muscles bulging and their eyes wide and focused. His gaze fell on Jesse Owens, the Black American sprinter. Garland had seen Black men before, but not many and none like this man. Owens's physique seemed faultless, his eyes concentrated in a gaze of complete focus as he took his starting position. As Garland watched, swirls of searing colour began to flow from Owens's head, so dazzling Garland squinted against their brightness. Looking closer, he saw they were ribbons of gold.

"Owens is going to win this," he said to Johan, an image of the runner with the medal glowing somewhere deep in Garland's brain. "I just know it."

"The negro?" Johan spat the word out angrily. "You don't get it, do you? Not here. Not this race. This is the Olympics."

"Jo, I *know* it. He's going to win." He felt a fleeting stab of resentment at his friend's inability to look beyond the man's colour.

Johan was still looking at Garland with a mix of anger and suspicion when the starter's gun cracked.

The athletes ran in a blur, faster than Garland had ever seen anyone move before, but Jesse Owens was fastest. He accelerated rapidly in the final third of the race, bursting forward to win easily. Garland jumped and yelled, Johan glaring in stunned disbelief.

"A negro." His voice was laced with disgust. "Of all the people that could have won, it's a negro. And you knew?"

"A lucky guess maybe." Garland shrugged. "I don't suppose being a negro has much to do with it. He was just the fastest."

Johan turned to him with fire in his eyes.

"It's got everything to do with it, Gar. You really think someone like that is as good as one of us? You think the fastest man in the world is a negro? Impossible."

Garland shrugged again. He hadn't seen his friend for half a year, he didn't want to argue, but Johan's reaction irked him. Owens won the race. He didn't seem to cheat – how could he? – and the man was clearly in superb shape. A fast Aryan and a fast negro are both fast, Garland reasoned. Owens was just faster. He thought back to Johan's comments on Jews and his stomach churned once more.

Before he could speak again, he felt Johan grab his shoulder and saw him pointing to a figure standing in a box high and to the left of them in the huge stadium.

"There he is," Johan said. "The Fuehrer himself! That's one up on your Dr Goebbels I'm sure you'd agree?"

But Garland couldn't answer. He leant forward and vomited on his shoes, the black coffee and bread he had for breakfast now a grey mush at his feet. As his disorientation overwhelmed him, he fell sideways into a large German man who pushed him back, annoyed and muttering something about not handling his beer. Garland leant on his hands and knees and brought up more of his breakfast until his heaves were dry. The smell of burning rubber was back stronger than ever, filling his nostrils and his lungs. Johan helped him to his feet, his firm grip digging painfully into Garland's arms. He looked up to see the full stadium giving the Nazi salute, a sea of hands pointing skyward, straight fingers jabbing like daggers at the air as they chanted the Fuehrer's name.

"What are you doing?" Johan yelled. "If they think you're drunk they'll kick you out, and me with you. How will that look as a new officer in the SS? Shape yourself up!"

But Garland hardly heard. He opened his eyes and lost all balance again, the vision before him too terrifying. Adolf Hitler was standing in the box surrounded by his guards, lightning bolts of red, black, and brown flying in every direction from his rigid body. Around him everyone in the stadium was dead, a sea of rotten corpses with black sunken eyes, hands now maggot-covered claws still rigid in salute. Garland stared at their outstretched fingers, frigid and bony. The smell of death, rotten meat mixed with decay and dusty earth, hung like a burial shroud above the echo of their screams.

Garland sensed death touch every fibre of his body. It was a cold, sick feeling, as if he had swallowed a poisoned sliver of ice and felt it spread like a plague through every cell, every organ, encasing his heart in a frozen tomb. As his consciousness faded, the whispering English voice returned, the words becoming louder and clearer as the world around him turned black. *Help me*, it said. A desperate, weak voice that echoed and bounced around the chasm of his thoughts.

Garland closed his eyes and slipped into the darkness.

Chapter Eleven

RICHARD - 2022

Richard knew he was elsewhere. In this place, memories were fleeting, thoughts were gluey. He was both present and absent, a ghost in everything but name.

He was bound to a bed, but his mind wavered between his own and that of the other man. The young boy. He'd watched the world through his eyes, unable to control or communicate, just viewing the world around him as one would watch a movie. Except this cinema was completely immersive, and Richard was strapped to a bed, unable to look away. In more lucid moments he knew it was a deep-set dream, powered by hospital drugs and his otherworldly abilities.

Every now and again he'd feel himself inside his own body rather than that of Garland Lund, the young Norwegian in Berlin. There was something familiar about Garland's powers, something important. A connection he couldn't understand. And his name, it couldn't be a coincidence.

He opened his eyes and a dreamlike scene unravelled before him. He could see his hospital bed and the wires and machines that surrounded him. But he wasn't in a hospital room. He was in a forest, surrounded by trees. Instead of a sky overhead, bright colours swirled and danced.

Richard closed his eyes tightly and screamed for help. He wanted to be awake once more and away from this strangest of realities. He willed himself to break out of this dream, not wanting to see any more of the horrors that were unfolding before Garland's eyes.

But as he screamed in his silent voice, the branches of the trees around him simply swayed to an unheard tune, and Richard knew it was useless. There was a reason he was here, he could feel it surging inside him. An energy, a purpose.

He knew he had to wait.

Chapter Twelve

JOHAN - 1936

The Mercedes's suspension turned the long road to Oranienburg into a plush carpet, the wheels rolling effortlessly towards their destination. Johan sat in the passenger seat, enjoying the feel of the leather and the smoothness of the ride. He thought the car, a masterpiece of German engineering, looked like something from science fiction, the curved line of the bodywork a thing of beauty. Johan could imagine the Mercedes transporting people around the moon, if man were to ever visit.

He had heard Hitler wanted as many Germans as possible to own a car, to make them affordable even to ordinary workers. To Johan, the ambition captured everything that was special about the country, an innovative government bringing joy to its citizens who in turn were ready to work for the greater good.

What a time to be alive!

Johan was proud to call himself a part of the German community and not just a bystander.

He was a protector of rights, an enforcer of laws. He felt like a king in his uniform and vowed to do it justice, to repay the faith this great nation had shown in him.

The car turned sharply and began to slow as Johan gazed out of the window at a row of beautiful detached houses. A man in full SS uniform, clipping colourful flowers on his front lawn, waved and Johan sheepishly returned the gesture.

"Who do these houses belong to?" Johan asked the driver.

"To our officers." The man kept his eyes on the road. "The brave souls who look after our great camp here in Oranienburg."

He pulled the Mercedes to a halt outside an imposing home with large bay windows and a perfectly tended garden. The lawn, fringed by billowing clouds of phlox in purple and red, was impossibly green.

"This one, Mr Olsen, is yours." The driver turned and smiled at Johan, amused by his passenger's gaping jaw.

"They said they would provide accommodation but this is. . ."

Johan couldn't finish the sentence, the words fading away to stunned silence.

He pulled his suitcase from the boot and put it on the porch. The house was perfect, one he could never afford unless he was promoted all the way to the office of Hitler himself. His first thought was Garland, what his best friend would make of it, the reflex reaction to think of his old orphanage brother whenever there was a story to tell. But thinking of Garland brought troubling memories of the last time they had met. Twice now Johan had seen him overcome by something Garland couldn't – or wouldn't – explain. Maybe an illness had engulfed him. Maybe he was just weak and naïve, too fragile to see the true ways of the world and too easily stressed. Looked at in isolation, Garland's sudden episode on the train could easily be explained by panic, an extreme reaction to the start of a new life. But the second at the stadium? They were in no danger there, only part of something historic and spine-tingling. Then there was Garland's prediction the negro would win. He had been so convinced. Johan reasoned Garland had either made a lucky guess or studied more of the negro's form than he had let on. What other explanation was there?

Johan could feel them drifting apart, the uneasiness when they were together in Berlin, Garland's attacks a shadow creeping across their friendship.

But Johan wasn't ready to abandon Garland just yet. He vowed he would meet him again and this time convince him to see a doctor. Something about the guarded way Garland dealt with the episodes suggested he knew more than he was telling, that there was something he feared Johan would not understand or accept.

"Don't get settled in just yet," the driver said through the wound-down window, snapping Johan out of his thoughts. "You need to see the office."

The last word came with heavy exaggeration and a smirk.

The Mercedes drove down a long road made of soil and lined with large trees that seemed to lean towards the ground, their long branches swaying ominously, as if they held secrets Johan would never know.

The driver parked and Johan stepped from car as a man in full SS uniform approached. Johan recognised the lightning bolts and the two squares on his insignia. The man was short and his face was slender, jagged as if cut from solid stone. Behind rounded glasses shone eyes that were both bright and cold, sparkling icily as Johan snapped out a salute.

"Welcome, trooper. You must be Johan Olsen." His tone was formal and hard, and his face remained stern.

"Yes, sir," Johan replied.

"My name is Bernt Schulz. I am camp commander. You come highly recommended from Dachau. Can I ask you a question, Olsen?"

Johan nodded briskly. "Yes, sir."

"How ambitious are you, trooper?"

"Very, sir. I want to serve Germany and Hitler. I want to make Germany great."

"Your feelings on Jews?"

"Rats, sir."

"Rats?" Schulz raised his eyebrows and peered over his rounded spectacles. "Please explain."

"Yes, sir. My training officer used to say they were rats. They should be treated as such. But he said the main difference between rats and Jews was that you could control the Jews more, sir. Make them useful before they die. Make them work. For Germany, sir."

For the first time some of Schulz's flintiness softened.

"Excellent! Yes, very good. I think you will like it here, soldier. Are you married, Olsen?"

"No, sir."

"You must get married." Schulz made it sound like an order. "Our children are our future, Olsen. Everything we do, every act, every fibre of our being must be poured into the progression of this great country. I will ensure you have a wife before the year is over. A young Aryan such as yourself. You will be highly prized amongst the beautiful women."

"Yes, sir. Thank you, sir."

"Good boy." Schulz gave him a tight, two second smile. "Let me take you on the grand tour. Welcome to Sachsenhausen."

Chapter Thirteen

GARLAND - 1939

Although Garland wasn't usually one for heavy drinking, the beer was flowing to celebrate the end of the company's summer season. They had already been booked to return for the lead-up to Christmas, but for now Garland had a whole two months off. Better still, he had managed to save enough money to go on a trip, perhaps even to join Gianni in travelling to Italy. Garland had long been seduced by his friend's tales of fine food, velvet-smooth wine and thick green olives sampled under a perfect Roman sun.

But his travel plans could wait. Tonight was all about celebrating with his colleagues from the theatre company, a toast to the end of a successful run in one of Berlin's greatest theatres.

"You have been brilliant," Tomas told him as he drained his tankard. "I'm proud to say I made my move when I overheard you and your pal that night in the beer house. Chance, I know, but of course, I take full credit."

Garland looked over at Tomas and smiled. He owed the man a huge debt, the experience of performing with the company better than he could have imagined. Everyone in the troop was wonderful to work with, and audiences loved them. Steadily the performances had been moulded around Garland's special talents, his fluid movement and ballet dancer's precision. What they made look spur of the moment on stage had taken endless hours of practice and patience. Garland truly felt love for these people.

"Excuse me, Mr Lund." The unfamiliar voice came from behind Garland. He turned to see a man of around the same age as himself. He was tall, dark haired and wore a dazzling smile, full of white teeth. "Can I buy you a drink? I've been to watch the show three times, and I just think it's exquisite. I hope you don't mind me saying?"

Like many who perform for a living, Garland never found praise and adulation a chore.

"No, not at all," he told the stranger. "You are too kind, my friend."

The man's smile broadened as he extended his arm and shook Garland's hand.

"Please, call me Hans."

"Garland. Please, join us. It's always nice to meet someone who appreciates our work."

They shared several drinks, the conversation natural and easy and still flowing by the time the rest of the company headed for home.

"So, what brings a nice boy like you to a horrible place like this?" Hans asked.

"Berlin? I love it here. There's so much more for me than in Norway."

"If I were you I'd go straight back," Hans said, his tone so abrupt that Garland flinched. "It's just that. . . Look, I'm a Berliner and I love the place. . . the city, the people, the streets."

He waved his hand towards Friedrichstrasse outside the bar, still bustling and thrumming with people despite the late hour.

"But the Nazis are squeezing the life out of Germany."

Garland raised both eyebrows, caught by the sudden change in mood that made his beer-filled head spin.

He thought of Johan working in the heart of the Nazi enforcement, his sudden determination about the Jews' place at the bottom of society. His stories of violence. He remembered with a shiver the visions that tormented him, the arena of emaciated dead saluting Adolf Hitler as bolts of coloured lightning flew from his body. "You're a Nazi supporter then," Hans was saying now. "Most people are, I suppose."

"No, not at all," Garland told him. "It's just different to hear someone say what you're saying."

Hans threw a glance around the near-empty bar.

"Berlin wasn't perfect before Hitler. There were a lot of things wrong. But the freedom, the expression, the belief that anyone could do anything? The hope? It's been stolen from us. Our identity has been ripped out."

Even through the fuzz of alcohol, Garland could see the hurt in Hans's eyes.

"Hans, I'm going to tell you something I've never told anybody before." He pursed his lips in concentration. "Something I can barely think about logically but is happening to me all the same. I know I don't know you, I just. . . I need to tell someone, someone who might understand."

"Intriguing." Hans stood and put his hand gently on Garland's shoulder. "This calls for two more beers."

Garland could have changed his mind in that moment, slipped from the bar and kept his secrets safely locked away.

But he wanted to talk, needed to share what he was suffering.

When Hans returned with their freshened steins, Garland let the floodgates open. He relived all that he had seen on the train and in the streets and at the stadium, the sickening smell of burning and the screams that came with his visions. He told him about Johan, about their orphanage, and how they were slowly being pulled apart.

Finally, he talked about his premonition, not guessing but *knowing* Jesse Owens would win the sprint.

Hans had listened to Garland's breathless tale in silence, the perfect listener who never interrupted, who let the words and the story flow.

Now as Garland reached the end, sweating with the effort of the telling, Hans stared seriously for a few seconds before breaking into a smile.

"Well, well, well. Sounds like we have a regular psychic in our midst."

Garland thought he sensed derision, the finger of fun poking at his ribs. "Don't take the piss." He dropped his gaze. "It took a lot to tell you that."

Hans shook his head and rested smooth, thin fingers on Garland's hand. "You misunderstand me, my friend." His voice reassuring. "I appreciate being the person you told. I know it can't have been easy. . . but can you truly see the future?"

Garland thought again about the visions, the images that seemed so real.

"I knew who would win that race but that's been the only time," he told Hans. "Mainly I just get a really bad feeling coming over me, the things I see, the colours and the feelings of so much despair and sadness. They paralyse me. If it's a gift, it's one I don't want."

Hans raised his stein and drank through the thin line of foam. "I think there'll be a plausible explanation for all of this," he said, resting the glass carefully back on the table. "My cousin used to suffer from panic attacks. He would vomit, pass out, it would overwhelm him until he calmed down. You moved to another country at a young age, made a life in a city that could scare anyone at first. It sounds like anxiety to me."

"It doesn't feel like that," Garland shot back, sharper than he intended. "And what about the race?"

Hans shrugged and showed Garland his palms.

"Owens is a brilliant athlete. One look and you can tell he's got something special about him. Sorry to shatter your illusions, my friend, but I do not think that you can see the future."

Garland gave a weary smile. He thought – *knew* – there was more to it, something that anxiety and panic attacks couldn't explain away.

But he had spent too long talking about it, and for tonight at least, the river had run its course.

"Okay," Garland said. "I'm drunk. I need to go home."

They headed along Friedrichstrasse towards the hostel. Hans, who lived another thirty minutes' walk beyond Garland's lodgings, offered to see him back to his door.

"Do you really think the Nazis are bad?" Garland asked as they approached the hostel.

"I don't doubt it," Hans answered without missing a beat. "They're all about power and control. They hate the Jews, but what did the Jews ever do to them? Nazis have changed the fabric of Berlin. Hell, they are changing the landscape of Germany and of Europe itself.

Losing the war was the worst thing to happen to us, Garland. Germany fell and now Adolf Hitler is blowing over the ashes. He is in charge of rebuilding us, but he is completely the wrong man to do it. War is coming again, Garland. Berlin will be in ruins this time, of that I am sure."

Garland listened to his new friend, unsure whether what he was hearing was an ill-informed political rant or a genuine foretaste of a harrowing future. He had heard of the Nazis' more extreme measures and their persecution of Jews, but what government didn't have some kind of policy of oppression? It seemed wrong, but it was something Garland had no control over. He saw his hostel ahead and turned to Hans.

"Thanks for a great night and those beers. We'll have to do it again sometime."

The men hugged on the dark, cold street, and as Garland began to break the embrace, Hans planted a warm kiss on his lips.

Garland froze, stunned by the suddenness of the contact and the realisation that it felt good. Instinctively he kissed back, enjoying the closeness in the cool night air, but as his senses returned he drew away.

"What are you doing?" Garland's words were etched with panic. "I didn't. . . I don't. . ."

Hans's face became taut and pale, his mouth a twisted, angry line.

"Oh I get it." The voice a low, hateful whisper. "You think you can lead me on, pretty boy? Kiss and run?"

"No, it's not like that." Garland's mind was scrambling to save him. "I like you, but. . ."

"Forget it. You're just like the rest of them. The Nazis. Those who think homosexuals are the scum of society. That Jews are there to be beaten, worse than murderers and criminals. I've got no shame in who I am. Maybe you ought to look at yourself in the mirror and really think about who you are."

Garland felt his own anger rise like a storm wave and he pushed Hans away. "You kissed me!" he yelled, slurring the words. "Why are you angry at me?"

Without warning Hans swung an arm. The blow was hard and fast and cracked Garland on the jaw. He made no sound as he fell backwards, hit the wall and slumped to the ground. Even through the haze of alcohol Garland felt hot pain pulsing down the side of his face. He heard the drum of Hans's shoes on the concrete street as he ran into the distance.

Garland wept until sleep consumed him and his chin rested on his chest, his chest heaving rhythmically in drunken snores.

Garland woke in a cold sweat, the last ripples of another nightmare ebbing away like black water. The dreams were getting worse, a wave of boiling lava rolling from a hellish inferno.

Each nightmare was more terrifying than the last, filled with death and suffering. In every one, Garland wore a dirty, oversized striped jacket and trousers, so real he could smell the damp filth and sweat that rose from them, the stench catching his breath.

This time he had been standing at the gallows, balanced on a stained wooden stool with a noose around his neck. Johan was beside him. Garland was inching his head against the rough rope, searching for his friend's eyes, when Johan kicked the stool away. Garland felt the noose snap tight, his legs flailing in a drowning fight for air. Each second swung him closer to an agonising death. When he awoke, panting and wet, he could still feel the pressure on his neck. His breath came in panicked snatches as the echoes of the dream slowly faded, leaving a cold, sickly feeling that writhed in his gut and spread to his brain.

He rose from his sweat-soaked bed and looked into a tall mirror set upon an old wooden cabinet in the dormitory. It had been weeks now, but the blow from Hans had left its mark. A deep ridge curved above his lip, and his nose was slightly misshapen.

But the mental wounds were worse. Garland thought they would improve with time, but his mind wouldn't shut down the ordeal, endlessly racing to make sense of what had happened. The night with

Hans had been an unexpected pleasure, the sense of a natural connection growing stronger and stronger, the relief Garland had felt at finally telling someone else about his garish visions. The kiss had come from nowhere, but Garland had responded, his reaction confusing him even more. What happened next had thrown him into free fall. He kept reliving the sudden change, the poison that laced Hans's words and lit hate in his eyes. The blow had hurt him, but the tear in his emotions was worse. Garland had felt his confidence leaking away, his optimism punctured and gnawing fear left in its place. Hans was homosexual. Was Garland also homosexual? It was something he'd thought before, those thoughts so deeply rooted in his brain that he'd hidden them from himself, ignored the gentle stabbing of them and boxed them away in his psyche. More than ever he felt desperately homesick.

He had drifted apart from Johan, the very person who persuaded him to move to Germany. He still found relief in performing, the moments on stage a chance to escape and lose himself. But what Hans had done, leaving him a mess of blood and confusion on that deserted street, was with him night and day.

Garland remembered waking in agony in the gutter in the early morning darkness and staggering home, still drunk and too shocked to know how long he had lain there. Back at the hostel, he had hidden his swollen face from Gianni, rolling over in his bed and muttering that he had the flu, that Gianni should keep away if didn't want to be suffering the same. Garland had stayed in bed all day, sleeping and crying in a restless cycle that left him strung out and exhausted. In the weeks that followed, Garland's face recovered but his morose mood always roamed beneath the surface. He no longer knew who he could trust, and he was wary of friendly strangers. Beneath the physical pain and fear, Garland realised he had begun to question the very essence of who he was.

He thought again about Hans's attack and knew the time had come to seek help. He wanted to tell someone about what had happened, needed someone to listen without judgement.

Homosexuals in Berlin were beaten. They were dismissed as low beings, only above Jews in social status due to the fact there was a glimmer of hope they could be rehabilitated. Garland fell back on his cot, tears welling in his eyes and streaming across his cheeks. He rose again when he remembered his rehearsal was in a couple of hours and with it came an idea.

I could tell Tomas.

Their friendship had grown strong over the two years he'd spent performing with the *Idiotentruppe*. Training for the show was tough, and they had been spending hours together each day. Garland saw the older man as a mentor, a wise role model, whilst Tomas seemed to be mutually fond of Garland. Tomas was a typical Berliner. He liked nothing more than a wurst washed down with a stein and to share the humour that bubbled amongst close friends. He was reliable and strong. No one crossed him. He was tough enough for people to see he was no pushover, but inside the hard shell was a man of warmth. When Garland thought of Tomas, he pictured a soft, nurturing soul. If anyone could share Garland's story, his confusion and his pain, it was Tomas.

Training was typically gruelling. The Idiotentruppe's new routine centred around Garland, which delighted him but doubled his exertions. They had two weeks left before opening the new show, and they were nowhere near performance ready. After the session, Tomas and Garland sat in the changing room and shared a cigarette. It had become an unspoken custom, regulating their heavy breathing after the intense period of exercise. The changing room was a small, shabby space, with two wooden chairs in front of a side table and a hanger for clothes pushed against the wall. The air in the room, as always, was thick with smoke.

"What's on your mind, kid?" Tomas asked.

Garland looked back, wide-eyed.

"You think I can't tell when someone's got something bothering them?" Tomas said without giving Garland the chance to respond. "You can fool others, but not me. So, what was it? Unrequited love? Homesick? Family issues? Make sure it's out of your system before we open. Can't have you looking as sad as this under the lights, pal."

Garland drew heavily on the cigarette and blew smoke towards the yellowing ceiling.

Now or never, Garland. Make up your mind

"Something strange happened to me a few weeks ago."

Tomas raised his eyebrows. "Ah, a story. Intriguing. I must know more!"

He flipped another cigarette from his packet and into his mouth. Garland watched as flame lit the cigarette end bright red.

"I'd had a few drinks," Garland began hesitantly, committing to his decision. "And I met a man."

Garland told Tomas about his night with Hans, about the beers and the conversation and finally, stuttering as he spoke, about the illicit kiss and Hans's violent reaction when Garland pulled away.

As he told the story, he watched Tomas's mouth shift from a boyish smirk to a flat expression. By the time Garland fell silent, Tomas's eyes had narrowed, his lips pursed.

Garland filled the awkwardness with the statement that he'd been hiding in a locked box in his own mind for the duration of his adult life. The feelings and questions he'd suppressed. The emotion he'd kept locked away.

"I think I might have. . . feelings for men."

Tomas lit another cigarette and exhaled, puffing out the first plumes of smoke in short bursts. "I never told you about your predecessor did I, Garland?"

Garland shook his head.

"He was a young Austrian, no older than yourself. A talented boy, also like yourself. Simon was his name. Worked in theatres since he could remember. His father before him was a great actor, used to tread the boards in the early 1910s, before the war took his life in 1917."

Garland scratched his head. "But how is this. . ."

"Don't interrupt me," Tomas silenced him. "Simon was brilliant and I took him under my wing. Trained him, trusted him. But he let me down. He was in a relationship with another man. So I had to ask him to leave. As I have to ask the same of you."

Garland was poleaxed, the cold bluntness and certainty too much for him to process. He shook his head and felt his eyes fill with tears.

"But why for God's sake? I'm not the same. I'm not even sure I'm queer, I'm really not, Tomas. I might not be, maybe I just need to. . ."

As Garland's words faded to nothingness, Tomas stared upwards, his steady gaze aimed at a target somewhere above Garland's head.

"I can't take the risk. I've been fooled before. We've had dignitaries come and see us over the years. Goebbels himself when you were here! You think they'd let us continue if we had a queer in the ranks? We've worked too hard for this next show but two weeks more training, two months performing and then you're gone."

Still not looking Garland in the eye, Tomas stubbed out the

remains of his cigarette in the ceramic ashtray, stood stiffly and walked out of the room.

Garland sat in the silence, his hands gripping the wooden chair, his cigarette hung loosely from his mouth until the embers began to warm his lips. He spat the cigarette to the floor and let out a long guttural shriek, an agonised wail that rose from the pit of his gut.

The sound seemed to rebound around the room, a living thing let loose as the atmosphere began to thin and the walls started to curve. The heavy ashtray shook, gently at first and then violently from side to side until it jerked upward from the side table and trembled half a metre in the air. For long seconds it hung motionless as if held by an unseen hand that finally sent it crashing to the floor, shattering in a cloud of dust and ash.

Garland stopped screaming and slumped onto his knees, sobbing.

Chapter Fourteen

JOHAN - 1939

War had broken out in Europe, and Sachsenhausen was a buzzing hub of activity.

Johan could feel it in the air around camp and see it in the eyes of the various ranks of SS guards. Those who had survived the Great War, and those who glorified the men who fought bravely against Germany's enemies, now had a purpose. For too long they had sat idle whilst their great country spiralled into a depression of debt and despair. Germany had become a slave, nothing more than a captive to those who defeated her in the last war, but now they were better, stronger, more organised. These men would see Germany reach her true potential. It would be a noble vengeance delivered without mercy, a second chance to show the world the greatness of the Reich.

It was a young guard that Johan didn't recognise that broke the news. He ran into the refectory, holding a newspaper aloft, red-faced and breathing heavily.

"We're at war!" he yelled as hundreds of heads turned, all eyes on the newspaper still in the air. "Britain has declared war!"

A moment of shocked silence gave way to the low rumble of murmuring that grew into a tumult of shouts and cheers. People jumped from their seats and shook hands. Others began singing patriotic anthems. Johan took it all in. It was as if the young guard's few short words had injected pure adrenaline into the atmosphere of the canteen.

"What does this mean for us?" Johan asked Schubert, sitting opposite and calmly dipping a hunk of buttered bread into his soup.

"We're about to get very busy," Schubert replied, a wide grin lighting up his face.

Schubert was right. Johan thought work at Sachsenhausen was demanding before, but now the camp thrummed like a giant machine at full power. The SS training camp next door swarmed with new recruits, a mix of men and women of all ages who arrived from every corner of Germany and beyond. It made Johan feel good to know he already occupied a place in the SS, a coveted position they longed to share.

Important-looking men in dark suits walked to the administration buildings. Schulz went from dealing with prisoners to attending meeting after meeting. There was even a rumour that Heinrich Himmler himself, the great Reichsfuehrer of the SS, was visiting to discuss the future of Germany and the importance of Sachsenhausen to the growth of the empire.

The prisoner population increased, slowly at first but then in a torrent that made it hard to keep up. First came the Jews, then the homosexuals. They arrived in their hundreds each day. Some of Johan's fellow guards were sent to fight on the frontlines with the soldiers of the Wehrmacht, but Johan was happy to be told he was staying. He had grown comfortable, settled in the camp and his beautiful house in Oranienburg, enjoying the camaraderie amongst the guards, the responsibility of keeping the growing ranks of prisoners in line. His life in the SS was everything he had hoped for and expected.

As the war effort kicked in, food rations for the prisoners – already undernourished skeletons – were cut drastically. Johan knew the move would send them even more swiftly to their death, but given the number of new inmates now flowing through the gates, it seemed a sensible move.

A few days after the young guard's announcement, Schulz gathered all guards together outside Tower A and delivered a speech.

"It's been coming, and it's finally here," he began. "We are at war. The British, the French. . . they stand in the way of the expansion of the Reich. Never has it been more important for our project to succeed. And for this to happen I need each and every one of you."

Johan watched Schulz. The puffed-out chest, the intense eyes, the rousing voice. He listened to each word as the camp commander spoke.

"We will see changes," Schulz continued. "More prisoners will walk through our gates. More guards will be recruited. More barracks will be constructed. You are the best of the best. You may not be out there on the front line, facing the enemy. But the importance of your work to the Third Reich is unparalleled. The German war effort depends on your management of the people who live and die within these walls. You are the future of Germany, and you will be remembered when our enemies are crushed and our empire reigns over the world.

"Adolf Hitler himself thanks you for your work. The Fuehrer has kept a close eye on our operation, and he is delighted with our progress. Now, let's win this war. Heil Hitler!"

The guards replied in unison, hundreds of flat hands angling into the air. "Heil Hitler!" The moment caused goose bumps to spring up on Johan's raised arm and hairs tingled on the back of his neck.

A wave of excitement had rippled amongst the guards for weeks after Schulz's speech. If German patriotism was strong before, it grew into a molten-hot bundle of energy once the war was underway. Johan was not a natural-born German, but no one could have been prouder. He loved his adopted country now more than ever.

That devotion was on his mind again as he worked the night shift, patrolling the eastern perimeter of Sachsenhausen under a star-filled sky. Johan gazed at the heavens, the same stars that sparkled over Oslo, over London, over Paris. He thought about what had brought him here, to be standing, a rifle in his hand, wrapped in the thick overcoat of the SS, the feared insignia and the great German eagle on his cap.

He hadn't known war was coming when he moved to Berlin, but he was glad it was here. He was at the forefront of the creation of a new empire. He wanted to prove his worth in the strongest military organisation in the world. In Hitler they had a leader none could match. In men like Schulz and Weber before him, Johan had found role models, strong men with stronger ideals, men who were willing to die for what they believed in.

Together they had led an Oslo orphan to a place at the high table. Johan swore to the great constellations he would never let them down. He would do whatever was asked of him, whatever was necessary to progress the German nation. It was the least he could do to repay them. He belonged to Germany now.

He passed Schubert, who winked at him, and Johan smiled back. He walked on and with his fingers traced the outline of the stitched swastika on his uniform again and again.

For the first time in his life, Johan Olsen knew how it felt to truly belong.

Chapter Fifteen

GARLAND - 1939

War. It was in the streets, in the air. It was in the bars, in the restaurants, in the hostel. Everywhere Garland looked. Every other word he heard.

It was panic, worry, anxiety. He saw it on the faces of the Berliners. He saw it in the lines of people who queued to sign up to fight.

War had arrived in Germany again with familiar enemies. The British. The French. They were attacking Germany, and Berlin was alive with energy. It was something tangible, as if Garland could reach out and grab it.

For the second time in just over twenty years, Germany would battle. Garland didn't know the reasons, the politics behind it. He knew Hitler had been pushing into other countries, but he hadn't taken much notice. He didn't read newspapers, he just listened to others talk. And since the hideous visions at the stadium, he had tried to keep Hitler out of his mind.

It was Gianni who first broke the news. He was sweating, having sprinted back from his shift at the Taverne.

"Garland, Garland." Gianni had gasped breathlessly as he entered the hostel. "Europe is at war again."

Garland shook his head and looked back to Gianni blankly.

"Garland, this is bad. Very bad."

"What do you mean? What will happen?"

"We're not German, *compagno*. What if they ask us to leave? Or if they ask us to fight?"

Garland lay back on his bunk. He certainly didn't want to fight. He had heard the stories from Johan. Whatever hardness a man had to possess to be a soldier, he knew he didn't have it. He didn't think he could take a man's life. Being sent back to Norway wouldn't be so bad. He'd become used to Berlin, but Oslo was still his home. It was the first place he thought of whenever he felt down and, with his sacking from the Idiotentruppe, he had been feeling extremely low.

"What about our countries?" he asked Gianni after a few seconds of silence. "Will we need to fight for them?"

Gianni brushed his hand through his hair and sighed. "Who knows? I don't know how it works. But war ruins everything, Garland. It only takes. Your father. My family. So much loss."

"Is it safe out there?" Garland asked, gesturing to the city, which bustled noisily outside the window.

Gianni nodded. "Some are excited. Some want to fight. Others are fearful for their business. Seadog Willy sent me home early. Nobody wants to go and eat when war breaks out. Everyone wants to be at home, listening to the radio, talking to their families."

"What happens next?" Garland asked.

"Your guess is as good as mine."

Garland walked out into the city the next evening with Gianni and everything felt different. A light-grey cloud hung over Berlin, translucent and gloomy.

His theatre work seemed a distant memory. Garland had performed well over the last two weeks of his stay with Der Idiotentruppe, but he didn't dazzle the audience as he had before. The thought of his expulsion from the group hung heavy on his shoulders. When they finished their final show, Garland had become hysterical, sobbing and begging Tomas to reconsider. But Tomas had refused. He told Garland he was lucky he didn't report his crime to the authorities and that he was breaking the law himself by turning a blind eye.

Garland and Gianni headed to the Taverne for the evening shift. Garland had been back washing pots on weekends, under the watchful eye of the disgusting Seadog Willy, in return for a few Reichsmarks and some leftover food. The big German was one of the most hideous men he had ever met. Willy had been a chef on a German U-boat in the first war, and his military background was plain in everything he did. It was also the reason for the blue tattoos that covered his bulky arms, skulls and crossbones, anchors, and eagles in rough designs somehow livid with rage. Willy's swarthy face was blotchy and bloated and he had the cool eyes of a killer.

Garland hated him, but it was the only work he could find and at least he didn't go hungry.

They walked across the city and every so often Gianni would nudge Garland to point out something taking place on the Berlin streets. A drunken fight outside a bar. A lover's tiff at an open door. A Jew being taken away by the Gestapo. At every corner there seemed to be a scene. Gianni viewed it all as a spectator, something to gawp at as they walked to the restaurant. But to Garland, they were sights to fear. They made him feel cold inside.

War seemed to have injected a big rush into the Berliners. Wherever they were going, people pushed past in their hurry, as if time itself was the enemy. They dashed in and out of houses, bustled into stores and offices, darted from the busy pavements into alehouses thrumming with the noise of eager voices.

Garland became sucked into each conversation. The same topic was on everyone's lips, the same words on a loop. . . War. Fighting. Bombs. Air raids. Rations.

War left no one untouched but meant different things to different people. For some it brought back harrowing memories of the first war, the heartache and hunger and ultimate shame. For others it was a source of excited pride, the whole country pulling together to take on the world.

But as much as Garland had become close to Berlin, Germany didn't belong to him and he didn't belong to her.

They entered the Taverne and Gianni pulled on his server's apron. Garland walked over to the sink.

The room darkened, and the wide figure of Seadog Willy appeared. His eyes were bloodshot and he staggered, a flask in his left hand.

"Go home," he said, shooting Gianni and Garland a look of contempt.

Gianni's face dropped. "Why, boss? No customers?"

"I'm closing, you worm." Willy hurled the flask across the room and it doused Garland and Gianni with whisky.

"But. . . what about my job? I—"

Willy didn't give him the chance to finish his sentence. He grabbed Gianni by his apron and shoved him against the wall. Willy's thick forearm pushed into Gianni's throat and Garland could see his friend's face turning red.

"You're hurting him!" Garland yelled.

Seadog Willy dropped Gianni, who crumpled in a heap against the kitchen wall, gasping. Willy turned to Garland and picked up a meat cleaver.

"You filthy, foreign scum." Veins were pulsing at his temples. "I didn't want you here in the first place. We're at war, you fucking idiots. Go and fight. There's no role for me in the German army anymore, but youth is wasted on queers like you. Get out of my sight before I cut your throats."

Seadog Willy held the cleaver above his head and both Garland and Gianni scrambled from the kitchen into the teeming city streets.

They ran around three corners without looking back, finally stopping in an alleyway. Gianni peered around the edge of the wall to make sure Willy hadn't given chase.

"Don't worry," Garland said, panting. "He wouldn't be able to keep up. What the hell's the matter with him?"

Gianni shook his head. "He's always been wild, but with the war, something's snapped. He wants to fight again. He wants to go back out to sea. I guess they told him he was too old."

"He's insane!" Garland said. "How did you survive working for him for so long?"

Gianni shrugged and mimed empty pockets with his hands.

"Money. Food. And now I have no job. I'm not sure where either's going to come from. He may be a crazy, but he gave me work."

Garland nodded. "Well, you and me both need to find something now."

"Unless they will have us," Gianni said. He pointed to a series of patriotic posters that were tacked to the brick wall of the alleyway.

Garland looked closely at one, a heroic depiction of a helmeted soldier staring to the distance. Two bolts of lightning spelt out the unmistakable emblem of the SS. It was a call for people to join and as he looked at the fearless soldier he thought of Johan. His orphan brother, already serving Germany, wore the very same uniform as the hero on the poster. It wasn't something Garland wanted.

"Fancy it?" Gianni asked, as if reading his mind.

Garland shook his head and continued down the line of posters, amongst them a grandiose image of Hitler, *One Nation One Empire One Leader* boldly proclaimed on the paper, which had begun to curl at the edges. The sight of the German leader made Garland feel sick. Hot bile rose in his throat and his vision began to sway in and out of focus. He watched Hitler move on the poster, his dark eyes burning into Garland's. He wanted to look away, but couldn't. He saw the young SS soldier in the call to arms turn and raise his gun as other posters on the wall came alive. Jews depicted as devils blew steam from their nostrils, and Garland could feel the air turn warm.

He bent double, swallowing the bile, and gasped.

"Garland! Garland, are you okay?" Gianni rubbed Garland's back. "Come, let's go back to the hostel."

Garland nodded and they made their way out of the alleyway into the throng of people streaming along the street. The sun had set and only the thin glare of streetlights illuminated the city.

Above them, aeroplanes droned towards the west. Garland gulped, there was change in the air, and he could see black and red flashes streaking across his vision, as if hell itself was trying to break through into the living world.

Chapter Sixteen

RICHARD - 2022

Richard found his awareness returning once more.

He forced his eyes open. Hoping to see Sandy. Hoping for his nightmare to be over. He didn't want to be there. He looked above and saw the coloured lights swirling, an effervescent tornado building in the shimmering sky. All around him, bright stars glittered, and the dark leaves on trees swayed hypnotically.

Richard cried, the frustration seeping from him without tears. He tried to move his hand but couldn't, so his eyes followed the smooth movement of the colours above.

He thought about screaming for help, to hope he could somehow force Garland to hear him, but thought against it. What could Garland do? He was probably a figment of Richard's imagination, a character born from the concentration camp tour in Berlin before the darkness had consumed him. And even if he did exist, what could a boy from the 1930s do to help him? If anything, it was Garland that would need the help.

Richard pondered the thought and gradually slipped back into darkness.

Chapter Seventeen

JOHAN - 1939

It was three years into his posting at Sachsenhausen that Johan first acquired his *Der Bestatter* moniker.

It had been an unseasonably cold night, and Schulz was in a furious mood, calling an unscheduled roll-call at three in the morning as frost coated the camp and sparkled under the black sky.

The prisoners had been in the courtyard for an hour and a half, watching the jagged patterns of frost forming on the concrete floor beneath their feet, when one of them collapsed. Schulz had watched silently, smirking and swigging from a silver flask emblazoned with a bevelled swastika. He'd been waiting for someone to crack. Now here it was. . . and one of the homosexuals at that.

He strode over to the prisoner, his heavy leather boots crunching the frost beneath his feet.

"Do you need some assistance?" Schulz asked, offering a gloved hand.

The prisoner nodded and raised his arm. He was shaking violently, his breath forming wispy bursts of cloud in the icy air.

"Are you cold?" Schulz asked, slowly pulling back his hand, the fingers always just out of the prisoner's reach.

The man nodded his head and cried.

"We can't have that, can we?" There was a gleam in Schulz's eye, reflecting the lamps that lit the yard in a harsh artificial glow.

He pulled out another flask from his thick coat pocket, twisted off the lid and poured the contents over the prisoner. Johan smelt it immediately. Petrol.

The prisoner shook his head and cried louder, harder.

"There, there," Schulz said, grinning as he emptied the flask. "We need to warm you up now, don't we?"

He slid the flask back in his deep pocket and pulled out a silver-coloured lighter decorated with another ornate swastika.

He flipped open the top and flicked the flint with his thumb. The prisoner breathed heavily, cold tears falling down his face as his chest rose and fell. His eyes were watching the flame as it wavered from side to side in the dawn breeze. He was still shaking and his oily skin gleamed under the petrol coating.

Schulz seemed to draw energy from the man, feeding on his fear. The grin on his face grew wider as he moved the flame in a teasing arc.

Suddenly he feigned to move it towards the prisoner, who flinched. Schulz unleashed a booming laugh that echoed into the night, and he kicked the prisoner in the face with his boot. Johan watched as several teeth flew across the yard, fleetingly caught in the camp's harsh floodlights.

Schulz leant forward and put the flame to the prisoner's uniform.

It went up immediately, an explosion of yellow and orange fire that quickly engulfed him. Writhing in the searing heat, the prisoner cried out in short yelps. Johan thought he sounded more like a panicked monkey than a man burning to death.

As the flames grew higher and wider, Johan smelt it, the roasting flesh. It hit the back of his throat and made his stomach lurch, but he couldn't show it. He had to keep his strength in front of the prisoners and his fellow guards.

Schulz continued to laugh as the man finally fell silent and stopped moving.

"Are you warmer now?" he asked the burning corpse, spitting as he spoke.

Schulz put a cigarette in his mouth, bent over the man and lit it on the flames that still flickered from his body. He inhaled and blew the smoke into the chill air.

"Best cigarette I ever tasted," Schulz said, looking down as the melting skin blackened, popping and shrinking with snapping sounds that ricocheted off the walls.

When another prisoner gasped, Schulz turned to him and put the cigarette out on his eye. The man tried to push him away but Schulz drew his revolver, straightened his arm and shot him. The prisoner slumped to the ground, Johan watching gun smoke wisp upwards from the bullet hole in the man's forehead.

Seven more prisoners died in the yard that night at Schulz's hands. Several more were admitted to the medical barracks with hypothermia.

The bodies were gathered, as was customary, by three prisoners barely able to shift the weight. They heaved them in wheelbarrows to the edge of the camp. When they were finished, Schulz made them stand against the outer wall. He shot all three in the back of the head, and their bodies were added to the rest.

Schulz turned to Johan and the six other guards who stood in a line behind him, his bright blue eyes sparkling beneath the floodlights. His eyebrows were arched, giving his angular face a pensive look.

"We need a driver to take this waste to Berlin Crematorium. I'll ring in advance. They all died of natural causes, of course. A volunteer, please, to load these into the back of a vehicle and to offload them at the cemetery?"

Johan looked at his colleagues. He noticed mouths downturn, eyes twitch, the thought of disposing of twelve dead bodies apparently a little too much for even the toughest of the SS guards. Transporting corpses was prisoner duty, not the work of guards. This isn't what they'd signed up for.

Johan took a deep breath and raised his hand. "I'll do it."

Schulz offered him a thin smile. "Excellent. But this is a two-man job."

He walked down the line of guards, the same glint from the roll-call back in his eye, his cruelty manifest in a cold, soulless glare. The low squeak of his leather boots creaking as he walked made a menacing soundtrack, his gait part measured march, part arrogant strut.

Schulz stopped in front of Albert Becker. Becker was one of the newer recruits, and his first few weeks at the camp had been littered with mistakes. He was too lenient, too easily led by some of the more powerful prisoners, especially those *kapos*, the self-administrated functionary prisoners promoted to be "in charge" of their barracks.

In the camp's social club, Becker was teased mercilessly by the older guards. In his own early days, Johan had handled the teasing well, giving it back without crossing a line. But Becker shied away, looking at his boots as guards mocked his slender appearance and sensitive nature. He'd quickly acquired the nickname *Der Arschgeige*, something Johan amusingly translated as "arse violin." It was generally felt demotion was on the cards for Becker if he didn't start impressing soon.

"Becker. You go with Olsen. Drop the waste at the crematorium. Bring the truck back in one piece by nine o'clock. No fuck-ups." Schulz glared at Olsen and shifted his cold eyes back to Becker. "Understood?"

"Yes, sir," both men replied in unison.

"Heil Hitler," Schulz yelled.

"Heil Hitler," all guards replied together.

"Olsen, Becker. . . get to work," Schulz commanded. "All others, dismissed."

The guards began to disperse, and Johan walked over to the pile of bodies. His eyes were transfixed by the still-smoking remains of the prisoner torched to death. He looked over at Becker who was gulping hard against the nausea that had turned his face to chalk. Der Arschgeige wasn't going to have the stomach for this job.

Johan walked over to the burnt remains and, in one movement, scooped up the charred body and put it over his shoulder as if he were a fireman saving a woman from a burning building. The corpse was still warm and Johan wondered if it would permanently ruin his uniform. He felt parts of blackened skin fall from the man's legs. Cloth and flesh had fused into one sickening mess, and large open sores oozed all over the body. The man's head was a weeping globe, hairless and lolling from side to side. Johan moved his hand upwards to keep the head steady, worried it would tumble off.

He walked towards the vehicle compound with the corpse over his shoulder but then stopped. He turned to look back and every single guard was standing still watching him. Schubert looked on, eyebrows raised. Schulz stood smoking a cigarette. The camp commander was illuminated by the rising sun over the eastern horizon of the camp.

Johan turned back to his work. He approached the truck, still with the heavy corpse over his shoulder, and used the keys to open the back doors. Straining with the effort, he hauled the body inside with a brittle crunching of bone and a puff of ashen dust.

He brushed his hands together and walked back to the pile of bodies. Becker was trying to pull one of the dead by the legs. Johan shoved past him and dragged another body over his shoulder, walking back to the compound. He repeated the task, his muscles cramping with the effort. By the time they loaded the truck, Becker had clumsily dragged two bodies. Johan had carried all the rest.

The other guards were still watching and Johan realised the expression on their faces was awe.

"I'll drive," he told Becker, who was still visibly shaken.

"No," Becker replied. "I still need to prove myself, Olsen. I wanted to be a guard, to do my duty for Germany. I didn't expect to deal with stuff like this, but I need to learn how to do it, otherwise they'll kick me out. They're watching us. If they see you drive away, they'll think I'm not pulling my weight."

"You're *not* pulling your weight, Becker," Johan hissed. "Okay, you drive. You can offload when we get there, and if you put your back into it, I'll report favourably. Agreed?"

Becker nodded, but Johan could see tears forming in the corners of his eyes.

They climbed into the truck, Becker found first gear and they drove out of the tree-lined avenue that led into Oranienburg and towards Berlin. Sachsenhausen, now bathed in auburn light from the morning sun, slowly disappeared into the horizon behind them.

In the back of the SS van, twelve bodies gently bounced over the bumps in the road.

Chapter Eighteen

GARLAND - 1939

Berlin took on a different sheen when viewed through the eyes of one suffering from depression. Garland knew that now. Seeing the city at war only made it worse.

The bright, vibrant streets became grey and hard. People who had always been warm and welcoming seemed unfriendly, disinterested. The squares and avenues felt suddenly ugly, fraught with danger. Military vehicles tore across the city, the sound of aeroplane engines chugged constantly overhead, and every day there were lines of volunteers signing up to fight for Adolf Hitler and the Fatherland.

Garland had no intention of enlisting. Instead, he walked the streets looking for work, the last of his wages from the theatre quickly dwindling away.

There were no longer many openings in the bars or restaurants, and none of the theatres were taking people on in any capacity, never mind the stage. Gianni was in a similar quandary. Italy hadn't joined the war, although it seemed likely, so they had both decided to wait. The SS would either come to deport them or force them to fight. The thought of going to the front line made Garland shudder. He wasn't a coward, far from it, but he had heard the stories from the Great War. Thousands of men running across fields to certain death, cut down for a cause they knew nothing about, freezing in muddy trenches or held like animals in disease-ridden prisoner camps.

How many mothers had mourned their sons? How many shell-shocked soldiers had watched their closest friends slaughtered?

"No thanks," Garland muttered as he passed another long line of excited young men with enrolment papers grasped in their hands.

He continued walking, reaching Chausseestrasse where the buildings loomed large and grey, and the bustle of the street left him feeling vulnerable and uneasy.

The rich smell of baking bread made Garland's stomach grumble. He would have to buy something cheap or scrounge food from Gianni if he was going to make his money last.

He walked on, kicking stones and smoking cigarettes as he stared at his worn boots pounding the concrete beneath.

"Excuse me, boy."

Garland turned to see a man beside a large portable oven in a shop doorway.

"Boy, you look like you've got some muscles on you, could you help us out for a few Reichsmarks in your hand?"

Garland walked towards him and saw another figure, a young man around his own age, sitting awkwardly on the pavement.

"I'm Mr Kori," the older man said "My assistant here has pulled a muscle in his back and I need someone to help me take this into this butcher's shop. Could you lend a hand?"

"Sure," Garland replied, smiling at the sudden stroke of luck.

Kori was in his forties, with blackish-grey hair and a neat moustache. He was tall and slender and impeccably dressed in a well-cut suit, a gold watch and chain glinting at his breast pocket. Garland helped him move the heavy oven whilst Kori explained his business. He produced ovens and incinerators, mostly for disposing of animal carcasses, and was successful enough to now map out a significant expansion. Kori planned to make vast industrial-scale ovens and heating systems for churches and other large stone-built buildings. Garland listened intently.

As they left the butcher's shop after an hour of heavy lifting, Kori dropped a few loose coins into Garland's pocket. They said their goodbyes, Kori shaking his hand firmly before they parted ways and walked in opposite directions.

Suddenly Garland swivelled and ran back to the businessman.

"Sir," he said breathlessly. "You wouldn't have anything more permanent, would you? Even just a few hours a week? I'm a fast learner and I'm fit and strong."

Kori smiled, looking Garland up and down, weighing him with his eyes. "Why not?" he said after a pause. "One of my workers has just signed up to fight. Report to my office at Potsdamer Strasse, eight o'clock sharp tomorrow morning. We'll go through your duties and what I expect. Call it a trial."

They shook hands again. "Thank you, Mr Kori. You won't regret this."

Garland skipped away down noisy Chausseestrasse, the Reichsmarks now in his hand, a smile on his face and a new spring in his step.

It might not be dancing in front of a crowd with his name in lights, but his life was getting back on track. He had the chance of a job, and he was going to grasp it with both hands. For now, whatever horrors the war would bring could wait.

Garland arrived at the Potsdamer Strasse offices twenty minutes early and Kori, visibly impressed, shook his hand firmly and gave him the grand tour.

Kori showed him the workshop where eight men hammered noisily at steel, sparks flying, and engineers used complicated machinery to drill features onto the body of a huge oven. The thick smell of oil, the industrial clanking of the noisy machinery and the workers' intense concentration combined to make the place almost intimidating. It all felt a million miles from the quiet fishing ports of Oslo, a brave new world Garland was entering wide-eyed and nervous.

Kori took him around the warehouse. Ovens in dark cast iron and shiny steel were stacked side by side in all shapes and sizes. There were small portable models, industrial ovens for kitchens and, in a larger part of the warehouse, huge incinerators twice as tall as Garland and over six feet wide.

"What are they?" Garland asked. A cold sweat was forming at the top of his head and a crisp smell of burning had begun to flicker at the edge of his senses.

"They're for the crematoria," Kori replied. "We're in the human disposal business too."

Kori explained there were several clients in the city who paid well for the incinerators.

"There's always business in death," he told Garland. "Unfortunately, the war means this is as true as ever. More killing, more death, more business."

The word *death* echoed back and forth in Garland's mind and he began to feel dizzy as an unstoppable force dragged his eyes towards the incinerators. Black clouds now swirled from their yawning mouths, the smoke shaping into tortured skulls which floated and warped in turmoil. When a shrill scream pierced his head Garland swayed on his feet, and Kori put an arm out to steady him.

"Are you all right, son?" he asked.

Garland looked in Kori's eyes and saw flames soaring higher and higher. The blaze grew until Kori disappeared and instead Garland was trapped in the smoking steel walls of a shrinking room, yellow and red fire dancing wildly as the space around him compressed with slow, steady movements. Garland was inside one of Kori's incinerators, the heat unbearable. All around were burning bodies wearing striped uniforms that melted and fused to their skin, the corpses disintegrating to dusty bone and ash.

A man opposite him staggered closer, his nose bubbling like hot wax and his eyeballs leaking streams of fire that dribbled down his cheeks.

"Leave," the man said in a hellish growl, a low guttural sound that thundered around the incinerator before the vision ebbed away, and Garland was back in Kori's warehouse. Garland felt his knotted stomach uncoil and his balance return.

"Sorry, I haven't eaten, sir."

Kori slapped his back. "We can't have that, can we? Let's get you some wurst and sauerkraut and get some energy back inside you. Don't tell me you're so hard-up you couldn't afford to eat?"

Garland didn't have chance to answer before Kori whisked him to the small canteen. Traces of the visions still rippled like aftershocks, but Garland realised he was ravenous. The wurst was heavenly, rich juices bursting from its skin as Garland attacked each bite with animal greed.

He washed it down with freshly squeezed orange juice, sat back and let out a slow breath.

Kori eyed him with a crooked smile. His eyes were kind, the crow's feet at their edges spreading to give his face a safe, fatherly appearance.

"Better?" Kori asked.

Garland opened his mouth to speak and unleashed a loud belch, immediately slapping his hand to his lips.

Kori narrowed his eyes in mock disdain, and then they both crumbled into helpless laughter.

Over the coming months, Garland settled into his new role. His shifts mainly involved helping Kori's son Otto deliver ovens and incinerators to businesses scattered around the city. Otto was rough around the edges and wise to the world. He possessed the same kind eyes as his father, but with an added glint of mischief. He smoked a pipe, causing the pleasant odour of rich tobacco to constantly accompany him.

Otto was a born adventurer, a man who swore his current occupation was only temporary, despite working for his father for the past six years. His conversation, in between sucking on the pipe, centred around *Die Frauen* and all the various women he'd met. Women in bars, women in theatres, even women at work whilst he was delivering gas ovens. Women wearing tights, women wearing skirts, women who danced, women who laughed. Otto told Garland his favourite place on a woman's body (the top of the backside) and the unlikely locations where a delicate mole could be found (the inner thigh). He talked about moving to Italy where Die Frauen were dark and sexy and slim, not like the sturdier, light-skinned German women.

It was in between delivering a cast iron oven to a restaurant in Mitte and dropping off an animal incinerator at a farm on the outskirts of the city that Otto almost crashed. He'd been talking and lighting his pipe, not concentrating on the road, when he drifted into the wrong lane. The tyres screeched and Otto gasped as he pulled at the wheel, turning their van 180 degrees across the road. Garland watched as a small military-green truck missed them by inches. The truck swerved as its driver fought desperately for control before it hit a lamppost, careered off the road and rolled onto its roof with a sickening crunch and a hiss. Bystanders screamed, other drivers slammed on their brakes and people came running from the doorways of nearby shops and alehouses. From the side of the road, amongst the frozen pedestrians, a woman screamed.

Garland's jaw gaped and his stomach lurched as he watched the scene unfold. "Can. . . can you see that?" he asked Otto, pointing forward.

Otto nodded gravely, his expression confirming to Garland this wasn't another hallucination.

The truck's back doors had burst open and several corpses now lay tumbled across the road.

Chapter Nineteen

JOHAN - 1940

Johan stirred slowly but the fog hung heavy. His head had slammed into the dashboard, and now sharp pain moved like a heartbeat behind his eyes.

Everything was the wrong way up. The rooftops of buildings hung downwards, touching the blue sky beneath them as if they were about to fall into a huge still-water sea. When his muddled senses began to clear, he realised he was upside down, his body crumpled against the roof of the truck.

He heard the hiss of smoke or steam escaping from the engine and groggily turned to Becker.

Becker's nose was flowing with blood, and Johan could already see an egg-sized lump rising on his forehead.

"It wasn't my fault," Becker groaned, turning his wide eyes to Johan.

"I know," Johan replied, "but now we've got to get out of here."

He winced in pain as he unfastened his seatbelt, braced himself and put his heavy SS boot through the cracked windscreen. It shattered immediately. Johan struggled free and hauled Becker behind him, the pair finally outside the truck with their hands on their knees, catching their breath.

Johan looked up at the van that had run them off the road, but just as his vision was focusing on the two blurry figures inside, its engine suddenly revved and it sped away with its tyres screeching.

Johan stumbled forward.

"Bastards!" His rage ignited. "Let's get them, Becker, let's jump in a car and—

"Olsen," Becker said, his eyes fixed on the back of the truck. He grasped a handful of Johan's shirt and tugged it. "I think we've got bigger problems."

All twelve bodies had fallen from the back of the upturned truck and lay scattered on the busy street.

Becker put his hand to his mouth and gave a muffled sob.

The dead were sprawled in a grotesque still life, arms and legs splayed and jaws open. Johan spotted the burnt corpse, the man's white skull visible behind his ruined face, strands of stringy muscle like blackened webbing.

The sight was ghastly and the smell even worse. People of the street had their hands over their mouth, others covered their eyes. Women cried into the shoulders of their husbands. Children wailed, their shrill sobs piercing the air.

Johan pulled out a handkerchief and clamped it across his nose. He glanced at Becker, whose hand was still over his mouth, his eyes wet and bloodshot.

"What do we do now?" Becker asked, his voice trembling. "The truck's wrecked."

Johan looked again the dead and the bystanders huddled by the roadside, the horror before them almost hypnotic.

Think, for God's sake. Think.

When Johan spoke his voice was firm and commanding.

"Go into one of those shops and borrow their phone," he told Becker. "Call the camp office and ask them to get the mechanics here as soon as they can."

Becker shook his head, beads of sweat flying from his brow despite the cold air. "But the prisoners. . ."

Johan cut him off.

"We've got a load of tarpaulin in the back of the truck. I'll cover the bodies. These people will lose it if they've got to look at them any longer."

The SS arrived within the hour. A repair crew worked on the truck for three hours whilst the road stayed closed and the bodies remained shrouded from any more prying civilian eyes.

The SS officer in charge grunted at them.

"It's in a bad way, but it's drivable." He was a hard-faced man of few words. "Which one of you pricks was driving?"

Becker tentatively began to raise a hand but Johan grabbed it and stopped him.

"There was a lunatic heading straight at us," Johan said, pointing at the black tyre tracks on the road. "They got away when we were still dazed."

"I see," the officer replied. "You were lucky to get out alive."

Johan heard the truck splutter and fire as one of the mechanics gave a thumbs up from under the bonnet.

"It seems your vehicle is now fixed." The officer's thin smile taunted them. "Interesting cargo you're carrying there, gentlemen. A shame people had to see it. You boys are from Sachsenhausen, yes?"

Johan nodded. He heard Becker exhale sharply next to him.

"Bernt Schulz is a good friend of mine. Tell him I said hello. In fact, I might give him a call, just to discuss this little incident. Have a good day, boys. No more accidents, yes?"

"No, sir. Thank you, sir," Johan replied.

Johan and Becker began walking toward the truck.

"Oh, and boys?" They turned to face the officer. "Find the people in that van, shake off your daze and shoot them between the eyes."

"Yes, sir," Becker snapped back.

"Heil Hitler." The officer's arm flashed out in salute.

"Heil Hitler," Johan and Becker answered.

"Let's get to work," Johan said, walking towards the line of dead men hidden under the heavy sheet. He made sure no one was still watching and uncovered three of the bodies. One was the charred corpse.

Becker shook his head and went down on one knee. He vomited onto the road.

Johan sighed and began to haul the corpses back into the truck. After fifteen minutes of heaving, grunting and hard effort, he was shutting the truck doors and brushing his hands. This time he would make sure the dead were still.

Johan drove as they headed back to Sachsenhausen from the crematorium; Becker unwilling to get into more trouble, Johan not trusting him to stay calm behind the wheel.

When they returned to the camp, Schulz greeted them at the gates wearing a humourless smile. He led them to his office and sat them down. He took his seat opposite and began carefully cleaning his pistol with a pipe cleaner and a white handkerchief. A cigar hung loosely from the corner of his mouth, puffing thick rings of grey smoke into the small room. Johan could feel his heart flutter and his breaths become shorter.

Schulz's eyes glittered.

"Well, tell me what happened. Who drove?"

"I did," Becker replied, his voice shaking.

Schulz continued working methodically on his pistol. Johan and Becker's eyes followed the commander's fingers as they delicately ran the handkerchief over the nose, handle, trigger and hammer.

"It was the fault of another vehicle," Johan interjected.

Becker nodded, his head bobbing in strong, exaggerated movements.

Schulz was still carefully polishing the gun, and when he spoke again, his voice was calm and measured.

"No." The tone was almost serene. "There have been too many mistakes. The good people of Berlin shouldn't be exposed to this underbelly, this necessary but repulsive work that lays the foundations of their lives. And thanks to you" – he stopped cleaning the pistol and pointed it at Becker - "they now have an insight into what it takes. They will ask questions that don't need asking. I watched you as Olsen moved the bodies from the camp to the van. You hardly lifted a finger. We have given you chance after chance, Becker. And you continue to let us down. Can I ask you a question?"

Becker nodded and gulped at the same time.

"Are you familiar with the Roman Empire, Becker?"

Becker gulped again. "Not really, sir."

"It was the zenith of human civilisation. Hordes of warriors, strategists, workers, engineers, creators, destructors. When a Roman army was guilty of misconduct, they employed what they called *decimation.* Do you know what that means? No, of course you don't.

Every tenth man was killed whilst the rest watched. It meant that a large number of people were punished, whilst the others were warned that actions have consequences. The human race went backwards after their empire fell, and you can see why. That discipline is nowhere to be seen in modern times, even in our great SS. But we're changing things. Under Hitler, we are slowly bringing it back. We're going to make Germany the greatest empire since Rome. Do you believe that, boys?"

He pointed his pistol at Becker, then at Johan, and back to Becker. Schulz had a wild glint in his eyes, an inhuman sparkle that was both bright and ominous. His eyes fixed on Becker and his voice became sharp and abrupt. "Are you cut out to be in the SS?"

But Becker didn't have the chance to answer.

Schulz pulled the trigger and put a bullet through his forehead, splattering the wall behind him with a soupy mixture of blood, skull and brain. Becker's eyes contorted with shock before they rolled, lifeless and empty. His body slumped, slowly sinking in his seat and then tumbling backwards to the floor until it was still. A pool of blood grew beneath his head, and the air filled with its unmistakable smell, tangy and bitter.

Schulz calmly went back to cleaning his pistol. Johan watched his every move intently, straining to control his emotions.

"He wasn't SS material," Schulz said, eyeing Johan whilst he continued to caress the gun barrel. "My official report will say that he used his pistol on himself, under the duress of my reprimand. And if required, your story will corroborate that. Understood?"

Johan caught his breath and coughed. "Yes, sir."

Schulz stopped cleaning his pistol and pointed the gun at Johan.

"I was impressed with your handling of the bodies." The commander smiled. "The men saw you. They're calling you Der Bestatter."

The Undertaker, Johan translated in his head.

"Thank you, sir. Anything for the Fatherland." He concentrated on his breathing as he spoke.

"Good. *Good.* Heil Hitler!" Schulz extended a straight arm in the air.

"Heil Hitler!" Johan replied, returning the gesture.

"Dismissed."

Johan stood, saluted and walked towards his house. He felt bad for Becker, but he wasn't up to it. He was always going to fail, and in the SS, that meant failing the German people. The citizens entrusted their safety to the mighty Schutzstaffel. Commander Schulz had delivered peace to Becker. He had shown him mercy.

Now Johan thought of Schulz's personal praise, a small smile stretching into a beaming grin that lit his face.

He walked towards the Sachsenhausen social club. Outside a young officer was kissing a woman, and the building was thrumming with light and music. It was Friday night, the guards not on shift enjoying their downtime. Johan felt the weight of the gruelling day but decided to stay, to relax with a couple of drinks and show his face. He was still a relative new boy compared to some in the camp, and he knew plenty of the older guards – drinkers themselves – judged the character of a man by his capacity to hold his beer. He pushed open the door and walked in.

The scene that greeted him caught him by surprise. He had been in the club a few times, but it was never like this. Men stood shoulder to shoulder such was the lack of space. Clusters of glossy women, sneaked in from nearby towns, draped themselves across officers. Beer flew in the air and most people in the heaving room were soaked in ale or sweat or both. A thick-set, ruddy-faced woman stood on stage and sang traditional German songs. She held a tankard of beer and it sloshed along with her movements.

Johan fought his way to the bar and had just ordered a tankard when he felt a hefty shove to his side.

"This one's on me." It was the guard Schubert. "I've never seen anyone haul bodies off like you did. We're all impressed. The boys have been talking about it all day."

The background noise was so loud Johan could feel Schubert's breath as he shouted into his ear.

A group of off-duty guards near the bar spotted Johan and pushed their way over. They were drunk and slurring but treated Johan like a hero, crowding around him, jumping up and down, and splashing beer from the tankards raised high above their heads.

Johan grinned, and as others spotted him, a raucous chant rang out across the room.

"Der Bestatter! Der Bestatter! Der Bestatter!"

The singer on stage, drowned out in the mêlée, picked up the word and joined in as Johan was lifted high above the cheering crowd.

"Der Bestatter, Der Bestatter, Der Bestatter."

Chapter Twenty

GARLAND - 1940

Otto was silent for the first few minutes driving away, but Garland could hear his breathing, rapid and short, as Berlin's grey roads unravelled in front of them.

He took a route full of unnecessary turns and detours, glancing often in his mirrors, peering nervously down side streets and back alleys.

"That truck," he began at last, his words a sharp burst that matched his breathing. "It was SS, wasn't it?"

Garland shook his head. "I doubt that."

"But I saw the passenger's uniform," Otto insisted. "It was SS and now we're in deep shit. You think they saw us? You think they know?"

"Don't panic," Garland told him. "I really don't think so."

Otto fell back into his edgy silence as Garland stared out of the window, watching Berlin life go by. He hadn't thought about the SS. Why would they have dead bodies in a truck? More likely it was a hospital van or from an undertaker.

Remembering the corpses made Garland's stomach lurch. He gripped the door handle and squeezed his eyes shut. The familiar smell of burning rubber returned on a rolling wave of heat. He pictured the emaciated bodies, every face contorted with terror, thin skin wrapped around bone. The striped clothes hung around them like filthy sacks, and now Garland could pick out a coppery odour drifting under the smell of fire.

A flood of colour and movement exploded behind his eyes, and when he opened them, he saw the road ahead was red with running blood. Cars coming the opposite way sent it in a wet splatter across the van's windscreen. It rolled down the high buildings that towered over the sidewalks and gathered in shimmering red pools. People walking past dripped with it. The blood ran from their fingers, covered their faces. Garland coughed, the pungent stench filling his mouth and nose, and rubbed at his stinging eyes.

He flinched as a huge stone eagle swooped from the top of a nearby building, its vast wings beating silently as it circled and soared skyward again. Crimson rain was falling in heavy drops, battering the van, the sound a dark drum beat.

This is hell.

A giant swastika flew from its position on a dripping red flag, writhing and growing until its shadow plunged the van momentarily into darkness.

Garland had choked back the bile burning his throat and closed his eyes tight once more, but when he felt dull thumping all around him, he forced himself to look.

The tortured ghosts of weeping men, women and children were banging on the van with dirty fists, their eyes black hollows, their skin porcelain and cold. Their mouths were open in a wordless howl, and Garland felt himself falling into that endless, empty silence. Death was close.

Garland glanced over at Otto but he stared forward, his face still. He didn't even seem to be breathing, just frozen in time as the horror unfolded.

Garland looked out through the windscreen. Five shapes lay flat on the bonnet, juddering and twisting to take form as he watched, a raggedy man and a woman with three children, bony and frail. They wore striped grey and black uniforms with numbers and coloured triangles on their breasts, the uniforms now sodden under the crimson deluge.

Garland felt a blast of searing heat on his back and swivelled to look at the rear of the van.

Every oven was on, raging with amber flames. They stung and sizzled at his face, but Garland couldn't move, couldn't look away. The stench of charcoal and sulphur was suffocating, yet his eyes stayed locked on the inferno where the same five skeletal wraiths were now screaming and reaching out to him.

Garland felt his own tears hissing to steam in the monstrous heat, the thick droplets of blood still drumming the van roof. He strained and slowly moved his body around, the motion grinding and awkward like turning a rusty screw.

He looked down at his lap and moaned.

He was wearing the same striped uniform, the coarse fabric scratching at his skin.

He moved his hand to his chest and gasped as his fingers traced leathery skin pulled tight over bone where there had been flesh and muscle. Garland was as thin and sunken as the wretched spectres still beating at the van. He had closed his eyes again, and was praying for the vision to end, when he heard the windscreen smash. He looked as one fist then another punched through the shattered glass. Blood swept in, lapping over Garland and swirling like a whirlpool, whilst behind him he heard the ovens roar.

The thick blood ignited with a dull *whump* and engulfed him, the flames blackened purple and devouring.

Garland threw back his head and unleashed an inhuman scream.

When he opened his eyes, it was all gone. The flames, the blood, the skin-and-bone torments in their striped uniforms. Garland had no idea how long the visions had lasted, maybe only seconds that felt like hours stretching into a lifetime.

"What the hell!" Otto's voice was high and panicked as he pulled the van over and stared at Garland, panting and leaking sweat beside him. "You scared the shit out of me screaming like that. I thought you'd seen them, the SS."

"I. . ." Garland spluttered. He couldn't explain what he had seen, couldn't let Otto think he was crazy. He needed this job. "Sorry I must have fallen asleep, a bad dream. . ."

Otto studied him, as beads of sweat trickled down Garland's temple.

"Look, we're both shaken up," he said. "Who wouldn't be? Let's just keep the whole thing to ourselves, no need to tell anyone, especially my old man. He's well-thought-of around here, and being an enemy of the SS wouldn't exactly be good for business."

Garland nodded. His breathing slowed, and although he could still feel the heat on his face, he put his hand on his stomach and felt strong, supple flesh.

"I'm fine," Garland replied. "Let's finish these deliveries and get back to the shop. Let's try and forget we ever saw. . ."

He left the sentence unfinished, fearful he would be thrown back into that living hell.

Otto grinned and started the van. "Good man."

Raindrops began to fall from the Berlin sky. Garland was relieved to see they were colourless as they speckled the windscreen and weaved their drunken journey down the glass.

They delivered two more ovens without incident and were in better spirits by the time they returned to Kori's shop.

Otto was teasing Garland about his Norwegian roots as they opened the door and walked in, but what they saw left them silent and rooted to the spot.

Kori was standing in his workshop, speaking to a man in an SS uniform.

Otto's face blanched. He began shaking his head.

"Father. I can explain. It was. . ."

"You're late," Kori stopped him. "I was hoping you would be here an hour ago. This is Officer Kruger. He's here to talk business."

"Business?" Otto replied, still shaking. "What's happened?"

"Nothing, boy, what are you talking about?" He turned to Kruger. "I apologise for my son, Officer. He's not usually this stupid."

Kruger turned to fix his dark eyes on Otto and Garland.

"My commander heard that Kori ovens are the best in Berlin." He let his gaze sweep the shop. "We need to commission a series of the very largest for. . . disposal."

Garland felt the visions from the van growing restless as his head began to swim.

"Disposal of what?" The words were out before Garland could stop them.

Kruger recoiled and Kori's eyes widened in shock, Otto shaking like an addict without a fix.

"It's SS business." Kruger's voice was a whip. "Sometimes keeping young men like you safe means we have to keep secrets."

Kori shot Garland a look then turned smoothly back to Kruger.

"Please may I see your plans?"

Kruger unfurled a blue roll of paper across the workshop table.

Garland saw one long German word at the top of the plans.

SACHSENHAUSEN.

He ran over to the workshop basin and was violently sick.

Chapter Twenty-One

JOHAN - 1941

Given his grisly reputation, Johan's talent for execution seemed like a calling. As Der Bestatter, he was the go-to man for killing and disposing of prisoners. Following the truck debacle, the commanding officers were more careful. First came the firing squad. A trench was dug just outside the camp walls and lined with planks of wood and stone to catch stray bullets. An unwritten agreement was struck with Oranienburg cemetery that they would pick the bodies up and bury the dead, for a tidy sum.

And with the camp's population rising, the need for discipline also grew.

That was fine with Johan, always a believer in setting an example, and he was feeling happy with the world when Commander Schulz called him to his office one balmy morning.

Ever since the day the bodies tumbled from the truck, there had been a different glint in Schulz's eyes when he addressed Johan. It was bright and focused and carried, Johan was thrilled to realise, genuine respect. He sat across from the commander in the dusty office, which was adorned with bright-red Nazi flags. Framed images of Hitler, Schulz himself and what appeared to be a sketch of Julius Caesar hung symmetrically on the walls alongside various posters about Jews.

"I have a new assignment for you, Olsen." Schulz smiled. "We will find out just how well you handle a firearm."

The corner of Johan's mouth twitched. He had been expecting the call, the camp buzzing with rumours of important building work and a new role for Der Bestatter.

"I scored highly in training, sir." Johan remembered his success on the range. "It wasn't as strong as my physical assessment but it—"

"Yes, yes," Schulz interrupted with a wave of his hand. "I know about your training. Every SS man in here has had that. That's not what I'm talking about."

Johan raised his eyebrows and wrinkled his nose. "Sir?"

"You're a fine man, Olsen," Schulz told him. "A brave officer who isn't afraid to get his hands dirty. You have a future here. In Berlin. In Germany. People like you, physical people, have gone very far indeed."

Schulz paused to take a cigarette from an open packet on his desk, Johan recognising the swastika'd lighter the commander now flicked into flame.

"Tell me." Schulz spoke again. "Have you ever fired a weapon for its very purpose? To extinguish a human life that stands before you?"

Johan shook his head. "No, sir."

"How would you feel about it?" Schulz eyes had narrowed. "Pointing a weapon, pulling the trigger and seeing someone's life evaporate before your eyes? The power of exiting someone from the world. It's a power that exalts some, destroys others. It all depends on character, the true strength of the soul."

Schulz reached forward and patted Johan's chest twice. It was hard enough to make Johan flinch.

"Do you have the heart, my Norwegian friend? Is it robust enough to deal with the awesome power of ending life? To look a man directly in his wide, tearful eyes, hear his pleas for mercy and put a bullet into his brain? To see him slump backwards, blood, brain, and bone gushing from his wound, shit and piss flowing from his body?"

When Johan nodded the movement was sharp, confident.

"I was born for it, sir." Johan's tone had certainty, no hint of doubt. "I'll thrive on the responsibility, on the power."

Schulz stared back at him for a few seconds. To Johan it felt like an hour as the commander's hard, square features faced him and those blue eyes burnt like lasers. Everything in Johan's body urged him to look away until he could feel his own his eyes begin to ache.

A fleeting vision of the Oslofjord and lazy fishing boats flashed in his mind. It was gone before he could even think about how much he missed Oslo.

"Excellent!" Schulz said abruptly, clasping his hand on his knee with a smack.

"You're assigned to our new firing squad, along with four other suitable men. You're the first I've approached. How does that make you feel?"

Johan was trying to take in the magnitude of his good fortune, the kudos his new role would bring.

"Very proud, sir." A warm rush of delight rose in his heart, "It will be an honour to relinquish Germany of those who do not deserve to walk on her earth."

Schulz threw back his head back and laughed. Johan could see the thick black hair that sprouted from his nostrils.

"Spoken like the Fuehrer himself."

"Heil Hitler!" Johan shouted, shooting his flat palm in the air with a straight arm.

"Heil Hitler," Schulz replied. He grinned, his thin lips forming a crescent, reminding Johan of a dying worm, curling on fresh soil.

Although the executions were more frequent than Johan expected, he had been calm about the work.

Exterminating rats, he had said to himself as he was preparing the first time. *Just getting rid of the vermin.*

He thought back to his training and his conversation with Officer Weber. These weren't people they were killing, they were barely human at all, a subspecies not capable of living or thinking to the standards of others. He was putting them out of their misery, relieving them of hopeless lives always destined to end in failure. Besides, his bullet was only one of five that would kill the prisoner. Can a man be a murderer when another's shot may have been the one to end the life? It was even said some of the rifles were loaded with blanks.

The first person in front of the firing squad was a communist; someone who had been stirring up trouble amongst the prisoners. Johan didn't even know his name. It didn't matter.

He stood in formation with the four other guards in a deep pit that had been excavated northwest of the camp, just beyond the walls. Wooden panels had been positioned all around, and the prisoner had been placed in front of several layers of wood. He had been offered a blindfold but declined. He wanted to look his killers in the eye, courage that Johan found both impressive and disconcerting. He wasn't sure if he wanted to return the sentiment.

"Aim!" Schulz shouted.

Johan could just see the commander's long leather boots in his line of vision, planted on the higher, sandy ground. Schulz's shadow stretched over the pit, ominous and dark.

Johan didn't know if it was the sound-proof structure or the magnitude of the moment, but he felt an eerie silence as he raised his weapon. A stiff breeze blew grains of sand above the pit, and strands of Johan's hair gently lifted.

He rested his cheek on the rifle and closed one eye, aiming at the prisoner's chest. Somewhere above, a man cleared his throat.

"Fire!" Schulz yelled.

The crack of the five rifles was deafening, a salvo that seemed to ripple and rumble through the air.

Johan raised his eyes from the barrel and watched the prisoner, peppered with holes seeping red across his chest, slump backwards. The man landed on his backside, then sank to his left, his shoulder and head touching the ground.

His eyes never closed.

From the moment the *aim* command had been given, Johan had been holding his breath. Now he exhaled sharply.

He looked again at the prisoner. There was something about a dead man's eyes. They were devoid of the brightness that conveys energy, emotion, wisdom. When death arrives it is the eyes that first betray, the eyes that signal the soul is gone, long before the body begins its journey to destruction.

Johan had quickly got used to killing. The dead all deserved it, otherwise why would they be here? But seeing a man's life force slip away – watching the eyes glaze and grey – was harder. Johan was always grateful for those who closed their eyes tight on the point of death and kept them shut. It was easier that way.

Time continued, as did the executions, and the firing squad found themselves mobilised on an almost daily basis.

Johan saw every dead man fall.

Some screamed, pathetic cowards who squealed like girls as death approached.

Others fed on their last flash of rage, the shouters who bared their teeth and swore vengeance with curses from beyond the grave.

The repenters said sorry over and over again, hoping the forgiving arms of mercy would save them even as Johan and the squad levelled their weapons.

Johan kept a grudging respect for the stoics, the men who silently took the shots and slumped against the back wall, no weeping or bravado, no howling at the moon.

Neither the creed of the prisoner nor the colour of the triangle they wore on their uniform made a difference. Execution removed all the boundaries, made every one of the condemned an equal. Whether they cursed, cried or calmly met their fate, they all ended up with their insides oozing through the bullet holes and blood drizzling down their chins. Johan often thought they looked like dead clowns with hastily applied red make-up.

On one cold morning, when the red sun was only slowly emerging on the horizon to the east of Sachsenhausen, the firing squad had been assembled to execute a well-known and well-liked prisoner. Ernst Schneider was a kapo. He'd been imprisoned as a communist, a trade unionist whose crime had been to lobby for improved pay and working conditions. Even the guards liked Ernst Schneider. He wasn't a Jew and he wasn't a homosexual. He was a German, and not a bad one at that, just a man who was prepared to stand up for fairness.

Ernst was never violent, and he wasn't the sort to oppose the progression of the Reich. He had simply wanted a better deal, not for himself but his fellow workers. Within the camp he was a leader, a man with influence and respect amongst the other prisoners. He must also, Johan was sure, be foolish to stand up to the government? Why fight a battle he could never win?

The firing squad didn't know why Commander Schulz had decided Ernst had to die, and it wasn't their place to question.

Johan exchanged glances with a couple of them. Kruger, the same age as Johan and who had arrived at Sachsenhausen at the same time, looked back with a *what can we do?* expression. Lange, an older solider who had fought in the Great War, looked at Johan and arched the brows that rested above sad eyes. Johan returned the looks, sending his own regret as best as he could,

Schubert was the guard tasked with marching Ernst Schneider down to the pit, the prisoner's hands already tied. Schubert called Kruger forward and then climbed back to a position overlooking the trench.

"Would you like a cover on your head, Ernst?" Kruger asked. Even at the point of execution, using Ernst's name spoke volumes about his standing.

"No," Ernst told him evenly. "I want to look my killers in the eye, thank you very much."

Schulz had taken up his own position about the pit and now his harsh voice boomed out.

"Does the prisoner have any last words?"

Ernst Schneider gazed up at Schulz and grinned. His teeth were stained with dried blood, collateral damage from whatever altercation had led to his arrest, Johan presumed.

"Words?" Ernst repeated. "What is there left to say? A cigarette would be nice though."

Schulz regarded him for several seconds before nodding to Kruger. The guard flicked a cigarette out of his breast pocket, placed it gently between Ernst's lips, and lit it with a match, cupping his hand around the fluttering flame to shield it from the cool breeze.

Ernst took two short rasping draws and blew smoke from the opposite side of his mouth.

"On second thought I will say this," his voice distorted by the cigarette jiggling between his lips. "This country - *my* country - is going to shit. Hitler, the man you all worship, is evil. Germany will fall and blood will be shed. The people will rise. . ."

Schulz had already heard enough.

"Ready!" he yelled towards the firing squad.

Johan checked his rifle and raised it. Without moving his head, he glanced to his right and noticed Kruger's eyes were sparkling, welled tears catching the dawn light. He could hear his breathing rise and fall in a rollercoaster rhythm, erratic and fast. Ernst was still speaking, rambling now about the sins of Hitler and the damnation that would be Nazi Germany's future.

"Aim!"

Johan placed his sight on Ernst's chest.

"Fire!"

Five shots rang out as one, the deafening report echoing away into the still-shadowed distance. Ernst sank screaming to the ground, gasping and flailing violently, feet kicking up gravel and sand from the ground.

Johan heard Kruger begin to sob. He looked at his feet, unsure of what to do next, and still had his eyes down when another gunshot crackled across the growing dawn.

His eyes darted towards the source of the sound and he saw Schulz looking down from his position above the ditch, thin slivers of smoke escaping from his pistol.

Ernst was dead and Johan was glad. He didn't deserve to spend the last few seconds of his life in agony.

Now for the first time since they had dug it, Schulz made his way to the bottom of the killing pit. Johan felt his shoulders slump in unison with the rest of the firing squad.

Schulz kicked Ernst's body, the loud crack of ribs as clear as the pistol shot. He looked at the wooden boards behind where Ernst had stood, using his finger to assess the damage. Then, without hesitation, he dragged Ernst's body up by the front of his striped uniform, pushed it against the makeshift wooden wall and dug his fingers into the red wounds still streaming with blood. Johan heard a wet squelch as Schulz pulled out two bullets. He pushed Ernst's body backwards and watched it fall ungracefully, legs splayed in different directions, tongue poking from lips drawn back in a red grimace.

Schulz turned to the firing squad, blood running down his fingers and dripping onto the ground.

"Two hits."

The five men in the firing squad stared back blankly.

"Two hits," Schulz repeated, "and three misses. Two bullets lodged in his chest, three in the wall."

Johan could see Kruger twitch out of the corner of his eye. No one had been given blanks this time.

"The first time anyone has missed, and yet three of you don't hit the target." Schulz took off his hat off and scratched his slick, neatly combed black hair in an exaggerated motion. "I don't understand."

He shook his head and studied the squad standing silent before him.

"You train. You're talented marksmen selected especially for this honour. Yet three of you missed. Very, very strange."

Schulz looked up at each of the men in turn. His cold eyes drilled into Johan who felt a shudder run through his body. Johan's bullet had hit, he was sure of that. His aim had never wavered from Ernst's chest. He hadn't liked doing it, but orders were orders.

"You all knew him?" Schulz asked. He was two yards from the firing squad, who still stood in formation. He walked up to them one by one, his face right in front of theirs. When it was his turn, Johan could smell bitter coffee and a sour hint of whisky on the commander's hot breath. Schulz moved to Kruger, who winced. Schulz, a man who could scent fear like a starving wolf tracking its prey, edged even closer and laced his voice with venom.

"Did you miss the prisoner, Kruger?"

Johan glanced and saw Kruger's bottom lip begin to curl, a toddler's tremble that looked pathetic on the guard's ashen face.

"Did you miss the fucking prisoner, you fucking traitor!"

Shultz shouted the words so loudly every syllable seemed to roll like a small earthquake across the camp.

Kruger nodded slowly, tears streaking his cheeks, silver lines of liquid light in the rising sun.

Schulz raised his pistol and pressed the barrel on Kruger's forehead.

"Did you miss on purpose, you queer piece of shit?" Schulz yelled, his face reddening.

Johan could hear muffled sobs elsewhere in the line of men. Someone else had cracked, and Schulz's eyes darted menacingly to the side.

"Weak!" he spat. "Snivelling, pathetic maggots pretending to be men that Germany could respect and trust."

He raised the pistol high and brought it down with savage force to split open Kruger's nose. Still sobbing, the guard crumbled to his knees, blood running in two thick streams onto his chin and chest.

Schulz made his way back up the bank and turned to Schubert.

"These men need a leave of absence," he looked again towards the pit. "We need to think again."

Johan didn't yet know it, but the days of the firing squad were nearing the end. Executions would soon become more efficient, more clinical, and more regular.

Sachsenhausen was about to begin killing for real.

Chapter Twenty-Two

GARLAND - 1941

It was a frosty night in December when Garland's life changed forever.

He still hadn't been pulled into the German war effort, no one had shipped him back to Norway, and even the trauma of the incident with Hans had slowly moved somewhere more distant in his mind. The kiss had left Garland confused about his own feelings, but he continued to block them out, concentrating on enjoying himself and even taking a couple of handsome girls on dates as distractions.

Friday night on the tiles had become a regular thing. He had been earning a decent wage at Kori's for six month now, and with Christmas on its way, even war's relentless undercurrent of fear couldn't dampen the merriment Garland sensed in the city.

He had become quite a regular on the Berlin nightlife scene. Garland still lived in the hostel, but that freed up Reichsmarks for weekends. He had made a large circle of friends, he could eat at reasonable restaurants, and although it stung his pride at first, he even began visiting the city's theatres.

Kori was a kind, honest employer, and the work meant Garland had discovered the nooks and crannies of Berlin. His job also gave him a view of how the city's industries and trades worked even harder in war. . . the bakeries, butchers, factories, and crematoria all playing their part in the patriotic effort.

Kori had continued his contract with the SS, but it was shrouded in mystery. Garland and Otto were kept away. Kori himself spent hours poring over plans, briefing the engineers, making sure the ovens matched the precise measurements dictated by the SS and even going with the SS to personally install them himself. Garland was relieved to be playing no part, for reasons he could never share. Every now and again he saw the ovens turn on, flames licking at the sides and those same melting faces emerging from the heat. He stayed silent and fought the sickness even when the thick stench of human flesh burning was almost overwhelming.

Like most other Fridays, Garland and Otto began their night in a bar along Friedrichstrasse and continued along their regular route, drinking frothy beer and shots of strong Polish vodka. Garland enjoyed the release. The drinks left his head spinning but dulled his senses and helped numb the visions which seemed to be getting stronger and stronger. When he was drunk, he no longer noticed the colours that swarmed at the corners of his eyes. The hellish images that plagued him when he saw the ovens, the swastikas, the SS emblem were washed away by the alcohol. Garland was himself again, happy and relaxed. When he was in the bars with their bright lights and noise he felt normal, that he was living life to the full.

He had left Otto and was walking to meet Gianni at another bar when he bumped into Hans.

Garland felt ice form in his heart and then melt into fire. Hans was in full army uniform. Garland gritted his teeth and felt pain run through his body. Even through the steins and shots, he could see black swirls form above Hans's head, thick and ominous.

The two men stood, three yards apart, staring at each other. Garland's eyes flicked upwards, the dark plumes making shapes of skulls, swastikas and grotesque figures that looked like demons. Hans broke the silence.

"Garland, I. . . I'm. . ."

". . .going to punch me again?" Garland finished, his words slurred.

Hans looked at his feet. "I'm sorry. I was. . . confused, frightened."

"You don't think I was fucking frightened?" Garland snapped. "In a strange city, hit by someone I thought was being friendly?"

"Let me make it up to you," Hans said. He put out a hand which Garland ignored. "Come, I'll buy you a drink and explain."

They talked for hours and, as each second went by, with every sentence Hans muttered, Garland softened. They drank beers, washed down with more vodka shots. Soon Garland was smiling. Then laughing.

"As you can see, I've been conscripted," Hans said, setting another empty shot glass on their table. "Against my will, obviously, but I'm lucky enough to have a simple administrative role in the army so far. The green battlefields of France haven't called yet."

He picked up his stein and smiled.

"What about you? Have you escaped Herr Hitler's grasp? Still treading the boards?"

Garland lowered his head and shook it drunkenly. "No. I got fired."

Hans reeled, his lips pursed. "Fired? What the hell. . ."

"I told them what happened with you. They thought I was a homosexual."

Hans nodded sombrely, his narrowed eyes fixed on Garland. "I'm sorry."

"Sorry for what?" Garland asked, the anger suddenly reignited. "For punching my face or for helping me get kicked out of the career I loved?"

Garland watched a watery film cloud Hans's eyes.

"We live in strange times, Garland," he replied. "Sometimes being what you are is one of the biggest battles. The war with yourself is the hardest one to win."

"You're homosexual?" Garland asked.

"As, I suspect, are you."

The two men looked each other for long seconds before Garland broke eye contact and stared down at his hands, the fingers shifting nervously.

"How do you know you are? I mean, I. . . I don't know if I am or not."

"If you weren't, why would you wonder about it?" Hans asked. "It's something I've denied to myself time and time again. People like us, we used to be free but not anymore. They're arresting queers right across Germany, locking us up just for what we are. Why is it anyone's business? Even some SS are queers themselves."

People Like Us.

The phrase stuck in Garland's drink-muddled mind and made him feel faint. He wasn't ready to confront whatever foreign emotions he was hiding even from himself.

He rushed outside the bar and threw up on the Friedrichstrasse pavement.

Hans had followed and put a hand on his back.

"It's okay," he said softly. "It's a lot to take in, and we've had a lot to drink."

Garland stood and faced Hans under the bright streetlight. Passers-by stared briefly before hurrying on their way to the busy bars. Hans was a handsome man. His square jaw was dashed with dark stubble, a lock of his black hair hung delicately over his forehead and his eyebrows arched in a way that made him look both strong and innocent.

They smiled and Hans offered Garland a mint. They lit cigarettes and silently watched the smoke rise and drift to nothingness in the night air.

"Crazy times," Hans said after a while. "Hitler, Jews, a new Germany and another senseless war. I still haven't changed my mind about it, Garland. If I were you, I'd already be back in Norway."

Garland smiled, still watching the grey smoke shift under the streetlight's glare.

"But I'm glad you're not."

Garland looked over at Hans and they both laughed. Garland pushed him in the shoulder. "I still haven't got you back for that lucky punch you landed."

Hans pushed him back playfully. "I'd like to see you try."

Hans took off, running down an alleyway. Garland, stumbling, caught up with him and threw his arms around his neck. They both tumbled to the ground, laughing, and scuffling for a few seconds before they came face-to-face. Garland was on top. He had pinned Hans's arms so he couldn't move. Hans's hair fell to one side, a rich curtain that moved to reveal his sculpted features.

Garland inched his mouth closer and let it hover above Hans's lips. He felt his tongue tingle. A flurry of butterflies flew from his stomach to his heart and filled his brain, an explosion of colour.

Garland closed the last of the distance, the kiss slow and soft as a wave of euphoria began to sweep through his body.

The blow to his ribs was short and sharp.

Three figures stood above them, darkness masking their features. Garland's head spun and he struggled to focus.

He had rolled away so he and Hans were both lying on their backs.

"These fucking queers," the one in the middle said, the voice familiar. He bent to look at them, his face still shadowed. "Running to a dirty back alley to do their business."

He spat each word. The man was large and Garland could make out thick hair silhouetted against the harsh light. He was chewing tobacco, giving his breath a rich, bitter smell. "You're scum," he said, breathing in hitches, enjoying the situation. "And an army soldier at that. You should be ashamed of yourself, queer."

Hans gave a high shriek of agony as the man kicked him hard between the legs. The two others stepped forward, all three kicking Garland and Hans as they curled helpless on the cold concrete. Every blow sent white-hot pain shooting across Garland's body. He shut his eyes and waited for the onslaught to end, stinging tears running fast down his cheeks.

It felt like hours. It was probably seconds. Garland opened his eyes to see the man in the middle haul Hans up by his army lapel and shove him against the stone wall.

"What you got to say for yourself, queer soldier?"

He punched Hans's stomach. Hans bent double and then slowly straightened up.

"Fuck you," he said, spittle flying from his lips.

The three men looked at each other, wide-eyed. Garland pushed himself up by his elbows and felt pain arrow through his shoulder. "Hans. . ." His voice sounded raw.

He saw Hans's eyes lock onto his own in the dim light. "Run Garland," he mouthed. "Run."

Then Hans turned and began throwing his fists. Garland watched him swing wildly with a force that must have been driven by a lifetime of white-hot rage, every slight and insult distilled into the moment. As Garland rose to his feet, he saw one of the men fall, blood gushing from his face. Another staggered away, clutching his ribs and moaning in pain. Now the ringleader was reeling too, Hans's savage, swinging hook breaking his cheek as easily as delicate china. Hans grabbed him in a headlock and looked at Garland as he punched the man's face again and again.

"Garland, go." He panted. "This is my payback to you." Blood ran from his nose and his swollen knuckles. "This is me saying. . ."

Garland caught the glint of light, a silver burst in the semidarkness, and saw the knife in the man's hand.

"Hans!" Garland shouted

He leapt forward but it was too late. The man drove the knife upwards into Hans's throat, the blade slicing a clean gash that threw blood in an arc against the alleyway wall.

Garland saw Hans slump to the ground, saw life leave his open eyes and stood frozen as a shimmering, milk-white cloud rose from Hans's body. It soared towards the night sky, trailing a rainbow of bright colours. Hans watched it merge with the stars above and disappear.

He turned to face the knife-man, his blade bathed in red and blood running down his wrist.

"I know you." The man hissed as he raised the glistening knife. "I know where you live, Garland Lund."

Seadog Willy stepped from the shadows and into the glare of the streetlight as Garland turned and fled.

He covered the length of Friedrichstrasse, a blur of yellow, blue and green lights, throwing frightened glances over his shoulder. He thought he could hear Willy shouting above the street noise and the sound of his own shoes slapping the concrete. He let the wet tears fall down his face, the night breeze pushing them into his mouth, leaving a salty, bitter taste.

Scenes from the alleyway replayed in his head. . . Seadog Willy's eyes, shadowed and unrepentant; blood exploding against the wall; the life force leaving Hans's body. Another romantic moment terminated by violence. Murder. Was it a sign? Garland slowed and finally stopped, doubled over and gulping air. Around him, the Berlin streets seemed full of danger. He closed his eyes as images whipped like a cyclone behind his fluttering lids. . . Thick black swastikas on blood-red Nazi flags. Soulless eagles gliding on marble wings. Men, women and children melting in a furnace that never went out.

And with the memories came the heavy, choking smell of burning flesh.

Chapter Twenty-Three

JOHAN - 1941

"The problem, Olsen, is that men are men." Schulz leant back, balancing his chair on its two rear legs. "They are human, with all the flaws that brings. As much as we hate to admit it, we are flawed. You are. I am. Both flawed."

Johan watched him rock gently. It was something Schulz did often, and Johan thought one day he would tip over. The notorious SS officer reduced to an undignified heap, those huge leather boots peddling helplessly in the air.

The image would have made him chuckle but for Schulz's hair-trigger temper. The camp commander was a cold killer, devoid of empathy or reason. He would probably shoot everyone in the room rather than live with the embarrassment. Johan shut off the scene and watched Schulz blow thick smoke rings from a cigar into the air.

"Some men are very comfortable delivering death," he continued, his voice muffled by the smoke. "But most simply aren't wired up that way. When the five of you stood in front of that commie, the only one I saw with steel in their eyes was you."

Johan stifled a cough, the smoke in the room thickening by the second.

Schulz went on. "I never watch the prisoners die, Olsen. All of my attention is on the shooters, and you were the only one I could trust. The only one! When the others come back, they'll be off execution duty. But I want you to stay."

Johan felt a surge of relief, not just for his own place in the firing squad but that the others were being spared. In the world of the SS, a *leave of absence* could easily mean a spell locked up in the camp.

"Thank you, sir," Johan replied.

Schulz dropped his chair forward and stubbed his cigar out in a spray of red sparks.

"Not enough of us are natural killers," he said. "Too many feel responsible when they look a man in the eye and end his life. It weighs them down, Olsen, preys on their mind like a circling hawk waiting to swoop. Some lose sleep. Some lose their minds."

Schulz stretched and resumed his balancing act, the chair creaking in gentle protest.

"Ernst Schneider was a good man." The commander smiled. "He did nothing wrong, but he played his part in my test. I knew the men liked him. I needed to know who could follow my orders without question."

Johan nodded. It was something he had suspected, knowing how much Schulz enjoyed mind games. Sacrificing Schneider had been just another move.

"I'm pleased I didn't let you down, sir," Johan said, relieved Schulz couldn't see through his own guilt. He remembered the sleepless nights in his bunk, the faces of those he had killed haunting him. He had thought of the mothers, brothers, fathers, children the dead had left behind. He heard their screams. He saw their empty eyes.

"Executions in the camp are going to become more regular." Schulz sounded excited, energised. "That's why we've devised a new way, a genius method that means no one is responsible for death."

"Sir?" Johan was intrigued, Schulz's words a riddle.

The commander rocked forward, took another cigar from an open packet on his desk, and made a show of lighting it in a series of long, slow draws.

"We need a way of killing that is smooth on the minds and souls of weak men," Schulz said. "If it were up to us, we'd dispose of these vermin with our bare hands, no?"

Johan smiled, warmed by the compliment. "Yes, sir."

Fresh clouds of smoke swirled above their heads, making Johan's eyes itch. Somewhere in the distance a man screamed. But neither Schulz nor Johan appeared to notice.

It was several weeks later that Schulz finally unveiled his grand execution plan, first discovering the scheme had been more ambitious than he had realised. The delay meant executions had stayed with the firing squad, although now its members – including Johan – were to be rotated. Johan felt it was another chance for Schulz to study all of the men, to see who had the cold eyes he wanted and who had the human fallibility of empathy he despised so much. They were all on trial. Shit, with a leader as unpredictable as Schulz, everyone at Sachsenhausen was on trial round the clock.

The commander ushered Johan into his office after roll-call. Johan could feel the glare of the other guards on his back as he followed Schulz. He knew they were jealous. He was one of Schulz's favourites, but they didn't see the other side. More exposure to Schulz meant increased danger. More time in his office meant more opportunity to say or do the wrong thing. And letting Schulz down would mean quick and pitiless death, favourite or not.

Johan sometimes wondered if the commander's high regard was worth putting his head in the lion's mouth.

Schulz pushed open the heavy iron door to his cramped office. Johan had been surprised he had chosen such a small space when there were other much larger rooms with more comfort. But the lack of comfort was precisely what Schulz wanted. When he dragged people into his office, he wanted the nicotine-stained walls to close in on them. Even the eye-catching images he hung from the walls had been carefully chosen, drawing even the most focused men like magnets and giving Schulz the excuse to beat them for a split second's inattention. Several guards had left Schulz's office bleeding and injured. Others, like Becker, never left his office alive.

Danger and death seeped out of every crack in the small room, as heavy and ominous as the thick cigar smoke that once again gathered above their heads.

Self-preservation meant Johan was always on full alert and his concentration was razor sharp as Schulz excitedly pulled out a large sheet of paper and smoothed it onto the wooden table. It was a building plan, an architect's detailed drawing that Johan couldn't understand, a maze of corridors linking to large rooms.

"Do you know what you're looking at, boy?" Schulz asked, his cigar hanging from the corner of his mouth. A large piece of ash fell onto the sheet and Schulz hurriedly brushed it onto the floor.

Johan shook his head nervously.

"This is the most revolutionary innovation in the history of executions," Schulz said proudly. "The men call the industrial yard *Station Z*, is that right?"

"Yes, sir," Johan replied, his eyebrows lifting in surprise. It was an in-joke amongst the officers. Prisoners came into the camp at Tower A and left at Station Z, their spirits rising away from the hellish confines of Sachsenhausen.

"I like it," Schulz said. "Humour is good for the men. It's healthy. Always better for a man to laugh than cry, Olsen. Words to live by, my Aryan friend."

"I'll remember, sir."

And Johan would remember until the day he died in a pine forest twenty miles outside Berlin.

"Good," Schulz continued. "This will be a masterpiece, a building of efficient human disposal, when I can get good enough builders to put it up. The plans don't convey the genius of what will happen inside these corridors though."

Johan listened intently, switching his gaze from Schulz to the plans.

"This method of execution ensures no accountability," Schulz told him. "There will be no emotional dilemmas for the executioner, no one will feel like they have personally killed anyone. Imagine that! Murder without a conscience. Death without a man's cold touch."

"But. . ." Johan brushed his hands on the plans, captivated. "How?"

Schulz spoke quickly, tracing his finger across the sketched-out corridors on the cigar-stained paper as smoke massed like storm clouds under the discoloured ceiling.

The weeks and months went by, and Johan continued to work hard to impress his commander.

He watched Schulz, forever swigging from his steel flask, torture and kill more prisoners, amusing himself with different methods so he never got bored. His favourite tests were those of endurance and humiliation, especially the cruel simplicity of making roll-call prisoners stand for hours in the freezing night. He stripped the inmates of their dignity until they no longer felt like human beings. They were treated like dogs so eventually they acted like dogs, many becoming feral, no more than animals reduced to shaking, nervous shadows.

Another Schulz favourite was drowning. There was something in the power of it he found particularly satisfying. The smaller the amount of water the better, Schulz believed. Johan had watched him drown a prisoner in a puddle of water, but the commander's preferred method was in the urinal, black gloves gripping a prisoner's skull to drive it downwards, the stinking piss-filled bowl filling with red from the victim's broken nose. Schulz's eyes would blaze as foamy bubbles rose from the gurgling prisoner who was swallowing urine until there was a final gulp and a violent twitch of his body.

Other methods of killing appealed to Schulz's more visceral, violent side. He was the proud owner of a samurai sword, brought as a gift by a Japanese delegation who a visibly proud Schulz had given a tour of the facilities. The finely-crafted sword was a weapon reserved for premeditated execution, a dispatch for a prisoner who Schulz had particularly hated and toyed with over a long period of time.

There was one inmate, a Jew whose lazy eye had been enough to make him a target, Schulz had cut in half from the crown downwards. The blade, which Schulz spent hours sharpening and polishing, had sliced through the prisoner's skull as easily as a man would walk through thin mist. Johan had watched the Jew's head split perfectly in two, like a specimen a doctor might keep in a jar. Even then he was sure he had seen the man's life leave him, a life that seemed to disappear slowly from his eyes as if it was playing catch-up with his dying body. Johan was both appalled and fascinated. The watching prisoners were silent with fright.

Although he never indulged himself in the same way, Johan had also disposed of some of the prisoners. *Rats*, he repeated like a mantra as he killed them. He wasn't absolutely ruthless like Schulz; he didn't kill for fun. Death was a last resort when he sensed a ripple of disrespect. A guard's authority was everything. He lived or died by it. There were over fifteen thousand prisoners in Sachsenhausen and only one thousand officers. There was always the chance of an uprising, even if the insurgents would be a skeletal army of broken men challenging strong, healthy SS soldiers trained only to win. It was laughable, but the weight of numbers made it possible, especially if an overpowered guard was to surrender their weapon.

Levels of fear had to be maintained, and Johan would have been failing if he had instilled anything less than dread in his prisoners.

He had lost count of the ones who had died at his hand. Schulz would be appalled to know he still carried a little of each man with him, phantoms that crept through the nights he couldn't sleep, staring at the dark ceiling and listening to a song thrush outside his window whistling its late song.

Fear was something you created in others but it was contagious, Johan knew, a fast-spreading virus only the very strongest could resist. Was it weakness? Was it a crack in the most solid of armour, that let fear crawl inside?

Often the song thrush had long fallen silent by the time Johan drifted off to sleep.

Chapter Twenty-Four

GARLAND - 1941

It was Christmas Eve when they came for Garland.

He'd woken up feeling ill, another night out punished with a sickly hangover, the familiar cloak of anxiety wrapping around him like a shroud.

Maybe with a clear head he would have paid more attention to the warnings, the phantom smells and sounds, the Nazi flag slithering red and black like something alive, the ghostly figures in their striped uniforms marching, falling, burning. In the months and years to come, Garland would revisit the signs and wonder what might have happened if he had heeded their warnings.

Could he have taken a different path? Could he have made it back to Oslo or found safety in another country? He would never know.

As Garland, shaking and unsteady, pulled on his clothes, he heard a commotion and looked to the dormitory entrance. Three uniformed Gestapo officers were making their way into the room.

"What now?" a man to his left said. "More inspections?"

"Probably looking for Jews," another replied. "Or queers. I heard they've started rounding them up now."

"No Jews in here, officers," the first man shouted.

The Gestapo men scanned the room before one of them barked six simple words.

"We are here for Garland Lund."

Garland felt his face turn ashen white. Colours skirted around the edge of his vision and the burning smell engulfed his senses. Flames licked at the walls, but when he turned to look they disappeared, his sight fuzzy and out of focus. In front of their bunks, Garland watched the other boarders change in a heartbeat, one moment stick-thin creatures in tatty stripes, the next back to normal, the changes a slide-show running at breakneck speed.

"Which one of you maggots is Lund!" The officer spat the words out like a bad taste.

Garland tentatively raised his hand. The dozen or so others in the dormitory looked and stared. The slide-show started again, a blurry switchback that left Garland dizzy.

"Garland Lund, we have come here to take you into protective custody. Under paragraph 175 of the German Criminal Code."

Garland was thrown, caught off balance. He heard gasps around the room, the short intakes of breath a cacophony of soft noise. They all knew what a 175er was.

Garland steadied himself, trying to focus. He met the officer's stare. "Protection from what?"

The officer stepped towards him, a big man whose shoulders tested the seams of his heavy coat.

"You're coming with us. Now."

"I don't understand," Garland's whole body was trembling, panic and adrenaline beginning to run free.

He felt the walls start to shake as fear turned to anger. "I've done nothing wrong!" he yelled.

As Garland's voice rose, the whole building shook, the motion almost knocking him off his feet. He saw a jagged crack suddenly zig-zag across the wall opposite, plaster splintering in a burst of chalky dust. The Gestapo officers turned, one of them walking to the wall and tracing the crack with his finger.

"Was this here earlier?"

"You can see that?" Garland asked. His anger had faded and the fear had returned.

The officer shook his head.

"Fucking queer," he said and grabbed Garland's arm.

The words fell like a thunderbolt on the residents still thrown by the tremor that had shaken the building.

"You are a queer? That's why they're taking you away?"

It was Gianni, staring in numb disbelief.

The gasps and whispers gathered like a strong desert wind, the muttered accusations swirling in its teeth.

Garland didn't respond, his jaw hanging slack as he was dragged backwards by two of the officers. His head spun with colours, smells and vivid hallucinations. He could see Gianni looking at him, his arms spread and his mouth open so wide it looked as if he were about to sing an aria. Another time and place, Garland would have been doubled up with laughter.

"Officers, no," Gianni called after them. "He's not homosexual. I know him. He is a friend."

Gianni ran up to one of the Gestapo men but was met with a fist clad in a black leather glove. Garland saw him slump against the dormitory wall, his face twisted in fear and blood running from his mouth.

The officers tightened their grip and hauled Garland out of the room and down the hostel stairs.

He never saw Gianni again.

Garland spent three cold, lonely nights in a cell before being promptly convicted as guilty of contravening paragraph 175. He was pushed outside where two SS officers met him and dragged him away.

Passers-by stopped in their tracks. Garland could feel their eyes burning into him as he was frog-marched up Friedrichstrasse with his arms behind his back. He had a sudden and furious thought about what Seadog Willy was doing and whether his crime would go unpunished, whilst Garland was arrested for nothing.

The officers smelt of alcohol and sickly-sweet sweat. One of them, Garland noticed, was about his own age.

It could have been Johan.

Garland was hit by a jolt of hate for Nazi Germany and a sudden dislike for his friend, a feeling that caught him by surprise. His brother from the orphanage had always been there when no one else cared.

"Where are you taking me?" he asked, panic making his voice high and shrill.

One of the officers planted a swift, hard punch to the side of Garland's face. He could taste warm blood and spat red on the pavement, rage once more moving somewhere deep inside, ready to rise.

"We'll work the homosexuality out of you, queer," the officer sneered. "We'll cure you with labour."

"Labour? I don't understand."

"Quiet or the next blow will send you to your grave. I'll make hard labour feel like a wet dream."

Johan had spoken about his posting at the work camp first near Munich. Garland felt vomit rising in his throat.

"There's been a mistake. I'm not supposed to be here."

Garland felt a huge crack as the other officer smashed a truncheon against the side of his face.

His legs buckled but the officers still pulled him along with ease, his feet dragging noisily across the sidewalk.

"You queers all say the same thing, just like the Jews and commies," the officer taunted. "*I'm not supposed to be here.*"

He made his voice a pleading, childlike squeal before a thin smile lifted the corner of his mouth and his eyes sparkled underneath his dark cap.

"You're right." He studied Garland like a rat in a lab test. "You're *not* supposed to be here. You need to fuck off out of Germany. Better still, stay and be run into the ground. I think you're going to like Sachsenhausen, queer boy."

When he ruffled Garland's blond hair, Garland could feel the wedding ring scrape his scalp.

Sachsenhausen. That word again. As the black letters floated in front of his eyes, he saw they were lined by a red border dripping blood. He could smell it, rich and bitter. The letters disappeared, and the stench of burning flesh returned, stronger than ever. Garland began to cry, his head on his heaving chest.

They reached Friedrichstrasse train station, commuters staring in silent judgement, watching a criminal being led to justice. Garland saw their expressions and found no pity in their eyes. As they reached the grey concrete platform, the haze of cigarette smoke a milky fog around them, Garland noticed others in the custody of the SS. The captives all looked dishevelled, confused. One Jewish-looking man had a swollen eye leaking blood. Garland glanced up to see menacing, dark colours swirling within the smoke. He felt sick and faint.

A long train of connected carriages, seemingly infinite, rolled into the station and eventually came to a grinding halt. Steam filled the air, carrying an acrid smell of petrol that made Garland wretch. He made out the destination on the card in the window, etched in thick black letters. *Oranienburg.*

Garland was marched to the rear of the train, along with the other prisoners, and manhandled into the packed carriage. Commuters and day trippers with downturned mouths and narrowed eyes shot him daggers. One woman spat at Garland, the stringy saliva drooping from his lapel.

He was led to a seat and slumped down as the train began moving with a shudder.

"Don't cry, boy."

Garland heard the softly spoken words and felt a hand on his shoulder.

He followed the voice and saw an older man in his midfifties whose thick black hair and beard were striped with silvery grey streaks.

"What's happening? Where are we going?" Garland asked him, his words muffled by sobs and his swollen cheek.

"We are going away," the man answered. "To a camp."

"A labour camp?" The words flashed in front of his eyes again, formed in black as if torn from the seams of existence itself. *Sachsenhausen.* A chasm leading straight to hell.

"Yes, so I am told. We are enemies of Germany now, boy. What did you do?"

Garland shook his head. "The 175. They think I am a homosexual."

"Ah yes." The man nodded. "I am a Jew, my friend. Of that I cannot change and I am immeasurably guilty. I fought for Germany in the Great War and have lived in Berlin my entire life. Yet now I am the enemy. Such is life."

"What will happen to us there?" Garland asked, even though he already knew. He had heard the stories from Johan, the whispered rumours in the bars and restaurants.

And he had suffered the visions, tasted the darkness and the pain that was to come.

"We'll be put to work until they see fit to dispose of us, one way or another." The man looked sharply at Garland and smiled without humour. "But you have blond hair and blue eyes. You're not German. Sweden?"

"Norway," Garland corrected.

"Maybe it will be easier for you." The man was looking him up and down. "Me? I am an old Jew. This is the last place I will live and the place I will die."

Garland looked at the man's eyes. They were a bright hazel now dulled by a sadness that made Garland's tears fall again. This was the reality. This day of all days, Christmas Eve, he was going to be locked up in a camp where death was likely and suffering certain. He cursed himself for ignoring the signs, for not understanding what the visions and the waking nightmares were trying to tell him. He remembered the premonition at the Olympic Stadium, knowing absolutely that Jesse Owens would win. Garland made a promise to himself. He would learn to understand. He would read the visions, decipher the signs, no matter how hard they were to face. He would live his life by them. They *meant* something, he knew that now. Garland thought about the other things he could not explain, the ceramic ashtray that defied gravity and the tremor that shook the hostel. Those weren't hallucinations or warnings. They were real. Something simmered inside him, an unfathomable energy that came from his mind and body. He couldn't understand it, but somehow he would learn to control it.

The train rolled on, stopping at stations on the way, passengers coming and going but the carriages still crammed and stifling. Garland knew they were heading east but he had never been this far out of the city.

After an hour the train came to a halt, spewing steam behind it. No matter what awaited him in this place, he would be happy to leave the carriage, the smell of body odour and urine unbearable in the suffocating heat. Garland and the other prisoners were herded down long streets. More passers-by stared. Some spat, some yelled obscenities. Garland was squinting into the midday glare when a man ahead burst from the long line and ran. He sprinted less than twenty yards before the air rang with a loud crack. The man fell face down in a growing puddle of deep red, sunlight bouncing from its surface in a blinding flash. The officer who shot him ordered two other prisoners to drag the body the rest of the way to the camp.

Garland walked on, still numbed by the brutal nonchalance of the execution when Sachsenhausen finally came into view.

His first sense as the distance closed was absolute greyness. He had never seen a duller, more gloomy building, as if its designer's brief had been only to deliver despair. Large poles held razor-sharp barbed wire, and tall turrets were placed at regular intervals on the high wall that surrounded the camp. As Garland breathed in, he could smell gun smoke and see the long noses of rifles in the turrets, each manned by a dark figure whose features Garland couldn't make out. He saw the bright-red Nazi flags draped over the wall and felt his stomach lurch. Another smell lay under the drift of cordite, something more sinister, a human odour but not the peppery sweat of exertion. This smell was an emotion, something tangible that Garland could feel in his heart.

The air around the camp was still, and when Garland looked to the skies, there were no birds. The place seemed empty of life. An army truck rolled towards the camp and the troops inside hurled German insults at the prisoners, the officers leading the doomed procession laughing and gesturing crudely in response.

Sachsenhausen was looming closer when a sudden gust of wind blew sand into Garland's eyes, the gritty sting like acid as they began to water.

When he opened them, he could make out the entrance to the camp, and the forms of the gunmen on the watchtowers were sharper. He saw the two closest swivel their weapons to cover the convoy's approach. It was a reminder of the power of these men, the ability to pull a trigger and end dozens of lives in seconds.

The camp was an ugly contrast to the charming town that sat next to it, like a stubborn wart on a pleasant face, an aberration in the world.

As they walked closer, Garland felt sickness sweeping from the pit of his stomach. He looked again at the empty grey sky and saw the colour darken, huge clouds pregnant with malevolent life boiling black, ready to rupture over the camp like a slit belly unloading stinking guts on the ground below.

When he turned to the old Jewish man, he looked out of focus and blurry.

"There's a storm over the camp," Garland said, slurring his words.

He watched the man scan the sky and shrug.

"What you talking about, son?" he said. "It's a terrible day, but it's bright enough for Christmastime. No storm here."

Garland followed the man's gaze and watched the vast cloud swell until it had blacked out every trace of sky, its shadow throwing darkness over Oranienburg. The cloud swirled and formed shapes that loomed towards the ground. . . skulls shrieking a banshee wail, serpents of black flame hunting human skeletons, the contorted face of a Nazi officer howling like a wolf at the edge of a corpse-filled trench. Finally Garland saw his own face in the cloud, his mouth a gaping chasm, screaming.

Garland fell forward, his face scraping on the gravelled road.

"Get the fuck up," the officer in front of him yelled. "No time for resting, queer!"

Garland pushed himself unsteadily to his feet, vomiting with a noisy splatter. The officer looked at him and smiled.

"You're not going to last five minutes in Sachsenhausen, pretty boy."

That word again. The letters flashed before Garland's face, then faded to nothing. He looked at the sky again, but the cloud had gone, replaced by bright winter light.

The prisoners were led along a grassy path to a building with a white tower. Garland made out the black outline of a machine gun. It was pointed away from them this time, looking down at what Garland presumed was the camp. They approached large iron gates emblazoned with decorative letters.

Arbeit macht frei.

"Work will set you free," Garland translated aloud.

The old man looked at him with yellowed, weary eyes. "Won't it just," he said. "Won't it just."

"What does it mean?" Garland asked. "The more we work, the more likely it is we'll get out?"

The old man laughed. It was a dry, crackly chuckle that made his lungs rattle. "That's what they'll want us to think," he replied. "That's exactly what they want."

Garland looked at the gates, towering and dark, and felt the urge to run. He would be shot and killed in a heartbeat but would that be worse than what lay beyond the gates?

They opened with a metallic scream and Garland walked through, glancing nervously at the old Jew by his side. The man grabbed his hand, his dry skin thin and papery. In that instant, Garland saw the man's life replay in his mind. He came from a good family, a place of love. A caring mother and father, close siblings, successful children and the joy of grandchildren. There was light in his life, but Garland knew it was dying. What had been a glorious beacon was now a solitary flame flickering in coarse winds. He was near the end. Garland wasn't sure why he knew, but he did.

The gatehouse cast a dark shadow on them as they passed underneath, and the camp came into clear view. Garland saw rows and rows of rectangular one-story buildings. They were wooden and solid, dotted around the otherwise barren field like huge upturned gravestones. Hordes of prisoners wore baggy grey uniforms, and Garland's stomach lurched again. The uniforms were striped. Memories of the visions flooded his head, the suffering and agony and flame-filled slaughter.

The officer shoved him forward and Garland almost lost his footing, stumbling upright and pulling himself together.

The men were forced to remove their clothes and possessions. Garland stood naked in the sunny yard, the unfamiliar chill of winter air on his bare skin, and looked around at the other prisoners. He locked eyes briefly with the old Jewish man who still held the empty look of despair, resigned to a fate he could not escape.

"What are you looking at!" the officer screamed at the old man. "Are you looking at the queer? You're a queer-Jew, are you?"

"No, sir," the Jewish man said firmly.

"Are you disagreeing with me, queer-Jew?"

"No, sir."

Garland noticed the guard was smiling. It was a cruel expression, full of cold humour. He was still smiling when he kicked the old man in the genitals and again when he smashed his fist into the back of his head, five more blows raining down as the man lay silent on the ground. The guard barked an order, and two rake-thin prisoners in baggy uniforms scurried to carry away the old man motionless on a wooden stretcher. Garland saw light leave his body in a thin cloud and dissolve into the air.

He would often think about the old man, a strong and proud human being whose life was senselessly snuffed out at the hands of a fanatical regime satisfied his kind was no longer viable in the modern world.

As soon as the body had been removed, the guards separated all the men into lines made up of Jews, political prisoners, antisocial offenders, criminals and homosexuals. Garland reluctantly joined the final line after seeing another man beaten into it by the same guard who had turned on the old Jew. Their heads were then shaved, Garland watching blankly as his blond locks fell at his feet. The hair was gathered up and taken away by more emaciated prisoners in the same grubby stripes.

Finally, the guards gave the men uniforms of their own, thin cotton overcoats and trousers with faded black and white stripes. There was no check on sizes, something that amused the guards, and one made a point of giving a tall man a uniform so small it burst at the seams, his long arms stretching out from the sleeves and his stomach exposed. Once the guards had stopped laughing, his tormentor broke his nose with a single punch for good measure.

"You'll get your numbers and triangles soon, you worthless pieces of shit," the officer yelled. Garland watched as a trail of thin black smoke curled out of his mouth, not sure anymore if what he was seeing was real or illusion. He felt if he looked hard enough, the smoke was spelling out the words the sadistic bastard was saying, but the effort made his head hurt. He breathed in deeply and closed his eyes. He felt reality slipping away.

"Your name no longer belongs to you," the officer continued. "From now on, your name, your arse and everything else belongs to Germany. You no longer exist other than to serve the Fuehrer. Heil Hitler!"

He ended with a straight-armed salute.

Garland looked at the sky, his head pounding. The sun was low, illuminating the camp and turning the grey buildings striking shades of yellow and orange. The mild light reflected from windows and washed over the sandy ground. Curls of barbed wire reflected glints of silver, and Garland's eyes traced the high wall which framed the perimeter of Sachsenhausen.

He closed his eyes tight whilst a thought planted itself in his mind, as permanent and solid as the concrete blocks which laid the foundations of this bleak place.

His life would never be the same again.

Chapter Twenty-Five

JOHAN - 1941

Christmas Day in Sachsenhausen. Johan woke and walked through the gates. In Oslo, he had never been blessed with money, lavish gifts or the warmth of a traditional family Christmas. Yet everything had just seemed better for the day. People were in good spirits, small tokens would be shared, even the food tasted special. He whistled the traditional *Jeg Er Saa Glad* as his boots crunched against the frosty ground.

"Merry Christmas," he said with a smile as he saw Kruger walking towards him. Kruger was twirling his keys on his fingers. He didn't smile back.

"Difficult shift?" Johan asked. Sometimes the graveyard duty was hard. The prisoners suffered night terrors or tried to escape. Often there were more killings through the night. Kruger was one of the more warm-blooded of the SS, a more sociable sort who liked to eat, drink and make merry in the bar. The paunch that strained against his uniform, along with the red blotches across his nose and cheeks, were a testament.

"Have you seen Schulz yet?" Kruger asked. His face was baggy and tired.

Johan shook his head. "Just walking in. Thought I'd come in early, see the festivities."

Kruger scoffed and Johan saw a flash of his normal joviality. "No festivities here," Kruger replied. "Schulz is like a man possessed. He's been on that medication. He's worked forty-eight hours straight."

Johan nodded and rubbed his chin. Schulz was *still* working? Johan had seen him at the end of his last shift. The medication must be strong. Schulz had told Johan about something they had been experimenting with, a crystal formula that would fuel Germany's march towards their enemies, a drug that would make them superhuman, an army able to march infinitely without feeling tired. Every man would have the strength of a lion and no sense of fear, soldiers reborn as a force of unstoppable machines. Schulz had been sampling the crystals for himself, if Kruger was right.

Johan slapped him on the back and walked through Tower A's gates into the courtyard. The sight that greeted him was unfathomable. He stared as his mind assembled the flurry of pictures it was receiving from his eyes, trying to make some sense of the whole.

Schulz was looking at Johan, a huge grin on his face. His ever-pristine uniform was dark with bloodstains. In his right hand he held the samurai sword. In his left was a severed human head. Blood fell from it, and its expression sagged. The head looked like a macabre mask, its hooded lids hanging over lifeless eyes.

"Olsen! Olsen!" Schulz yelled.

Johan walked towards him gingerly.

"Happy Christmas!"

Schulz lobbed the head, blood spraying in a large circle as it looped in the air. Johan caught it, and the blood splattered his trousers. He winced. The coppery stench would linger on his uniform for the rest of his shift.

Johan looked down at the atrocity in his hands. The drooping eyes stared back. It felt weighty, its skin pale. It didn't look real and Johan tried to tell himself it wasn't.

"Der Bestatter, you won't have a problem getting rid of that for me, will you?" Schulz made the words a challenge. "Oh and you may as well cart the rest of him too. We've just had a delivery, and I'm keen to test it out. I'll meet you at the industrial yard."

Johan put the head under his arm and snorted a sharp chuckle when he pictured the comic horror scene, blood still dripping from the severed head he carried.

He walked over to the headless body. The stripes of the dead man's uniform were barely recognisable, his entire shirt stained dark crimson. Johan bent and hauled the body over his shoulder. His muscles strained, and he could feel his calves burning, but the other officers were watching. He had a reputation to uphold. Der Bestatter, going about his business. No fear. A model of strength that could handle anything. The guards couldn't know he was already haunted by the sight of the dead man's eyes and the heavy feel of the severed head. Johan's legs burned from his ankles to his backside, and his shoulder was on fire, the pain flaring like molten sun spots.

Suddenly he stumbled, the headless body falling on top of him as they landed in a gory heap on the ground. The head rolled away, leaving a watery red semicircle on the sandy earth. Johan pushed himself into the press-up position and got back to his feet. He felt the mocking eyes of every guard and prisoner and his heart sank. A show of weakness. A pathetic failure in front of them all. He wanted the bloodstained ground to open up and swallow him, wanted to take Schulz's gleaming sword and throw himself onto the waiting blade.

He picked up the head, grabbed the corpse by the leg, and dragged it along. He could feel joints popping out of sockets and hear the flesh scrape on the gritty surface, grimacing with the exertion as he made his way across the camp.

When Johan reached Station Z, Schulz was standing with a broad grin. Station Z had been completely transformed. The pit was still there for the firing squad, but a whole structure had been built. Johan recognised it from the plans that Schulz had laid out in his office.

"Well done, Olsen," Schulz said. "Unorthodox but a good effort all the same. Many would have given up or asked for help, but not you. You don't possess that gene that makes lesser men concede.

Whatever it takes you will always do. An admirable quality in a young soldier."

Johan allowed himself a relieved smile. If Schulz still admired him so would the men. The prisoners' respect he could quickly and coldly restore, if that was needed.

"Thank you, sir," he replied breathlessly. "I should have been able to carry him over my shoulder, but. . ."

"Yes, yes, enough of that," Schulz waved his hand. "I have something to show you." His eyes glinted with malice. "Bring that Jewish pig."

Johan steeled himself and dragged the body, clasping the severed head under his arm.

Show no weakness!

He walked through a door to a large room. Johan could smell a pleasant odour of freshly cut wood mingled with brick dust. He pulled the corpse around a corner, through two more doors, struggling with every step, forcing himself to ignore the pain.

He turned a sharp corner and followed Schulz down a corridor, the commander's fast pace unusually jerky and quick for a man in his fifties.

They came out in a large stone room with high ceilings. Huge steel ovens lined the far walls, so new they gleamed despite the lack of light.

Schulz turned around, his arms in the air, like a conductor encouraging an orchestra to their crescendo. His eyes were wide and wild, thin strands of hair askew on top of his sweaty forehead. His jaw jutted, his teeth grinding in a mechanical side-to-side motion. When he spoke the words were a tumult.

"This is the jewel in the crown of Sachsenhausen." He gestured grandly around the room, a mix of love and almost fatherly pride across his face. "No more cemeteries. No more vanloads of dead vermin. Instead, we burn and commit these worthless specimens back to the earth. Recycling, Olsen, that's what I call it. Yes! Their final contribution to this great country will be to layer the earth with their ashes. It's the least these fucking parasites can do. And I, Bernt Schulz, will be the man to lay them to rest."

He walked over to the ovens and began to stroke them. Johan raised his eyebrows when he saw Schulz turn and kiss one of the incinerators with something close to tenderness.

"These beautiful machines," Schulz went on. "They will facilitate the dawn of a new era. Hitler himself has directed us to burn all our dead, Olsen. All of them."

Schulz laughed. It was a high-pitched titter that seemed at odds with his tough demeanour. He was on another planet this morning. Johan began to wonder how long the commander had been awake.

"Come, feel its power."

Johan walked over to the ovens. They were emblazoned with large letters spelling *KORI*, presumably the manufacturer. He placed his hand on the surface, the feel of the cold steel giving him chills, an icy tinkle that ran across the surface of his skin as stiff goose bumps rose. There was something disorienting about the coolness of something that would become an inferno of human remains. He grabbed the oven door and pulled it open. It was solid and well-made, the work of a craftsman who knew his trade.

"British-made?" Johan asked Schulz.

The commander's face dropped and he spat out a thick, green-brown globule that smacked the sandy ground.

"Scum," he said, out the corner of his mouth, his teeth bared as he spoke. "Nothing in this camp is British-made, Olsen. How could we trust them to make anything we have to rely on? Those rats. Those enemies of Germany. Fuck their men, fuck their leaders and fuck their steel. I'd rather get something from a Jew or a Roma, believe me."

Schulz's good humour returned as his hand once more caressed the steel.

"Everything in here is German-made," he said. "Even better, most are built here in Berlin, the best of the best of the best. We are the foremost labour camp in the Reich, the most important place in Germany. And we will only have the best."

Johan listened to the rousing speech and felt the wildness that seemed to radiate from Schulz.

The commander pulled his hip flask from his jacket pocket and took a large hit. His hands shook as he held the flask. He looked like a man who was already half over the edge.

"They are very impressive, sir," Johan said, attempting to guide the conversation back to something approaching normal. "I can see now they're German. Excellent craftsmanship."

He closed an oven door after he spoke, imagining the horrors they would hold in the weeks, months and years to come. The smell of newly-forged steel wouldn't last, in its place the permanent, unforgettable smell of human flesh on fire. Johan's stomach rolled. He shook the thought away and looked into Schulz's wild eyes. "I can't wait to see these in action."

Schulz grinned and ran his hand through his thin hair, which had become increasingly streaked with grey over the last year.

"Happy Christmas, Olsen."

Schulz opened one of the giant oven doors, a beam of yellow sunlight bouncing across the room. It was his turn to heave the headless body, droplets of sweat trickling from his brow as he did. Johan helped him, grabbing the legs. They both pushed the body into the furnace. A proud grimace broke on Schulz's face, now glistening with perspiration, as he lit a rag with his lighter and stoked the fire.

They both stepped back as the body burnt inside, filling the room with acrid clouds of dark smoke. Johan afforded a sideways glance to the camp commander and saw his eyes blaze with excitement, the licking flames reflecting wildly in his eyes.

He was back in Schulz's office. Schulz searched clumsily through a drawer of odds and ends until he pulled out a jar containing large white crystals that sparkled in the dim, smoky light.

"This is the future of the German force, my Aryan friend," he said, using a monocle to inspect the jar. The crystals looked part pharmaceutical, part jewel, like a precious diamond buried in snow.

Schulz placed a glistening lump on the table between them and used the butt of his pistol to crush it into powder. He worked the thin end of the pistol to shuffle the lumpy substance into thick lines. Johan watched Schulz's eyes grow wide with concentration, his hands still shaking. Every few seconds, a drop of sweat would run down his hair and land on the table with a thin slap.

Once he had finished and four fat lines of powder sat sparkling dully on the table, Schulz raised his eyes to look at Johan. He breathed heavily, and Johan thought he could hear the commander's lungs inflate and deflate, his breath - as always - unpleasant with sour traces of whisky and tobacco.

"This, Olsen, is a weapon of the mind and body." Schulz looked at the lines. "This will make our men invincible. With this chemical enhancement, the German army will not be stopped by anyone. The legions of ancient Rome themselves could rise from the dead, and we would defeat them too."

Johan watched as Schulz pulled a metal tube from his pocket, bent over the table and snorted one of the large lines up his right nostril. He put his head backwards and Johan saw the veins and the pocked, thin skin sag on the commander's neck. When he dropped his head back level with Johan's, his eyes were even brighter and his nose was as red as a freshly picked strawberry. Schulz coughed, a hacking, guttural sound that made Johan cringe.

Schulz lit a cigar and grinned. His teeth were yellow with shades of black creeping up the edges. Johan had a vision of what the commander would look like in the near future, if he lived that long. Black, rotten teeth, dark pits for eyes, skin sagging further, jowls flabby and loose like a drooling hound.

Schulz waved his hand over the table and his eyes twinkled. "Now, your turn."

"Sir, I'm on shift, I don't think I can —"

"Bullshit!" Schulz yelled, a sound that sent a cold film of fear crackling over Johan's skin. "Do you know how many officers would give their souls to be in your position? You have the chance to be everything a man could dream to be. Invincible. Immortal."

He held up the tube. Johan could see traces of dried blood at its edges and swallowed. His eyes found Schulz's pistol on the table, inches away from the powder. The drug was the lesser of two evils.

"Another Christmas present, boy. You shall be the first of my men to try this enhancement."

Johan put the bloodied pipe to his nose and took the powder.

The shift sped by in a haze. Schulz was right, the drug made Johan feel invincible, a God amongst mortals whose power was limitless. Halfway through his shift, shortly after four o'clock on that Christmas Day, Johan killed a man. It was one of the homosexuals, wearing his pink triangle with the number 9617. Johan would remember the number, in more sober moments, as he tried to sleep at night, the digits passing slowly before his eyes along with images of the dead man's face.

Johan learnt killing came easy in the moment but always returned to haunt him. Each man who died at his hands came back. The list wasn't long, not compared to a psychopath like Schulz's, but it trailed enough guilt to plague his mind when it reached the darker recesses of doubt and regret.

This killing had simple beginnings. Johan was chaperoning a group of prisoners from their work detail to their block. He asked them to move more quickly, and 9617 had glared at him. At least, Johan thought it was a glare. The prisoner had narrowed eyes, but after taking the powder, Johan's awareness was sky high. He had a superhuman ability to pick up on microexpressions, a minute twist at the corner of the mouth, a flicker of darkness on a face, an insolent spark in a pair of eyes. He could read the exact meaning behind every tic and twitch, and it was always ill-natured. Men, Johan reasoned, were simple beings, whether Nazi, Jewish or homosexual. They ate, they shit and they tried to get to the top.

And a man in Johan's position? He was there to be shot at by those below him but desperate to climb upwards. They were all out to get him, and he needed to be on his guard. The queer had glared and Johan had seen it. As well as his number and his pulverised face, it was the glare that would torment Johan when he battled insomnia in those dark hours after the song thrush had finished its sweet melody. A time when doubts, anxieties and regrets would consume him like a fire raging in the space between consciousness and sleep. His dreams would be even worse, pitiless journeys to a soulless hinterland that left Johan's chest burning in agony and his eyes wet with tears.

He had grabbed 9617 by the back of the neck. He was a small, wiry man, and his uniform was baggy as Johan snatched a fistful of the rough material. He rammed his other fist into the prisoner's cheek and felt it shatter against his knuckles. The man had fallen, his thin body barely making a sound as it hit the ground. The blood spray and the screams that pierced the afternoon silence seemed to energise Johan. He could feel pleasure ripple through his body as others looked on. Der Bestatter going about his business. Cold sweat emerged under the hair on his head, every strand like a thrumming wire standing briskly on its end.

He leant over the prisoner, who was crying face down, and flipped him onto his back. The man's mouth and chin were covered with the blood streaming from his cheek. It only took one more blow to end his life. Johan simply stamped his boot on the man's face, rage and pleasure surging through him like matching bullets from an invisible gun. This man who thought he could match Johan. A queer who thought he could glare at him and live. The new world would have no tolerance for people like 9617, subhumans whose existence contradicted the very purpose of life itself.

Johan lifted his boot and saw lifeless eyes above what remained of the man's nose, a mess of tissue around two blood-caked, crimson holes.

In that moment Johan considered the contradiction of fresh blood flowing from the face of a dead man. Soon 9617 would be ashes, but for now his body was in that strange transition between life and death. It existed still, but his life force had disappeared.

Johan wiped his boot on the ground and looked at the smeared footprint it left behind. When he glanced up, the group of prisoners he was herding all stared.

"Let this be a lesson," Johan yelled. "Any other fucker who stares at me like that, this is what happens."

He pointed at a prisoner whose face had blanched.

"Drag this sorry queer to the infirmary."

He pointed to three more prisoners who wore pink triangles.

"Go for water and mops," he told them. "Clean this dirty blood before someone gets an infection."

He looked each prisoner in the eye, hunting for signs of disobedience.

But all he saw was the dark taciturnity of fear.

Chapter Twenty-Six

GARLAND - 1941

The rough material of his oversized uniform scratched against his skin, giving Garland a constant itchy sensation on his arms, legs and torso. He assumed he would simply get used to the feeling in time, although he hoped he wouldn't have to. He had thought again of speaking out on the lies that had landed him in this horrible place but stopped himself. He'd been served enough warnings.

He looked at the breast of his uniform and saw the number N2871 and a pink triangle. He had no idea what it meant. As he looked across to the other prisoners, he noticed different coloured triangles above their numbers. Most of them were red, some purple, green, yellow and black.

Garland gasped when he first saw his accommodation block. One long building housed hundreds of inmates, crammed together so tightly they were almost shoulder to shoulder. A rotten stench hung constantly in the air.. There were three beds to each bunk and at least two hundred bunks packed into the relatively small space.

"Grab your bunks, you rats," a stern German voice from behind him yelled. There was a shuffle of feet as people looked to secure the best bed. Garland found a bed towards the middle of the cold, dusty room.

"Do you mind if I take the lower bunk?" asked a small man with a pink triangle on a uniform many sizes too big. "I don't like heights very much, I'm afraid."

"Of course," Garland said. "I'll take the next one up." Garland looked at the bed and saw it was alive with large black bugs, a moving sheet completely covering the wooden base. Cringing, he brushed them onto the rough pine floor, which was covered with hay. It smelt like a neglected barn.

"What does the triangle mean?" Garland asked.

"Pink means homosexual," the man answered. "Not that I am, of course. I had a fight with a jerk in a bar last week. He was chatting up my girlfriend, and I told him to get lost. He came at me, and I beat him up good. The next day I'm getting arrested for being a queer. You?"

"Similar," Garland lied. "They just brought me here without letting me explain."

"No explaining to be done here, friend. You're N2871 now. You must be from Norway. Is that what the N stands for?"

"Yes, I suppose. I mean, yes, I am from Norway. I was living in Berlin."

"Lucky you." The man held out his hand. "I'm Kurt. Back in the old world, I was a shoemaker in Brandenburg. Nice to meet you."

"Garland Lund."

They shook hands and both men lay on their bunks.

"Kurt?" Garland asked, staring at the wooden planks that made up the bunk above him. "Will we get out of here?"

"One way or the other." Kurt sighed. "One way or the other."

Garland was dozing, a restless half-sleep, when one of the guards yelled into the room.

"Break time is over, prisoners! Your work begins today."

They were led into the yard, and each man was allocated a job. It turned out that Kurt was a handy friend to have.

Kurt, a charming man whose line of work must have seen him sell thousands of pairs of shoes across Germany, was assigned to the shoemaking workshop. Such was his easy, affable, manner, he convinced a guard to take Garland with him, under the guise of a former apprentice shoemaker for Ludwig Reiter himself. Garland had never heard of Ludwig Reiter but assumed he was a big deal, as two guards discussed whether they could have not one but two 175ers working in an environment much coveted by other prisoners, albeit those consigned to the toughest of outdoor work.

Kurt's charm worked, and both men headed to the workshop under strict warning that even a second of poor work or insolence would be punished by sending both men to a more severe detail.

The workshop smelt of sharp leather and oils. They began immediately, handmaking leather shoes. The shift lasted for hours, long after the sun had disappeared into the western horizon and Garland's fingers had begun to blister. By the end of the day he had made thirty-six pairs. An older man, on the other side of the room to Garland and Kurt, began to cry.

"I can't do this," he wailed. "You can't make us do this. My hands!"

The guards were quick. They surrounded the man and punched him to the ground, kicking and yelling abuse. Less than a minute later, one of the guards was dragging the man's beaten body out of the workshop. It was another early reminder for Garland to keep his head down and his mouth shut. He looked over at Kurt, and their eyes met in a silent agreement. They would say nothing.

At a time Garland guessed was around seven or eight, the guards dismissed them back to their blocks. He lay in his bunk, exhausted, trying to process the worst day of his life and contemplate the future. He had to tell them they had made a mistake, he had to run the risk of a beating, because if there was one slight chance of freedom he had to take it. He had to tell them he had only kissed one man, that he wasn't homosexual. Surely one kiss wasn't a crime worthy of this?

He needed to tell them about Seadog Willy murdering Hans, and he could mention Johan to the guards, maybe even talk about his encounter with Dr Goebbels. Anything that might help. Wasn't Johan stationed in Berlin now? Maybe he was even here. Maybe he could help.

He closed his eyes, the little sleep he managed littered with vivid dreams. He was lying in a hospital bed, hooked up to futuristic machines in a room covered with swastikas, a place as dark as a blackened soul leaking misery, despair and emptiness.

He saw a word appear in his dream, huge, black and aflame.

Sachsenhausen. Blood and melting flesh oozed from every letter before they swirled into a mound of blackness and formed a swastika, dripping with blood. Skeletal bodies roamed the nightmare, an army of the nearly dead, the barely living. He watched himself from above as he marched, marched, marched with the stricken army towards a huge precipice where flames rose above the edge, licking, seeking, enticing.

In his dream the scene faded to black, replaced by a thin green line going across his vision. It was made of tiny squares that jumped, the line moving like the outline of a huge wave or a graph's erratic rise and fall. A man's soft English voice called to him distantly, but he failed to make out the words.

Garland heard beeps before everything turned white.

Garland fell into a deep sleep in the minutes before an officer hurled open the door of the building and yelled for them to get out.

He rubbed his eyes and felt the pang of painful realisation, the swift feeling of his memory updating to the awful here and now, his *new normal.* Wood creaked as he rose from his bunk and dropped to the floor. Agony shot through his blistered hands, and his back burnt with pain.

One day in this hell and his body was broken. How many more days? How many more agonies? But that was the Nazi plan; Johan had told him when they met in Berlin. Killing prisoners would be too easy, too much of a waste. Working a man to his death was the most efficient way to end his life. Garland closed his eyes tightly. He had slept in his uniform, his skin now prickly and red raw. When he opened his eyes, they were full of tears. Johan's words from the small café off Friedrichstrasse echoed in his head.

The Jews and the queers, we give them the worst.

At the time it had seemed an overblown story from another world, a life so removed from Garland he had found it hard to really care. Why should he have? The brutality Johan described was part someone else's story, woven over coffee and cigarettes between the closest of friends. Had Garland worried about the nameless, faceless Jews and homosexuals dying naked, dignity stripped away like pieces of cheap clothing as they lay in their own blood? Had he winced at the pain of the Romani or the ritual humiliation of once-proud men? He couldn't remember what his emotions had been as Johan described the camps, but now he felt the prisoners' suffering as a crushing weight. Guilt, compassion, and hate overwhelmed him alongside the utter hopelessness. His life would now be about fear, the constant dread that death was waiting around the corner. Would a bullet in the head be merciful? Was arousing a guard's anger the best way to go?

He walked to roll-call side by side with hundreds of men. They streamed out of every building, a sea of cropped heads bobbing. He could feel heat from the bodies. The sound of shuffling feet was like a train slowly chugging to its destination. Fear hung over the enormous group like a rain cloud, morose and malignant. Moans and groans punctuated the steady rhythm of weary footsteps, and Garland saw many of the prisoners were limping. People looked down as they walked, faces strained and lips pursed. They had been given only a few short hours sleep, a narrow window of respite from the brutality and dread. Now another day in this man-made hell was already upon them.

They came under the shadow of Tower A, the machine gunner perched on top like a Roman emperor surveying slaves below him. Garland watched as the guard swung the gun from left to right. He stared at its long barrel and wondered if it would be better to hear the brittle rattle of bullets wiping out their miserable lives.

A mercy, he thought again.

An officer walked in front of them. He was old and his face was hard. Even from a hundred yards away, Garland thought he could see the man's eyes glistening with cruelty.

"Prisoners!" he yelled, his chest puffed out. "Roll-call!"

The man was like a cartoon character, but nothing here was comic. Garland focused on him and became slightly dizzy, his own eyes flickering as he zoomed in so close he could see the officer's heart beating in his chest. For Garland everything slowed down as a kapo from each of the blocks began the roll-call, all of Garland's concentration locked on that callous, unfeeling heart. In that instant, Garland could see the man's soul. It was inky and ringed with black flames drawing strength from the misery of the prisoners in front of him. His soul was a demon feeding on their fear, like bread and water to a starving man.

"Schulz," Garland said, loud enough for the prisoners either side to look at him in shock. The word had flown into his head and out of his mouth in a split second, a sneeze that couldn't be contained.

A skinny prisoner whose cropped hair was bright red nudged him in the side.

"Psycho Schulz more like," he whispered.

"N2871," the kapo in charge of Garland's barrack yelled. He was a tubby man with thick dark hair and a red triangle on his breast, 610 underneath.

"N2871!" he shouted again, when only silence greeted him.

Garland felt another nudge to his ribs.

"That's you, idiot." It was skinny red. "You got a death wish?"

"Here," Garland said, his eyes wide.

The kapo narrowed his own and wrote something on the paper in his hands before continuing the roll-call.

"Be careful," skinny red whispered. "Fats there looks like a chubby waste of space, but get on the wrong side of him and he'll shop you to Schulz as fast as it takes a bullet to leave a rifle."

He looked at Garland's uniform and winced.

"And he hates queers. You should stay out of his way."

"Too late," Garland said, nodding towards the kapo who was storming towards them.

Fats shoved two prisoners out the way and pushed his face into Garland's on a blast of spoilt meat and stale tobacco.

"You talk during roll-call again and I'll gut you," Fats said, his lips drawn back to expose his gums and his crooked teeth, "You think I'm just another one of you? I'm in charge of your fucking barracks, you dirty queer. You show some respect or I'll tell Schulz. Either he'll end your life or I will."

The man's thick jowls shook as he spoke, and Garland found himself having to stifle a nervous laugh. Sweating and bloated, the kapo would be nothing if his pseudoimportance here was removed. Garland looked at his brown eyes, the lids hooded like half-moons, and thought he resembled a sleepy dog.

Garland nodded. In the corner of his vision he could see Schulz staring at him as Fats glared and slowly walked away.

Roll-call was dispersed and Garland made his way to the shoe factory, working through pain that had him choking back tears. Every minute seemed to drag and, in his mind, random images came and went like the blinding pops of a camera flash. . . swastikas, black alphabet smoke, and gaunt prisoners marching towards a forest. Everything, like the camp itself, was godforsaken and clouded in fear.

By the time the shop manager told them to break for lunch, Garland was already broken in mind and body. His knuckles throbbed and ground like rust-ruined pistons, his arms two knotted lines of constant hurt.

He queued in the camp kitchen where two officers stood before a wooden table, dishing something out of a tall metal container. By the time he grabbed a bowl and spoon and joined the line, there were at least fifty men in front of him. He saw the skinny redhead hanging back. He joined Garland in the queue and delivered a nudge to Garland's ribs that was fast becoming his trademark.

"The trick is to stay near the end of the line," he whispered. "None of the new ones cotton on for a while, and some people are so starving they just want to run to the front."

"Why?" Garland asked.

"They think they're getting the best, the freshest stuff, but we'll get the cream," skinny red grinned. "Whatever soup they give us, the top is just water. The best bit, the chunks, all sits at the bottom. They might think we're getting the dregs, but all they're getting is a shitty hot drink."

He laughed so dryly it sounded like bones grating together, and he nudged Garland's ribs once more.

"Thanks for the advice," Garland replied. "What's your name?"

"Ginger," he said. "And you?"

"Garland."

Ginger looked down and frowned. It was the first time Garland had seen him lose his humour since he'd met him that morning.

"It's a tough place, this," he said, still staring at the ground. "I've seen men killed for nothing. People collapse under the weight of their own illness. I've seen guards murder people for just looking at them the wrong way. Or not looking at them. It's hell in here, and for a homosexual like you. . ."

He paused as Garland shot him a look.

"Hey I'm not judging you," Ginger went on. "I'm a thief and they put me in the worst jail in the world. But for people who wear the pink, it's hell on earth."

They shuffled forwards as the line moved. Garland learnt about Ginger's life as a pickpocket in Berlin and was surprised they had never crossed paths. They had drunk in the same pubs. Ginger had even heard of the Idiotentruppe.

They reached the table and Ginger smiled as he pulled out two bowls. He looked over and winked at Garland as he received two servings. Garland's portion was reasonable, and Ginger had been right, there was something mushy at the bottom, although he wasn't entirely sure what it was. He slurped it, watching Ginger go to work on his bowls.

As Ginger wiped his mouth and tucked the bowls and spoons back into unseen pockets deep in his uniform, he clapped Garland on the back.

"Stick with me in here, Garland. There's a few tricks that'll make your life easier."

He pointed at the pink triangle on Garland's chest.

"And with the colour of that," he continued, "you're gonna need all the help you can get."

Garland's fingers traced the rough outline of the triangle and he exhaled deeply. It was time to go back to his shift.

Chapter Twenty-Seven

RICHARD - 2022

Richard awoke, suddenly aware of returning to his own body. His real body. *His.*

He opened his eyes to blurry images around him. People wearing white. He heard the intermittent beep of a machine next to him and felt the strange sensation of tubes and wires going into his body. Or were they coming out?

He couldn't think straight.

And then he thought of Sandy. The man he loved so dearly. He strained his eyes to see him, to catch a glimpse, if he was in this strange room. But his focus refused to refine above the blur of people wearing white.

He knew he was in a hospital, probably in a coma. He squeezed his eyes tight, willing his brain to see. Willing the images to become clear so he could see exactly where he lay. To see Sandy again.

When he opened them, he could see clearly. But he wasn't in a hospital. The blurry figures had disappeared. He was in the middle of a pine forest, in a clearing. A tangy aroma of sap hung in the air and a cool breeze shimmied past the hundreds of tall, thin trees. Morning dew glistened on outstretched brown branches, a layer of glitter that reflected a strange sky overhead.

Richard was beneath a swirling torrent of colour yet again. It was like a sky from another world, somewhere distant, beyond the Milky Way, unseen by any human eye. Reds, yellows, blues, greens, oranges and myriad colours he couldn't name converged together in a patterned swirl above him that seemed to breathe in and out with his heartbeat.

Richard took a deep breath and closed his eyes. Another hallucination, surely. But a respite from seeing through the eyes of the Norwegian boy. The camp and the atrocities. The dream within a dream that he willed himself to wake from. When he was Garland Lund, he felt every blow, every emotion, a deep connection that ran through the blood in his veins.

When he opened his eyes, the colours still swirled over the tops of the giant trees. But a sweet sound whistled over the breeze, in a pitch which was both soft and sublime.

A bird had perched on a stumpy nearby branch and had begun its morning chorus, its breast proudly puffed outwards, a beautiful spotted pattern, brown dots on yellowed feathers.

The bird sang to Richard and he listened with glee. He heard the tune and understood its wordless message. And when he closed his eyes, this time he drifted deeply into sleep, thinking of Sandy.

Thankful for the existence of love.

Chapter Twenty-Eight

JOHAN - 1942

The prisoners lined up in front of Johan and his fellow guards in their thousands. Under the glow of the thin morning light, it was an impressive sight.

They were confronted with a brutal existence, one of work, of disease, of misery, and wore the hardened, vacant expressions of defeat. Johan wondered if they could any longer keep track of time, if they even knew what day it was. Did birthdays, anniversaries, and religious events come and go without them knowing? Johan found it hard to believe their faith still mattered, praying to a God that had cast them into these shadows. Even the most religious seemed broken in mind as well as body. A strong mind can compensate for much. Without it in a place like Sachsenhausen, a bleak future was all that awaited.

Johan let the thoughts run as he looked out over the prisoners during roll-call. They were watching executions, Schubert taking pleasure in instructing them to hang their fellow inmates at the gallows. Schulz stood on top of Tower A, looking down with a wry smirk.

Johan watched the prisoners' faces. Rows and rows of thin skulls with empty eyes staring back. He only saw hate in the newest of prisoners, in most he saw nothing. They were shells of human beings. Johan had quickly learnt to date a man's entry into the camp just by the way he looked. Gaunt cheeks, hollows around the eyes, narrowed shoulders. But most of all it was the emptiness on their faces. The men who had been there the longest were all the same. They had been drained of their very humanity, and it would never return.

Johan looked out across the sea of dirty men, waves of striped uniforms, the flashes of faded red, black, pink and green triangles. A stiff breeze carried the stench of the nearly dead. Johan had got used to it, the rotten, sour smell like spoilt vegetables. Compared to the odour from the incinerators it was a perfume. Cooking flesh had a sulphurous odour all of its own. Once it had drifted into your senses it left something inside you, a memory that returned on the dark nights when the moon shone its dim light through the rain-battered windows and the song thrush had long finished its last note. It was a smell no man ever forgot.

Johan noted that even the ice-hearted Schulz, who thought nothing of ending a man's life with his bare hands, covered his nose with a handkerchief when the incinerators burnt. No, the spoilt smell of twenty thousand half-dead men was easy by comparison.

As he scanned them, Johan spotted the new prisoners, the ones with fresh faces, thick meat on their jowls and something more than defeat in their eyes. They might have been told their stay would be temporary. Now the brickworks had been built, that was probably no longer a lie. Certainly they would not leave Sachsenhausen alive. How long they survived would depend only on their durability and will to live. The *Klinkerwerk* had been directed by Schulz, one of his masterplans devised somewhere between the lines of white powder and shots of German whisky. *The largest brickworks in the world,* Schulz had told Johan. His callous eyes glimmered when he snorted the powder, sweat glistening on his forehead in the mellow smoky light. The Klinkerwerk would be the core of the rebuilding of a German world. Starting with Berlin, the Reich would grow outwards, built on the blood and sweat of a billion broken men. The empire would rule the world, it would consume all in its wake. Johan had listened to the commander's impassioned vision of the future, his intense fervour hitting Johan like a strong wind that buffeted his soul around the tiny office.

The Klinkerwerk would literally provide the building blocks for the empire's glorious rise, the prisoners working and dying there no more than an expendable resource. Schulz had beamed as he talked about their workload. He would generously give the prisoners five hours sleep after eighteen hour shifts interrupted only by a brief lunch break. The labour would be unbearable and so would the heat from furnaces blasting prisoners with only their flimsy uniforms for protection. Most of all, the Klinkerwerk would destroy wills and souls.

Johan stared out over the army of prisoners again. Schulz's workforce. Most of them were already almost finished. Slaving in the brickworks would see them fall in their thousands.

He looked down at his black boots. He was indifferent to the suffering of these men, people who had been placed here through no decision of his own. He was at Sachsenhausen to do his duty, to take orders from his superiors and to keep law and order, nothing more, nothing less. There were times, deep in the nights when sleep wouldn't come, that doubt crept into his mind. It was like a blow from a spear that found the chink in a suit of armour, the wound sharp and unexpected. But in the morning, looking in the mirror in his pressed uniform, everything seemed brighter. Johan would gaze out of his window and watch green leaves shiver like sprites on the trees. There were good things in the world and mostly he considered himself worthy of his place. He had travelled across Europe to serve a country in need, a nation at war with enemies who wanted to stop Germany's rightful rise to domination. And Johan had no doubt the Reich would prevail. The British, the French, the rest of their allies, they could never comprehend the might of the German war machine. If they did, they would lay down their arms and let the empire sweep over them.

Schulz had reshuffled roles to get the brickworks in full swing, and hundreds of guards had been given extra assignments. Johan had taken full advantage. The Klinkerwerk was over the canal, and escorting so many prisoners back and forth was important work. Some would try to escape once they were outside the camp walls. Others would struggle to stagger back even after a single shift.

The overtime payments had come in useful for Johan now that he had met Gerda.

He had first noticed her at a dance in East Berlin, one he had attended with several of his Sachsenhausen colleagues. She was the most beautiful woman Johan had ever seen. Her skin was perfect, like buttermilk, soft and pale. Her lashes seemed to curl endlessly back on themselves, bringing out her blue eyes, two aquamarine jewels sparkling on a white sea. She was tall and slender, her long dark hair tumbling effortlessly on her shoulders.

But it was her personality that shone through, her humanity like sunlight streaking through clouds. She spoke in a soft Berlin accent and held her chest with her hand when she discussed anything that had touched her, which was often. Positivity burst from her, something she could never have stemmed even if she had wanted to. They left the dance hand in hand that night and kissed under a flickering Berlin streetlight. As Johan walked her to her mother's house, they passed a homeless vagrant on the street. Gerda stopped to speak to him. She gave him a few Reichsmarks, then offered up her expensive fur coat. When Johan had questioned her sanity, the response had been instant.

He needs it more than I do.

Through the months that followed they became closer, Johan discovering something new every time they went to dances or coffee shops where Gerda would reveal more and more of the woman behind the beauty. Johan saw the way the corners of her mouth curled into her cheeks each time she smiled, the way she would laugh by delicately inhaling, the hollow at her throat that showcased the dazzling array of necklaces she wore, a different one each time they met.

Johan learnt Gerda's wealthy father had died on a field in France near the end of the Great War. She had been a baby when he was killed, and her mother had brought her up to see beauty in everything. *Beauty is infinite,* her mother had told her, *but fleeting in its individual presence. You need to identify it, appreciate it, and move on.*

Although Gerda admired men in the military, and cooed whenever she saw Johan in full uniform, she had refused to speak about politics and war. Often, Johan's conversations strayed to the camp, the government, Adolf Hitler and the German war effort. Each time, Gerda had put a finger softly to his lips.

"War is work, Johan," she said. "Let's use our time for pleasure. For beauty. I don't want to talk about anything ugly when we're together. I have no desire to understand or learn about what's happening in the minds and hearts of warmongers. I just want to learn about the heart of Johan Olsen."

They dated for some time and Johan's affection grew. It was a life away from Sachsenhausen. As the weeks and months passed, he had something else to occupy his mind. Soon, the work within Sachsenhausen was exactly that: work. He found himself smiling again. As time went by, he didn't even feel the urge to talk about work or the war with Gerda; there was an explosion of colour in Johan's life. Whilst his ambitions of belonging and achievement were satisfied by his move to Berlin and his SS role, Gerda unlocked something inside Johan that he didn't realise was there. Something that sat deep inside him, that had been waiting patiently for years. And now it was gradually being released. He brimmed with love, and it lifted him to a higher plane.

Gerda was the woman he would marry, he was sure of that the first time he met her and became more certain each time she spoke, every time those dimples appeared when he said something to make her laugh.

The overtime from the Klinkerwerk shifts would help him buy the engagement ring Gerda deserved. He wanted to see the expression on her face when he opened the box, one knee planted on the ground. The SS had told him to find a wife as soon as he could, but none of the female *Aufseherin* SS guards, who worked at nearby subcamps, appealed to him. A few of Johan's colleagues had settled down with Aufseherin but Johan found most of them too masculine, too hard to the ways of the world. No one had caught his eye. Until Gerda.

He had written to Garland for the first time in months, telling how he was in love, how Gerda made him feel.

Although their last meeting had ended on a sour note, he still cared for Garland like the orphan brother he was. He felt his previous annoyance with his friend fade, overtaken by his newfound zest for life and for love. He hoped Garland had also found someone. He had vowed to meet up with him when he was next on leave, but his commitment to Gerda and the overtime made it difficult.

He thought of Gerda now as his eyes scanned again the thousands of broken men.

Johan had enough spirit to fill every empty vessel in front of him, but he needed it. Working with death on a daily basis could grind down any man. Even Schulz seemed to be slipping steadily into insanity the more power and powder washed through him. But with his life and love outside the grey walls of Sachsenhausen, Johan found balance restored.

Gerda made him feel like a good person again. The song thrush's shrill tune still lasted until midnight, but now it carried redemption and hope. His sleep was long and dreamless, and he woke feeling refreshed, ready for anything that lay ahead.

Schulz had been speaking but Johan's mind had drifted. Now he saw the prisoners were being split up. He was given a group of fifty shambling men, mainly Jews and homosexuals, for the long walk to the Klinkerwerk. As he led them towards the open gates of Tower A, he glanced at another group being taken to the boot-testing track, another Schulz initiative. The commander was going to test the wonder powder on prisoners who would bear the heaviest load a German soldier would be expected to carry and wear army boots crafted on-site. The prisoners would be given huge doses of the powder and, if Schulz was right, they would become supermen with inhuman strength and stamina.

Schulz had always been passionate as he explained the nature of the camp's output. The prisoners created everything and everything was to further the German cause. Most of them would die, but each man's footprint, even the lowest of the low, would be left on the German machine. It was genius, Johan had thought. Building an empire using the very enemies they were stamping out.

He looked at the hundred or so men assigned to the boot-testing track. Schulz had chosen well. They all looked fairly strong and with souls still intact.

As he glanced back, he saw a flash of blond hair on a prisoner's slight frame and tilted his head. His mind raced. *That looks like. . .*

His concentration was broken by one of his prisoners sprinting out past the gates and across the path, his long strides making impressive ground away from the camp.

Johan raised his rifle, but it wasn't necessary. A burst of gunfire cracked the air from the top of Tower A, and the prisoner's uniform was peppered with jagged red holes.

Johan watched him slump face first into the grit, his face skidding on the ground, and gave a thumbs-up signal toward the watchtower. But when he glanced up, the guard was draped over the wooden edge of the turret, his hands and arms spread as blood streamed from his stomach, splattering the pristine white wood on the side of the building.

The officer swayed and then fell to the ground with a sickening thump. His neck was twisted at an impossible angle and intestines slipped from a strip of flesh torn from his stomach, steam rising as warm blood and human offal met the cold air, his body curled in a crudely drawn letter D.

Johan glared at the rest of the prisoners as they began hurriedly shuffling toward the Klinkerwerk.

Chapter Twenty-Nine

GARLAND - 1942

Garland stood at roll-call, shivering in the morning breeze. He had lost count of the days and weeks he had been in the camp.

Schulz stood in front of them, and as always, Garland could feel the man's power, a malevolence pumped by a heart black and cold.

He listened as Schulz explained where some of them would be working from now on, the Klinkerwerk.

Toiling in a brickworks sounded a hard slog but so was the shoemaking, and in a place where daily routine was gradually wearing away his spirit, part of Garland would welcome the change if he was assigned there.

Schulz told them to wait for their numbers to be called.

A guard walked up to him and Garland could smell his cologne, the scent transporting him back to a distant and forgotten world of bars, dances and city life. He breathed in so deeply that the aftershave's sharp, alcohol sting hit back of his throat. It was a momentary escape to a happy place. The guard looked at him warily.

"You have a problem, N2871?"

Garland shook his head briskly. "No, sir!"

The guard's stare lingered for a few seconds before he diverted his eyes to a scrap of paper in his hands, the writing crudely scrawled with thick pencil.

"Boot-testing track for you." A sly smile grew on the guard's face as he looked at the triangle on Garland's breast. "Perfect job for a 175er," he sneered. "You'll last five minutes you lowlife piece of dog shit."

When the guard spat in his face, Garland watched the soft plug of saliva come towards him in slow motion. He could see every tiny line and crack on the guard's bone-dry lips and, in those stretched-out seconds, knew that behind them sat stained and brittle teeth. The guard had shut his eyes as he fired the spittle and now Garland felt the impact. He let the saliva drip from his nose to the ground, aware that moving his hand to wipe it away would lead to a beating or worse. His nose twitched. The guard held his stare, and although his eyes burnt with the strain, Garland fought the desperate urge to look away.

With a grunt the guard ordered him to the western side of the roll-call area and strode away. Only then did Garland wipe his nose and face with his sleeve.

He walked to where he had been told and looked around at the groups quickly forming. He nodded as Kurt joined him but noticed Ginger approach another gathering where prisoners were muttering they had the Klinkerwerk assignment. Garland felt a pang of jealousy as he realised they would walk outside the camp. Every day in Sachsenhausen brought more of the same agony, the mindless violence and cruelty that reduced human beings to animals, no longer men with names but subbeings identified only by numbers and coloured triangles. The idea of going beyond the grey walls to the leafy streets around Oranienburg pulled like a siren's haunting call. Outside he might see birds flying in the open sky, civilians going to work, neighbours talking about the weather or shopping together for bread and milk. He hadn't been a prisoner at Sachsenhausen for long, but already the humdrum moments of an ordinary existence seemed rich beyond Garland's dreams. He knew part of his spirit had already slipped away. He felt like a rocky cliff face being battered by roaring waves. Steadily his will would erode until he ended up as hollow as all the rest. Sleep was a luxury and always broken, fatigue a constant shadow that engulfed him.

Garland was still looking towards the Klinkerwerk prisoners when his eye caught something, a blur of grey that became a man bolting from the group. Garland watched him as he ran. He willed him to go faster, to run through the trees, through the flat German land and out to safety, to a life beyond the hard walls of Sachsenhausen.

Garland closed his eyes and felt a sensation of weightlessness surround him. A spectrum of vivid colours swirled, and when he opened his eyes again, they were no longer his own. He was the escaping prisoner, heart pounding as the slender trees whooshed past him and the path unfolded in front of his pounding feet. Garland lived the prisoner's exhilaration and hope, a wide smile lighting a face he knew could not be his own but somehow was. Images of the man's wife and children, his simple family home in a village on the southern edge of Berlin, flashed in Garland's mind. He heard horses whinnying in a newly varnished barn and watched bees delicately land on pastel-coloured flowers growing wild at the edge of a silver-dappled stream. He saw beauty and life as he brought forward the face of the man's wife. She was a brunette with a toothy grin framed by bright red lipstick. Her hair was tied in a bun and she had eyes that glittered with kindness. Garland could taste the memory of her kiss, the smell of her skin as they made love under a vast and starless sky. When the shooting began Garland heard nothing, no report or recoil as a blackout curtain dropped silently before his eyes. He felt the bone in his shoulder shatter, felt the path of every bullet as it tore through his flesh, the unspeakable pain as his stomach and bowel were ripped open, boring through his genitals from behind. He felt himself fall forward in this borrowed, dying body, skin tearing from his face as he hit the ground, blood rising in his throat.

Garland doubled up in pain and vomited thick, gloopy puddles of red. He watched them spread across the sandy gravel by his feet, his eyes once again his own. Dizziness overcame him and he sank to his knees, two guards now rushing over. Garland looked to Tower A, the guard there grinning, a submachine gun smoking in his hands. Blood still pouring from his mouth, Garland focused on the man as a blistering fury washed through his senses.

He breathed in and out, the old smell of burning rubber rising as the world around him slowed again. He could hear the voices of the guards as they looked at the prisoner's bullet-riddled body, the scene shimmering before him. When he was younger, Garland had stared at the auroras in the night sky, awestruck as they danced in their greens, blues and purples, as if God himself was painting the heavens with colour. It was captivating and filled him with hope. And now Garland rode those same magical skyscapes as his mind travelled, gracefully swooping over the prisoners and guards, gliding across the grey walls of Sachsenhausen and upwards into the endless blue. He looked down at the tower guard, a hard-drinking veteran reeking of whisky and cordite, eyes like glaciers and a nose pocked with red craters.

Garland forced his way into the man's consciousness as the aurora's perfect lights faded to black and dark red. He whispered somewhere deep inside him, a lulling hiss as the man reached into his belt and pulled out a knife. Garland could see the morning light bounce from the sleek blade and for the first time could sense the guard's fear. It wasn't just a feeling, it was something more, something tangible. The word that came to Garland was *fungus*. It seemed to appear and grow, mutating and slipping through the guard's body, injecting poison into his veins. Garland dug deeper, searching for the man's essence, the doorway to his ruined soul, as the fungus took over. The guard closed his eyes and sank the knife into his own stomach. Garland felt the hot flash of pain but this time it was positive. He left the guard's body as it was falling, flying back over the camp to merge like a shadow with the form – his form – still on its side on the cold ground.

"He's coming round." The voice echoed from far away as Garland slowly opened his eyes. He saw the grim faces of two guards and hauled himself to his feet, wiping his mouth with the back of his hand. A streak of bright red blood ran from his thumb to his wrist, and he was swaying slightly. He looked towards Tower A where men were dragging two corpses through the gates, one of them in a striped uniform, the other in the black of the SS.

"There's no point sending this one to boot testing," one of guards said. "He wouldn't last five minutes. Anyone spewing blood probably hasn't got long left anyway. What about the infirmary?"

The other guard reached forward and brushed dirt from Garland's uniform.

"Look, he's a 175er." The guard jabbed at the pink triangle on Garland's chest. "They wouldn't let him through the door."

He slammed a hand on Garland's shoulder, the force almost making his legs buckle.

"Are you dying, boy? Should I put you out of your misery?" The guard made a finger gun and aimed at a spot between Garland's eyes. "Where was your last duty?"

Garland tried to pull himself together but when he spoke the words came out dry, like ancient rocks grinding together.

"The shoemaking workshop, sir."

The guard looked at his colleague and nodded.

"A queer in the shoemaking workshop. Nice job if you can get it, eh? Let's throw him back there." He shrugged. "If he's dying he might as well do it making the fucking shoes not testing them."

He laughed at his own joke and looked at Garland again.

"We're not gonna learn anything from this half-dead queer even if he does take the pills."

The other guard nodded and ordered Garland to the shoe workshop.

"Now let's pick another poor bastard to test those boots."

Garland trudged towards the workshop. He could still feel the burn of blood at the back of his throat, and his stomach throbbed, but all he could think about was the tower guard. Garland wasn't sure what had happened, but he knew it felt right. Carried by the aurora, he had moved with his mind, transported himself from his own body and made another man's bend to his will. Rage seemed to be the trigger, but if he could control the power, if he could find the switch to flick it on and off as he chose. . . Garland felt a surge of adrenaline.

Could this be his way out? Could he somehow take both his mind and body beyond the camp walls, spirit himself past the watchtower and the guards toting their rifles? Even as the possibilities played out, another thought ignited. He had to find Johan. Could he reach out to him wherever he was, send a mental call for his help? Garland knew time wasn't on his side.

He looked back at the men who were being taken to the boot-testing track. Kurt was being fitted with the biggest backpack Garland had ever seen. The guards were handing out pills. Somewhere in the distance, the group of prisoners assigned to the Klinkerwerk were being marched through the gates. He could make out Ginger's slight frame and red-topped head before they disappeared out of sight.

Garland never saw Kurt or Ginger again.

He looked over to Tower A where two prisoners on their hands and knees were cleaning the stains the dead had left behind. Somewhere a rifle fired out a round. Screams echoed around the camp.

Garland felt a tear form in his eye as the harsh weight of reality – his reality – came crashing down. How many more hours, days, nights could he endure? When would Sachsenhausen's darkness take him? He closed his eyes and balled his fists. He had to fight. Garland vowed he would perfect the ability he had found within his own mind, his aurora-guided gift bestowed by a power he could not comprehend. Surely he had been touched for a reason. If fate existed, Garland's was clear. He had something supernatural inside him, an invisible force unseen by the thousands sharing Sachsenhausen's hell. Garland didn't know if any of them deserved to be there, but he knew that no human being deserved the karma they had been handed.

As he approached the workshop, he looked to the east and saw the sun rise. He felt an energy pulse through him from the sun's rays, not a fungus or a poison but a blinding brightness, righteousness that settled on him like a calling.

He walked into the workshop and began making shoes once more.

Chapter Thirty

JOHAN - 1942

Johan had been at the Klinkerwerk for a month, and it was even more brutal than he had expected.

He had already seen over fifty prisoners die in the building and more of them perish back at the camp, husks of men taken by exhaustion and sickness.

The Klinkerwerk was huge. Prisoners worked round the clock to maximise production regardless of the death toll, convoys of trains and trucks delivering supplies and shipping out the bricks to wherever the Germans were building their empire. Being at the heart of it made Johan proud.

He would often sit in Schulz's office, listening to the commander ranting about the rise of the Nazis across Europe. Schulz would regale him with endless stories about Adolf Hitler, never missing the chance to name-drop the Fuehrer and relive the numerous dinners and drinks they had shared, wives and colleagues in tow.

Johan had watched footage of Hitler delivering spine-tingling speeches at rallies where the rapt crowds seemed infinite. He had seen him with his own eyes at the Olympics, although Garland had spoilt the moment. Hitler was a true giant amongst men, a leader for the ages. No matter what his beloved Gerda thought, Johan considered it an honour to be alive in this revolutionary time, to be at the command of someone destined to be a legend forever revered in the centuries to come.

Schulz constantly compared Hitler to his hero Julius Caesar, heading an unstoppable empire that would further and enrich the lives of its citizens with wisdom, innovation and a single unshakeable belief. Hitler, Schulz had said, was ultimately in charge of the Klinkerwerk. The Fuehrer was fanatical about the process, the science behind the production, the art of the architecture and the skill of the plant's ingenious designers.

"He sat opposite and looked me in the eyes," Schulz had said to Johan, grey-blue smoke circling the air above his head. "He told me, and these were his words, 'The empire will not be built on beauty, it will not be built with guns and war and death. The empire will be built much more simply than that.'"

Schulz had paused and affected a grandiose voice for the finale.

"'It will be built with bricks!'"

Schulz had sat back, watching Johan's reaction.

"As simple as that, Olsen," he had said, clapping his knee as he spoke. "If you understand that, you understand the empire. This factory will be the jewel in the German crown. It will be

Sachsenhausen's crowning glory, and we sit at the pinnacle of that. How does that make you feel? An orphan from Norway, serving Hitler himself."

Johan had found himself swept up in the moment. "Fantastic, sir," he had gushed. "I love the country and I love Berlin."

"Berlin, nonsense," Schulz had scoffed. "This is bigger than Berlin, bigger than even Germany. Soon we will be in the centre of the world."

Johan scanned the Klinkerwerk as his mind floated back to that conversation. *The centre of the world.* It did make him feel fantastic, he hadn't been lying, and those feelings justified everything. Moving from Oslo, the rigorous SS training, his stationing in Sachsenhausen and his continued hard work. Maybe one day he would take a place in the German government himself, setting policies, making decisions, winning wars. And it would all be built with bricks. Nothing more, nothing less.

He watched the prisoners work. Every time someone slacked, he would take a match to the end of his pistol and hold the flame to the metal until he saw a faint red glow on the black circular muzzle. Then he would walk up to the prisoner and say, "Faster." He wouldn't yell or curse. One word delivered in a normal voice. Then, when the prisoner looked up, Johan would hold the muzzle to the man's cheek. They would scream but they would always take the pain. They knew better than to flinch away from the pistol when the barrel was firmly in their face. The slackers would be marked and warned no man would make it to three marks. Most of them walked around the works with one or two red burn scars on their cheeks. It was enough to keep them working at speed.

Every so often, Johan would watch the Hohenzollern Canal outside the Klinkerwerk. The glistening water made him want to be elsewhere, far away from the hundreds of unwashed prisoners under his order. The canal was lined with trees and shrubs that made up the Lehnitz Lock, and every couple of days a narrow boat chugged happily along. Johan regarded the picture-book scene as a reminder of the idyllic future that awaited them. Once the groundwork was finished, the German Empire would rise. Sachsenhausen's bricks would be those foundations. Johan knew their workforce was unreliable, untrustworthy. They had homosexuals, Jews, thieves and commies in their ranks. But to Johan there was always a beautiful irony that those who were never going to be part of the Reich would be instrumental in its growth. It was a thought that warmed him. It made the cruelty worth it. The end goal was surely worth the suffering. He was doing his job, serving the Reich. It was right and righteous. Otherwise why would he have been assigned it? Gerda was a woman, she could never understand the hard face of war, but Johan was a soldier. He knew the truth.

He watched a heron land on the canal and pluck a fish from the water before flying away. The hunt was graceful for such a cumbersome bird, its surprising elegance bringing a smile to Johan's face.

He turned his focus back to the prisoners. The pink triangles made up most of the Klinkerwerk labourers. They were generally fitter and younger than the Jews when they arrived at the camp, and Johan assumed they were the least educated. A clever man was worthless in Sachsenhausen and they often meant trouble. Only the hand-picked kapos, usually hand-picked criminals, were the ones who required any intelligence. The rest were best used for brawn. Even the flabbiest or the scrawniest prisoners developed strong biceps in the Klinkerwerk, the muscles like bound ropes under their skin.

Schulz himself had decreed homosexuals should take priority for Klinkerwerk duty. No matter how wild his eyes or erratic his behaviour, Schulz was always thinking about the next step. He wanted to be rid of the homosexuals, an idea with which Johan was fully on board. Johan couldn't understand their ungodly nature. Although they posed no threat to him, they disturbed him greatly. He would often look in their eyes, searching for something, some common physical mark or character trait they all shared. But whilst the Jews and the Roma had the same physical characteristics, the queers all looked different. It made Johan believe their minds must be diseased, possessed by an invisible enemy, dark and demonic. These godless men could wander the world undetected. Johan hoped his SS colleagues hunting them across the country and beyond would be able to identify and eliminate them before they spread their evil throughout the new empire. He worried what the world would look like if such devils walked free.

Schulz himself visited the Klinkerwerk on the fourth week after it opened. Johan had ordered six of the "pink" workforce to run around tidying up, sweeping dust into corners and making sure the tools were all in the right places. Johan had gathered together his section, now comprising sixty prisoners, that morning in a roll-call of his own.

"My boss is coming for an inspection today. I think you know him." He had looked into the eyes of the first few men before him and saw the cold glaze of fear. Prisoners winced at the mere hint of Schulz's existence. "He makes me look like Christ himself, not that you sinners would know anything about Jesus."

When the men's eyes lowered to the floor, Johan tightened his fists.

"Look at me, you maggots!" Johan saw eyes snap warily his way. "I need to impress Commander Schulz, which means you need to impress him. You think I've been tough on you before today? You haven't seen anything. Fuck this up and I will fuck your entire lives. I know by now you're probably not scared of dying, but let me down and you will feel more agony than you could ever imagine. I will wring those demons out of your rotten homosexual bodies until you'll beg me to put a bullet in your head. Do you understand?"

The prisoners in front of him muttered. Johan yelled again, this time twice as loud. "Do you fucking rats understand!?"

"Yes, sir," they replied in unison.

"Good. Good." His voice softened. "Today it's Commander Schulz. Tomorrow it could be Herr Hitler himself. Now get to work."

They dispersed as Johan watched, going to their assigned tasks. Johan's eyes scanned the room, focused and searching for anything out of place.

Thirty minutes passed and Johan saw the shadowy figure of Schulz walk across the Klinkerwerk. His gait was jerky, and even as he approached, Johan could see the sparkling whites of his eyes form thirty yards away. Schulz, as always these days, was high as a kite. A thick cigar hung from the corner of his mouth, and fat clouds of smoke billowed from its burning end.

His smile broadened as he neared, and Johan could see his teeth, which were blackened and sharpened into hideous points, clasp against the thick butt of the cigar.

"Olsen, my boy," he said as he clapped Johan on the back. "How's it going?"

"Good, sir." Johan nodded. "Would you like the grand tour?"

Schulz shook his head and Johan saw sweat fly. The commander's eyes were bright but his skin was saggy and grey. He looked like a man on the cusp of a terminal illness.

"No need, boy. I know this place inside out. I helped plan it remember?"

He clasped his hand on the nape of Johan's neck and squeezed it tight.

"Hitler himself would be proud of the way we run this place. Bricks, Olsen! Bricks are the new gold, you know that?"

Johan smiled and nodded. "Yes, sir."

"How are you finding the workforce? Are all these deviants easy to control?"

"Yes, sir, with a bit of force." Johan scanned the room again. "When they're scared, they're easier to manage."

"Yes!" Schulz exclaimed, jumping slightly in the air. "Yes, Olsen. Rule with a fist of iron, boy. It's the only way. What about the trek over here?"

Schulz's change of tack caught Johan off guard for a moment.

He thought about the walk, part of the day he enjoyed, marching and making the prisoners sing pro-Nazi songs.

He had lost a couple of them on the way, but that was to be expected. One had died of exhaustion, his fellow prisoners carrying his lifeless body in a barrow back to the camp. Another had tried to escape across the canal. Johan had aimed his rifle and shot him dead, the bullet hitting the back of his head with a fine spray of blood. He had waited until the next day before ordering two of his prisoners to drag the sodden, bloated body from the water. Rats had already gnawed the man's flesh and chewed out his eyeballs, leaving bloody gaping holes in their place. The man's tongue protruded from his mouth, which had tuned purple in the cold water. Fragments of skull poked through the hole in his forehead.

It was a message to the rest of them. *Try to escape and you will die. The water and the rats will consume what's left of your miserable, sinful body.*

"It's a long way, but it's good for the men, I think," Johan said.

Schulz narrowed his eyes and frowned. "I'm not so sure, Olsen."

Johan turned to him. "Why?" He asked abruptly, before remembering himself. "Er. . . sir," he added.

"Think about your training. Efficiency is the key when it comes to the growth of our empire. The very existence of this factory is testament to its importance. I've already reduced roll-call to morning and evening to avoid the interruption of work duties. This walk not only damages these workers, it eats into their working time."

Johan frowned again and, paradoxically, nodded in agreement. "Okay," he replied, "but the camp is two miles away, and the Klinkerwerk are here. The only solution is. . ."

"To build a camp on-site for the prisoners to sleep," Schulz finished for him. "We need to keep them here. They need to breathe this place, and the more that come to the main camp, the more we can send here."

Johan inhaled, thinking of the walk, the two times a day he felt part of the outside world again. The shimmering water of the canal. The green and yellow reeds that grew tall next to the water. The narrow boats that floated peacefully by.

"An excellent idea, sir."

Schulz grinned and an unhinged expression grew on his face. "If you play your cards right, you could be camp leader over here."

Johan looked back at his commander, barely able to stifle a beaming grin, and nodded. "It would be an honour, sir."

The overtime payments had mounted up, and before long, Johan had enough cash to buy Gerda an engagement ring that matched his devotion and her beauty. The move was sanctioned by Schulz after Johan had described Gerda's moneyed background and a father amongst the Great War's glorious dead.

Johan walked onto the main street in Oranienburg towards the jewellers. The atmosphere had changed in Berlin once the war had begun, and now Johan wore his uniform when he had leave from the camp. How else would civilians know he was different? The SS commanded fear and respect.

He strolled through the streets, past a paperboy who bowed respectfully. Johan nodded back, reading the headline scrawled in bold, black letters. PARIS SURRENDERS. Johan smiled, thinking of his German comrades. He pictured celebrations, singing and dancing amongst the gun smoke, the soldiers quaffing French wine and eating their precious cheese. He knew a few of the men who had been sent to fight and felt a pang of jealousy as he read the headline. Whilst he had been keeping order in Berlin, they had been heroes growing the empire abroad.

There was a buzz in the air, a mixture of nervous energy and excitement. Johan could almost see it. Steps quickened around him, children ran and pointed at him in his finely pressed uniform, young men smoking cigarettes disappeared back into alehouses as Johan approached. Older men, no doubt veterans of the Great War, thanked him as he walked past. One who was riding his bike along the main road dismounted and offered Johan his hand.

"Thank you, young man. Thank you for saving us all."

Johan soaked up the atmosphere as his boots rhythmically tapped the concrete. He watched a ray of sunlight blaze through even the thickest branches of a tree, bathing the entire street in warmth.

He found the jewellers. The shopfront was shabby, varnished in faded green, but the name on top had been freshly painted over. *Kramer's Jewels* was now written in large black letters. Johan could still smell a faint trace of the oily paint in the breeze. The shop must, until recently, have belonged to another trader.

He walked through the door and was pleased to see the man he assumed was Kramer stand when he saw him.

"A pleasure to meet you, officer," Kramer said. "What can I do for you today?"

Johan returned the greeting and glanced over his shoulder.

"For a few weeks now I've been admiring that beautiful diamond ring in the window."

Kramer scampered to the shopfront with a bunch of keys jangling as he moved. He unlocked the cage that protected the display and with exaggerated reverence brought the boxed ring to Johan. The diamond sparkled in the sun that broke through the southern skies, casting bright light throughout the shop. Johan took the box and picked up the ring delicately. A sharp stab of worry squeezed his heart. Would it be good enough for Gerda, a woman who lit up every room she entered?

"What's the story behind the stone?" Johan asked as he held it to the light. It seemed to burst with a spectrum of a million colours.

Kramer scratched his head and furrowed his brow. "I will need to check the records, sir, I'm sorry."

"How long have you run this shop?"

"Only a few months, sir, but I have good knowledge of jewels and stones."

Johan took his eyes from the diamond and looked at Kramer, the shopkeeper betraying his rising nerves.

"Who owned it before?"

"A Jewish fellow who was imprisoned, as you will probably know," Kramer rushed. "I bought all of the stock with my life savings, sir. A wonderful opportunity for an honest German worker. The ring was being stored out the back."

Johan nodded. "Diamonds are rare these days, with the war effort and everything. There can't be many rings like this around?"

A woman Johan took to be Kramer's wife appeared with a logbook, written in a neat, calligraphic hand. Her face was stern. Cold eyes peered over half-moon glasses and her thin face had an expression of callousness that ran from her wrinkled forehead to her narrow jaw-line.

"A diamond ring was seized and bought from an auction," she said. "It belonged to a lady of Berlin, Lady Abraham. Your people stripped her of everything she owned, including her precious engagement ring, bought for her by her husband who died fighting for Germany in the Great War. The diamond was removed and repurposed."

Johan nodded. *A Jew's ring.* Could he bring himself to buy it, to look at it on Gerda's finger every day, knowing it had belonged to a Jew? After all, before Hitler came to power many of them had money and some evidently had good taste. They may be enemies of the Reich, but they knew fine jewels when they saw them.

Johan's eyes twinkled back at the spectrum that shone from the diamond as he gently circled it in his fingers.

"How much?" he asked, not taking his eyes from the perfect stone's glinting light.

Kramer's eyes shifted sideways to his wife, who was still looking over her half-moon glasses, her chin pointed downwards.

"Four thousand," she replied.

Johan glanced up. He felt a familiar power surge through him, the feeling of strength that filled him when he addressed the prisoners.

"It's too much," he replied sharply.

"Well shop elsewhere, officer. There are plenty of jewellers in West Berlin who'd welcome your bartering skills. This was a diamond that belonged to a lady of high social standing."

"A Jewish pig!" Johan yelled across the shop. "It should be half the price, knowing that it came from the finger of a Jew!"

Kramer shuddered at the sudden venom and volume in Johan's voice, but his wife was unafraid.

"It is full price and a good one at that," she fired back.

Johan looked at her stoic face whilst his own hung with anxiety and unease. It was obvious who was both the brains and brawn behind the operation.

"This shop has been here for over forty years," Kramer's wife continued. "They took the Jews away and I persuaded my husband to sell our house and take care of it. The previous owner was a good man, a good friend to us. I – we – felt it was our duty to keep it running. What you have in your hands is one of our prize stones. It will not be sold cheaply today or any other day to an officer of the SS, a kaiser, or to Adolf Hitler himself."

Johan felt the blood rise from the pit of his stomach. Fire erupted inside him.

"How dare you speak that way," he said, taking a step forward. "I could take you right now and throw you in Sachsenhausen."

Kramer's wife was unmoved. She stared at the ring then turned her unflinching eyes to Johan.

"On what grounds, officer?" The words were taunting. "We are not Jews. My husband isn't homosexual. We are German nationals. You can throw me into one of your camps, work me to death, kill me. But what cause do you have?"

Images of Schulz flashed in Johan's mind. He felt himself channelling his commander.

"Your words defile the government. They betray the Reich."

Kramer's wife tutted and spat onto the wooden bench in front of her. "Pah. I work hard, I pay my taxes to the war effort. My husband served in the Great War. If Germany wins or loses, we'll still be here, making ends meet, serving the local people. You're not German are you, officer?"

The question slid into Johan like a stiletto blade.

He pulled his SS issue knife from his side pocket and brandished it. Kramer gasped and recoiled, as if the knife had somehow already wounded him.

His wife glanced at him with a mix of pity and disgust before settling her gaze to the knife in Johan's hand.

"You have three options," Johan said, his tone slow and deliberate. "Number one, you give me the ring at a price that befits the current economic climate and the chequered history of the object. Number two, I leave with the ring, and your only recompense is a cell in Sachsenhausen, where you will end as ashes. Number three, I use this knife on both of you right here and tell everyone the truth, that you are enemies of the state."

He stared at the Kramers, shifting from one to the other every two seconds. He realised later, when he relived the moment, that his movements were in time with his heartbeat.

He looked at the blade in front of him and then up to the jeweller and his wife. Even Frau Kramer's eyes began to glisten with fear. Johan's mind suddenly filled with an image of Gerda. Beautiful, honest Gerda. How would she feel if she saw him behaving in this way, to buy a ring for her? Would she accept it as a gift? Or would she too show that look of intense fear?

He felt the hand that held the knife begin to shake, and his own eyes welled up. He exhaled and the faces of the Kramers simply dropped in more fear. The unpredictability of an SS officer was more a warning than a comfort.

Johan placed the knife back in his pocket and afforded a forced smile.

"Let's start again," he said. "It's a beautiful ring. I'll pay what you ask."

Frau Kramer eyed him suspiciously. Herr Kramer leant forward, expecting a deception, a sick joke that would lead Johan to pull out the blade once more.

"I was a little heavy-handed and I apologise to you both," Johan continued. Again, he thought of Gerda. What she would want him to do. This was about her, after all. This was all about her. "You are good people. I made a mistake."

He drew a roll of money from his inside coat pocket, counted four thousand Reichsmarks, and handed the notes to Kramer. He took them and put them in his till.

Johan snapped closed the ring box and put it in his other inside pocket, tapping it lightly when it was safely tucked away.

"Well, it's been nice doing business with you," he said apologetically. "Have a good day."

He opened the door, the bell chiming as the noise from the street rushed into the quiet shop, and stepped out.

As he walked past the window, the Kramers were staring at him, their mouths open. He flashed them a white smile and strode on, affecting a slight spring in his step as he made his way home.

"Yes. Oh yes, Johan, of course I will."

The whole restaurant burst into spontaneous applause. Several of the other customers clapped Johan on the back and some mocked him with jovial comments, that there was still time to change his mind. Drinks appeared from all angles until six bottles of fine German wine stood on his table.

Johan had used more of his overtime money to book the best restaurant in the whole of Berlin, a place so luxurious it was said Hitler himself was known to eat there and Marika Roekk would be regularly wined and dined in between filming. The food was the best Johan had ever tasted, and the restaurant itself exquisite, a beautiful building classily decorated.

But it all paled into insignificance when he stared into Gerda's eyes. They were bright blue and sometimes Johan swore that if he looked deeply enough he could actually see her kindness. Not in the colour or any kind of sparkle, but a tangible matter that represented all that was good. It reminded him of more serene times, sitting with Garland on the weather-beaten wood of the Oslo docks as emerald waves lapped by their shoes. There was an unparalleled calm to it that he had never considered until something in Gerda's eyes settled the same contentment in his heart. He watched the dimples appear on her cheeks as she smiled. She was a goddess, placed on earth for him, a lesser mortal whose life was being enriched day after day.

"You like the ring?" he asked, still down on one knee.

Gerda nodded, her hair falling lazily over her forehead as she moved.

"It's beautiful, but Johan you shouldn't have. It must have cost a fortune."

"You're worth it," he replied with a smile. His mind flashed back to Kramer's shop. The bitter memory of his behaviour contrasted by the sweet pride he felt in paying full price and walking away a more merciful, better person. The person Gerda would want him to be.

He rose to his feet and kissed Gerda on the lips. It was a soft, heavenly touch that made the top of his head tingle.

"So you'll move in with me, in my house in Oranienburg?"

"We'll see," she replied, smiling. "Maybe we can find somewhere more central? But shall we wait until the war is over now?"

Johan's face dropped in disappointment as he shook his head.

"No, we can't wait. I don't know how long it'll last. And my orders are all at Sachsenhausen. I need to live close."

Gerda brushed the hair away from her forehead so it sat behind her ears.

"I'm not sure I want to live so close to a prison camp. I hear stories, Johan. I don't want a place like that on my doorstep."

"There's no danger, Gerda," Johan reassured her. "The prisoners work all day, every day. They're no trouble. We keep them in line. You have nothing to be scared about."

Gerda pulled a dark lock from behind her ear and twizzled it around her fingers. When she let go, it bounced, the curl unravelling before springing back straight.

"That's not what I meant. Let's drop talk of the future and enjoy the here and now."

She put a wine glass in his hand and then picked up her own. "A toast to our future happiness." She raised her glass. "Mr and Mrs Olsen-to-be, wherever that bright and beautiful journey may take us."

Johan lifted his glass and clinked it gently with Gerda's.

"To us."

He drank and smiled, but when he looked into his Gerda's eyes something reflected back that he had never seen before. It was a sharp, underlying glint of emotion he had seen in the eyes of hundreds of prisoners. He had always taken it for respect, but now he realised it was something else. Something he had seen in the eyes of the Kramers, even when he'd corrected himself and paid full price.

What he saw was fear.

Chapter Thirty-One

GARLAND - 1943

Every second in the place seemed to last a lifetime, but strangely the weeks and months at Sachsenhausen went by quickly. Garland had used his fingernails to carve a notch into the soft wood of his bedframe as each day went by, and now it looked like it had been used by a rat to sharpen its teeth.

He had got used to the shoemaking work. Although his hands still throbbed and stiffened at night, they became hardened and his body assimilated itself to the daily routine. And of course he could have been assigned worse roles. Even his bed, which crawled with huge black lice, became somewhere he slept reasonably amongst the endless noise of hundreds of other men, their snores and nightmare cries a soundtrack that no longer kept him awake.

The bitter winter nights were so cold Garland would will himself to sleep so he could escape the shivering of his body and the tinny chattering of his teeth. Sleep was the great off-switch, the time any man could be somewhere else. For those few hours at night, Garland was free. Free from the guards, free from the cold and free from the shoe factory. When sleep came he no longer had to wear the pink triangle and the nameless numbers that now defined him. Garland would dream vividly, each time the aurora's lights carrying him, his spirit dancing with the bright colours, through the skies to faraway lands, across rolling turquoise oceans and auburn fields, a welcome breeze under the hot blaze of the sun.

Opening his eyes in the morning was the worst part of each day. That sinking realisation, the moment sleep left and reality kicked in the same grinding routine of roll-calls, death and needless violence, guards screaming and the gunshots that pierced the air and made his heart jump, leaving a trail of ice from his chest to his brain. Each guard was cruel but some were worse than others, monsters ready to end life on a whim.

Garland had already witnessed the murders of over sixty men, all at the hands of guards. Others he saw worked to death. Friends, like Ginger and Kurt, came and went without explanation, only whispers and gossip left behind. Some were released back to the Berlin streets, but most weren't afforded such kindness.

Garland thought often of Ginger, a man he had only known for a short time but who had taught him so much.

He had told Garland to always stand in the middle section of the formation for roll-call, so he could take a piss without the guards seeing. The ruse became well-known and prisoners jostling for position took regular beatings from any watchful guards.

Ginger also showed Garland how to beg for more food, asking construction crews sometimes working at Sachsenhausen to throw bread crusts over the walls. Once a whole pickled egg had been tossed into the camp. It had landed in the grit but Ginger had dusted it off and allowed Garland a bite. It tasted heavenly, although the vinegar had stung his ulcers. It would become an anecdote Ginger would often share, and as the story gained momentum amongst the prisoners, one egg would become a dozen until finally a whole jar had come flying across the wall complete with wursts and ale. Even Garland couldn't accurately recall what was true anymore.

Garland's heart had sunk when Ginger vanished, and the rumour spread that he had been shot trying to escape the Klinkerwerk. One version had him diving into the canal and staying underwater for over a minute before surfacing so close to the far bank he could almost touch it. His luck ran out when a guard saw him break the water, the bullet to Ginger's head single and deadly. Garland hoped the story was a mistake, hoped his friend had scrambled the bank and run to a new life.

Hope was all he had.

Kurt had been Garland's first friend in Sachsenhausen. He would keep himself sane with exercise, nightly press-ups and star jumps before bed. He would earn cigarettes from the other prisoners by performing haircuts and cleaning duties on Sundays, when the prisoners weren't expected to work. Garland was told Kurt had collapsed from exhaustion at boot testing and been taken to the infirmary. If the version was right, Garland hoped Kurt had been released, but he knew it was unlikely.

Cruelty existed in every form a mind, sane or otherwise, could imagine. There were no dark corners where devils were hiding, it was all out in the open. Evil didn't lurk at Sachsenhausen, it strolled, strutted and bustled around in plain sight. It even had a colour, a smoky dark crimson. Garland could see it out the corner of his eye. It billowed like smoke, a noxious gas hanging in the air. He was the only one who could see it, but he knew others felt it, even if they stayed silent. It was the reason birds never flew over the camp. Malevolence hung around it, pregnant and sinful, and the guards were its manifestation.

Some of the kapos were just as bad. They enjoyed special privileges and some even considered the guards as friends, although Garland was doubtful that would stick outside the camp's unforgiving walls.

Fats, the kapo in charge of Garland's barrack, had taken an instant dislike to Garland. Hell, every prisoner with half a brain stayed away from the pink triangles. If the various classes of prisoners made up a society, the homosexuals were only above Jews, the most despised. And even the Jews stayed away from the queers, fearful of a more severe beating. It was the criminals with green triangles and the political prisoners with red who were more favoured by both prisoners and guards.

Fats was a commie, wearing his red triangle with a warped sense of pride. He must have been receiving some special treatment, Garland was sure. His ample gut strained against his big uniform, and when he screamed in Garland's face, he smelt of meat and beer. Garland had seen neither in Sachsenhausen.

Fats bullied the pink triangles in his barrack, assaulting and humiliating them with or without provocation. Garland himself had taken more than one gratuitous punch to the face. One blow had broken his nose, and when Garland reset it in his bunk, he cried out so loudly a prisoner a few beds away had thrown a handful of lice at him in protest.

Fats had even taken bowls and spoons from a couple of the homosexuals. Each prisoner was issued just one of each, and once they were gone, they were gone for good. Garland had seen men simply hold out a cupped hand as boiling, watery soup was poured onto them, the fluid spilling through cracks in their fingers. It was a ghastly sight, watching skeletal men desperately slurping at their scalded palms.

Since the Klinkerwerk opened, and because the pink triangles made up most of its workforce, the guards had stopped doing anything that led to the injury or direct death of homosexual prisoners.

Fats found the new directive hard to follow. The result was bittersweet. Garland and his fellow prisoners lived slightly easier, less fearful lives, but they knew the bigger picture. They were being kept in one piece for something worse. Although Garland himself had escaped the trauma of both the boot-testing track and the Klinkerwerk so far, he had heard the stories and seen the vacant look in the eyes of the men returning. Garland had watched their cheeks hollow until they were concave, seen the ribs and bones protrude from their bodies as if their skeletons were trying to break out of their own skin prisons.

He knew the Klinkerwerk would call for him one day. Each morning he woke, he prayed to God it wouldn't be today. The gaunt, soulless figures that shuffled back from their shifts were the lucky ones. He had seen corpses ferried to the camp in wheelbarrows every day. Some shot, some skeletal from exhaustion. Some still soaking wet and bloated from being drowned in the canal and left to rot for hours.

To the Nazis, the Klinkerwerk was the genius solution to their hatred of homosexuals. They would make them die in agony, all whilst making the very thing that would help move the Reich forwards.

Before he drifted to sleep, Garland would often think of the war. He would pray the British, French and Soviets would win, just to defeat these evil men who could treat their fellow human beings with such cruelty. But who was to say they were any better? Maybe it was the world that was a cruel place, and people were naturally evil. He'd had word that Germany now occupied Norway, and it made him weep with sadness and anger.

Garland stuck closely to the others wearing pink, more out of necessity than design, but he became good friends with three of them. They even swapped beds to be nearer each other, a move that suited the other prisoners who wanted nothing to do with the ungodly scum of the camp.

Gustave, a Frenchman who had been living in East Berlin, was everything Garland had hoped a real-life Frenchman would be. His dark, cropped hair and his beard were thick and wiry, and even though he was only in his early twenties, both were streaked with silver. Gustave would often have remnants from the day's soup caught in his coarse facial hairs, a comic contrast as he ranted in his passionate Gallic way, causing the group to laugh uncontrollably. He also talked endlessly about food. . . cheese, beef, pork, veal, and the herbs, spices and sauces that made a meal much more than just the sum of things that sat on a plate.

Whenever he spoke of beautiful food, Gustave would kiss the back of his hands, as if his lips had to touch something, anything, to imagine the taste. Out of all the prisoners Garland knew, it was Gustave who was most aggrieved at their miserable meals. It was something that insulted him and the very nature of what food represented. He reminded Garland of his old Italian roommate

Gianni. They shared many traits, from their passion for fine food to their love for their home countries.

Gustave spoke of the magnificent view from the top of the Eiffel Tower, the cathedrals of Paris, and the city's unequalled nightlife. He had moved to Berlin when he was nineteen to become a singer and had sung professionally in the Berlin clubs. As a prisoner, he had even performed in the Sachsenhausen canteen, a building he dubbed the Green Monster in honour of its colour and the hideous men it entertained.

He spoke freely and openly about the variety of men he had known. Men dressed as women, muscular men, tough soldiers, soft-skinned men whose touch was delicate and sensitive, Africans whose hair would bristle when he ran his fingers through it.

Garland was surprised to hear a man speak so openly about his feelings, but Gustave was unashamed, some would even say proud. Considering the grave results of homosexual relationships, Garland barely thought it possible. It was a constant source of bemusement to the others that Gustave was so effeminate and good-humoured the guards laid off him a little more than the rest of the 175ers. They could define him, Garland supposed, and although they were disgusted with what he was, they couldn't help but laugh at his exaggerated whingeing and the contrast of his thick beard with his soft femininity. They gave him an administrative role sorting out the possessions of new arrivals, probably the best job any prisoner wearing pink had ever been assigned.

Hugo was from Berlin, and shared Garland's love of humour. He had not been openly homosexual. He was all too aware of the risks, the prejudice, the persecution and the beatings, never mind the same-sex criminality. Hugo had been in a secretive, long-term relationship with a married man that had become quite the scandal of 1940 when the affair was exposed in the local newspapers. Hugo had been arrested and jailed shortly after. He was a quiet, shy fellow with a wickedly dry sense of humour and a talent for impressions. His impersonation of Fats was a perfect parody that left the other prisoners in hysterics. He was the kind of man that withered in big crowds and fell silent if someone new came into a group. But within trusted company, he was loud, funny, and jovial. He reminded Garland of the friends he had left behind in Oslo and some of his colleagues in the Idiotentruppe. Hugo was assigned the shoe workshop with Garland and the two became closer each day.

Max, his other firm friend in the camp, was born in Berlin and had never strayed from the city. Oranienburg was the furthest he had ever travelled. Max had been orphaned at the age of five. His father had been killed at the Somme whilst his mother had contracted tuberculosis and died before she could reach hospital. Max was taken in by his uncle, a nightclub owner from central Berlin, and had run errands for him from a young age, riding his bike to deliver packages and messages to business partners all over the city. He began drinking and smoking when he was ten and by twelve he worked the Berlin streets as a *Strichjunge*, serving his uncle's homosexual clientele. In return, his uncle gave him a few marks for pocket money, along with all the Polish vodka he could drink and as many American cigarettes as his young lungs could inhale. By the time his uncle died a brutal death in a Berlin back alley, stabbed in the throat by a rival nightclub owner, Max was a strapping teenager. He had taken beatings and abuse and been plied with every drug on the streets of Berlin, but he still stood, scarred but unbroken. Eventually Max was arrested for repeated acts of prostitution and sent to Sachsenhausen. He had a coldness forged by his upbringing, a childhood lost and a life beyond the understanding of his peers.

Max went about his business in Sachsenhausen as if the walls and gun towers were a mirage, walking briskly with purpose, as if he could be heading to a building site or a bar to meet friends. When Max looked at someone, his eyes burnt through them to an unseen spot somewhere in the far distance. Even on the camp's scant provisions, his muscles were thick and the stubble that seemed a fixture on his chiselled jaw made him look heroic, more soldier than prisoner. He had a fierce intensity but underneath it rested a kind nature. The guards eyed him with cautious disdain, Garland assumed because of his physical presence, and had moved him from detail to detail. He had started in construction, digging trenches and building new accommodation units. Then he had been moved to the Klinkerwerk, not working in the factory but carrying bricks to the boats that arrived every day on the canal.

Garland thought Max was being spared. His physicality, even for a homosexual, was something to be prized. Garland imagined him as a gladiator in ancient Rome, slaying tigers and putting rivals to the sword as the Colosseum rose in acclaim.

It struck Garland three weeks after he had met Max. He was falling in love with him. Something glinted in those hard eyes, fire and ice merged together. Garland was sure the full spectrum of the aurora danced within his irises.

Max was the one who made Garland discover his true sexuality. Perhaps he had always known, but it was within the grey, soulless confines of Sachsenhausen, under those barren and birdless skies, that he accepted the truth.

He had spent tortured nights thinking about the injustice of his arrest, falsely accused of holding feelings that were not his own. But after Max, he had felt an awakening both painful and wonderful. He was homosexual. A queer. A 175er. He wore the pink and he wore it rightfully.

Garland would drift into sleep seeing visions of Max's face, his dazzling eyes sparkling against the night. And by the time his mind soared away on the aurora's majestic lights, he had a smile on his face and a feeling of liberation. It was freedom in the toughest labour camp in Berlin. He was frightened, but the fear energised him, propelled him to new heights. And on those nights, his dreams carried him further and further, past the moon and the stars to ancient galaxies that stretched to infinity. Speeding through the cosmos, Garland felt nothing would ever matter again.

It was one frosty February morning, shortly after he had opened his eyes and the aurora's voyage became a hazy memory, that Garland's real life turned on its head.

He heard Fats's familiar voice, yelling at them to get up for roll-call.

He sat and dropped the five feet to the floor, his calves holding strong as his knees bent to steady himself. He smiled at Max and clapped Hugo on the back.

"Another day, boys. One at a time. *En dag av gangen* as we'd say back in Oslo."

He sat on the bottom bunk to pull on his shoes and saw Gustave watching him, his eyebrows arched.

"What's up, Gus?" Garland asked. "Something wrong?"

"I forgot to tell you," Gustave said. "There's a guard. A tough son of a bitch. He looks like you but taller and much broader. Ice blond hair. They call him Olsen."

Garland's eyes widened and his mouth hung open, his brain trying to process each word Gustave had said. Then he closed his eyes and felt a wide smile break on his face. He sprang to his feet and ran to the kapo.

"I need to see a guard, how can I do it? How do I go about it?"

Fats looked at him with narrowed brown eyes, his head jerked to the side.

Then the kapo laughed. It was a heavy sound which seemed to rise from his swollen belly. When he looked back to Garland, he raised his hand and slapped him hard across the face.

The blow sent Garland reeling backwards, his skin burning.

"What was that for?" Garland demanded, rubbing at his cheek. "I just said I need to speak. . ."

Fats took one step forward and punched Garland in the face, knocking him to the floor. As Garland lay on his back, the world spinning around him, he saw Max leaping for the kapo.

What followed was hazy and played out in front of Garland's eyes in frames, like the jerky movies he and Johan had seen in the Oslo cinema. . . Max swinging his fists, his eyes wide and fixed, a wild animal launching onto prey; something on Fats's face breaking in spray of crimson; Gus and Hugo running over, holding Max back; Max breaking free as a scrum of prisoners waded in, arms and legs flailing. Dust filled the churning air and black mites scurried to the safety of the barracks' nooks and crannies.

Garland heard the shouts as the guards burst through the door, but he couldn't make out the words. When another prisoner landed on him, Garland let the scene close to darkness.

"Who the fuck do you think you are?"

Every syllable sent a wave of pain through Garland's head, and he realised it was the guard Kruger. He remembered him from Kori's workshop, a lifetime ago in another world.

"A 175er starting a fist-fight?" Kruger's chubby face came into focus. "A few months ago I'd have drowned you in the fucking toilet. You're lucky we need you to work."

Kruger grabbed him by the back of his shirt and dragged him out of the barracks.

"Solitary confinement," Kruger told him. "You know what that means, Norwegian queer?"

Kruger hauled him into a room that was dark, the air heavy with a strong sulphurous odour. The only light came in a thin sliver from beyond the doorway and the entrance to the barracks. It illuminated half of Kruger's face, leaving the other half in darkness. As he looked at the guard's thin gash of a mouth and crooked nose, set below two narrow eyes, Garland thought how ugly the human face could be. Kruger's hair was shaggy, poking out from under his cap like a cheap rug.

He pushed Garland inside, shut the door and pulled open a narrow plate that sent a block of light into the room. Kruger's pale eyes shone briefly through the gap then disappeared and Garland could see his thin lips instead. They began to move.

"You touch any wall, you die. You even think about leaning against anything, I drag you out of here and I put a knife in your brain. You understand?"

The mouth disappeared and the cold eyes returned. Garland believed him.

The light disappeared and darkness engulfed Garland, the only sound the delicate rhythm of his own breathing.

Seconds melted into hours and the darkness began to creep into his mind. Every now and again Kruger would open the hatch and peer through. To Garland, it was a floating eyeball, a disembodied entity there to watch. When it left, it plunged him into darkness once more.

The isolation had a strange effect. Garland's muscles ached from standing still, and every fibre of his being willed him to sit or slump against the wall. But his mind stopped him. How long had it been? He couldn't even guess. The eyeball came again, bathed in light. He thought he heard Kruger yell words but couldn't be sure. The eye left and darkness swallowed the light. Garland's thoughts sped like traffic on a busy road, each bringing its own layer of fear. Johan was here, but how could Garland reach him? What lay in wait when he was out of solitary? And what about Max who had escalated the incident to a full-scale riot? Not for the first time, Garland wondered how he himself would die in this place.

The walls called out again to be touched, to feel the weight of his body. They throbbed eagerly in the blackness, and Garland lost his sense of spatial perception. Were the walls even there at all? If he reached out would his hands touch only the void? Was there something lurking malevolently beyond, waiting patiently for him to move? Or would his hand touch solid wall before Kruger dragged him out and beat him to death?

Garland closed his eyes. If anything was going to help, it was the aurora inside him. He willed it forward, beckoned it to come. Moving into the bodies of the running prisoner and tower guard had left him exhausted, mentally and physically. He had never tried to control the lights again and told no one, not even his friends, what had happened. They wouldn't understand. Even Johan had reacted strangely to his *turns*, as he'd called them. Keeping his secret made him feel alone.

But with control could the possibilities be endless? Could he transport himself to a bird and fly free, alone and unchained? He imagined drifting over snow-capped mountains, drinking from crystal-blue lakes whose depths were endless.

He closed his eyes tighter and focused, blocking everything else from his mind. But the aurora never came. There were no dancing colours, just the darkness and the beating of his heart.

Garland opened his eyes and he was somewhere else.

Everything was white. . . the walls, his clothes, the artificial light. He had the sense he was surrounded by tall trees, the environment familiar. The room had expanded and Garland realised he was lying in a bed. His body wouldn't move but his mind was aware. A strange electronic screen was next to the bed, with a green line and a series of numbers that Garland remembered from his dreams.

The green line jumped suddenly and he felt agitated.

Then the eye appeared. It floated in front of him on the white wall, bathed not by light but darkness. It watched him for seconds, minutes, hours. Time had frozen, it meant nothing.

Garland closed his own eyes tight again. He could hear the beep of the machine and see the green line even though his eyelids were squeezed shut. It jolted rhythmically, a sharp beep each time it rose. Then it flattened to one solid line and the beep became a long, constant noise. Garland felt the breath leave his body and panicked.

He heard that familiar English voice speak his name. The voice that came to him in his dreams and from the periphery of his visions. It was soft and calming. This time it was close, closer than he'd ever felt it.

"Hang in there, son. Use your talent. Use your power. Listen to the colours. Find your brother."

He recoiled suddenly. The voice was coming from his own mouth. It was his voice. He heard a strong breeze blow the trees and felt his hair – how did he now have a full head of hair? – blow over his face.

When he opened his eyes the white walls and light were gone.

He ran his hands over his body and felt an odd pang of relief that it was his own. He didn't know where he'd been or *who* he'd been.

Garland spent the rest of his time in solitary trying to meditate, concentrating on his own breathing. The discipline calmed him.

Even the floating eye faded into the background until it returned for a final time, and the iron door was heaved open.

"Get out of there, queer!" the guard yelled. Garland felt light-headed, the sudden light too much for his eyes. He was hauled out and thrown, tumbling face first to the ground.

"Back to work, maggot!"

The shift was even harder than normal. Garland's body ached, and when his work rate dropped, a guard beat him around the shoulders with a truncheon. Garland managed snatched words with Gustave as they were packing shoes into boxes.

"How was it?" Gustave asked.

"Hell," Garland told him. "I don't even know how long I was in there."

When Gustave said it had been no more than a couple of hours Garland shook his head in disbelief.

Two hours. To Garland it had felt more like two days.

"Did anyone else get punished?" he asked.

Gustave rubbed his chin, a dark shadow momentarily cast on his face.

"Max got it bad. The guards battered him and then threw him in a cell like yours. I came to work. I just hope he got let out, the same as you."

Garland spent the rest of his shift in anxious silence. When it was over, he quickened his step, almost sprinting back to the barracks despite the cramps that burnt in his legs. Unusually, guards were standing at the entrance, blocking the way.

Officer Schubert stepped forward. He wore a wide grin when he saw Johan and Gustave approach.

"Hello, pink boys. One of your kind is over there. The big one, the troublemaker."

Schubert motioned to a spot to his left and Garland rushed over.

Max's wrists had been clamped to a wooden structure. His arms were behind his back and his body hung below. He was alive, but his face was an image of agony, a gory mess that made Garland wretch. Max's teeth were clenched and his head was shaking, his eyes shut so tight Garland could see deep lines stretching across to his temples. Huge veins pulsated around his muscular chest, and his hands sat three feet above his hanging head, his bare feet teetering only inches from the ground. The force of the savage restraint had torn his shoulders from their sockets and they poked out at unnatural angles. Garland thought he looked like a creature from a horror tale, gnarled and inhuman.

When Garland moved to take Max's weight a guard punched him to the floor, and he was dragged groggily into the barracks. Gustave and Hugo helped him to his bunk where he curled up and cried.

After a few minutes, Max was thrown in too, his body skidding face first along the filthy surface. His arms hung loosely by his sides, and his bloody face smeared a red trail on the floor.

Garland rushed to him and screamed at the other prisoners to help. They ignored him. Garland looked up and saw fear and defeat across their gaunt faces.

"What's wrong with you people? This could have been you? Do you think he deserved this?"

The prisoners began to walk away, their heads down. They knew Garland was right but wanted no part in it. They had all suffered enough for their own so-called sins against Germany. Why would they suffer more for another man?

Hugo and Gustave joined Garland and they gently carried Max to his bunk. Garland looked at his shoulders, misshapen and loose.

"Max," Garland said softly. "Max, can you hear me? Can you understand me? It's Garland."

Max nodded, beads of blood falling from his nose and the gashes on his cheeks.

"Max, I'm going to do something that is going to hurt a lot, but we need to do it. And I'm going to need to do it twice. Do you understand?"

Garland picked up a stray piece of wood from the floor. He had done this once before, when they had been fourteen at the orphanage and Johan had fallen from a tree. The orphanage master had guided him, no doubt not wanting to get his own hands dirty with a lowly orphan boy. He hoped he could remember how to do it.

"Bite down on this."

Once Max had the wood in his mouth Garland took his left arm and gently ran his fingers upwards as Max flinched. Sweat ran down Max's face, mixing with the blood.

Garland felt the right spot and quickly shifted the arm upwards. He heard a loud *click* as Max jerked in a spasm. Max sobbed softly around the wood held tight between his teeth. The veins around his arms and neck pulsated, his muscles tight and tense.

"Well done," Garland said quietly. He stroked Max's cheek with the back of his hand. When he brought it away, it was wet and red.

He pushed Max's right arm back into its socket, but this time it was clumsier, and he needed two attempts, the bone grinding as Max screamed in pain.

"It's all over," Garland told him. "All done."

He spent the night by Max's side, cleaning his wounds with cold water and a wet rag that began white but was soon saturated with blood. He thought of the Englishman's words which had seemed to flow from his own mouth. He thought of Johan and the power of the aurora which flowed from another world into his own veins. But most of all he thought of Max, broken and soft.

Then in the weak light of a grey dawn, amongst the steady drone of snores, he leant forward and kissed Max on his temple. He watched a smile crack into Max's ruined face.

Garland let his own tears flow silent until morning and they were sent to work again.

Chapter Thirty-Two

RICHARD - 2022

Richard's fleeting moments of consciousness, where he found himself in his own body once more, in the shadow of hundreds of pine trees, always came with a surge of excitement and knowing. The familiarity would come quicker and quicker, until now, he was immediately aware that he was back in his own body.

The colours danced above him, this time framed with darkness. A memory flashed in his mind, a cold ferry trip with Sandy to see the majestic northern lights. Nature's magnificent show for humans to gape at in awe, a work of art on a canvas of dark sky. He thought again of Sandy and wondered where he was. Whether he was so deep in his dream that his husband was lost forever. It crossed Richard's mind for an awful moment that he might be dead, and he was experiencing the afterlife or some form of purgatory, although he dismissed it. He'd know. Surely he'd know?

And what of the boy? What of Garland in Sachsenhausen? The name, such a coincidence. A long-lost family member, perhaps. Or was Richard a reincarnation, looking back at a previous life, one much more wretched than the last, but still with the strange, otherworldly ability that gave him the means to sense things that were about to happen.

Richard's thoughts were broken by a tremor. The world around him shook and the colours swirled more violently, an effervescent storm above. Then, the light descended, submerging him until all he could see was a bright white light.

Then a shaking sensation. His body convulsed. He had the feeling of being taken over. He felt his head move and his eyes scan.

He wasn't alone.

"Garland?" Richard asked softly. His voice, spoken aloud, seemed to echo, carried on a light breeze in this strange, alien place amongst the trees.

He didn't receive an answer. But he knew, he *felt*, that the boy was present. Realisation flashed before him, as strong and as clear as the memory of Richard and Sandy standing in amazement below the dancing northern lights as they reflected gracefully from the cold North Sea. He had to help Garland. There had to be a reason that their two lives had crashed together in this strange, fantastical fashion. He was here to guide this boy through his trauma. Garland and Johan were in the same camp, Richard knew it. He didn't know how he knew, maybe it was the gift. But Garland Lund's salvation lay with Johan Olsen. He just knew it, there was a symmetry, something in the way the colours danced, something in the way the bird sang its cheerful tune. Johan was Garland's only ticket to survival.

Richard focused, concentrating his whole body, channelling all the energy of his very soul into every word.

Hang in there, son. Use your talent. Use your power. Listen to the colours. Find your brother.

He heard no reply, but he knew Garland had heard him. He felt the words being received and interpreted. And with the effort, Richard slumped back into his bed and into an immediate sleep, aware of being alone once more, the colours above him swirling into darkness.

Chapter Thirty-Three

JOHAN - 1944

It was teeming with rain, the water falling relentlessly in thick drops that bounced from the ground and splashed in the muddy puddles forming quickly all around.

Johan led the prisoners, his rifle hanging nonchalantly in his soaking hands, unaware it would be his last trip to the Klinkerwerk.

He surveyed the leafy horizon for danger. A man passed on a bike in the distance, warily eyeing the troupe of slender men in striped uniforms. The shift was nothing out of the ordinary. Johan hit a 175er in the face with the butt of his rifle for working too slowly, and the rest made sure they redoubled their efforts. For the first time, the action came uneasily, especially when he saw that familiar look of fear sat darkly in the eyes of the prisoners. What had once been the source of power had begun to feel dirty, actions that required to be washed off if Johan's soul were to live beyond the harsh requirements of his SS role. But, even so, he had a job to do, and Johan made a conscious effort to dismiss such feelings as weakness. Feelings that could stand in the way of doing a good job.

Work on the new camp next to the Klinkerwerk was underway, prisoners labouring with Schulz himself supervising, no doubt inspired by the Fuehrer's own fascination with architecture.

Johan saluted the commander as he passed. Schulz had a roll of papers in his hand, a pencil behind his ear and a fat cigar dangling from the corner of his mouth. He was yelling at a hapless prisoner, and Johan noticed Schulz's hand was caressing his belt, where he kept his pistol. When he saw Johan, Schulz seemed to forget all about the prisoner and turned to salute back. His eyes were now bloodshot and yellowing, and Johan noticed the straight-armed gesture had developed a significant tremor. He had become more and more concerned about Schulz's behaviour over the past few weeks. He was still taking the powder, and Johan guessed he was snorting bigger doses as his tolerance rose. The flask, too, was making more frequent trips to the commander's thirsty mouth.

Johan watched him from across the path. Schulz cut a shambolic figure. He had heard mutterings from some of the guards, murmurings in the quiet moments when people passed each other on shift handovers or loose-lipped chats when the officers had one too many in the social club.

Schulz has lost it.

He was addicted to the very drugs intended for experimentation on prisoners walking themselves to death at the boot-testing track.

Johan had never worked a shift there but he had known guards who did. The track was Schulz's idea and it epitomised his Sachsenhausen philosophy. He had assigned the most sadistic guards to oversee it, men without care or mercy. Johan had heard all about it over beers with Schubert, who he had come to know well. The more he learnt about Schubert the warier he became.

Schubert had grown up on the Berlin streets, orphaned after the Great War, killed men in street fights with his bare fists and was a criminal in all but name. How he was allowed into the SS Johan never knew and didn't feel inclined to ask.

Every inch of Schubert screamed violence and rage. He had been running the boot-testing track since it began with a team of assistants who never seemed to stay long. Johan wasn't sure whether their transfer requests were the result of Schubert's psychopathic intensity or the trauma of the detail itself. Both sounded pretty unbearable to Johan.

There were over a 150 prisoners put on the testing track, all provided with army-issue German boots and backpacks full of sand, set to the maximum weight a German soldier was expected to carry. Terrain was laid out on a semicircular track, consisting of broken stones, sand, and concrete. Most prisoners were handed boots a couple of sizes too small, to maximise their discomfort. They were each given pills, a new form of amphetamine developed by the top scientists in Germany. The same drug that Schulz crushed onto his office table and sucked up each nostril until his pupils were as big as black lumps of coal.

The prisoners would change within minutes, Schubert told him over a foaming stein at the social club. The surge of energy was so strong he had regularly needed to stamp down on some who had forgotten he was in charge. Johan had nodded. He'd had to *deal* with his fair share of prisoners, losing count of the number he had killed, but if the rumours were true, Schubert rivalled Schulz himself for kill count. Regardless, none of the original boot testers had survived. On average, ten men died every day, and at the end of every shift, Schubert would examine each boot and note the effect of the heavy impact. They always outlasted the men who wore them. That was guaranteed.

It was this thought that circled within his mind as he saw Schulz's shaky arm tilt skywards, and his glazed, half-distant eyes gaze back at him. Schulz's insistence on overseeing the building of the new barracks wasn't that bizarre in itself. But his sheer enthusiasm, his excitement as every brick was laid, and his lack of leadership in the main camp led to more dark whispers amongst the men in the social club. Johan's own meetings with Schulz in his smoky office had become shorter and shorter, the commander struggling to hold one thread of conversation at a time. Something always came crashing like lightning to divert his attention, an idea or detail that he had forgotten, and he would either send Johan out or bounce from the office to some unknown destination. His speech had become faster, and he permanently reeked of a combination of alcohol and oily sweat.

Johan knew Schulz was no longer fit to be camp leader. The drink and drugs had wrecked his decision-making, and his appearance was becoming more and more unhealthy. Johan realised, as he studied him now across the path, he had lost respect for Schulz both as a man and a commander. He could barely lead himself, never mind a camp of nearly three thousand SS soldiers.

Schulz's decline would prey on Johan most strongly at night, the restless hours when his thoughts would race and he analysed the bigger picture. He recalled the men he had killed with Schulz as his inspiration and mentor, the prisoners who had meekly crumbled before him. The unfettered power had been a source of pleasure. Now it lit a smouldering sense of discomfort.

Johan often relived the encounter with the Kramers, the fear in the jeweller's eyes and the cool, unbridled hate flowing from his wife like a melting ice cap. But most of all he thought of Schulz and how much his opinion of the commander had changed. A feeling would begin in the base of his stomach and rise like acid on a burning path to his brain, where it festered black and malignant. It made Johan nauseous and cold, sticky ribbons of sweat rolled down his temples. This was more than general anxiety, more than vague stress and uncertainty. Schulz's deterioration was the root cause, and the image his mind would always go back to. Schulz had made all the killing, all the barbaric cruelty and abuse, seem right. The desperate, pathetic prisoners had deserved nothing more.

Now something had followed the commander's decline like a ghost whispering weakness in Johan's ear. It was an emotion that could bring the hardest to their knees, the seedling of an idea that could destroy dynasties and raze empires to the ground. The feeling was growing, expanding, drilling deeper with every long, sleepless night, the awful offspring of guilt and torment, an evil entity that haunted the best of men.

Johan would lie awake and say its name.

Doubt.

Johan's appetite declined and Gerda began to notice a hollow dip in his cheeks. She was concerned, worried their impending wedding was playing on his mind. But in truth, his head was too full of the horrors of the camp, and the blood on his own hands, to consider matters of the heart. Johan loved her, but every week brought more madness from Schulz, more suffering for the prisoners.

One night, Gerda woke to find Johan standing in the middle of the bedroom, eyes closed, motioning as if he was washing his hands. When she shook his arm he gently pushed her away, muttering something she couldn't make out.

When she asked him about it the next morning, Johan had blamed tiredness and the ever-growing demands of the Klinkerwerk. Inside, though, he knew. The blood on his hands that used to feel necessary, justified by the greater good and the progression of the Fatherland, now marked him like a demonic stain. Had he been duped by unhinged people like Schulz? Was Hitler himself nothing more than a control freak, screaming and shouting his way to power, condemning whole peoples to a prolonged and painful death whilst he squeezed everything from them in the name of a country that wasn't even his own?

Germany wasn't Johan's country either, yet he had served it loyally and blindly. The men he had killed in the name of the Reich were countless. And what of the others? The ones whose deaths he had been part of, the firing squads where no man was burdened with the scorching touch of guilt. Johan felt their vengeful spirits slithering on his body and dipping into his mind when the night stretched slowly to morning.

Doubt had opened a door that could not be closed. If Johan tried to leave, they would ask why. What was the alternative? Fighting on the front line? Leaving Gerda behind and risking his life for a cause he had begun to question? Johan realised he barely knew the cause at all. Schulz's rhetoric and passion had swallowed him up, but now even thinking about it made him dizzy.

When the first Soviet prisoners arrived at Sachsenhausen, they came in their thousands. Schulz had to expand the camp again to accommodate them. Cramming them into the existing barracks wasn't feasible. The Soviets were tough bastards with hard jaws and eyes of steel. For the first time, Johan heard the word he had only associated with other camps, something distant and surreal he had hoped would never find him.

Extermination.

Whereas Johan could convince himself Jews were traitors and 175ers were blasphemers, the Soviets were just men, plain and simple. He tried to conjure them as demons deserving to die but he couldn't. All he could see were men, nothing more.

The swarm of Soviets, prisoners of the war, changed Sachsenhausen immediately. There was a threatening air, a tangible malevolence that hung over the camp. For the first time since he had come to Germany, Johan, Der Bestatter himself, was scared. He knew Schulz, even through the fog of drink and powder, felt it too. For the SS of Sachsenhausen, extermination became the number one priority.

The Soviets had been brought to Sachsenhausen deliberately, Schulz volunteering to test a new method of killing. Schulz had unveiled his plan to Johan personally, walking him through the rooms and corridors of Station Z. Even when it had been newly built, something about the place filled Johan's heart with ice. It felt haunted.

Johan remembered places when he was younger that scared him for no discernible reason other than his colourful imagination. He recalled especially the dark and dank basement of the orphanage. It was used to keep paperwork in dozens of boxes as well as cleaning materials. Each time he was sent there for chores, Johan couldn't wait to sprint back up the stairs, his mind tormenting him with flickering images, movements in black corners, the shadow of an unseen evil. The same fear struck him in Station Z, leaving a cold film of sweat across his forehead.

Schulz didn't seem afflicted with the same fright as he led Johan around the unit. At one point, the commander's expression was so intense Johan thought he was going to make him a martyr and execute him there and then, the first man to die in the killing zone. Schulz was so deranged he would probably see it as an honour.

The plan was convoluted and again had a lack of personal accountability at its heart. One guard would dress as a doctor and greet the prisoner in an office decked out with the instruments, charts and paraphernalia you would expect to see in such a place. He would pretend to take some standard details, ask a few questions and ascertain whether the prisoner had any gold teeth worth salvaging. Finally, the prisoner would be led to a soundproofed room and asked to stand with his back against a wall to be measured. When the prisoner was in place the "doctor" would tap on the table, a signal for a hidden guard to poke the nose of his pistol through a hole behind the measuring stick and put a bullet in the back of the prisoner's head.

The guard wearing the white coat, faking his role as a doctor, should feel no responsibility. He didn't pull the trigger.

For the guard who took the kill shot, he would never see the prisoner, only a faceless, nameless victim. Accountability wasn't even shared, it disappeared. And that suited Schulz fine.

Johan saw it was the small details that made the scheme so typical of the crazed commander. Music, for example, would play gently in the background so the prisoner was relaxed, and the sound of the gunshot was masked. None of the panic, shouting and desperation of a man about to face the firing squad. No realisation from other prisoners in the waiting room what fate awaited them.

Johan performed as both doctor and shooter, and at first it was easy work. Despite his rising feelings against Sachsenhausen's senseless murder, firing at the back of the head of a man he couldn't see bothered him little at first. Just an order to follow. In truth, he preferred acting as the doctor, a role demanding a warmer approach that was never otherwise required at Sachsenhausen. Johan found donning the white coat and stethoscope a welcome distraction from camp life. He felt like an actor on the stage and it reminded him warmly of Garland, a natural performer made for the footlights and acclaim. Johan missed his old friend. He wondered what his orphan brother would make of him now, a major cog in a killing machine sending hundreds of men to an early death. With each thought of

Garland came a stab of guilt at his role. And then, he thought of Gerda. He always thought of Gerda.

Johan walked past Schulz and led the prisoners away from the Klinkerwerk and back to the main camp. The doubt gnawed at him in a way only the worst emotions can, chewing him from the inside out. Gerda was away tonight, so Johan headed to the social club after his shift to ease his conscience. It was a Friday, so he knew it would be full. How better to restore a man's faith than being around others in the same shoes?

Johan was relying on drink more and more lately but told himself it did no harm. He knew now why so many of the older guards swigged from flasks. It smoothed the rough edges of the job. It restored humanity in men who committed inhuman acts.

The club was packed and noisy, the patrons shoulder to shoulder beneath a constant cloud of thick smoke. Johan was given several slaps on the back as he walked in, men he knew from shifts and different details across the camp.

He ordered a beer at the bar and noticed Schubert standing near him, along with a young, fresh-faced recruit eyeing Schubert with a starstruck expression.

Schubert appeared bored and his eyes lit up when he spotted Johan.

"Ah, Olsen," he said and gestured towards the recruit. "This is Stollen. He's just finished his first week and offered to buy me a beer, fancy that. Stollen, this is my good friend Johan Olsen."

Johan shook Stollen's clammy hand. His grip was limp and he wore a dumb expression.

"You're the Norwegian!" He sounded like an excited schoolboy. "Der Bestatter! I've heard of you."

Johan smiled widely, surprised at its sincerity. "Yes, that's me."

Stollen flushed. "Then I'll buy you a drink too. I know this is going to sound odd, but men like you are the reason I joined."

Stollen signalled to the barman for another beer and scraped some coins from his pocket. Johan could see from his reddened cheeks he had either been at the bar for a while or couldn't hold his drink. Looking closer, Johan decided it was probably the latter.

"I'll tell you something Officer Schubert did today," Stollen clapped his hand on Schubert's shoulder, an action that caused Schubert to flinch. He was always on guard.

Johan drank his beer and nodded to give Stollen the go ahead to begin his story.

"There was a queer talking at roll-call. He was giving one of the kapos hell. So Schubert goes over and decides to fuck with him. He takes off his cap, chucks it into the custody zone, and tells him to get it. So this 175er has the choice: step out-of-bounds and be shot dead or refuse the order of an officer and be shot dead. One-way ticket, whatever he did. Different train, same destination. Genius."

A story like that a few weeks ago would have brushed off Johan's conscience without a second thought. But even as Stollen reached the end Johan felt a chill shoot down his spine.

"What did he do? The 175er?" Johan asked. He grabbed his beer and took a large swig. He knew the prisoner was dead. He had heard gunfire at roll-call that morning. He heard it every morning.

"What do you think? When Officer Schubert is asking you to do something, you don't fucking say no! He went to get the cap, Schubert gives the hand signal to the nearest tower, and the queer gets pumped full of bullets. He'll be cooked by now. Auf Wiedersehen, Uranian!"

Schubert grinned wryly. "He wrecked my cap too. Three bullets went clean through it. Have to order another out my own wages. Imagine that."

Stollen laughed, belched and sloshed beer down his uniform.

Entertainment at the club was often provided by prisoners. Sometimes if there was enough interest, the canteen, a bulky green building that could accommodate larger crowds, would be used for events instead. They would put on plays, sing and dance, and some of the German prisoners would even tell jokes in one-man stand-up routines. On a previous Friday night, a kapo had performed an impression of Schulz whilst the commander was in the audience, something Johan watched in both horror and amusement. He was surprised how good-natured Schulz had been, roaring with laughter and loudly congratulating the prisoner afterwards.

Schulz must have been in a generous mood that night, although Johan wasn't sure he had seen the prisoner again. He wondered if the man had disappeared back into the ever-growing Sachsenhausen population or if Schulz's sense of humour had taken a U-turn in the days that followed.

Now Johan watched the camp's sports and social officer, a popular round-faced, ruddy-cheeked fellow named Richter, walk to the raised stage at the opposite end of the room and clear his throat. After a few seconds, the crowd quietened and turned to face him.

Richter was a showman who liked to introduce the acts with aplomb, even though they were worthless prisoners, and tonight was no exception.

"Ladies and gentlemen, our entertainment this evening comes in the form of a stunning solo gymnastics performance. This prisoner hails from the glittering fjords of Norway, where he was a star on the rise before he came to join us in Sachsenhausen. He leaps, he bends, he makes moves you and I couldn't match in our dreams. Gentlemen, welcome, the Dancing Norwegian."

Richter withdrew to the side as a slight figure entered.

Johan put down his beer and tried to focus through the thick smoky cloud as music began and the man jumped, stretched and twisted across the stage. He remembered the flash of blond he had seen the day the guard fell from Tower A. His pulse raced.

Even through the tobacco fog he knew those fluid movements, the fair shade of hair now cropped closely to the dancer's skull. Although the frame was wirier than the last time he had seen him, he recognised his build, the length of his arms and legs, the effortless movements of every limb. The crowd in the club were watching in silence, held by the brief vignette of beauty in the vilest of settings.

Johan watched his best friend, his orphan brother, dance on the Sachsenhausen stage and his heart filled with ice.

Chapter Thirty-Four

GARLAND - 1944

Garland awoke with a start, his heart racing. The aurora had carried him away again, but this time there was an ominous tone to his dreams, the brightness fading to a smoky dark with evil licking at its edges.

He jumped from his bunk and brushed the black lice from his body, so thin now that it was ridged with bone. He looked at his friends. Max slept, his face still scarred and swollen from the beating a few weeks ago. Gustave was stretching, rousing as the red morning sun peeked through the window. Hugo was already awake, pulling on his ill-fitting striped uniform.

But there was something wrong with his face.

"What's the matter?" Hugo asked, buttoning his shirt whilst Garland stared at him.

Garland tried to speak but he couldn't. Hugo's head was a gory mess, a huge crater exposing white skull where it had caved inwards, dark blood covering his left eye and running down the side of his face.

Garland lurched forward. He could see wisps of black rising from the floor and the world spun. He saw Max and Gustave rise from their beds, felt hands on his shoulders as he closed his eyes and slumped to the floor. He could hear yelling in German, followed by the loud crack of a rifle. The screams, which Garland could see, were inky colours shooting across his vision.

When he opened his eyes, Hugo's face had returned to normal.

"What's wrong, Garland?" It was Max, stroking his head. Other prisoners had gathered around. It wasn't unusual to see a man lose his mind, and it wasn't the first time Garland had collapsed. Now as he struggled to his feet, he saw Fats watching, black eyes staring under arched brows.

Garland looked closely at Hugo. The crater in his skull had gone, but there was a fine black mist surrounding him. His eyes were grey.

Somewhere in the distance a crow cawed, a sound Garland couldn't remember ever hearing in Sachsenhausen.

"Hugo," Garland began, his voice cracked and dry. "Be careful today."

Hugo frowned and laughed nervously. "Me? Why?"

Max looked up at Hugo and nodded. "Did you see something, Garland?"

Garland had finally told Max about the visions. He hadn't mentioned the aurora, how it had carried him into the bodies of the escaping prisoner and the SS gunner, but he had described the rest. . .

Jesse Owens, the swastikas and flags that came alive, skeletal wraiths clawing through furnace flames, the soul-wrenching premonitions that left him sick with panic and fear. Max seemed to believe him, but Garland wasn't sure if he was being polite. He had considered trying to show Max but nerves always got the better of him. So many things could go wrong.

"What are you on about, Garland?" Gus asked. "You're scaring him."

"I'm not scared," Hugo told them, but his hands shook as he tied his boot laces.

Garland looked over at the thousands in formation for roll-call. As always, they made a perfect semicircle, and with so many new arrivals, the sight was even more impressive.

The legions of Soviets had changed the atmosphere in the camp not just for the guards but the prisoners too. They pretty much kept to their own, but the influx of so many had made food scarcer and space almost non-existent. Garland could also sense something new, a mood that hung over Sachsenhausen, a foreboding that seemed to touch the SS as well as the prisoners.

The war, too, felt closer and intensified day by day. Garland could hear aeroplanes and distant bombs, even the shouts of soldiers. He didn't know whether they were real or a part of his gift. He never asked the others if they could hear the same.

As he stood in line his mind kept rolling back to Hugo. Even now, standing three metres away, Garland could see a thin mist moving around him. The effect was like someone drawing on a cigarette or cigar, but the smoke was dark, odourless, and only Garland could see it. Something was going to happen, Garland knew, but he was powerless. He prayed Hugo would do nothing to put himself in danger, willed his instinct to be wrong this time, even though it never had been.

Fats did the roll-call for their barracks, as he did each day, under the watchful eye of the SS and Tower A's machine gun pointed towards them, hanging over the prisoners like the sword of Damocles. It was always a fraught way to begin the day, the ranks of men at the mercy of brutal guards happy to begin as they meant to go on.

Fats walked the line of prisoners, reading out numbers, but his expression changed when he reached Garland, Gustave, Max and Hugo. He stared in their faces one by one, the kapo's rancid breath like a toxin Garland could almost taste. He shut his eyes.

"We all know you 175ers are here, don't we?" Fats's face contorted in a scowl. "Whatever the fuck that episode was this morning, the sooner you're in the ground, the better."

Garland thought the kapo resembled a cartoon devil, his slick black hair like horns above his lined forehead. Unlike the rest, Fats had avoided the head shave, one of the perks of the job. But it still crawled with lice.

He moved to Max, insulting his size and his lack of intelligence, and called Gus a snail-eating French sheep fucker. Gus smiled and Fats cracked him across the mouth with the back of his hand.

Then Fats came to Hugo.

"And you." The taunting began. "You call yourself a Berliner? You're an insult to Berlin. You are shit on the great city's shoe. You don't even deserve to be German. Fiddling with married men. I hope they cut off your cock and shove it down your throat before they bury you. If your mother's alive she'll wish the same you piece. —"

Hugo landed the head butt with a movement so quick and unexpected Fats didn't even have time to blink. His nose shattered with a single, sickening crack and he reeled backwards as a young guard ran over. He looked like a fresh recruit.

"What's going on?" he asked Fats. "You're in charge over here. Why can't you control them?"

The kapo began to speak but he was gurgling his own blood and the guard couldn't understand.

Schubert, who had been watching from a distance, walked over.

"I'll deal with this, Stollen," Schubert told the young officer. "Which one of you attacked this man?"

Garland grimaced. He stepped forward. "I did."

"Tut, tut, N2871." Schubert was already enjoying himself. "You know you have to treat this man like you would treat a guard. He is our representative in your barracks."

He paused and brandished his pistol. "Now, do I need to make an example of you?"

Garland's eyes darted to Fats. He could see the flicker of confusion, the kapo's dark pupils darting one way then the other. Garland willed him to stay silent, imagined deep in his mind a needle and thread sewing Fats's lips together. Fats was trying to talk but he couldn't. All that came from his closed mouth was a jumble of hisses and high-pitched squeaks. Garland fought back a smile. It was working.

"What the hell's wrong with you?" Schubert was thrown. "What the. . ."

"It was me," Hugo had suddenly stepped forward. "I did it."

He was looking Schubert straight in the eye. The mist around him grew thicker, darker.

"No, Hugo!" Garland yelled.

Schubert pointed the pistol at Garland. "Shut up."

He looked back to Fats, sweating and confused. The shock of seeing Hugo move had broken Garland's concentration and Fats began to talk.

"He's right." The kapo spat blood at his feet. "The Norwegian was covering for the other queer."

Schubert moved until he was nose to nose with Garland. His eyes were wild.

"Does this excite you, boy? A man of the SS being so close? I bet you'd love me, wouldn't you, blondie?"

Schubert grinned and punched Garland in the face, the skin on his cheek splitting in a spray of crimson. Garland saw hundreds of heads turn to watch as he fell backwards to the ground.

"But you?" Schubert spun to Hugo, holding the stage like a Broadway veteran.

Schubert put his left hand on Hugo's throat and Garland saw the black mist thicken and rise, a boiling cloud that left the two men blurred and shapeless. To Garland it looked like a show from his old theatre world, a backlit scene complete with dry ice and an atmosphere that promised tragedy.

"You would've let your friend take a beating for your mistake." Schubert's voice was rich and carried across the ranks of prisoners. "You're the lowest of the low. A queer by name and nature. A German but a man unworthy of the privilege, unworthy of being called a man at all."

He let go of Hugo and walked away as Garland sat up. The mist was so dense he struggled to make out Hugo's face, but he knew what was coming. He had seen it already.

When he was thirty yards away, Schubert took off his cap and threw it towards the electrified fence which lined the perimeter of the camp. It landed on the grey stones next to the fence, a place out-of-bounds for all prisoners. *The death strip.*

Schubert turned back to face Hugo.

"Pick up my cap, queer."

Hugo stared back. "But. . . but. . ."

"Pick up the fucking cap!" Schubert yelled, his voice an earthquake.

No one moved as Hugo stepped towards the perimeter. He nodded at Garland, Max and Gustave as he walked slowly past, mouthing "Sorry" to Garland when their eyes met.

"Hurry you queer piece of shit!" Schubert yelled. The morning light blazed in his eyes and Garland thought he looked inhuman, a monster from another world.

Hugo paused at the edge of the perimeter and glanced over at Schubert.

Schubert gestured for him to continue. Hugo closed his eyes and put his right foot forward, gravel crunching in the silence as Schubert raised his hand.

The gunfire from the watchtower above was a sudden and deafening explosion.

Hugo's body crumpled to the ground and Garland saw a pool of blood grow beneath his head. The black mist that had surrounded him faded to a thin white and then gradually disappeared.

Schubert and Stollen walked away, laughing.

Garland cried silently. The tears flowed diagonally across his cheeks and dripped on the sandy ground. He had known but was powerless, able to see his friend's future but not to save him. He couldn't understand why his gift was so cruel. He had to use it to get him and his friends out of this hell, but until he could harness what lived inside him, nothing would change. He looked up at the gaunt faces of Max and Gustave. Would they be next? Would Garland see their broken corpses whilst they still lived and breathed? He thought of the words from the unseen Englishman, a message from beyond his consciousness, and again considered that Johan was moving somewhere in the vast, sprawling camp. He had to find him, whatever it took.

Garland pulled himself to his feet and thought of Richter, the jovial, chubby guard who ran the social club. His mind ticked on.

There was no time to mourn Hugo. The prisoners were ordered to their work even as his body was still lying where it had fallen. Garland and Gustave had to live with their grief and labour as if nothing had happened.

Garland saw his chance to speak to Gustave during a short break.

"You've sung in the club, haven't you?"

Gustave looked back, confused.

"Garland that's a weird question." His eyes were bloodshot. "I don't even feel like talking after what I've just seen. I'd rather ask you how you knew. How you. . ."

Garland stared at the blue, birdless sky.

"I've never told you this but I have. . . feelings. Visions. I sometimes sense when something's going to happen, something bad."

Gustave shook his head. "I know you tried to stop it, but I just don't understand. You're. . . psychic?"

Garland felt bone-tired just talking. "I don't know what I am. There's other stuff too. I can move things, sometimes, but I don't know how it happens."

"You have to use it!" Gustave had suddenly come alive. "You must. You could get us out of here. You could save us all!"

"Don't you think I've thought about that?" Garland heard the snap in his voice. "I don't understand it myself. It could do more harm than good. It could get us all killed."

Gustave stared at the floor. "We're dead anyway, friend. What could be worse than this?"

Garland nodded, glad he had told Gustave but stressed by the pressure of being some kind of saviour.

"So, about the guard's social club? And the canteen?"

Gustave stroked his striped beard. "Ah. The Green Monster. Stay away from there, Garland. Some don't make it out, you know. Those guards are even bigger devils with a few beers inside them. That place has seen more horror than the Klinkerwerk itself, I bet."

"The guard you told me about," Garland said. "It must be Johan. I have to find him, Gus. That could be our ticket out of here. Not magic, not visions. But my friend in the SS."

Gustave laughed, holding his belly. It was a humourless chuckle, dry and soft.

"You think the SS are friends to people like us? If he was your friend in an old life, he's not now. You think he'd risk his own life for yours? Never mind mine? No, this is hopeless. I'd rather go with your gift."

Garland had never considered Johan deserting him, even though they had drifted over the years. Would his orphan brother really become his enemy? Garland found it impossible to believe.

"There was a comedian once," Gustave said "A German, trade union man who was a kapo like Fats. He went on stage at the Green Monster and did impressions of Schulz. Everything was okay on the night and crazy Schulz even laughed. Then one morning they found the kapo hanging from a pole. His mouth had been slit wide open like a massive grin."

Garland swallowed and fell silent for a few seconds. "Gus, trust me, please. Johan will help. He's the closest thing to family I've ever had. We came to Berlin together. He owes me. And he *will* help. I promise."

"Okay." Gustave sighed, still not convinced. "What do you want me to do?"

Garland said four words.

"Get me an audition."

Richter was chatting to a group of other guards outside a barrack block when Gustave made his move.

"Sir," he said, approaching gingerly. "May I ask a question?"

The guards bristled but Richter, smiling as always, gestured for them to be calm and turned to face Gustave.

"How is my favourite French singer?" Richter asked. The man emitted warmth. Without the uniform no one would pick him as SS, another cold-blooded killer with evil in his heart. Gustave said talking to Richter made him feel human again.

"I'm okay thanks, sir. I was wondering if I could ask you a favour."

The guards around them laughed, and Richter himself slapped his knee and chuckled. "What kind of *favour* can a lowly SS officer like myself do for an important Frenchman like you?"

Gus smiled and bowed his head as he spoke. "I was wondering if you had a slot for an entertainer over the next couple of days."

Richter raised his eyebrows and nodded. "You are a fantastic singer, boy. Wonderful! I have a spot for tonight. That's if you aren't otherwise engaged?"

He smiled as he said it, and the guards behind him laughed like sycophants.

"It's not for me, Officer Richter. It's for my friend."

Gustave gestured and Garland stepped forward. The guards bristled again but Richter's smile remained between his red chubby cheeks.

"And who is this?" Richter looked Garland up and down.

"My name is Garland Lund, sir."

Richter put a puzzled look on his face.

"Lund," he said. "Not a German name. Or French."

"Norwegian, sir. I'm from Oslo."

Richter was still smiling. "And how are you going to entertain our officers tonight, Mr Lund of Norway?"

Garland held his nerve, the other guards staring and silent.

"I dance, sir. I was one of the best in Norway."

Richter nodded, his cheeks wobbling as he did. One of the guards behind cooed mockingly, but Richter waved his hand to silence him. Garland was amazed someone with such a gentle, friendly demeanour could hold such sway.

Richter studied Garland like a livestock judge in a show ring.

"I have to say, boy, the men aren't really into dancing. Singing, comedy, drama, perhaps. But dancing? You look like a slip of a boy too, hardly built for ballet."

Garland had a vision of himself in his prime.

Was that really me?

"You'd be surprised, sir, although I was fitter when I worked in the Berlin theatres."

"Berlin theatres as well as Norway?" Richter looked impressed. "You must be good, my blond friend."

"Yes, sir. I once met Dr Goebbels himself. It was a proud day." Garland swallowed. It had been true at the time.

The guards fell silent and for the first time Richter's smile disappeared, the warmth suddenly chilled like a lone cloud passing the sun on a summer's day.

"Goebbels, you say?" He turned to the guards and when he looked back at Gustave he was smiling again. "Well it sounds like you've unearthed a gem for us here."

He put his cheerful gaze on Garland.

"Let's see what you've got, Mr Lund of Norway. No music. No stage. Just here and now. I'll give you one go and if I'm impressed, I'll put you on tonight."

"Thank you, sir. You won't regret it."

Garland stepped back and looked down at the gritty, sandy surface only a few metres wide. His usual ballet wouldn't cut it in front of a room full of drunk murderers. Brutal men wouldn't want to see grace. They needed to be wowed a different way.

He threw his body around, flipping, somersaulting and spinning to a soundtrack in his own head. As he danced he felt the air carry his body. He was skinny but his limbs felt supple and his muscles were hardened after months of constant labour. He twisted, raised himself on his toes, soared high through the air and swirled gracefully to the finale, rolling to spring back to his feet. He could see the blazing colours of the aurora in his peripheral vision, and he felt a surge of energy, positive emotions flying to his brain.

When he finished, the only sounds were nearby crickets and the distant drone of an overhead plane turning towards Berlin. Richter broke the silence by clashing his palms together in a loud, bellowing clap. The guards joined him. Others who had watched from a distance, prisoners and guards alike, stared in awe.

Gustave smiled and nodded. Then he began clapping, too.

Garland's calves and arms were seizing up, dehydration causing agonising cramps, but he grinned against the pain.

"Exquisite!" Richter yelled over his claps. "I'll put you on the list tonight. Report to the club at 1900 hours prompt."

Garland half bowed, a throwback to the stages of Oslo and Berlin.

"Thank you, sir. I'll look forward to it."

Garland and Gustave made their way back to their barracks. Although Hugo's death lay heavy, Garland's performance had been an unexpected bright spot on the blackest of days.

More importantly, Garland hoped to finally see Johan and ask for his help. It had to work. The alternatives didn't bear thinking about.

Getting inside the Green Monster was easier than Garland expected. He had given his name to the guards lining the approach to the building, which lay just beyond Tower A. As he got closer, he took in its structure. From the outside the building was nondescript; it could have been another barracks inside the walls of the prison. Like many buildings in Sachsenhausen, it formed an L-shape. Unlike others, it was painted in a dirty shade of green. Garland wondered why the SS had picked such an unattractive colour, almost camouflaging the building against the trees and grass that framed it. Several long windows lined the side of the club and Garland could see the outlines of officers drinking from giant steins. It took him back, momentarily, to his days with Gianni in the bustling Friedrichstrasse bars. What would that busy street look like now, in the midst of war? And what about Gianni? Would he have been called to fight for Italy, allies of the Germans? Would he still be talking about opera and the finest Italian food? Would he even be alive?

Garland shook off the memories and began walking. A set of brick steps led to the social club's main entrance where three officers eyed him with disdain as he approached.

"Name?" one of them yelled. He held a scruffy sheet of paper covered with scrawled German.

"Garland Lund. Dancer."

Using his name again felt dangerous and strange.

The officer with the paper looked him up and down, and Garland watched his eyes settle on the pink triangle on his chest. The officer broke out into a grin.

"Of course. What other pursuit would a queer take up? Get in here then, maggot. We'll show you where to go."

Another guard led him to a small, shabby changing room.

"But I don't have any. . ."

"Costume?" It was Richter. He passed Garland a white T-shirt and what looked like a pair of baggy football shorts. "Not the best but they will have to do."

Richter stared at the ceiling, the plaster cracked and flaking like egg shell.

"Ballet." There was a melancholy as he said the word. "It was always my favourite, in the old days. I used to go every night in Berlin with some of my closest friends. We'd dress to the nines and paint the town red. Theatre, cabaret, and, of course, the ballet."

He paused and studied Garland with admiration, Garland uncomfortable with something he once would have welcomed.

"Your audition was tremendous young man," Richter told him. "As good as any ballet I've seen in the city. A talented and good-looking Norwegian like you shouldn't be in here."

Garland stood straighter, his chest firm.

"Thank you, sir. I never thought I belonged in here either."

Garland took a breath and seized the moment.

"My best friend, my brother, not my real brother but. . . he's called Johan Olsen. He's a guard here, sir. If only I could just speak to him?"

Richter's eyes widened and his jaw fell. "You know Der Bestatter?"

Garland translated in his head. *The Undertaker.* Was it a joke? What kind of man had Johan become?

He nodded.

"A fine officer," Richter said. "Quiet. Intense. One of Commander Schulz's favourites. Your friend is a strong man who can hold his ale and haul dead bodies to the incinerator like he was carrying a basket of bread to his grandmother's house."

Garland tried to hide his shock and ignore the nausea building in his gut.

"Nothing fazes him," Richter went on. "You really think he can get you out of here?"

Garland felt his eyes fill and brushed at them quickly. "I'm hoping so, sir. I'm really hoping so."

Richter reached forward to rest his hand on Garland's shoulder, the pressure light but reassuring.

"Never hope, young man." His voice was touched with sadness again. "Hope is dangerous in here. It's what can finally snap a man's will. A little hope you perhaps can survive. But when hope turns into something tangible, something you can touch, that's when the danger begins."

Richter squeezed Garland's shoulder and dropped his hand. "You're crossing that line, boy," he went on. "Your hope is already too big. I know Der Bestatter. He's a cold fish. I'm not sure he's the same man you remember. I advise that you let go of your hope a little."

Garland looked to the floor. "Hope is all I've got, Mr Richter. My brother is here and he owes me."

Richter nodded and clapped his hands once, a gesture that seemed to say, "Warning over, the rest is up to you."

"Then I wish you the best of luck, boy." Richter smiled but what Garland saw was sympathy not humour.

"Get changed and be ready to perform in around twenty minutes. Then I'll arrange for you to see your friend. But don't say I didn't warn you."

Richter left the room and Garland listened to his pounding heart. Its rhythm sounded like hope. Forbidden and dangerous as it was.

He came onto the stage surrounded by thick smoke. Garland took a moment to realise it came from dozens of cigarettes and cigars not one of his visions. There were at least sixty people in the room. Richter had announced him like an old-time master of ceremonies then stepped away, leaving Garland alone. It felt good to be out of the striped uniform, away from the pink triangle and the number that defined his existence. His dance outfit was soft and comfortable against his skin.

A single spotlight shone directly on him, darkening the faces in the crowd and playing through the smoke that swirled around him. He performed the same solo he had danced for Richter and the guards but this time he had music. The sound was exquisite. It was the first time Garland had heard any real music since he came to the camp, and as he leapt, pivoted, and somersaulted across the stage, he felt every note thrum through his body. Garland moved smoothly through the routine and felt the colours of the aurora lifting him, running in his veins like life blood. They energised him, made him fluid, and he felt himself rising on a force beyond his understanding, an energy that pulled his soul higher and higher.

When he finished, stance strong and hands in the air, there was silence. Then Garland heard the familiar sound of Richter's booming clap, and like a ripple on a mill pond, the shouts and ovation began.

Garland held a bow but ignored the applause, his eyes scanning the room in vain for Johan's blond hair and bulky shoulders. It was too dark and smoky even from the elevated stage.

He felt a hand on his arm and Richter led him back to the same small room.

"Wunderbar!" he said as he went to close the door. "You've got some talent, boy. Now, wait here and I'll go and get your friend."

Garland was already pumped with adrenaline. Now he felt breathless and faint, the aurora's electric touch tingling all over him and the spectrum of lights flickering in the corner of his vision.

The door opened with a creak. Richter stepped in and gestured to Garland. Then the tall, muscular frame of Johan walked into the room. It seemed to happen in slow motion. He looked bigger in his uniform, and Garland's racing heart seemed to jump and sink simultaneously. That uniform he had come to hate, wrapped around the person he had loved more than anything in his life.

They embraced. It was a strong, tight hug that only lasted seconds but could have been hours. Johan tapped Garland on his back with both hands. Garland began to cry.

"Garland. What are you doing here? Why. . . ?"

Garland looked into Johan's eyes. They seemed different somehow, greyer and colder. It was as if something inside the Johan he used to know had died, a part of his humanity shed like a snake squirming out of its dead skin. The sight made Garland weep more.

"You've got to get me out, Johan," he pleaded through his tears. "I'll die in here."

Johan glanced behind him, but Richter had slipped silently from the room.

"What did you do Garland?" Johan wiped at the tears on Garland's cheeks. "I don't understand."

Garland was silent and then blurted out the words. "They thought I was homosexual."

Johan raked a hand over his thick blond hair and slowly shook his head like a man grappling with the mysteries of the universe.

"But, Garland, that's. . . Why would they think that?"

"I. . . I don't know." The words seemed to catch in Garland's throat. "Someone told them, someone. . ."

Garland hitched a heavy, tearful breath. "Help me, Johan, just help me, please."

Chapter Thirty-Five

JOHAN - 1944

Johan's head was spinning. It was too much information to process at once, and the beers had made his judgement cloudier than the smoke that hung over his head.

Garland was here. A convicted prisoner at Sachsenhausen. His brother from the orphanage. His best friend.

Johan had rushed to see Richter as soon as the applause began, pushing his way to the opposite side of the room, spilling beer and taking a few angry shoves as he bustled through. Richter had been expecting him, a smile on his fat, rosy face as he led him to a small changing room.

Johan hadn't seen Garland for years, and his appearance had shocked him. The cotton T-shirt clung to Garland's sweat-soaked body. Johan could count the bones in his ribcage and see his breastbone move up and down with each ragged, rattling breath. Garland's shoulders were jagged blades, and his face was gaunt, concave cheeks and dark, hollow sockets holding dull blue eyes.

By the look of Garland, he had been in Sachsenhausen a while. How could Johan not have known? How had he never noticed him? He had felt his own tears well as he held his friend, his brother.

The reunion had been brief but those short minutes played over and over like an endless loop for Johan.

Garland had been wrongly arrested for homosexuality. It wasn't uncommon, people falsely reporting others they had a grudge against. Maybe it was his dancing. Johan cursed himself for not being more vigilant, for not warning Garland that ballet might be too flamboyant for a man in Nazi Germany. Sharp pangs of guilt stabbed at his insides. Johan had brought Garland from a safe and happy life in Norway to a war-torn country that had thrown him in with the rats.

Rats.

Johan had learnt to see the prisoners as vermin when he began at Dachau. Now he could see them as men, human beings like Garland in his ruined, emaciated body. He would likely die and, marked as a homosexual, the Klinkerwerk beckoned. It would finish him sooner or later. Johan had at least warned Garland about that.

"What's your work detail?" he had asked him.

"I'm a shoemaker." Garland had lifted his hands to show the ragged, calloused skin on his palms and the gnarled bones of his knuckles.

"That's not the worst detail, believe me," Johan told him. "Avoid the Klinkerwerk, Garland. That's where I am. Avoid it at all costs. And you wear the pink. . . of all the colours you wear the pink."

They had hugged each other again, Johan holding Garland more gently, frightened he would snap in his hands.

"I have to go but I'll do something," Johan had told him. "I'll get you out of here, Garland. I promise."

Johan had walked from the room, turning to smile at Garland and closing the door behind him. Richter was standing in the passageway.

"He's a good boy," Richter said. "It's true, I suppose. You were orphans together? Like brothers?"

Johan had nodded glumly.

"And you'll try and get him out of here? Der Bestatter helping a homosexual to get himself released. It's quite a story."

Johan had nodded again. "I promised him."

Johan had slipped out through the back exit of the club, a cool breeze biting his cheeks as he inhaled the night air.

Walking home he thought about Garland and how he could set him free. But an image of Schulz and the blood-red blade of a samurai sword took root in his mind.

Gerda took so long to answer Johan was about to hang up when he finally heard her voice.

"You've been drinking," she said after his slurred greeting.

"Garland is here, he's in Sachsenhausen." Johan had blurted out the words, his voice choked.

He told Gerda about their meeting at the club, Garland's story and his pitiful appearance, and finally his promise to help.

"Oh Jo, what have you got yourself into?"

"He's a brother," Johan told her. "I brought him here."

"I'm not doubting it," Gerda said, softness now in her tone. "In fact, you have a bigger duty to help him than your German comrades."

The words worked like a key that unlocked something Johan had kept hidden, secrets that lay with him in his fearful, sleepless nights.

"Gerda." His voice wavered. "I'm starting to have. . ."

"You're having doubts."

Johan shut his eyes to hold back the tears and snatched a breath with a gurgling sound. Then he released it, a tormented wail that let loose every emotion he had kept so tightly in chains. All of the fear and guilt poured out of him like raging white water.

In Garland's sunken eyes Johan had seen human devastation, faced the horrors he had helped to orchestrate. He saw the evil he was part of and felt his heart split in two.

Johan was trapped, as much a prisoner in Sachsenhausen as the desperate souls who wore the stripes and triangles.

"Johan." Gerda's voice brought him back. "You've got to keep it together. I've never wanted to talk about your job, and I don't want to know the terrible things that happen in the camp, but you've just been a pawn in all of this."

Johan felt tiredness tearing at him and he yearned for the shut-off valve of sleep.

"It will be hard, but this is your chance," Gerda told him. "You've been given some power now, some control. You can try and rebalance everything."

Johan knew what he would be putting at stake, what he had to lose.

"I might die, Gerda. You don't know Schulz. He's a maniac."

Static bubbled on the line as he mentioned the commander's name, and Johan feared it was an omen.

He wondered out loud if, by giving up his own life, his sins would be forgiven.

"Only God can do that," Gerda told him. "But this is something you can do that's right. This isn't *my* Berlin. It's not *my* Germany anymore. And she was never yours, Johan. Fight the battle that's yours. Fight for your friend."

Johan understood now he had been beguiled by power, by his own need to belong. That was why he signed up, why he swallowed everything the Reich promised, but it was built on evil and lies. He needed to do what was right. It was time.

"I'm here for you," he heard Gerda say. "I'll get the first train tomorrow."

Johan cried more tears, and by the time he put down the phone, his eyes were raw and his throat burnt. He lay back on his bed and fell into a half-sleep, emotions running like raindrops down a window, one overtaking the other only to sink back and disappear in the growing pool.

He knew Gerda was right, and the strength of his love for her almost overwhelmed him. Knowing she would be waiting when all this was done was the light at the end of a long, bleak tunnel. Johan pictured her face and wished she was lying next to him, wanted her arms and her scent and her soft kisses.

Outside his window the song thrush fell silent as Johan drifted into deep sleep. He dreamt of Gerda and her beautiful smile. He couldn't know, but dreams were all he would have.

The next morning, Johan went to the camp early, despite it being his day off, and knocked on Schulz's office door. He knew the commander's routine. Schulz began overseeing work on the new Klinkerwerk barracks at nine each day, so Johan went in at seven to catch him.

The usual manic look was plastered on Schulz's face. He had lost weight, and the lines on his forehead had deepened. The bags around his eyes hung heavy and had a dark-purple tinge. Johan wondered if he ever slept.

The room was, as always, already clouded with cigar smoke and a sharp smell of urine drifted under the rich odour of tobacco. The office reeked of illness, of a man older than Schulz in the last throes of life. Johan stared into the commander's yellowing eyes and considered how he was steadily killing himself. The booze and pills were slow bullets from a gun Schulz himself had fired.

"What is it, Olsen? You pick a busy time."

"How is the construction going, sir?"

"It's going as well as it can with a workforce of the most incompetent imbeciles to ever walk the earth." Schulz's impatience was a bad sign. "So what can I do for you?"

Johan felt his stomach clench but he held his nerve.

"Sir, I'm sure you know how highly I respect you, and I hope I have earned your respect in return."

Schulz stared silently back at him, his dull eyes matching the walls that had faded to a dirty gold.

"There's a prisoner here," Johan continued. "Garland Lund. A man I grew up with in an Oslo orphanage. He's been wrongfully imprisoned."

Schulz let out a slow breath, and Johan could hear thick phlegm in his chest. His cheeks were covered with ruddy bumps and thin red lines. He stood and looked out of the tiny window, at the trees outside the camp.

"So, you're saying the Gestapo made a mistake?"

Johan silently considered the question for a few seconds, sensing a trap.

"No, sir. I believe he was falsely accused. The information the Gestapo acted on was incorrect. They did their duty honourably but. . ."

"And you want your friend freed."

Johan nodded. "Yes, sir."

"On what charge was he arrested?"

Johan swallowed hard, the words a barricade in his throat.

"Homosexuality, sir, but falsely accused, as I say."

"Are you sure?" Schulz had turned from the window to give Johan his full gaze. "Many choose to blaspheme, Olsen."

Johan nodded. "I know him as much as I know myself. He's not homosexual."

Schulz returned to his chair and reached for the cigar that was smouldering in the ashtray on his cluttered desk.

"Olsen, there are processes to follow. I need to involve the Gestapo. If I condone the release of a man on the say-so of a guard, it sets a precedent. You know that, don't you?"

"I think there's been confusion about his sexual preferences, sir." Johan held his ground. "He's a dancer, he was the best in Oslo, he. . ."

Schulz cut him off.

"You'll need to sign papers for the Gestapo. To vouch for him. The Gestapo administrator, Dannel, owes me a favour or two, he should be able to sort this out for your friend. But, Olsen, it will be on your head. And mine."

Johan felt light-headed with relief, stunned at Schulz's mercy as the commander spoke again.

"But if there's any hint he's homosexual, if you've misled me in any way, I'll throw you in there with the rats and I'll make you wear the pink. You'll be hauling bodies around with the stripes on your back. Do you hear me, Der Bestatter?"

"Yes, sir." Johan rose on shaky legs. "Thank you, sir. You won't regret it."

Schulz gave Johan a thin smile. "I'll ask one of the men to draw up the paperwork. Report back here at six tonight."

Johan walked out smiling, replaying Schulz's words again and again to convince himself what he had heard was real. He had secured Garland's freedom. His orphan brother's ordeal would be over with the scribble of his signature on a simple piece of paper. He couldn't believe his luck, couldn't believe the commander had agreed. Maybe the new barracks had left him distracted. He knew he was one of Schulz's favourites. Now one or both had helped save Garland's life.

Changing his own future would surely be harder. Men didn't just leave the SS. Johan had never heard of it happening. The only time a uniform was hung up was when the owner was in a wooden box. No one resigned of their own accord.

He strode through the dusty camp past rows and rows of prisoners. He looked at the numbers and triangles on the faded material they wore, human beings reduced to a line of figures and colours. He looked at their sallow, shrivelled faces, wrinkled beyond their years, men whose souls had long been ruined by Sachsenhausen. He looked at the ones who wore the pink triangles and wondered how many had been falsely accused. How many had lost everything, their friends, families, and occupations on a vengeful lie. He thought of the ones he had killed, the lives nonchalantly snatched away at his hands. The jeweller's wife's cold look of disdain swam into his mind.

Some men aren't cut out for killing, Schulz had once told him. Back then Johan believed that had applied to others, to weaker men. But as he watched the broken prisoners avoiding his eyes as they trudged to their back-breaking work detail, he realised it wasn't weakness. Weakness was blindly following orders and blaming someone else. Weakness was ending a helpless man's life and taking pleasure in it. True strength would have been to refuse or to show mercy.

He made his way to the shoe-making workshop. At least he could give Garland the good news. Garland's release would be a start towards Johan's own redemption, a step towards salvation. God may never forgive him, but maybe his best friend and brother would.

Johan spoke briefly to the workshop manager and requested a private word with Garland, whose eyes came alive when he saw him. Johan led him outside away from prying ears.

"You're going to be released, Garland!" Johan felt like he was shouting a whisper. "I just need to sign some papers to vouch you're not homosexual and that there was a mistake, and you'll be free!"

Garland's knees buckled and Johan shot out an arm to keep him upright, holding him steady and letting the realisation sink in. Garland tried to speak but couldn't find the words, catching his breath instead with a single, hitching sob. Johan stepped back when Garland tried to hug him, raising his palms and glancing around.

"Careful," Johan said. "You're still a prisoner and I'm still a guard, at least for now."

"You're quitting?" Garland finally found his voice.

Johan nodded and looked around again. "I'm going to try. I can't do this anymore. If they let me, I'll leave. We should go home, Garland, go back to Oslo."

Johan suddenly saw his future, a normal life where he was no longer Der Bestatter, a simple existence where men didn't shrink from him in fear and people like the jeweller's wife treated him with courtesy instead of hatred. Gerda would be the rock around the rest of his days.

"Johan, I need to ask another favour," Garland said "My friends. . ."

"Garland I can only help you." Johan stopped him. "Are you telling me they were all arrested on lies as well?"

Garland stared down at his shoes and slowly shook his head.

"No." He looked ready to cry again. "But it's still so unjust. They don't deserve to be here, Johan. None of them do."

Johan could see hurt wash over Garland's face, torn between his own freedom and his friends' endless misery.

"I don't want to sound ungrateful," Garland said. "And I'll never be able to thank you enough for saving me, never. Maybe I'll be able to help them from the outside."

Johan wondered whether Garland realised how much was at stake, that he was already risking his life to get Garland free.

"People do get released," he said. "They'll still have a chance."

It was true some prisoners were freed from Sachsenhausen, but the homosexuals, Johan knew, rarely left alive. And sooner or later, the Klinkerwerk would finish them off.

"I've got to see Schulz again tonight," Johan said. "Hopefully you'll get summoned and released. I'm going to offer my resignation."

The day passed slowly. Johan tended to his garden, listening to the birds as he worked and willing the clock to eat up the hours. He wanted to see Schulz again before the maniac had a chance to change his mind, and he was desperate to be with Gerda. Every so often Johan would look at the sun and try to drag it westwards, to force it down to the horizon in the direction of Berlin.

Missing Gerda had become a physical ache that never left him unless he was too drunk to feel anything. He couldn't wait to marry her, to start their new life in Oslo, to begin a family of their own. He could talk to her tonight, once he'd asked Schulz if he could resign. All those days in the commander's poky office with its dirty walls and smoke. All those times he had stared into Schulz's crazy eyes and feared for his life. Now he was putting his head in the lion's mouth again. He had to hope respect and his record would be enough.

With bird song surrounding him and the warmth of the sun caressing the back of his neck, Johan dropped his spade, sank to his knees and prayed.

His heart was racing when he entered the office, but as he had promised, Schulz had the paperwork ready on his desk. The commander was wearing a crooked smile and a fat cigar billowed smoke from the corner of his mouth.

"I've had it drawn up." He gestured towards the document. "It's to vouch that your friend, your brother as you describe, is not a homosexual and that the Gestapo made a mistake. If you sign the statement, I'll take this to our Gestapo administrator at once."

Johan looked at the paper with its elegantly-penned wording. He leant forward and signed in the space at the bottom of the page.

"Excellent," Schulz said. His eyes were wider, more feral than Johan had ever seen them. There was something about the tone of his voice too.

"Sir, I'd like to ask something whilst you've been good enough to process this," Johan said.

Schulz raised his eyebrows, beads of sweat gathering in his hair and the deep lines that crisscrossed his brow.

He's been at the powder again

"And what would that be, Olsen?"

"I'd like to resign, if possible." Johan kept his voice respectful but firm. "I'd like to go back to Oslo. I've given Germany all I have and loved being a loyal servant to the Reich."

The lie at least sounded convincing, Johan thought.

"I'm to be married and I'd like to settle back home. Germany has occupied Norway now so it's a good opportunity to return."

Schulz nodded and picked up the contract which now had Johan's scrawled signature at the bottom.

"I had this drawn up specially, Olsen." Schulz lifted the paper a little higher. "You really should read things before you sign them, boy."

Johan felt the beginnings of something uncertain stirring deep inside, a ripple of unease rushing towards panic and confusion.

"Sir?"

"I trusted you, Olsen." The ripple was becoming a wave. "I let you in. You were officer material. You could have filled my boots!"

Schulz paused, maybe from regret, more likely out of malice.

"And then you try to release a homosexual. A *known* homosexual."

Johan felt the tsunami crashing around him, laying waste to all those dreams, swallowing up his simple future.

"I have my ear to the ground." Schulz went on. "People tell me things. And now, once this homosexual is released, you want to defect to Oslo. Flee with him, I presume. I can turn a blind eye to a few things. I can accept that men, even officers of the SS, are flawed. But you, Olsen. *You!* One of my best men, a homosexual and a deserter. An enemy of Germany and a man I was foolish to trust. You no longer wish to be an officer? Your wish is granted."

Johan's heart filled with ice. He heard the heavy trample of boots nearing the door as he took the document from Schulz's hand and read.

I, Johan Olsen, testify that I believe beyond doubt that prisoner N2871 has been falsely arrested and imprisoned. I hereby accuse the SS and the German government of law-breaking themselves. If proved otherwise, I accept the consequences of my incorrect accusations and will hand myself to the authorities as a criminal of war, spreading anti-German propaganda."

Heart hammering in his chest, Johan let his eyes trace the signature at the bottom of the page. Schulz smiled and Johan saw the blackened teeth like weather-beaten tombstones.

"No, sir," Johan felt like a man trying to talk underwater. "I can explain. I'm not. . . I wasn't. . ."

He wished he could find the words, whisper a hurried a spell to turn back time like the fairy tales he had loved as a boy, anything to take himself to a place before Germany and Sachsenhausen and the empty faces of those broken, tortured souls. He closed his eyes and thought of Oslo and the orphanage, of his friend and his brother. His eyes filled with tears.

"There they are!" Schulz shouted, a tone like triumph in is his voice. "There are the tears of the weakling. I don't get many things wrong, Olsen, but I was wrong about you. You're a traitor to this great country, a filthy homosexual, no less. And now, Der Bestatter, you'll be put to work with the rest of the vermin."

The door swung open and several guards entered the office.

"Not a conventional way for a guard to be incarcerated, Olsen, I give you that. But as I said before, our Gestapo friend owes me a favour or two and he's happy to turn a blind eye."

Johan felt one of the guards grab his arms from behind as Schulz took something from a drawer in his desk and hurled it at Johan. Hands forced behind his back, Johan watched the striped uniform hit his chest and fall to the floor. It was tattered and rank with the stench of grimy sweat. Stitched to the front was a faded pink triangle.

Chapter Thirty-Six

GARLAND - 1944

Max turned his head sideways and his mouth formed a large O before he spoke.

"We're getting out of here? We're finally going to be. . ."

His words stopped abruptly when he saw Garland's face drop. Max put his hand on his shoulder, but Garland pushed it away.

"You're going to hate me, Max. He could only release me. He could only argue for one of us."

Silence fell for a few seconds, the only noise the faint thrum of an aeroplane to the west.

Max looked up to the sky.

"Of course," he said quietly. "How was he going to present a case for all of us? It wouldn't make any sense."

Then he smiled, only warmth in his eyes.

"You've got your chance though, Garland! You've got to take it."

Garland had told Max how Johan had arranged his freedom, convinced Schulz he had been wrongly accused and should never have been thrown behind Sachsenhausen's walls.

"We might not see each other again," Garland said now. "What if you never get out?"

Max held Garland's hand. "I could. I will! Maybe I'll escape. I'll dig a tunnel. Me and Gus, we'll bore our way out of here."

"Then you'll come and live in Oslo." Garland let himself enjoy the fantasy, even if it was only for these moments. "I'll show you the Oslofjord, the way the light glistens from the water. You should see it, Max. It looks like it's made of silk. I should never have left."

Max smiled again. "But then we would never have met. That's the one thing in this whole sorry shitshow I'll never regret. Don't you think? That's something to cling onto."

Garland squeezed Max's shoulder. "I'll wait for you. I'll try my best to get you out of here."

Max paused as if he was running a dilemma through his mind, uncertain and uneasy.

"Isn't there something else you could try, something you said was always with you, inside you somewhere?" Garland could see hope flicker in Max's eyes. "It won't be as risky outside the camp and if it works we could all be free, we could. . ."

"Don't get too excited." Garland stopped him. "I can try, but I don't want to promise you anything. I've let you down once already."

Max rested one hand over Garland's heart and the other over his own.

"You promise you'll try, and I promise I'll never leave your side once we're out of here."

Max pulled him so close their foreheads were almost touching. Garland looked at Max's face. It was hardened and still had the white and red scars from the beating he had suffered, but there were soft edges if you looked close enough. Max's eyes held a kindness, and his eyebrows danced above them when he spoke, his expressions vivid and alive. To Garland the permanent stubble that framed his jaw gave Max a rugged beauty that never faded even in Sachsenhausen's grey misery. Overwhelming love surged in Garland, molten lava boiling and rising.

He pulled Max's arm and led them to the back of their building. Max pushed Garland against the barracks' wooden wall and Garland felt his passion break free as they kissed, the dry roughness of their lips softening as they moved their mouths together in a slow exploration. Garland put his arms around Max and stroked every bone and tendon on his back, goose bumps of pleasure rippling across his own body as the lights of the aurora began to dance in the corner of his vision. He felt love for the first time and saw it as a colour as he kissed Max with his eyes closed, like staring at the sun too long and the world would blister with blinding light. He saw the aurora's reddish hue jump in curved lines and felt ecstasy flow from the top of his head, a force so strong Garland could see it shooting into space, bright and infinite, a comet forever blazing through the blackness. In that instant he realised love never died. It was always there, and now he felt his body reaching for more.

When the brightness suddenly faded and a thick, ugly mist began to rise, Garland tumbled like a tightrope walker plunging from the wire, his senses in free fall; his passion stopped dead as if ice water had been poured on a fire.

Garland opened his eyes and saw Fats.

"Well, well, well." The kapo's face was rigid with hate. "Look at what we have here."

Max swung his body around and raised his fist but Garland grabbed his arm.

"No, Max, he's not worth it. It's his word against ours."

Fats grinned and Garland could see his teeth, discoloured and jagged. Two guards walked from behind the barracks and stood next to Garland. They both brandished pistols.

Garland watched as black mist rose from the ground at his feet, dense and churning and bottomless.

Garland found himself back in solitary confinement in the same small room as before. Again he was ordered not to touch the walls, and the floating eyeball returned to the hatch at regular intervals. Garland's desperation was as dark as the room. Richter had been right. He had allowed himself to hope, to dream like a naïve fool who had learnt none of the lessons Sachsenhausen doled out every miserable day. Tears streamed down his face. Johan couldn't save him now. No one could. Even Johan's own life would be in danger if he had vouched for him.

Panic crawled over his body. Garland felt it gnawing and itching in the dank darkness. But what if Garland could still save himself? Could he summon whatever was inside and free himself? Free his friends? Even rescue Johan?

Garland closed his eyes and wished himself out of the room. He visualised his soul soaring high above the camp, climbing and climbing until the air became icy and gossamer thin.

He pictured Schulz and imagined the force – his force – filling the commander's wretched body. Garland had somehow controlled the turret guard with nothing more than his mind. Possessing Schulz would give him power over the whole camp.

Garland concentrated so hard his head began to ache but the aurora never came. He opened his eyes to the familiar darkness.

Garland focused again, channelling all of his anxiety and fear, pouring out every last atom of his anger. Then the room changed. It was bathed in light and Garland was lying in a white bed. The room had white walls and a white floor, and when he looked at his hands, some kind of tube was attached to his skin. He sat up, disoriented. Once more, he could see the tall trees that swayed gently around him. A man sat by his side. He was asleep. The same electronic screen, with its green jumping line, was rhythmically emitting high-pitched beeps.

Garland had the impression of waiting, but for what, he wasn't sure. He had been waiting a long time.

The Englishman's voice came through him again. He didn't hear it, it simply ebbed and flowed throughout his body, more energy than sound.

"Channel it. It's your only hope."

"I listened to you!" Garland replied wordlessly. "I found Johan! What else can I do!" His tone was livid, a bright red energy that fizzed from him like electricity.

"Keep the faith. Channel your energy. Find your strength. Ride the colours."

It was nonsense, Garland considered. Words and phrases in short sharp bursts, like a message from a telegram. Why should he listen? What could he learn when it was all so confusing?

Suddenly, the eyeball appeared and the shadows swirling around it plunged the white room and trees into deep shade.

Garland watched the eye narrow and heard a muffled voice behind the heavy door.

"Your disgusting boyfriend. He's dead."

Each word stabbed at his heart and he began to weep.

He knew it was true.

By the time Garland had been dragged out of solitary, it was nightfall. Max was dead. Garland somehow *felt* he had gone. He had tried so hard to find him, squeezing shut his eyes and seeking his energy, looking for some semblance of colour that would tell him Max was still close. But no signal came.

A guard took Garland by the back of his uniform and threw him down the steps onto the hard ground outside. His cheek skidded against the grit, skin tearing in a jagged line. He picked himself up and turned around to see the guard laughing. It was Stollen, the newer recruit. Stollen and the guards standing with him were gesturing for Garland to look around the corner, where the wooden gallows stood. He knew what was waiting, but still his feet began to slowly move.

Max's naked body was hanging by its neck. It swung gently like a grotesque pendulum, and fresh blood dripped from the toes.

Garland fell to his knees and vomited dark bile that stung his throat.

Max's neck was broken and twisted to an impossible angle, the friction marks around the noose red and raw. His muscular body swayed in the breeze. The movement was malevolent, taunting.

Garland wept with his head in his hands and cried out a single scream of anguish that sent the birds screeching from the trees beyond the camp. They circled and squawked in noisy protest.

Garland felt his anger rise.

The gallows on which Max's body hung began to shake, and Garland was aware of Stollen somewhere behind him, shouting in a dialect he couldn't understand.

The heavy gibbet moved with the groan of wood on wood, and moonlight glistened on Max's skin as the corpse began to pitch and spin. One of the gallow's posts split in two, shearing away with an ear-splitting shriek and flying through the air.

Stollen watched frozen as it fell, piercing his SS boot and spearing him to the ground, his frantic scream scattering the birds from the treetops again.

Garland heard but didn't see. His eyes rolled back as he rocked on his knees.

Now as his vision returned, he stood and saw Stollen, impaled and bleeding and with something shining in his wide eyes that Garland had only ever seen when he looked at prisoners, never in a guard. It was the cold, wild look of fear.

Garland kept walking as the other guards rushed to Stollen. He went back to his bunk, not even looking at the empty space where Max should have been resting. Garland ignored the lice and curled beneath his thin sheet. For the first time since he had been sent to Sachsenhausen, Garland's sleep was dreamless.

The guards had been too shocked to pin Stollen's injury on Garland. They saw he had never touched the gallows and blamed a sudden gust of wind none of them could now remember. Stollen knew otherwise but he was sedated in hospital waiting to have his left leg amputated below the knee.

"Are you okay?"

Gustave was working like an automaton on the shoes, his gnarled hands pulling material over machinery without looking. He had watched Garland rise silently from his bed that morning and walk to work without expression on his face.

Garland nodded at Gustave but said nothing.

"Every day we seem to lose someone we love," Gustave said. "First Hugo, now Max. Friends and brothers. It's too much."

Garland slowly exhaled.

"We were so close, Gus. So close. I've made up my mind now. I'm going."

Gus's eyes burnt into him. They were anxious and bright but alive with curiosity.

"What do you mean?" Gus asked.

"I've got one last trick up my sleeve."

Garland looked out of the narrow window. A sudden stiff breeze picked up sand and grit and shifted them in a low cloud, a microstorm that shimmied across the yard. Garland focused and zoomed in until he could see every tiny stone. He lifted them easily, then chose a few larger pebbles, plucking them effortlessly from the ground. He let the storm play like a whirlpool in the air, then summoned the white-hot rage Max's murder had ignited. He let it build, a black hole sucking up all the energy around him, and blasted the spinning cloud against the window. Garland heard the glass shatter and felt his eyes roll from white to normal as his mind and body realigned. The first thing he saw was Gustave's ashen face.

"You? You did that?"

Outside, a group of SS rushed over and others from inside the workshop joined them. Garland heard shouts from both sides of the window but he turned away. He recognised one of the guards from the gallows and heard him whispering about *strange things* that had been happening.

But Garland didn't smile, he didn't celebrate. He balled his hand into a fist and screwed up his face in concentration. The remaining glass on the window shattered in an explosion of tiny shards that stabbed like needles at the guards standing in their path. Garland had his back to the scene but he could still see it.

His fury rose like hot steam, but now Garland controlled it.

"You know who's always the most dangerous man, Gus?" Garland could feel his voice change, as if it belonged to someone else, more guttural and gritty.

Gus shook his head.

"The man who's got nothing left to lose."

Garland walked out of the workshop towards the barracks.

Chapter Thirty-Seven

JOHAN - 1944

Johan sat in his cell, his head in his hands. His first month as a prisoner in Sachsenhausen had been a living hell, although the word *living* felt too positive for what he was experiencing.

After his arrest, he had been marched directly to the cellblock, ironically a place he had never worked as a guard. The prison was designed in a T-shape so the guards could see all three of the long corridors from the junction in the middle. The doors were made of heavy blue-painted iron, each with a small slot for the guards to peer inside, which they did at regular intervals. It was a prison for the purpose of holding people of value. Johan knew he had none. Another of Schulz's mind games no doubt.

He spent long days between his four narrow walls, beneath the low prison ceiling. Only the lice-infested Hessian blanket, the creaky metal bed, and the infinite chasm of his own thoughts kept him company.

Johan considered how a man's mind was so deep, even in a tiny room it was like having an entire universe at your disposal. And the more Johan sat, the more thoughts he conjured. Memories, mistakes, different paths he could have taken, each possible decision creating an alternative outcome. And in the cold nights, when Johan's body shivered against the abrasive bedding, his mind would wander to the darkest places, the infinite tunnels where the blackest results festered and all eventualities were surrounded by hellish fire.

He thought of Garland and the hope he had held out to him, lifesaving water in the furnace heat of a desert. The image of Garland's disbelieving face haunted him, his orphan brother's blue eyes lighting up with relief as Johan delivered his ticket to freedom. Those words had been a mirage, just like his dreams of waking to the glistening emerald fjord and Oslo's red-tiled rooftops in a milky morning light.

Sometimes Johan thought about Garland's strange turns, the sudden attacks that left him sickly and faint. Was he ill or overcome by anxiety, as Johan had always suspected? Then there was his prediction at the Olympic Stadium, the absolute conviction that Owens would win the sprint. Was that some kind of channel to hidden powers that Johan could not understand? Garland's episodes had only begun when they left Oslo. Were they warnings that had foolishly been ignored, signals from someone or something that their future would become so dark? Johan could never know. The more possibilities he explored the more deranged they became and the sharper the pain behind his eyes grew.

Thinking of Gerda was a torture all of its own. He knew he had lost her forever, that he would never see her again. In the end he hadn't even been granted a simple goodbye. For Gerda there would be no farewell embrace, no last words. What would they have told her? That he had died on duty? That he had fled? He knew Schulz was breaking the law by imprisoning him without trial. No doubt a back-hander to the Gestapo administrator, some forged paperwork here, false testimonies from browbeaten guards, or a promise to keep it quiet if there was any inspection.

Johan's only consolation was Gerda's own spirit. She mistrusted the SS and the government. Hopefully she would challenge them. Perhaps she would even fight.

He thought of Gerda's soft skin and dark hair that always seemed to shine in any light. He pictured her smile and the way she would laugh as if nothing would ever matter so long as the world around her was full of goodness and wonder. He remembered her wisdom and her unerring resolution to do what was right. Most of all, Johan remembered her warmth, the natural feeling when their bodies entwined, and the comfort that always filled him.

Of course he fretted about what Gerda's life had become without him. Sometimes his mind told him Schulz had ordered her dead and Johan would see Gerda, her head lolled to one side, a single bullet-hole between her eyes, dried blood stiffening her hair. The longer the image stayed with him the worse it became. Maggots feasting, rats gnawing, that perfect skin rotting to blue, yellow and finally black, the stench of his dead fiancée becoming one with the earth.

Even jealousy was too cruel to leave Johan alone. If she had been spared would Gerda have moved on to another man? Johan couldn't stop himself seeing someone else making her laugh, someone else firing the warmth in her eyes, someone who would love her through long winter nights when passion left her body damp and musky.

Johan also thought of Schulz. The man he once admired was a psychopath, an unhinged addict who lived without empathy or remorse. That he had been the commander's favourite made Johan feel stained soul-deep. He had been told in Dachau that the Jews and the homosexuals were subhumans, vermin to be exterminated, the last drops of life squeezed out of them to oil the cogs of the great German machine. It was a credo Schulz had him follow with every random act of barbaric cruelty. But Johan's doubts had long hardened into a new truth. The prisoners were the brave men. They had been ripped from their families and sent to suffer the blazing inferno of hell day in, day out. Men judged unworthy and godless, animals kept alive only whilst they were useful, enemies of the state not deserving of life.

But the Nazis were the real subhumans, Johan knew. Those who felt pleasure in the death, torment and pain of others.

Johan had been one of them and now he prayed every night for forgiveness. He closed his eyes and tried to remember the face of every man he had killed, but he could never recall them all. He hoped God would be merciful when Johan's own time came. He prayed he would have the chance to show there was goodness in his head and his heart.

When his mind finally fell quiet, in the rare moments it stilled, Johan would listen for the song thrush. To Johan the bird's melody was the sound of peace, the voice of God, and as Johan listened, he waited the first shrill message of forgiveness.

As the days passed, Johan's feelings about Garland shifted, as if they were being carried by unseen winds. One of those feelings was resentment. Freedom had been within their grasp but Garland had somehow brought everything crashing down around them. Was he really homosexual? Was he one of the men who sinned against God? But then, who was Johan to judge?

Whatever he had done, Garland was the reason Johan now found himself amongst the most guarded prisoners in the camp and wearing the pink himself.

Months went by in his cell. He heard people taken outside and the sound of gunfire from the edge of the camp, from the direction of Station Z. It was whispered there were now notable prisoners in the cells, including the son of Stalin himself.

Johan watched his skin hug his bones more tightly. His uniform became baggier and he felt his once-muscular shoulders shrink, until he was like a tall stick, a walking skeleton like the rest of them. He began to yearn for the day he would be taken to Station Z, measured by a doctor and shot painlessly in the back of the head. One bullet to rid him of his pain and his sins.

God may never forgive him, but Johan would soon be a part of His earth, flesh and bone degrading as it must. He took some comfort in that.

Early one morning, three guards, led by Schubert, opened the door and stomped into his cell. Johan scanned them wearily as they filled the space.

"Tut, tut, Olsen," Schubert said, smirking. "Sorry, I used your old name, the one you no longer own. I should say N70134, shouldn't I, 175er?"

Johan looked down to the cell floor. A fat louse shuffled past and Johan's eyes followed its zigzagged trail.

"We've got new work detail for you, prisoner, and we're sending you to general population," another guard said.

Johan grimaced, his mind conjuring images of the Klinkerwerk or the boot-testing track. He considered the irony and slumped his bony shoulders in resignation. It was no more than he deserved.

"It's a task that one with the reputation of Der Bestatter will love," Schubert added.

The other two guards grabbed Johan and pulled him to his feet.

"We're sending you somewhere you know well, queer-lover," Schubert said. "Come with us to Station Z."

Chapter Thirty-Eight

GARLAND - 1944

From the moment Garland laid eyes on him, he knew there was

something special about Johnnie Dodge.

A veteran of the first war, he had that look about him, one of old-fashioned heroism. Dodge came from a long line of important Americans, the grandson of a civil war hero, great-grandson of a congressman. And now he fought for the British, who had taken him in as one of their own. It was even said he was a relation of Winston Churchill himself through his mother's marriage.

Garland first saw him sauntering across the yard. He looked like he owned the place, more than any guard, more than anyone who Garland had ever seen walk through the shadowed metal of the Sachsenhausen gates.

He came with several other prisoners, and rumour had it no institution had been able to hold him. Johnnie had escaped his three previous camps, the last through an elaborate tunnel run. Johnnie and a group of British POWs had made it beyond the walls before they were recaptured.

Johnnie's demeanour oozed confidence. He had the manner of a man who wouldn't be staying long, and Garland absolutely knew that was right. He wasn't even sure if it was part of his *ability*. It was something everyone could see. He was a man Sachsenhausen wasn't fortress enough to contain.

He reminded Garland of a character from a superhero cartoon, dashing and cool and unflinchingly upbeat. He was the blend of two cultures that had long fascinated Garland, the stoic, good-humoured British and the tough, determined Americans.

Johnnie was treated like a celebrity in the camp, a chosen one walking amongst mortals. Garland watched him whenever he walked by and saw a bright white trail of mist sparkle behind him. Johnnie Dodge was different, no question.

So when he saw Johnnie having recreation time with other prisoners not far from the shoe workshop Garland's heart raced like a starstruck fan meeting a movie idol.

It took a couple of weeks before Johnnie spoke to Garland.

"I understand you're a shoesmith in here. Can you give me a hand with this?" Johnnie had asked, his New York accent dulled with a British upper-class shading. He gestured towards the shoe, where the stitching was coming loose, making the sole flap when he walked. Garland helped him silently, taking the leather and carefully realigning the two pieces and using some saliva and pinpoint accuracy to rethread the stitches. It wasn't perfect, but it worked.

"Why thanks very much, man. Don't say much do you?" Johnnie grinned.

Garland looked into his eyes. They were bright and blue and his neat moustache bristled as he spoke. His crooked smile was as natural as sunlight.

"You do speak English?" Johnnie was teasing him.

"Yes, sir."

Johnnie crumpled into hysterical laughter before a guard stared his way and barked an order. Johnnie slapped his knee and then looked at Garland apologetically.

"Don't worry about them. They don't like us milling around here. Probably think we'll influence the general population or somethin' like that. Anyhow, why the hell are you calling me *sir*? We're equals, you know that? We're both in this shithole together."

Garland nodded nervously. "I get that. I just. . . I heard you're the one who always escapes."

He cursed himself for saying something so stupid but Johnnie just grinned. Up close he was full of humour.

"They called the last one the Great Escape, you know that?"

Garland smiled back at him as he spoke. *You know that.* It was something Johnnie Dodge said a lot, as regular as punctuation at the end of a sentence.

"What's your name, friend? I don't work on numbers and letters. Americans don't work like that and us Brits sure don't either."

"Garland."

Johnnie's eyes lit up. "Garland?"

"It's British."

"I knew a man called Garland. One of the best damn blokes I ever fought with. Daniel, they called him. Dan Garland."

Garland stared at the gravelly floor as Johnnie's words hung between them. When he looked up he couldn't speak.

Johnnie grinned at him, slapped his back and went back to his work.

It was another three days before Garland had the courage to talk to Johnnie about the soldier who shared his name. Johnnie was nonchalantly wandering between barracks when Garland rushed up from behind him.

"Johnnie," he began, his voice wavering. "I wanted to ask you. About the soldier you mentioned."

Johnnie looked at him through squinted eyes and flashed his crooked smile. "Daniel Garland?"

Garland's heart rose and he could feel his scalp tingle with goose bumps.

"A great man," Johnnie said. "We fought together in the Royal Sussex, 16ᵗʰ Battalion. Took on the Germans in France. We'd huddle together in the trenches, share rations, light each other's cigarettes. A warrior and a gentleman and I miss him very much."

"What happened to him?" Garland could feel emotions boiling in his heart.

Johnnie's grin disappeared and he nodded slowly. "We lost him in '40 in France, or so I heard. He was shot. He'll have gone down fighting, that I know."

Garland stared at the dusty ground. Somewhere in the distance a gun fired, but neither man flinched.

"Why the interest?" Johnnie asked him. "Because you share his name?"

Garland's gaze remained fixed on the ground when he spoke. "Did he ever mention Norway?" As he finished, his eyes rose to meet Johnnie's.

Johnnie blew out a slow breath and nodded. "He went there, I know. Son, did you know Dan Garland? Is that why. . ."

Tears welled in Garland's eyes. "I never knew him, but he was my father. My mother gave me his last name."

"Ah, son." Johnnie shook his head. "I'm sorry. I thought you were just interested. God, I could murder a cigarette."

He stared into the distance, where guards were standing over something crumpled on the floor.

"Just know this." Johnnie spoke again. "Your father was a good man. One of the best. And I'm sure even in this crazy, messed-up world, he'd be proud of you."

Garland scoffed, surprising himself, and dropped his head again. Johnnie watched him and waited.

"Sorry but I don't think he would be." Garland's voice was thick with self-loathing. "He was a heroic soldier. I'm a prisoner, a homosexual. A criminal. I've never fought. I've just danced. What would a man like him make of me?"

The sun had climbed to its highest point of the day, washing Sachsenhausen with warmth and light. Johnnie nodded and looked towards the trees that lined the edge of the camp.

"Do you believe in fate, Garland?"

Garland stared back.

"Of course you do. You look like a reflective man. What would you say the chances are of the two of us being here under this beautiful German sky?"

Garland wiped a tear from his eyes as Johnnie spoke.

"I could tell you a million things about your father," he said. "I could talk about his humour and his kindness, how he would do anything for anyone. I could tell you about his strength and his courage."

Johnnie paused as if he was weighing the wisdom of what he was about to say next, unsure whether to go on.

"But there was something else too," he said at last. "Something about your father that none of us could explain. It was like he had another sense. He'd just know certain things. He'd know what was going to happen, and he'd go into these trances. He didn't like talking about it, but I knew it was something special. The French boys used to call him Nostradamus. He'd get these feelings, you see, these weird. . ."

Garland was rocking backwards and forwards, and his eyes had rolled to whites. He had been listening with his eyes closed but somehow *seeing* every word, the shape of each letter and the colours they created. And then he saw the face of his father. His brown hair was carefully gelled and his nose sloped downwards, like an emperor's. He wore a neat moustache and his blue eyes were bright and kind. The British army uniform was pristine. Garland could even sense his smell. It was warm and comforting, burning coals and sweet lavender mixed with talcum powder and aftershave. He heard his father's voice. His accent was all soft consonants and long vowels, the sound musical and compelling. Garland stood face-to-face with his father and stared into his eyes. He felt heat. The rhythmic beating of his heart was loud in his ears and in his own eyes, the aurora danced, its colours hurtling in circles looking for a way out.

The aurora bubbled inside him, and in the moment, Garland felt pure unconditional love.

He was reminded fleetingly of the mysterious Englishman who spoke to him in the pine forest. The vision faded and Garland was looking into Johnnie's eyes. Johnnie held him by the collar of his uniform and in that instant Garland was sucked into his world, images of Johnnie's life flashing before him.

He watched him digging through black earth and running through fields, the wind in his hair and the sun beating down on his tanned forehead.

"You'll escape," Garland said in a flat tone. "Your tunnel will set you free."

His voice was a soft monotone and his unblinking eyes never left Johnnie's as he narrated the vision playing silently in his mind.

"You'll receive the Military Cross and you'll bring the Nazis down, long after Germany falls. You'll be a bigger hero after the war than you were during it."

Johnnie had let go of Garland as the words ran like ticker tape, a future already designed and decided and his to live.

"Wow. You really are your father's boy, aren't you?"

Garland was leaving the workshop the next day when Johnnie met him and told Garland how he was going to escape from Sachsenhausen, as if he had forgotten Garland already knew.

"We've started digging," he whispered. "These guards have got lazy, Garland. They don't look and listen."

Johnnie told him the plan and the timescale.

"I'll get you out of here," he said. "I'll bring you along with us, take you back to England. You can meet Dan's family. *Your* family."

Garland smiled and used the back of his hand to dry his forehead, which was sticky with perspiration. He pictured himself in England, taken in by family, *his* family, no longer an orphan but the loved and respected son of a fallen war hero. Maybe he could make it happen, start again and build a new life.

But it wasn't Garland's story. This was Johnnie Dodge's path and his alone.

"It's a nice thought but I'd slow you down," Garland told him. "And I've got unfinished business here."

Johnnie smiled, and in that instant, Garland felt something new. He had found the man to fill the gap in his life, the father figure he had always needed. Suddenly he wanted to change his mind, to tell Johnnie Dodge he would go, he would tunnel out with them and feel the sun's touch on his forehead and the wind of freedom breeze through his hair. They would go far from Sachsenhausen, away from the guards and the bullets and the suffocating grey walls of the camp.

But Garland knew his own path had to be different.

"You're one in a million, son," Johnny said "You've got the gift even stronger than your father. You stay safe in here and if you change your mind. . ."

Johnnie paused and Garland imagined how they would look in another world, two friends chatting in a local park, soaking up the sun, sandwiches and cool lemonade ready to be unpacked. "I trust you, Garland, just like I trusted your father." Johnnie's voice brought Garland back. "We're planning to break out in the next few days."

Johnnie reached into his pocket and pulled out a chain carrying the emblem of St Christopher. It was silver and scratched and the engraved pendant was slightly bent.

"I want you to have this." Johnnie pressed it into Garland's hand and Garland wondered how Johnnie had managed to hide it from the guards. "My pastor gave it to me before I left the States. I've carried it for luck every time I've escaped, but this time I don't need it. You've seen what's next for me and you're a good man. I'm not scared, Garland."

Garland looked at the chain in his hand. He felt the cold zing of the silver on his palm, a pleasant contrast to the hot sun, and inspected the scratched engraving. Johnnie reached into his pocket again.

"Here," he said, handing him a soft sheet of torn paper. It had a London address scrawled in thick black ink. "When we get out of this, write to me. Come and stay. It's what your father would have wanted."

Johnnie stood up, and as Garland watched his tall frame stroll away, he thought about hope and what it meant to the prisoners of Sachsenhausen. Hope that one day they would be released. Hope that the next day would be better than the last. Hope that a guard wouldn't beat or kill them. Hope that they would survive and that the war would end.

But Johnnie Dodge had taught Garland there was something other than hope, something much more powerful.

Johnnie had taught him to have *faith*.

Garland watched him grow small in the distance and knew what he had to do.

Chapter Thirty-Nine

JOHAN - 1945

Station Z had frightened Johan when he worked as a guard, but nothing prepared him for the horror of the place as a prisoner.

His new role was body disposal, part of the *sonderkommando.* He would take a prisoner who had been shot, gassed or beaten, pluck the metal fillings from their mouth and carefully check the corpse for anything else that could be remotely valuable. Then he would open the giant door of the furnace, push the body inside, and fire up the greedy flames. Johan had to stand whilst the bodies burnt, living and breathing the smell of cooking flesh for hour after hour, every inch of him soaked with sweat. The stench and acrid smoke would hit the back of his throat, the guards always ready to dish out a kicking when he threw up. Once the furnace had done its work, Johan would pile the ashes into huge urns, the hot dust of men coating his tongue and stinging his eyes.

Every now and then, a family member would ask for the ashes, a privilege only afforded when the prisoner had been German or of a better standing than simply a Jew or a homosexual. But the remains were all intermingled and unidentifiable. The guards would simply order Johan to stuff any ashes into a small urn to hand to the prisoner's grieving relatives. Johan would often picture them being scattered around rivers, lakes, and other places of natural beauty where sentimental memories were the strongest. He would imagine grief-stricken widows holding the urns to their hearts then solemnly casting the combined remains of dozens of strangers into the air, all the while whispering tearful words of remembrance and love. It was all a façade, one that Johan knew mirrored the hypocrisy and deception of the Nazi regime. Even in the most poignant times they were there with their glimmering eyes and evil manipulation.

Johan still tried to find crumbs of comfort. Maybe somewhere, the souls of the Jews, homosexuals and Soviets would feel their mortal remains being cherished, even by a stranger, and it would mean something to them. Johan had come to doubt God played any part. He remembered the times he had feared divine judgement, had fallen to his knees praying for the Almighty's mercy and forgiveness. His feelings had changed since he had been incarcerated. How could any God let such atrocities happen? How could He have allowed such evil to gain control of a country, to manipulate its people and cause so much death and suffering?

The harrowing work stretched from weeks to months and all the while Johan was marked down as a homosexual himself. He would rub ash onto his uniform to dull the pink triangle. He hoped it would be mistaken for red or black. But they all knew. Even the others who wore the pink avoided him. In Sachsenhausen, he was the lowest of the low. In helping a homosexual, he had been declared one himself. In betraying Sachsenhausen and Schulz, he had betrayed all Germany. In being a former guard, he was hated by the other prisoners. Johan was alone amongst the thousands, every man an enemy. The guards would beat him and look away when kapos and even gangs of prisoners did the same.

Physically, Johan knew he was fading. He felt his cheeks become hollower and his eyes sink into his skull. His body had become angular and awkward, and his stomach so empty it would bloat. Johan had even stopped speaking. He would nod if guards gave an order and take his beatings stoically, without a word or whimper. He wanted to give the outside world nothing. In his mind, he was all but dead. Johan had considered suicide, a simple solution when he was surrounded by guards who could easily be goaded to shoot him on the spot. He could maybe use his thin bed sheet to fashion a noose or bolt from roll-call under the Tower A gunner's gaze. That would be a quick and merciful end. But it was an engineered death that Johan didn't believe he deserved. Instead, he had to endure. He had earned every dreadful, miserable second.

Around the camp Johan heard whispers, muted conversations that now carried the same message. The Allied forces were winning the war. All of Sachsenhausen could hear the low rumble of explosions coming from the city. Planes droned regularly overhead but few of them were German. There were even rumours the Klinkerwerk had been destroyed in an Allied bombing raid.

As each back-breaking day merged into another, Johan's mind was occupied by three things and three things only: Schulz, Garland and Gerda.

He hated Schulz. The man repulsed him. Each night in his bunk, Johan would close his eyes and picture the commander's face, his wild eyes, his rotten teeth, and the glimmering sweat that permanently glazed his wrinkled forehead. Johan would even conjure up the undercurrent of peppery urine that seemed to leak from Schulz's skin. He would feel the hatred surge through his body, shooting through his veins. It was an energy, and in Sachsenhausen that was a priceless commodity. Hatred made him want to launch himself off the bunk and sprint to Schulz's lodgings, to slowly throttle him with his bare hands. His pulse fluttered as he pictured life leaving the commander's crazed eyes. It would take Johan's heart several minutes to stop racing, and his mind would rarely relax enough to bring sleep, but the wakefulness was a price he was happy to pay.

And then there was Garland. The resentment in Johan had been consuming him, the anger at his orphan brother a constant companion. Garland had cost him everything. But for Garland, Johan would still be a guard. He would still have his beautiful Oranienburg home, the soothing tones of the song thrush outside his window and the blue skies of freedom above. But Johan hadn't been able to stay angry with Garland for long. He knew the suffering his friend and brother had endured. Johan had brought him to Berlin in the first place, and it was Johan who had been a willing part of the evil that had thrown Garland in Sachsenhausen. Johan would look each day for his face in the crowd but he never saw it. There were tens of thousands of prisoners in the camp now and not much room for socialising. He wondered if he would ever see him again. He hoped Garland was alive, wherever he was.

Gerda had become a bittersweet memory. Behind those shimmering eyes and skin as smooth as fresh peach, she had always known. She had loved Johan, that he believed, but he realised now there had been something bubbling underneath, a darkness that she tried to ignore but could never clear. Johan didn't think it was him she resented but everything that surrounded his life away from her. . . the SS, the government, and the onset of a war she didn't support or understand. On the nights when they drank wine and talked into the dawn, Gerda would sometimes let slip a belief or opinion, an innermost feeling she would normally keep hidden. On one of those long, dreamy nights she had talked of the hearts of men.

"All hearts beat as softly as anyone else's," she had told Johan. "But men coat their hearts in a hard, frozen shell, a fortress that holds it captive. And over time, the heart itself becomes frozen, starved of love and emotion, never to become warm again."

Johan had listened and tried to understand.

"The hearts of men," Gerda had said, "are engineered to deliver cruel acts."

Weeks after Gerda spoke those words the war had broken out and men began proving once again she had been right.

Johan pictured his own heart, encased in an icy fortress in his chest. Had Johan kept it captive whilst he let his cruelty run free or had his heart needed to be protected? How could a soft heart survive a place like Sachsenhausen or the sharp stab of lost love. Without walls of its own it would never recover.

Thinking about Schulz, Garland and Gerda helped Johan as he plundered and burnt the bodies of the dead, distractions through the constant horror of Station Z and its stench. Of course, distractions only went so far. Johan tried to avoid the empty eyes of the skeletal corpses but was always drawn to them. A dead body made him think of the human soul and the eyes were its window. Life left the eyes first, and without life, a body was just a sack of blood, tissue and bone. When the prisoners were killed did their souls fly free to another place? Were they simply drawn into the ether, a void of nothingness? Johan looked for answers in the glassy, vacant stares of the dead.

He remembered with shame how much he had despised the Jews when he first arrived in Germany. He had seen only subhumans who needed to be stamped out, not ordinary men, women and children living their lives. The bodies in the incinerators all burnt the same.

Jew or German, criminal or queer, communist or Romani. . . the inferno didn't care.

Johan had been wrong about the Jews, he knew that. But so had the whole of Germany. The nation had been misled, brainwashed. But that wasn't an excuse Johan could hold on to for long.

The dozens of dead he turned to ash each day made sure guilt would always be on his shoulder.

Johan hadn't killed these men, of course, and that alone gave him a small respite, but those who had already died at his hands never left him in peace. The guilt tortured him and he carried it each day, as if the body of every man hung on his back.

But Johan refused to feel sorry for himself. Whenever self-pity stirred he would think of Gerda and imagine the impregnable case around his heart. Every time he felt the prickle of tears he would shake them away. And when Sachsenhausen's darkness consumed him, Johan would set three words echoing in his head.

I deserve this.

Johan had been on sonderkommando duty for several months when Schulz paid him a visit. He could smell him before he saw him, even above the hot stench of the furnace. Johan heard the door open behind him and felt the light from outside wash over the incinerator room. He only turned to face Schulz when he heard his voice.

"I'm glad they kept you alive." Schulz's skin had broken out into sores, and he was swigging shakily from his silver flask. His bloodshot eyes were a pale shade of yellow, like freshly churned cream dashed with drops of blood. The sight of him made Johan's own blood boil. He felt himself shaking, a volcano ready to erupt.

"Ah, Der Bestatter." Schulz sounded drunk. "This was my idea, this assignment, my little joke."

The commander's humourless smile showed his blackened and crooked teeth. Johan closed his eyes for a second to keep his anger in check, his heart hammering at its fortress walls.

"I thought it might be better if you were dead. An example to the other guards. But that would be too easy. Too much paperwork that would be difficult to explain."

Johan didn't doubt it. Schulz wasn't wired to give anyone who disappointed him an easy way out.

"Do you know why you're really here?" Schulz took another swig from the flask. "It's not about being homosexual or trying to free your queer friend. That's sickening but I could maybe have let it pass. No, Der Bestatter, you're burning the filthy dead because you turned against the cause."

Schulz shook his head. "You were my favourite! I told you things that could have jeopardised my own position because I trusted you. But then you tell me you want to go, to leave the army in a time of war! That's desertion, Olsen, and deserters are shot."

Johan had barely spoken a word in weeks and his dry voice rattled with thick phlegm. "What do you want from me?"

"I want you to feel shame!" Schulz yelled so loud spittle flew from his lips, and liquid sloshed from his flask as he lurched towards Johan. "You could have been a hero of the SS but instead you're here, a worthless traitor shovelling dead vermin into these ovens. *Meine Ehre heisst Treue*! Honour! Loyalty! The SS code. Does it mean nothing to you, boy?"

Schulz drew his pistol and levelled it at Johan's face. For a second Johan felt a sharp stab of fear but it quickly gave way to calm. The insane tyrant who did so much to create him would be the one to take away his life and his daily suffering. It was almost poetic.

But instead of a bullet Johan got more of Schulz's ravings.

"Do you remember when I built this place?" The commander gestured grandly with the flask still in his hand. "I gave you the guided tour, even allowed you the honour of burning the first dead."

Schulz jammed the pistol in Johan's mouth and Johan watched the long barrel shake in front of him before he closed his eyes and waited for the permanent darkness. It was time and he was ready, no matter what hell had waiting on the other side.

The blow from the pistol butt split open his nose, and he fell backwards onto three corpses piled up for incineration.

"Deserter!" Schulz screamed above him. "Your final duty to the Reich is almost upon you." He spat in Johan's face. It was stringy and brown and webbed between his fingers when Johan wiped it away.

Schulz placed his pistol in its holster and opened the door, bathing the dark room in light so dazzling it stung Johan's eyes.

"Oh, before I forget." Schulz spun to face Johan, still on his back, blood streaming from his broken nose. "I had fun with your pretty fiancée before I put a bullet between her eyes." The words hit Johan like a sledgehammer to his stomach.

"She came to my office." Schulz was enjoying the memory and what it was doing to Johan. "Demanded your immediate release, yelling about how powerful her father is, how he would have me kicked out of Sachsenhausen and demoted. Me, who has the ear of the Fuehrer himself!"

Johan felt dizzy, and when Schulz grinned, he thought he could see the smile stretch from one ear to the other, demonic and taunting. Johan tried to scream but all that rose was bile and blood which he spat on the ground.

"I had the guards pin her down," Schulz went on. "The last act of her life was to feel a real man inside her."

Schulz paused as if he was running a replay through his head.

"Such a waste," he said at last. "It took one of my men an hour to clean her brains off the wall."

Johan pushed himself to his feet and stumbled towards Schulz, his arms out. Schulz didn't even reach for his pistol this time, just kicked Johan hard under the chin, sending teeth tumbling like poker dice across the concrete floor.

Johan peered up at the blurred figure of Schulz silhouetted against the blazing sun behind him.

"Here," Schulz said. "Something to remember her by."

Johan saw the commander's arm move and Gerda's engagement ring pinged on the ground before him, the diamond throwing a kaleidoscope of brilliant light around the room. Head pounding, he scurried and grabbed the ring with his fingers.

"Think of it as a short term loan," Schulz gave a low, throaty laugh. "Until someone finds it on your dead body and it comes back into my hands."

He slammed the door behind him and the sunlight vanished.

Johan looked at the ring, just as beautiful as the day he placed it on Gerda's finger. But now the only light it caught was the scorching red of the incinerator flames behind him.

In his bunk that night, he held the ring to his chest and felt his heart's frozen walls melt away, washing him with cold anguish. Johan's eyes ran with tears and his pain was building towards an unstoppable scream when he felt strong hands dragging him from the bed.

Johan hit the floor with a crunch, and the shadowed face of a guard he didn't recognise hovered in front of him, bending to grab his neck and punch him hard on the jaw. Johan's own fist clenched over the ring, so tight the diamond cut into the soft flesh of his palm and a thin stream of blood trickled down his forearm.

"I'll take it from here."

The voice sounded familiar and Johan felt someone haul him to his feet. Moments later he was out of the barracks and standing in the cool night air, Schubert's face inches from his own.

"You've got to stay calm," Schubert said, pushing Johan against the wall. "You've got to keep it together."

Johan shook his head and squinted through the blur of his tears, colours dancing in Schubert's eyes.

"Schubert? What are you. . ."

"It's Garland," Schubert's mouth whispered. "I'm getting us out of here tonight."

Chapter Forty

GARLAND - 1945

It had been another gruelling shift in the workshop and his body ached, yet Garland knew what he was planning would take him to his limits. He wished he felt stronger, but in Sachsenhausen, survival not strength was the best any of them could hope for. Bone deep exhaustion was their default setting, and Garland would have to hope he could overcome the tiredness.

He had decided night would be the best time to execute his plan. He would be in his bunk, so no one would know if he had collapsed or was just sleeping, and even with the glare of the Sachsenhausen spotlights, darkness offered more protection than daylight.

He would need to take his own body out of Sachsenhausen too. Otherwise he would be spending the rest of his life seeing the reflection of a sadistic SS guard every time he looked in the mirror.

He hadn't tried transporting into anyone else since he had somehow found himself *inside* the Tower A guard and driving a knife into his own body. That had been months ago, and looking back, Garland realised everything had happened without his control. He had *become* the guard in those moments but he had no idea how. This would be different. Garland would need to guide the gift within him, just as the Englishman in his visions had told him to. He had one chance and if he failed it would mean certain death. He wouldn't have the energy to fight. But Garland owed it to Johan to try.

He lay in his bunk and whispered a prayer, staring at the dark ceiling. Then he closed his eyes and willed his mind away from his body, picking at the seams that held them together, calling on his soul to fly from flesh and bone. When the colours arrived they floated and danced in a thousand shades, some that Garland couldn't recognise or even imagine. They lifted him and he heard singing, high and angelic, in words he didn't understand.

He looked down and saw not the floor of his barrack but Sachsenhausen sitting far below. The camp looked small and insignificant, washed beneath the harsh floodlights. He could see the gun towers and guards, each leaking black wisps of smoke he knew only he could see. He concentrated on Johan and found him immediately, the colours hovering in mid-air before plunging through one of the silent barracks. Garland saw his agony as light red with a glimmer of white, warm blood and ice forged together in pain. Johan was clutching something to his chest.

Garland left Johan and floated upwards, looking for a solitary guard. He found one sitting in a dark corner less than fifty yards from Johan's barracks, drawing on a cigarette and blowing smoke toward the starless sky. Garland watched the man like a falcon before the kill strike, suspended and still. Then in a heartbeat he was diving, tearing through a boiling vortex and into the guard's mind.

Garland felt a surge of pinprick pain and a sudden sensation he was suffocating, gasping for breath as the spectrum of lights faded and melted away. He sucked in air as his vision – real once more – slowly began to sharpen.

He struggled to his feet and yelped as he touched his face. He had forgotten the cigarette glowing red between the index and middle fingers of his right hand, the burn on his cheek already blistered and raw. It was a reminder his new form was as mortal and vulnerable as his own. He took a quick drag of the cigarette to calm his nerves.

Garland moved his hands around his body and was pleased. The man was well-built and strong, and Garland felt the power as he tightened one muscle then another. He reached into his pocket for his papers. *Schubert.* Garland felt a pulse of fear, a stab of panic breaking free. Of all the guards it had to be Schubert, one of the most sadistic psychopaths in Sachsenhausen.

Garland moved quickly, ironing out his unsteadiness as he hurried towards Johan's barracks. He heard a guard's raised voice as he got closer and broke into a run. When he threw open the door hundreds of prisoners turned to face him. Some were on their bunks, others were standing in small groups. All of them had eyes that were saucer-wide and fearful.

Garland felt a strange sense of power when the prisoners moved away from him, parting like the Red Sea as he walked into the room. When he reached the centre he saw a guard grappling with Johan.

"I'll take it from here," Garland said, the crisp German accent sounding alien on his lips. He used his strong arms to pull Johan to his feet and drag him towards him, the prisoners parting again. He felt a jolt of paranoia as those haunted eyes all stared. Sweat broke out on his forehead and temples, loosening the grip of the cap on his head.

Garland frog-marched Johan outside and pushed him against the side of the barracks, out of sight and in the shadows.

He looked into his friend's eyes. They were wide and wild. Something inside Johan had broken. He saw wisps of smoke, the colour of bloodstained blocks of ice. Blood dripped from Johan's balled fist.

"You've got to stay calm," Garland said in Schubert's voice, and pushed Johan against the wall. "You've got to keep it together."

"Schubert? What are you. . ."

"It's Garland," he whispered. "I'm getting us out of here tonight."

He tried pulling open Johan's fist, but it was like tearing apart a rock.

"What's this? It's hurting you."

Johan was staring at Garland as if he hadn't heard, a frightened man lost in a world he couldn't comprehend.

Another guard walked past and Garland clamped his hand over Johan's mouth. The guard looked over and smiled.

"Give that filthy traitor a beating from me, Schubert," he said and continued on his way.

Garland turned back to Johan. "You need to forget everything. You need to concentrate on one thing and one thing only: getting out of here. Look at me and focus."

He grabbed Johan by the collar of his scruffy uniform and shook him. "Don't try to understand, just believe what I'm saying. We'll have our whole lives to talk about it. Right now I need to get my body, get a vehicle, and get out of here."

He led Johan to a large water barrel beside a nearby building, looking around to make sure no one was watching. The barrel was half-full.

"Get in there," Garland said. "Wait for me and don't make a sound."

Garland helped him squeeze in, Johan a sleepwalker still mute and dazed. Garland hoped it wouldn't make him too cold. The last thing he needed was Johan falling ill and needing a doctor once they had escaped.

Johan crouched inside the barrel. The water came up to his neck and he held his mouth and nose just above the surface. Garland hoped the water would snap Johan back to his senses. He had never seen him so weak and helpless.

Once Johan was safely inside the container, Garland walked briskly away, glancing back twice to make sure Johan hadn't moved. He walked by a few guards and nodded, each passing second giving him more confidence.

He reached his own barracks and opened the door, heart racing as he walked past the hundreds of prisoners. Most of them were asleep, some snored, and those still awake watched him through bloodshot, fearful eyes. He could see the terror on their faces. They knew someone would be taken out. Garland came to his bunk and froze. His body was twitching on the bed, the whites of his eyes flickering and his chest jumping in electric-shock spasms. Garland swallowed hard against the chill washing over him. He picked up his body and with an effort slung it over his shoulder. Gustave hadn't stirred in his bunk. Garland kicked his leg to wake him.

"Gus," he whispered. Gustave's eyes flicked open and instantly widened. He began shaking his head and his jaw fell slack.

"Gus, it's me, Garland. I don't have time to explain, you just need to trust me. Come with me. This is it."

He grabbed the back of Gustave's neck, to make it more realistic. His muscles strained as he carried his own jerking body and manhandled Gustave out of the barracks. More prisoners were waking, the low murmurs and whispered curses rising. Garland kept moving and when he caught the black, hooded eyes of the kapo Fats, he ignored him. Fats would know better than to question an SS guard, especially one as brutal as Schubert.

Even with Schubert's strength, Garland felt his legs became heavy as he approached the barrel, Gustave following quietly at his side. He lowered his still-twitching body to the ground and pulled Johan, soaking and shivering, from the water. He beckoned Gustave and the three of them huddled low as Garland spoke quietly and quickly.

"There's no time for questions," Garland said. "All you need to do is trust me and do what I say, when I say it. I'm Garland. I'm your friend. And we're getting out of here. Are you both with me?"

He looked at Gus, whose eyes were now alert and sharp. Johan still seemed glazed and his shivering was getting worse. He needed to warm himself somehow but there was no time. They needed to go.

"Jo, what's the best way out of here? There are vehicles, at Station Z, aren't there? Where do they keep the keys?"

"I – in the a – admin office." Johan's words trembled and his face was ghost-white.

"Where is it?" Garland asked impatiently.

Johan pointed an unsteady finger to the imposing, darkened shape of Tower A.

"Y – you'll need to b – break in," he said. "It's locked a – at n – night."

"Okay," Garland replied. "Gus, give him your coat and huddle together. Stay low and for God's sake, don't move."

He darted for Tower A, stopping for a couple of seconds as the spotlight swept like a lighthouse beam across his path. Even a guard as renowned as Schubert might have to explain if he was caught where he wasn't supposed to be.

Garland reached the door to the lower offices of Tower A and pulled out the large ring of keys that had been heavy in his coat pocket. There were a dozen or more keys dangling. Garland started trying each in turn but decided it was taking too long. He removed his cap and used it to cushion his elbow, as he broke a window next to the door. The shattering sound was muffled but Garland still prayed it had gone unnoticed and froze in the silence. When he was confident no one was coming, he gently removed the shards of glass from the frame and hauled himself through. He found a torch attached to his belt and searched frantically for car keys, the torchlight throwing sinister shadows around the room. After a few seconds he stopped and breathed deeply. He would fail unless he stayed calm.

He looked again and as he moved the torch in a slow arc, a row of keys shone back from one of the walls. Each had a registration number written neatly on a tab above them. Garland took one and committed the number to memory, repeating it over and over in his head as he hurried back to the broken window and clambered out.

He walked quickly back to where Johan and Gustave were waiting – forcing himself not to run – but he knew something was wrong. A sensation of cold dread began in his heels and raced upwards, a sickening feeling that grew the closer he got to Johan and Gustave's hiding place.

When he turned the corner, six guards were waiting for him. Two of them held Johan and Gustave upright, pistols pointed at their heads, whilst Garland's body jerked on the ground. Fats walked out from behind the guards.

Something in Garland snapped. He launched himself at the kapo, all his hatred and venom exploding in a heartbeat. He saw a dark mist fall until the figures in front of him were only outlines, liquid shapes that swayed behind a film of red and black.

A single shot rang out, and Garland stopped dead as the dazzling lights of the aurora suddenly surrounded him. He was lifted to the skies, so high he thought he was being carried on angels' wings to the heavens, all his hate and fear dissolved. He would happily have gone there, the peace inside him overwhelming, his pain forgotten.

But he felt himself falling, dropping in a slow spiral towards the bright lights of the camp, back inside the grey walls of Sachsenhausen, and back to his own emaciated body now motionless on the ground. Schubert lay dead at his side.

Garland opened his eyes and vomited over the boots of one of the guards. He had time to smell the leather and dirt before the swinging kick and absolute darkness.

Chapter Forty-One

JOHAN - 1945

Johan found himself shackled, his mind racing over the night's events.

In the furore, he had shoved Gerda's ring in his britches and he could feel it dig into his groin. The pain was unpleasant but it was a sharp reminder that he still existed, for now at least.

He was back in the T-shaped cellblock on the floor next to Garland and the French prisoner. Their capture had happened too fast for Johan to process, and being submerged in the water had left him freezing and numb. He knew, though, their escape bid had been doomed to fail. Even if Garland had taken over the body of Schulz himself they would have struggled to get through the gates. And if the miracle had happened, if they had got past the guards and gun towers, where would they have gone? Rumours had spread that even Johnnie Dodge and the prisoners who fled with him had been cornered in the countryside and were already back in Sachsenhausen.

Johan strained his neck to look to his side. He wondered if Garland had one last card to play, whether his supernatural gift could still save them, but he was unconscious. Johan closed his eyes and tried to imagine the force that lay somewhere inside his brother, a power that allowed him to inhabit the body of another man, to predict the future. Johan felt the now-familiar shame that he had failed to protect him, that such a gifted soul had ended up in such a brutal place. Tears clouded Johan's eyes and his sorrow brought him back to Gerda, raped and murdered by the monster who would surely be there at his own death, which was imminent.

Johan's breath rattled in his chest, and when he coughed, a bubble of dark red phlegm covered his chin. Pain stabbed at his body, the aches like acute influenza, but he feared it was something worse. Johan could smell himself, too, a rank odour that seemed to drift up from his lungs, wet and rotten, like a fungus growing malignant and vile.

Johan was dying, but he knew whatever was eating away at him from the inside wouldn't take his life. That race would be won by the SS.

The very institution that brought him to Berlin would be the one that destroyed everything he loved.

Hours passed before the heavy cell door creaked open. Johan could only see the black leather boots stomping on the concrete floor. But he recognised the smell.

"Olsen, boy," Schulz sneered. "You never fail to disappoint me. You try to escape and take one of my best guards with you. I should have put a bullet between your fucking eyes when you first let me down."

When Schulz knelt beside him, Johan could taste his warm, rancid breath.

"I don't know how you persuaded Schubert to desert, but it will be the last thing you do."

Schulz looked across at Garland, who was stirring. "You queers will never see Oslo again. You'll only see death – and soon. I might even instruct the men to leave you half-alive so you can watch the flames devour your own flesh. That would be poetic, wouldn't it? An especially fitting end for Der Bestatter, no?"

Schulz laughed and then rose to his feet as the horn sounded outside to signal the morning roll-call. He nodded to the guards, who unshackled the three prisoners and hauled them to their feet.

"Come," Schulz said through his black grin. "The show is about to start."

Johan knew as soon as he entered the yard what was to come. Gallows had been hoisted in the middle of the yard and thousands of prisoners already stood in neat rows under the milky glow of the early morning sun. He shivered and coughed, his own body willing him to give up, to collapse and let the earth swallow him. He knew the end was coming.

He exchanged a glance with Garland. He still seemed distant and disconnected and his eyes sat in the middle of dark rings as a guard shoved them forwards.

They reached the scaffold and Gustave was strung up first, standing on a stool with the noose chafing at his neck. Schulz climbed a raised platform and yelled to the prisoners.

"This French queer tried to escape last night." His voice echoed across the yard. "Let his death be a message to anyone who disobeys, a warning to anyone who has the false courage to rise."

Schulz turned swiftly and kicked the stool from under Gustave's feet. There was a loud snap, and Gustave's dead body swung gently in the silence.

Johan glanced at Garland and saw he was crying. Then he looked at the prisoners. Thousands and thousands of broken men watching a corpse swing back and forth at the end of a rope. Johan hadn't known Gustave, but it didn't stop his heart from hurting.

Gustave's body was cut down and thrown into a wheelbarrow, no more dignity dead than alive.

Then Garland was led to the gallows and a noose yanked tight around his neck.

"A homosexual traitor and from Norway no less!" Schulz bellowed, revelling in the show. "They say he has special powers, but I don't believe in magic."

Schulz laughed and other guards joined in, some of them nervously.

"But just to be sure, I'd like your fellow traitor to kick away the stool."

Schulz turned to Johan and let the laughter fade as his face grew dark.

"You'll hang your orphan brother." Schulz expression was stone. "A final kill for Der Bestatter before you follow him to hell."

Johan shook his head. "I won't do it, never. No matter what you do to me."

Schulz drew his knife from its leather scabbard and moved quickly, his yellow eyes sepia and wide. Johan watched the commander approach in slow motion, his right arm high in the air and the knife blade gleaming in the sun.

Johan closed his eyes a heartbeat before white-hot pain ravaged his face and he was choking on his own blood. Only the arms of the guard kept him on his feet and when he opened his eyes, he saw Schulz holding up his severed nose like a trophy in front of the silent prisoners.

"What next?" Schulz shouted. "His ears?"

Johan looked down at the growing pool of blood. He felt dizzy. Sharp pain stabbed constantly at his face, worsened by the sting of a cool breeze.

"What do you say, Der Bestatter? Time to live up to your name?"

Johan began to speak but heard Garland on the gallows.

"Do it, Jo. Do it. I'll be okay. Everything will be okay."

"I can't," Johan yelled, foaming blood flying from his mouth. "I can't do it to you."

Garland stared at him and Johan saw colours swirl then vanish within the dark, hollow rings of Garland's eyes. Something moved inside his mind. It was compelling and confident and impossible to resist. He looked over to Schulz.

"I'll do it."

Johan staggered over to Garland, each step a draining effort, the cool morning breeze stinging his face.

He held on to Garland's legs and hugged them as a dozen guards raised their pistols.

"I'm sorry, brother. Sorry for everything. I love you and hope God can find some forgiveness for me."

"Do it!" Schulz yelled.

Johan sucked in another rattling breath and coughed a thick mixture of blood and phlegm. Then he let go of Garland's legs, took a step back and kicked the stool away. Johan turned his head and braced himself for the sound of Garland's neck snapping.

But the sound never came.

Instead, he heard thirty thousand men gasp as one, an army of lost and broken souls who would forever remember the chilly March morning of 1945 and what their disbelieving eyes had seen. Those who survived would tell their grandchildren about the man who would became a myth and a legend. The man they christened the Psychic of Sachsenhausen.

When Johan raised his head he gasped like the rest.

Garland was standing. Standing was the wrong word. He was *levitating*, the rope around his neck still loose and his feet planted firmly on thin air.

But it was Garland's eyes that held the crowd spellbound. They blazed with multi-coloured fire, a bright and vivid spectrum that shone and burnt into the cold blue sky.

Chapter Forty-Two

GARLAND - 1945

Garland looked down on Sachsenhausen far below, a grey smudge amidst the pastel greens and the dull silver sheen of the canal.

He looked towards Berlin and saw blood-red Nazi flags on fire, the black void of their swastikas melting in the flames. He saw Adolf Hitler, no longer the dark angel of his visions but a trembling old man, stooped and broken in the wreckage of his own godless dreams. Garland saw the smouldering Third Reich, built on suffering and hate, and threw back his head in a howl of rage. He saw men, women and children swept away in a jet-black maelstrom and gazed on their bones and ashes, wind-blown and high as mountains. He saw honourable men like Kori, pulled into the Nazis' malevolent machine. He saw war and death on land and sea, saw ocean floors whose sands were hidden by a million eyeless corpses and skies raining tears of scarlet blood. Death was all around and it fed on the evil that man had created against man. Garland saw it all in his mind. And he couldn't take it anymore.

There in the cool morning, above the place that had taken the best of him, he would let the aurora's vengeance run free.

He closed his eyes and felt a storm surge of pure power, all of his life leading to this moment, all he had failed to understand now pouring from him as a spectrum of glorious colour and light.

It was as much a part of him as the blood flowing through his veins. It was the trees, the stars, the sky, it was the force of existence, all colliding within his body.

Garland felt the morning sun on his flesh and the aurora absorbing its energy, charging itself, still growing.

He stared down at Sachsenhausen and *saw* it all even though his eyes were still closed, the evil that took place there every minute of every day.

Garland moved his mental gaze to the machine gun pointing at him from the top of Tower A. The aurora flared as he blew the tower apart in a fireball, and he saw the lives of the three guards flash before him as they fell. . . their childhoods, the hopes that never happened, the women who had once known their love. Garland watched their bodies hit the ground with a dull thump, twisted and glowing with flames.

He turned his focus to Station Z and it became an inferno, the ghosts of the evil done there rising through the orange forks of fire. Garland felt every act of depravity and murder they had suffered.

On the ground, guards ran frantically towards the gallows, and from high above, Garland heard the clatter of gunshots, watched the bullets moving in slow motion towards his body, small and motionless over the scaffold. He steered the bullets aside with ease and concentrated on the gates below Tower A, smiling as they flew open and tore away from their hinges.

"Run!" Garland shouted silently to the thousands of prisoners, sending the aurora across them in a shimmering wave. But the men stayed frozen, staring slack-jawed and wide-eyed.

A guard ran towards the scaffold firing wildly but Garland snapped his neck with his mind. His scanned the crowd and saw Fats begin to run, knocking prisoners out of his path until he tripped and landed on his back. The kapo's flabby jowls shook as he yelled at Garland to stop, begging him to have mercy. Garland could see him praying, kissing a crucifix that hung around his chubby neck, and watched Fats's pathetic existence replay like news reel. . . his career as a petty criminal, his abusive relationships with women and children, all the lying and cheating. The kapo was a bigger man inside Sachsenhausen than he had ever been outside. Maybe that was why he was so hateful, so drunk on the power.

Garland let his anger burn through him and watched Fats burst into flames, his flesh cooking as he thrashed and rolled on the ground. The prisoners around him stared until he was dead and smouldering.

Garland turned to Schulz still standing on the platform, firing his pistol as the mayhem raged around him, his silver flask empty in his other shaking hand. Garland let Schulz's story play out in his head, a young thug and a homosexual himself, a psychopath who tortured his family's pets and moved on to abuse men, women and children without a moment's remorse, a man at whose hands thousands had died. Garland saw each death, looked at the faces of the loved ones left behind and the children that would have followed, the generations of lives never to be born. He saw in Schulz absolute evil, stronger and more pure than he could ever imagine.

Garland closed on the commander's heart and saw it was already black and malignant, its arteries blocked with thick fat, swollen and diseased. He had only days to live but it would be a natural death. He deserved something more.

He threw the aurora at Schulz and began to see him slowly burn but thought of Johan and stopped. He would leave it to his brother to decide Schulz's final fate. Instead Garland snapped the commander's right leg with a crack that rang through the camp. Schulz screamed in agony as the guards and prisoners around him scattered. Pandemonium spread across Sachsenhausen. The air was thick with smoke and the sound of gunfire. Schulz was writhing on the ground but still had his pistol. He fired just as Garland was breaking his left leg, and Garland felt a sudden agony as the bullet entered his body.

Garland opened his eyes and felt the aurora bringing him down, its lights spiralling around the rope and noose which dissolved beneath them. He felt the weakness of his body as it dropped to the gallows's floor and watched the aurora slowly dissipate into the air. He was too tired now to move, every part of him empty and exhausted. Garland tried to focus, fighting against the oblivion lapping at his feet. He felt his eyelids tremor and drop as someone yelled from the distance, the sound drifting above all the noise and confusion. Garland forced open his eyes, squinting to see the guards around him lowering their rifles and turning towards the voice shouting one word over and over. It took him a moment to understand.

Evakuieren.

They were evacuating the camp.

Chapter Forty-Three

JOHAN - 1945

Johan watched Schulz laughing hysterically on the ground, thin strands of smoke drifting from his pistol. Johan wanted to rush to Garland, curled on the scaffold, his breathing shallow and eyes fluttering behind their lids, but Schulz was still a threat. Johan felt a cold cloak of hate envelop him, his body tensing and fists clenched into tight balls.

He stomped forward as Schulz pointed the pistol, sunlight bouncing from the barrel as it shook in his hand, and pulled the trigger. Johan felt the air move as the bullet passed his cheek, the sound of the gunshot a split second behind. Schulz aimed again but Johan kicked the pistol out of his hand with his bare feet and stood over him, snarling out his hate. Schulz only laughed harder.

Johan knelt down, his legs against Schulz's arms so he couldn't move, and put his face close to the crazed commander's. Blood dropped onto Schulz's forehead from the hole where Johan's nose used to be. Johan was spared the smell of rotten breath and piss-stained decay, the high odour of a body already dying inside.

"This is for Gerda." Johan delved for the diamond ring and lifted it in the air, the stone shooting a blinding spectrum of light that seemed alive in his hand.

He drove the ring into Schulz's right eye and watched it explode in a spray of red. Schulz howled, his face contorted in an agonised grimace that still carried the remains of his deranged grin. He jerked his head upwards and tried to push Johan away.

Johan raised his hand again and plunged the ring into Schulz's other eye, grinding the stone as the soft resistance gave way. Schulz was whimpering now, barely conscious as Johan returned the ring to its hiding place, braced himself on his knees and began to pummel Schulz's face. Each punch carried years of hate. Johan watched what were once features become a mush, a palette of oil paint in myriad shades of red, pink and orange. His fists fell rhythmically, one after the other until he had no feeling left in either hand. Teeth flew from the ruined crimson gash that had been Schulz's mouth, white, black and yellow shards spraying all around, until Johan's burning arms could swing no more.

He collapsed breathless onto Schulz who twitched and groaned, still alive but drowning in his own blood. Johan staggered to his feet. He saw a crowd of prisoners were watching and caught a glint of sunlight reflecting from the pistol on the ground. He bent to pick it up, cocked the hammer and pointed it at Schulz, willing his cramping arm to stop shaking. He walked closer and put the barrel to Schulz's face. He could see Schulz's chest heave slowly up and down and heard the death rattle deep in his lungs.

"My last kill," Johan said aloud. "I pity your soul when it arrives in hell."

He shot Schulz five times, sending each bullet into his head until the hammer clicked. He knew the first one had killed him because his chest became still but he kept firing, kept tearing the bullets into his brain, haunted by the thought Schulz could somehow return. After all he had seen that morning, anything was possible.

Johan dropped the pistol and sank to his knees as a hacking cough bent him double.

Then he looked at the scaffold.

Garland was writhing around holding his stomach, blood oozing from a bullet wound and pouring through his fingers. Schulz's final shot that had been meant for Johan. He crawled to Garland, every small movement an effort, and lay beside him, breathing heavy, tinny gasps. He took Garland's hand and squeezed it tightly.

"I love you, brother."

"I love you too." Garland's voice was a thick whisper.

The sound of boots moving quickly across the gravelly yard made Johan look up and he saw a group of guards trotting towards them. They stood over Johan and Garland and pointed their rifles.

Johan held Garland's hand tight, closed his eyes and listened to the metallic shift of the guns being loaded. He waited for the bullets that would finally free them. He hoped whatever was waiting would be better than Sachsenhausen's unrelenting horror.

But the shots never came.

Johan opened his eyes, squinting into the sun, and saw the guards had lowered their weapons. He pulled himself upwards and heard them talking about the Soviets getting close and disposing of evidence. One suggested killing the prisoners but they quickly agreed there were too many.

Johan felt as if he was drifting somewhere between sleep and wakefulness, no longer sure if the words were real or in his dreams.

"Orders from the top. Leave the ones who are too weak or ill to walk. March the rest out of the camp. Get them away from here."

Johan's vision was blurry but he saw one of the guards point his finger towards Garland and himself.

"What about these two? They're both nearly gone."

Johan heard a disembodied voice from behind.

"Take them but keep an eye on the strange one. Blindfold him in case he does anything. We need to get rid of any evidence. I don't know where but we need to go."

Johan closed his eyes and dreamt he had been forgiven.

They were walking in convoy and Johan realised he was next to Garland. He had no memory of leaving Sachsenhausen, no idea where they were being taken. A thin bandage now stretched around Johan's face and someone had tied another prison uniform roughly around Garland's stomach. It seemed to have stemmed the bleeding but Garland's face was porcelain white and his eyes surrounded by thick black rims. Around his lips were the red-brown specks of dried blood.

"Garland," Johan said. "You okay?"

Garland nodded.

They were walking in line with hundreds of other prisoners, guards shepherding them. Both Johan and Garland's hands were tied with thick rope. Every now and then, someone would stumble. Johan realised he was using Garland to steady himself.

He looked behind and saw the long line of gaunt bobbing heads. A guard eyed Garland nervously.

They were scared of him, Johan knew. After what happened at the gallows he could be capable of anything. Were they even scared to kill him?

They walked through woods on beaten dirt paths, past huge trees throwing blankets of deep shade and through barren fields and long grass. They passed gentle becks running amber in the dappled light and skirted a deserted lake that lay in a clearing. Those who fell exhausted were left behind. No one tried to carry them. No one had the strength.

Johan saw the sun dropping toward the horizon and thought they had been going northwards. They passed a row of cottages where nervous faces peeked from behind drawn curtains and in the distance, they could hear planes chugging through the darkening sky. Johan had tried to concentrate on the sounds of nature, the larks and crickets and the hidden animals that rustled through the undergrowth. He even thought he could hear the song thrush as they waded through a shallow stream and into a dark forest.

Then the guards suddenly ran. They disappeared in different directions, their panicked voices harsh and loud before fading into the distance. Johan looked over at Garland, too exhausted to speak, and watched other prisoners begin to scatter, some even finding the strength to run. Others collapsed where they stood.

Johan used his bound hands to inch Garland's blindfold from his eyes, and together they walked deeper into the forest. Garland led them, his face that of a gaunt ghost. Johan knew they were both nearing their end.

His own breath had become laboured, more water than air, and blood still leaked through the makeshift bandage across his nose. A headache thumped like a steel hammer behind his eyes.

He looked as Garland turned and in his eyes he saw the same spectrum of colours that had burnt so brightly over the gallows. Not as vivid but a glimmer, like an exotic fish gliding below the surface of clear waters. Garland gestured with his eyes towards a clearing ahead, and Johan knew that would be the place. He followed dreamily, half-awake and half sleepwalking. He could feel a cool breeze across his neck and with every step, his pain gradually faded. They stopped in a semicircular space amongst the tall pines, the sharp tang of sap hanging in the air. Johan felt the trees breathing and he breathed with them.

Johan's legs gave way below him. His knees buckled and he fell, bringing Garland down with him. They landed in a heap, arms and legs entwined. Johan stared at the sky. The last sparks of the setting sun had painted it purple, a velvet canvas dotted with far off stars that flickered and sparkled above.

He turned to Garland and saw the dazzling colours flow from his eyes and knew that all was well. He squeezed Garland's hand and felt warmth flow up his body. Garland's smile warmed Johan's heart, the casing of ice long melted away. Johan let his body float to the sound of the forest, the high trees so tall he could no longer see where they ended. They could have been ladders to heaven itself.

Johan heard a strange sound escape from his mouth and realised he was laughing. He remembered Schulz's words. *Always better to laugh than cry.* Not even the thought of Schulz and all his evil could spoil the beauty around him.

The loudest sound was the call of the song thrush. Johan saw it on a branch, its yellow and brown spotted chest puffed proudly above long slender legs, its beak open wide as it whistled its late tune.

The song thrush soothed him and he thought of Gerda, her bright eyes and infinite warmth, the smell of her hair when she lay with him, silky and fresher than a meadow soaked with the morning dew. He stared at the song thrush, singing to the backdrop of a million stars, and wondered at the miracle of the world around him. He thought of Norway, the green-turquoise lakes and crisp, pure air.

He turned away from the song thrush, and its ballad lifted him high beyond the trees. He felt euphoric, painless. He thought of Garland and felt the unconditional love of brothers, of two lives on a journey that was now coming to an end.

As he felt his soul fly, he heard the song thrush and searched its song for a message.

He listed in vain for forgiveness.

But as its melody took Johan away forever, the song thrush simply told Johan that he was loved, and always would be.

Chapter Forty-Four

GARLAND - 1945

Garland watched Johan die and smiled. He knew his brother had passed peacefully. Soon it would be his turn.

He had watched Johan's spirit climb high over the pine trees and into the night sky.

A tear fell down his cheek as he considered their journey, two orphans from Oslo whose futures were bonded by tragedy and suffering. That had been their fate.

Wincing with the effort, Garland pulled the St Christopher from his pocket and twirled it in his bloodstained fingers. He kissed it and thought of the father he would never see.

He looked down at his stomach and grimaced. He had lost too much blood. Every breath felt like it could be his last, and his head spun each time he moved.

Fleeting memories came and went. He thought of Max and remembered his love and his beauty. He said a prayer for Johan, the protective brother he had cherished his whole life.

Garland closed his eyes and began to dance across a stage in Oslo, old Mr Andersen smiling in the wings. Garland moved in time with music more beautiful than anything he had heard, his movements matching its grace and passion. All of his pain had disappeared. He was lighter than air itself as he spun and twirled and stood tall on the balls of his feet, pushing himself up with strong toes and jumping higher than ever before. He fell still under the hot lights as the cheers crashed down and soaked up the moment in a crescendo of ecstasy.

When he opened his eyes, the aurora shone all around him, its colours more radiant than ever.

He rose to his feet as a voice somewhere deep in the aurora beckoned him onwards. He knew he didn't need his body anymore, so he walked and left it behind. Garland easily climbed a small bank, the energy carrying him, pulling him towards a clearing that glowed under delicate moonbeams. He breathed in air that was crisp and light, and he remembered Norway.

Garland turned to see Johan and himself huddled together on the forest floor. They could have been a painting hung in a great hall, the work of a master capturing the height of human emotion on canvas.

He turned back to the clearing and could see what awaited him. The colours of the aurora had given way to intense artificial light which shone on a bed in the middle of the pine trees. Beside it were machines with green readings that emitted regular electronic beeps. Garland recognised the scene from his dreams and visions.

A single figure sat upright on the bed and turned to face Garland when he approached. He was older than Garland and wore clothes in a strange style, blue trousers and a checked-pattern shirt. He had kind eyes which warmed when he smiled.

The stranger extended his hand. He spoke with a familiar English accent.

"I'm Richard Garland. I've been waiting for you here. I've been waiting a long time."

Garland shook his hand and returned the smile. "The voice in my visions. Nice to meet you. I'm Garland Lund. We have the same name."

"I know," Richard said. "Daniel Garland was my great-grandfather. We are related, Garland. You've been walking for so long, my friend. You must be tired. Why don't you lie down?"

Garland nodded. "I'd like that."

He stretched out and looked up. The room and the bed and the Englishman were gone, the trees around him and the ground below once more engulfed in the aurora's swirling colours.

Garland looked at his hands but they weren't there. The aurora pulsated through him. He was nothing and everything, and as his consciousness soared, Garland danced towards an infinite light.

Epilogue

SANDY - 2022

When Richard opened his eyes and sat up, Sandy gasped and lurched to his feet, sending his chair tumbling noisily behind him, and reached for his husband's hands.

It had been over a year but Sandy had never lost hope, even when the doctors warned him Richard's chances of recovering were slim. Richard would sometimes blink or twitch, but those were only reflexes, they said.

But now as Sandy held him he had no doubt. Richard had woken from his coma. He wore a weak smile and his eyes glittered with awareness.

"Sandy," he said slowly.

Sandy hugged him and called out that Richard was awake, frightened to let him go or leave the room.

Sandy had been told, if Richard ever did revive, it could take years before he was anywhere near back to normal. There would be months of therapy to help him walk and talk again. Richard, they said, would have to relearn how to function as a human being.

But Sandy knew his husband was different. He had been touched by something special, a gift or a sixth sense that would always be beyond his understanding.

Sandy had never doubted. He had sold their house, given up his job and rented a tiny flat in Berlin. He had made every sacrifice because he had faith in Richard and the mystical energy that burnt inside him.

"My love," he said, staring into Richard's eyes. "You've been asleep a long time."

Stunned doctors and nurses rushed in and Sandy heard someone whisper *miracle* as machine readings were checked and a white-gowned consultant shone a torch beam at Richard's pupils.

Sandy reluctantly stepped outside whilst the medics ran their tests.

Now as he hurried back into the room he saw Richard propped against the pillows and sipping from a beaker of water. He looked as handsome as the day they married.

"Are you okay?" He was crying as he spoke.

Richard nodded and tears filled his eyes.

They embraced as though they would hold each other like statues cast in stone for all eternity.

Richard was the one to pull away. He gently held Sandy's face in his hands and kissed his lips. "I've been on a long journey, Sandy. I need to tell you about it."

He began to speak and Sandy listened to the story of the orphans of Oslo, their tragic lives and the suffering and strength of so many in the face of human evil.

When he looked into Richard's eyes, Sandy swore he could see a swirling rainbow of light shimmering back at him. The ever-changing colours whispered the word that was already burning in his heart.

Love.

Dedicated to the 200,000 prisoners who were incarcerated at Sachsenhausen, and the tens of thousands of men who wore pink triangles under the Third Reich.

If only the aurora could have lifted you to safety.

Sachsenhausen:

THE FACT BEHIND THE FICTION

I hope you enjoyed the story of Garland and Johan. *Enjoyed* is maybe too positive a word to describe what is intended to be a harrowing journey through hell, but you get what I mean.

It feels a large responsibility to tell the story of the camp, and I can't stress this too much, it is a work of fiction, and with it brings an element of massaging of the camp's true history.

As far as my knowledge stretches, at time of writing, this will be the first novel written about Sachsenhausen. This fact baffles me a little, as it is a fascinating place. Maybe the huge death toll and utter soullessness of places like Auschwitz make the crimes in Sachsenhausen seem unworthy of as much coverage, but I feel it has a strong story to tell. It was the administrative centre of all concentration camps in the Reich. It also had a large concentration of homosexual prisoners, something this novel focuses heavily on.

It may seem strange that I've given the tale a supernatural bent, something that may seem unnecessary given the true horror and its unrelenting circumstances, the infinite tales of human interest that no doubt could be spun from such a place, whether based on a true story or as a literary fictional piece. I gave Garland psychic and supernatural powers for the sake of hyperbole, a way of seeing and feeling the emotions he has. I feel it gives the story a nuance, and I hope it does justice to the 200,000 people who were incarcerated at the camp and the many, many people who died there.

So, now you're probably wondering, which bits are real? And where has the author exercised his creativity?

Only a couple of the characters in the book are based on real people, which I'll come to later.

I've been helped by the brilliant Ronan Spillane, a tour guide at Sachsenhausen, who has worked with me to shape the book into as accurate a story as possible, give or take a few slight diversions from what is likely.

First of all, Schulz, the psychopathic camp commander, is based on everyone and no one. He is a composite of many stories of commandants and a manifestation of the crazed Nazi philosophies, the power-hungry, hypocritical and criminal people in positions of power. In truth, the real camp commandants at Sachsenhausen could have novels based on them alone.

A good example of this is Karl Otto Koch, who would have been commandant when Johan first went to Sachsenhausen. His wife, Ilse Koch was the subject of 'sexploitation' movie *Ilse: Shewolf of the SS*. She was alleged to have had affairs with both officers and prisoners.

Koch himself was executed by firing squad by the SS for embezzlement.

It is unlikely Schulz would have been Sachsenhausen commandant for so long a time, but for simplicity of storytelling, he remained there throughout Johan's stint. Schulz was also unlikely to have carried out all the tasks described in the novel, but as a character he was a power-hungry control freak, so I brought him closer into the story.

An earlier draft of this novel was entitled Station Z, but I decided against it. As a horror author I worried people would mistakenly associate the Z with the zombie genre. I've been a little creative with the timelines of Station Z. It was actually built in 1942, after the experimentation in a wooden version of the building, when the Soviet prisoners were killed. Sadly, the use of SS guards dressed as doctors and the "measuring stick" execution method really did happen before being ditched as too inefficient. Sachsenhausen was used as a testing ground for executions, paving the way for the mass extermination of people across the Third Reich. It was indeed called Station Z as a dark, sick joke by the SS as people entered the camp through Tower A and met their end at Station Z. Schulz's violent use of a samurai sword was pure fiction, but a Japanese delegation from the Imperial Army did visit Sachsenhausen in December, 1937.

Homosexuals were often called '175ers' in Germany at the time the novel was set, because paragraph 175 of the German criminal code dealt with homosexuality. Normally a homosexual would be sentenced by a court to a specific amount of time in prison. After that time had been served, often, the '175er' would be taken into 'protective custody' by the Gestapo. Garland found himself having a couple of days in a cell for the purpose of the timeline of the story but, in reality, it would be unlikely that it would happen so fast.

Something Garland could have clung on to as a glimmer of hope: it was believed homosexuals could be rehabilitated, especially Ayran ones. In 1944, Heinrich Himmler set up a camp brothel where homosexual prisoners were forced to have sex with women as a 'cure' for their deviancy.

I understand 175er has since been reclaimed by the gay community and is printed on T-shirts. And rightly so.

Drug use was common in the Third Reich. Pervitin, known more commonly today as methamphetamine, was used by the army but it wasn't really such a secret military weapon, as made out in this novel, as it was actually sold in chemists. The SS, in conjunction with the Navy, did test drugs at the shoe test track but it was late 1944, rather than the earlier time suggested in the novel.

The brutal Klinkerwerks was real, although Schulz's drug-fuelled ravings about it being the biggest in the world are probably inaccurate. In fact, the Klinkerwerks actually ended up losing money due to the poor quality of the bricks being produced. It was certainly the worst place to work at Sachsenhausen though, due to the sheer number of people who died working there, most of them homosexuals. Johan heard correctly – the Klinkerwerks was destroyed by Allied bombs on 10 April, 1945, killing more than 200 prisoners.

In reality, it was highly unlikely that Johan could be accused of homosexuality and thrown into the camp so easily. Guards were often imprisoned in the camp for various issues such as going AWOL and would serve a month or so, but they were not assigned jobs or a triangle – in fact they were given better food and accommodation than other prisoners. Let's put this anomaly down to the psychopathy of Schulz and the betrayal he felt by Johan's will to go against the law.

Johan probably wouldn't have been brought to the cellblock as it was for high-value prisoners, but the facility was noteworthy enough for a mention in the novel.

Johnnie Dodge was a real person. Again, he was a part of Sachsenhausen's history I felt was worthy of inclusion and was even portrayed by Christopher Reeve in the Great Escape II: The Untold Story, as heroic a man as I've hopefully portrayed. I had to bend some probabilities to have Johnnie interact with Garland. British servicemen were kept in the cellblock, and it is unlikely that he would have been able to mingle with other prisoners. He was in Sachsenhausen in 1944, and on 23 September of that year, he escaped along with other prisoners. He spent over a month on the run thanks to some help from French slave labourers, but was ultimately arrested and returned to Sachsenhausen.

An interesting and honest fact about this book that was a strange coincidence (or maybe I temporarily had a touch of Garland's gift), I randomly picked the surname Schubert after a Google search of popular German surnames in the 1930s. Strangely, there was a Wilhelm Schubert stationed at Sachsenhausen from 1938 to 1942. His habit of shooting inmates led to his nickname "Pistols" and he was known for his sadistic excess, firing his service weapon when he got angry. Unsurprisingly, he worked as a guard at the Klinkerwerks, where he murdered many homosexual prisoners and took part in the killing of thousands of Soviet prisoners in the 'neck shot block' in 1941. Sometimes as an author when you write about the horrors of war, and try to put a fictional spin on past events, the two converge and convene, wrapping around each other until one is indistinguishable from the other. The Schubert of this novel grew from my own mind as a ruthless, sadistic beast. The real man sounds cut from exactly the same cloth, and it makes me break out in a shudder as I type.

There is so much more to say, but you reached the end of the novel a few pages ago, and if you would like to know more then you should visit Berlin and take a tour of Sachsenhausen. Berlin itself is one of the world's greatest cities, and her past is as fascinating as her future is exciting. Book a tour through one of their many excellent tour companies to discover more. There are myriad books about the history of Sachsenhausen, and all are worth a read. Take a look in the museum shop and learn about the fascinating, brutal history and one

Berlin – and Germany – have left for us to discover, remember and

learn about the horrors of the past that must not be repeated.

David Turton

2022

Acknowledgements

Thanks to all who have helped in the creation of this novel. I began writing it in 2017, so it's been five years in the making.

Firstly, thanks to my wife Vanessa for the two trips to Berlin that inspired this story. A great city that we will return to as soon as we can.

Thanks to Ravven White for taking this on for her brilliant publishing company. For her enthusiasm, her empathy, and her just overall brilliance. Thanks to the other Curious Corvids Mark Alexander McClish for the amazing cover, David Grinnell for the proofreading and my wonderful editor Anna Corbeaux. And to all the other Corvids at various stages of publication – best wishes from across the pond!

To Ronan Spillane and Insider Tours who pointed me in his direction. Thanks so much for ensuring this work of fiction didn't stray too far away from the awful reality of Sachsenhausen. And for your enthusiasm for the project during what was a busy time for you.

To Drew Dalton, who read an earlier draft of the novel and gave some key pieces of advice and encouragement. Keep doing what you do, Drew, you're a rock star.

Thanks to anyone who has shown an interest in my writing over the years, too many to mention, but you know who you are. And my local writing community including Glenda Young, Annie Doyle, Tony Kerr, Vic Watson, Alan Parkinson, all of Holmeside Writers and the legend that is Iain Rowan.

A huge acknowledgement goes to Garry Willey, an early editor of this story who moved it in a much better direction, sprinkling his 'magic dust' on the words, and Paul Jones who also helped shape it.

And a massive thanks to Tony 'Hutch' Hutchinson, a friend, fellow author and drinking partner all rolled into one!

Thanks to the women's football family. The players, the staff, but also the supporters who stand on the terraces no matter what the weather, the result, or the quality of the burgers. Whichever colours you're cheering on, all of you are heroes.

Thanks to my closest friends. Dave, Rob, Steve, Matt, Rich, Ben, Barry, Pete S, Chris M, Chris H and Louise, Emma, Luise, Lauren, Craig, Andy A, Pete E, Paul, Andy M, Dan, Carley - I hope I've remembered everyone.

And finally, thanks to my family, without who all this would be much harder. Vanessa, my mum and dad, Liam and Faith, Olivia, Claire, Lauren, Garry and Maddy, Ruth and Robert and the two brand new additions, Emma and River.

Thanks to everyone who has helped this story see the light of day.

- David

David Turton has been successful in selling over 30 short stories to websites, magazines, podcasts and anthologies and has been shortlisted and longlisted in the Sunderland Short Story Award 2019 and 2018 respectively. His debut novel, *The Malaise*, was released in December 2018. David lives by the sea in North East England with his family and enjoys horror movies, women's football and country walks.